BLOOD

AND ICE

LOIS H GRESH

2011

FIRST EDITION
10 9 8 7 6 5 4 3 2 1
Published in December 2010
ISBN: 1-934501-20-4
Printed in the U.S.A.

Published by Elder Signs Press
P.O. Box 389
Lake Orion, MI 48361-0389
www.eldersignspress.com

Dedicated to H.P. Lovecraft and At The Mountains of Madness

PROLOGUE

Antarctica: October 2015

THE COMPUTER SCREEN CRACKLED once. And then it went black.

And then: *Boom.*

The plastic lab walls rattled. Notebooks and screwdrivers rolled off the tables.

Sasha Karonski's chair wobbled. She grabbed the edge of her desk so she wouldn't topple over.

Nothing ever *boomed* in Antarctica, not in the middle of millions of square miles of ice and snow.

BOOM.

It was louder this time. From outside, a harsh scream rushed through the air and then abruptly fell silent. A cacophony of shrieks rang out.

Had something exploded on the runway?

Was it even remotely possible that the Amundsen-Scott Station was being attacked?

The South Pole wasn't the sort of place terrorists targeted. This was a scientific outpost, where nothing was top secret and nothing was related to military operations.

They couldn't be under attack. It made no sense.

But those screams–

Sasha shivered. The temperature outside was negative 45, but that wasn't why she was shivering. Her mind flew to the gold cross dangling between her breasts. *Dear God, Oh Holy One, Thou Art in Heaven, please forgive my sins . . .*

She couldn't remember the words!

Then came another explosion. This one was so massive the file cabinets and tables jumped up and down. Again, Sasha lurched, catching herself a second time. She gripped her desk and stared at the door, which was vibrating on its hinges. Outside, the screams escalated, and then suddenly, the computer monitor crashed to the floor and shattered. Damn skinny flat screen monitor; it didn't take much to damage hardware these days, everything was flimsy and put together so it would fall apart if you so much as blew on it. Still, the station was sitting on a block of ice *two miles thick*: it was solid and earthquakes here were unknown, so what had caused the explosions and what had caused the monitor to crash to the floor?

Sasha's skin prickled with fear, that tingle that sweeps over you when you know something is terribly wrong and you have the feeling things are only going to get worse.

And then the lights flickered and died. The room was as black as the Ross Sea in winter. Sasha knew if the power didn't return, she and the rest of the crew were in a lot of trouble.

The station was still operating with a skeletal winter staff, a few dozen researchers and technicians, and their only source of power was from the three generators running on JP-8 jet fuel. If all three failed, anyone injured would probably die before help could reach them from McMurdo or from the outside world.

Feeling her way along the desk to the lab bench and from there to the wall, Sasha stumbled toward the door that led outside. It was hard to move quickly in her South Pole gear: hat, goggles, face scarf, ten-pound parka, snow pants, insulated gloves, and boots. In the cramped lab, she tripped over cables and bumped into chairs.

She pushed open the door and peeked across the expanse of Antarctic ice. The glare of summer had hit the glacial plateau. After coping with the endless night of winter, February through October, Sasha was blinded every time she went outside now. Even her goggles didn't deflect the sun as it shimmered off the snow, the ice, and the clouds of crystals: diamond dust sparkling under the frozen lid of the sky. Sasha squinted at the snow whipping across the glacier, at the weird ice sculptures molded by the katabatic winds, at the black folds of the crevasses.

As her eyes adjusted to the glare, her first impulse was to run back into the lab and hide in a storage closet and weep. She was surrounded by the sort of nightmare she never thought she'd see; she was an MIT-trained physicist, not the sort of girl who might stumble across the massacre of all her friends.

And yet, there it was, and there was no denying what she was seeing. As her eyes swept over the scene, her limbs went numb, and for a few moments, she froze in place, unable to will her legs to move forward. It was hard not to cry. Everywhere she looked, Sasha saw hell. Blood was etched across the ice like spider webs. Blood was soaked into the snow. Legs, arms, hair, *heads:* bodies, and pieces of bodies were scattered in shreds by the runway, the equipment buildings, the recreation center, the food depository.

What had happened? How could this be real? What if the killer came after *her?*

Her mind raced. There was no place to hide in a small Antarctic station. The lunatics who had killed her friends would find her no matter what she did. Then a thought flashed through her mind: *someone else might still be alive.* She couldn't just hide and let another die out here. She'd never forgive herself.

There had to be survivors.

She scanned the vast plateau beyond the carnage, beyond the station. Nothing out *there* had changed: ice sculptures twisted toward the sky like broken fingers; the surface was a blinding sheet of ice, like a gigantic mirror reflecting the sun back upon itself. The scene was one of frigid beauty marred by death and loss.

She stepped from the station onto the ice. As the lab door closed behind her, she smelled the bodies—full blast, like burned meat on a grill, and she doubled over from nausea and gripped her stomach. She was going to throw up, she just knew it. She swallowed and swallowed, hoping the nausea would pass, and she clutched the railing by the door and blinked, trying to clear what *must* be a hallucination.

But the hallucination didn't clear, and the burned meat and nausea didn't go away.

The blood, the bodies, the arms, the gore was splattered every-where over the ice. It was a massacre, but there were no gunmen, no terrorists, no weapons. *Just all of her friends, dead.*

No, she saw, not *everyone* was dead. There *were* some survivors. A few guys limped over the carnage, and she thought she saw movement near one of the IceCube modules.

Halos shimmered around the sun as if angels were up there, watching over Antarctica. Apparently, the angels had been distracted and not watching very carefully today. Everywhere was beauty and death, blood and ice.

The greenhouse was intact, thank God, so they still had food. But the supplies and recreation building was burning, or rather, *what was left* of the building was burning.

They weren't particularly equipped for putting out fires here, but someone—she couldn't see who it was at this distance—was dousing the flames. He was using a hose that normally supplied hot water for drilling the IceCube neutrino observatory holes into the ice. The whole IceCube experiment, Sasha's life's work, now seemed trivial. In the face of death, who cared if neutrinos passed through the Earth from unknown sources in the universe? Sure, lately, the data was showing odd neutrino events that had intrigued her, but it would be a long time, probably years, before scientists analyzed the data sufficiently to know if they were seeing anything truly unusual.

"Over here!" someone called. She recognized the voice. It was An-toine Damar, one of the key lab technicians. He was waving his arms and trying to get her attention. She crunched over the ice, carefully avoiding frozen streaks of blood and body parts. She couldn't make out who had been killed and who survived; God it was awful, the faces blasted off or shredded on skulls, entire heads blown off necks and wedged in pockets of ice. Fighting down the bile, she made her way over to Antoine, who stood by one of the dozens of boreholes. On top of the hole was a digital optical module that was frozen into an IceTop tank. The entire IceCube experiment was basically an upside down telescope that peered through ice thousands of meters beneath the surface to gather information about outer space. As if it mattered now . . .

She forced her lips to move, forced herself to talk. "What hap-pened? Are there any clues?" She swallowed, unable to say more.

Antoine motioned for her to crouch down next to him by the equipment. She lowered herself to the ice. "All of the equipment is dead. It all crashed," he said. She stared, numb, at the optical module, which looked like a transparent globe filled with electronics, cables coiled beneath it like octopus tentacles. When she said nothing, he added as if to further explain the inexplicable, "The circuits are fried, Sasha."

Sasha shook her head, tried to focus on technology, tried to *care* about it. Finally, her mind cleared sufficiently to think. "How could all the circuits short out, Antoine? *How?* These things are tested to—" She paused. "They're tested to death."

"Yeah," he paused, too, "I've never seen anything like it before. But I'm not actually saying the circuits *shorted.* I'm saying they *literally fried.* Melted. Whatever hit—" he pointed to a half dozen bodies freezing in the snow— "whatever hit *them . . .* well, it hit the IceTop modules, too."

His voice grew soft, and he choked on his words. She could tell he was trying not to think about his dead friends, that he was using a technique that she often used. Talk about science to avoid thinking about emotions. "I don't know what happened, Sasha. I don't have a clue. I was on my computer when the blast hit. I ran outside and saw all this—" And then he stopped. His shoulders slumped, and he bowed his head; and she heard the muffled sobs. "Oh, Sasha, what happened?"

She placed a hand on his shoulder. Even if she had a clue, she couldn't answer because her own words were strangled in her throat. Ten yards behind Antoine, she saw Zhen Qing, or what was left of him. Poor guy, he was only twenty-two, even younger than Sasha. Zhen, an ace engineer fresh out of school. His legs and arms were shattered and laying in pools of blood far from his body.

Antoine turned slightly and saw Zhen, too, and then Antoine gripped Sasha's shoulders, and she fell back on the ice, and he fell on top of her; and then they were both laughing hysterically, and she knew it wasn't because anything was funny, but rather, because they had stepped inside a nightmare and laughter was the only release.

Holding onto each other, Sasha and Antoine stood and awkwardly pulled themselves together, and then she said through chattering teeth, "We have to find out how many are dead."

"We won't make it through the night without heat. I'd like to know what's left of the station."

Sasha nodded. It was only October, with Antarctica inching into summer: were enough guys left from the skeletal winter crew to fix the generators and get the communications up? Did they even *have* any generators or communications equipment left? The guy with the hose had to be using some sort of power.

Ash filtered down to the snow and ice, coating the blood with black flakes. The fire was out, and the supplies and recreation building was damaged but intact. Across the expanse of snow, the two-story drill building was okay, as were the red equipment trailers. The yellow cable repair tent had collapsed into the snow, and giant brown cables coiled around the tent like snakes.

Surreal. Sasha bit her lip, tasted the blood before it froze.

They were just emerging from the dark hood of the six-to-eight-month winter. It had been night twenty-four hours a day with temperatures down to negative 85 degrees, and with the wind chill to negative 120. The blizzards had been absolute hell: winds roaring at 100 miles per hour, ice raging across the bleak landscape and killing everything in their paths. Antoine and Sasha, and the rest of the winter crew, were more than ready to leave the South Pole and return to civilization. Now most of them wouldn't go home. The dead would spend eternity mummified in coffins beneath the ice.

"What are we going to do, Sasha?" Antoine's voice was calm again. The scientist was in control; the emotional human had been stifled. "The summer crew won't be here for a couple of weeks. We probably don't have any communications left. I think it's all been blown out."

"We don't know that for sure," she said. "Look, there's Rayna. Maybe she knows something."

Rayna Chubkoff was lifting small objects—fingers—from the ice and putting them on a stretcher. She was the only medical pro at the Amundsen-Scott IceCube Lab. Russian by birth, brilliant mind, a good doctor, Rayna also had the personality of, well, an ice cube. Sasha didn't like her much.

Sasha asked Antoine to check the generators and determine if any modules were still online and functioning, then made her way through the snow, ice, and dead bodies over to Rayna.

The young doctor turned from the stretcher, paused to acknowledge Sasha. Her face hidden by goggles and scarf, Rayna might have been scowling, angry, worried, or any mixture in between. There was no way to know, but her voice was cold, to the point, and sharp. "Before you ask, there are twelve dead. Nobody injured. Just dead."

With twelve dead, that meant only six people had survived. Sasha, Antoine, Rayna, the techs putting out the fires.

She asked Rayna to clue her in about the deaths, but the doctor wasn't much help. "I don't know what killed them," she said. "I was asleep when the blast hit, whatever it was."

"I thought maybe–" Sasha groped for the words, "maybe you could tell what hit us from the condition of the bodies . . . the people."

Rayna lowered her head. She was clearly rattled. She was in her twenties and had no experience with this sort of thing. She handled frostbites and minor cuts, headaches and mild illnesses. "Maybe I'll know more after the autopsies but I don't think so. It's clear that some people died from the blast and the fire. But as for the others, I don't know. It's like they were burned in place, not close to the explosion at all, but nearby. I'm afraid that I just don't know what happened."

"Have you contacted the Air Force?" Sasha asked.

"All my equipment is dead. All I can tell you is, in my quarters, everything short circuited and switched off. A lot of equipment went up in flames. Maybe you should see if you can fix the equipment, Sasha, and maybe you can get us some help."

Yeah, fix the equipment, that's what Sasha would do. Fix the equipment. Get her mind off the bodies, the blood. That was Rayna's domain.

"I'll do what I can," she said.

Rayna nodded and returned her attention to the head, torso, leg, and fingers on the stretcher. All in pieces: the hair singed off, the face half melted from fire, the blood-splattered skull glittering in the sun. It was Sarah Hermann, pretty, petite, engaged to be married next month in Maine. Sarah wasn't going to make it to her wedding. Sarah wasn't even going to make it home.

CHAPTER
ONE

Antarctica: December 9, 1902

ICE CRACKED, AND THE dusting of snow shifted on the seals dozing under the summer haze. Even from the 10,000-foot-high plateau deep within the continent, Fernando Le Sprague sensed the animals grunting and scratching themselves on the granite by the Ross Sea. He felt their keening, their anxiety as the intruders clubbed one of their young for a meal.

Penguins huddled on the Great Ice Barrier and gazed across the patchwork of floes, ready to bolt into the water if the intruders came too close. Icicles dripped from the ledge where the penguins squawked as they chased a white petrel bird until it finally flew into the breeze and left them alone.

The icicles called to Fernando, for they were part of him and all of his kind. A hibernal fraternity, knit together by wind and frost, they were the snow blankets, the drifts, the blizzards, the storms, and they were also the beauty: at times, radiant and dazzling; at times, stark and bleak; and always, vibrant and in control.

Intruders were never welcome here, and Fernando didn't understand why they came.

He turned now from the telescope, shuffling his nanoparticles into an ice statue of immense proportions: a ledge here, a curve there, caverns and crevasses splintering his body into a maze of planes and polygons. Beneath the Antarctic sun, Fernando was a god. Twinkling beneath the cloudscape and dripping water from his icicles, Fernando billowed frost into the sky: he knew that he was gorgeous, a crepuscular vapor tinged with red light. He flexed, and the miles of ice beneath him convulsed and sent tremors straight down to the sea.

His friends, Otto and Jean-Baptiste, also mutated, shuffling their particles in harmony with him, pushing their ice lobes into kinks and curls, thrusting their icicles into Fernando's cavities, wafting as mist across the plateau.

From afar, the intruders chopped the seal pup into chunks, spraying its blood across the snow. Fernando heard the knives grating the air, smelled the tinge of blood in the snow; heard boots fracturing ice, axes fracturing bones. The air vibrated as the mother wailed, rolled on her side and raised her flipper, and then slipped into the sea. Fernando felt the black water stir, felt the mother's teeth snapping, felt her bellowing as if she was right beside him.

It hurt.

Fernando shuddered. *I never want to become like the intruders. Such cruelty, such disregard for life. Such utter ruthlessness.*

An ice cube hit Fernando, shattering his outer ledges. He snapped back to attention and saw Jean-Baptiste splintering off another chunk of ice from his body and aiming it toward Fernando and Otto.

Fernando swept out of the way, causing a whiteout of the sky, and the cube hit Otto in his main flank. Poor Otto flew backward as a frozen fog, whining and shedding slivers of ice.

Fernando clobbered Jean-Baptiste with an eighty mile per hour gale, sending him careening down a hole in the ice. Within moments, Jean-Baptiste recovered from the surprise punch and spewed from the hole in an ice spray so thick it threw both Fernando and Otto half a mile away.

What a blast!

There wasn't much to do here on Earth, in this vast wasteland of ice. They'd been blasting each other with howling winds and blizzards since the radiation activated them many years ago.

For now, let the intruders do as they please. Soon enough, they'll go away again and leave us in peace, Fernando thought. In the meantime, he and his friends would play and enjoy themselves. Fernando hovered as a fog near Otto, and then Jean-Baptiste shot hail at the two of them before collapsing on the ground, laughing.

Otto started crying, and Jean-Baptiste clobbered him with a fierce wind and said, "You take all the fun out of everything, Otto. You're so pathetic. Grow up, would you?"

Fernando clasped frozen arches around both of his friends and squeezed Otto's slumped ice shelves, hoping to cheer him up a little.

Otto sniffled. He turned away from Jean-Baptiste, and he shook snow off his ice mantles as if shrugging off Jean-Baptiste's insults. Otto melted a little. Unlike Fernando and Jean-Baptiste, Otto didn't possess glimmering ice. Rather, he was dull and pasty, a frowning clot of slush. As usual, he tried to sound important. "Carsten told me that the ancestors have a mission for us. I think we should go back and ask him about it instead of playing like children."

"What kind of mission could we possibly have, Otto? We're nothing more than snow, and we've been stuck here for what feels like an eternity. Why would the ancestors want us to do anything *new?*" said Jean-Baptiste.

Yeah, thought Fernando, it was crazy to think that a bunch of misfits would have a mission in life. It was more likely that Carsten was picking up and interpreting stray signals from outer space again. The telescope was so old, it was probably showing Carsten things that weren't there. Playing along with what he saw as silliness, Fernando asked, "Does this supposed mission have to do with the intruders?"

"Not the intruders, no," said Otto. "It has to do with us. It's from the Fridarians, from our ancestors, and they don't know anything about the intruders. Besides, who cares about the intruders anyway?"

"Well, I care about them," said Fernando. "They keep invading our territory. A few come, then more follow. Soon, there will be too many of them. Think what will happen if they discover us, Otto. They're violent, and their blood lust is irrational."

Otto said, "But why should we care at all what the intruders do? They'll never discover us. We have all of Antarctica to ourselves. So what if some humans wander over the glaciers, fall into crevasses, and die of starvation or scurvy?"

Jean-Baptiste bared his icicles, and they glinted under the red sun.

"I say we do away with them. They eat *animals*, it's a bloody thing to do, that. It's shameful."

Fernando disagreed. "We should avoid them, or at worse, scare them away. Nothing more."

"Why do you think they keep coming here?" asked Otto.

"Maybe to eat the seals and penguins," suggested Fernando. "They seem to enjoy meat and blood."

"Maybe they come to make sure we don't get enough radiation to reproduce," said Jean-Baptiste.

"They don't know about us yet, so that's ridiculous, Jean-Baptiste. Besides, *we* don't really know how we reproduce. And besides, I don't see what their presence has to do with the amount of radiation in the air." Fernando paused, then added, "Fridare is a hundred light years away, which means our ancestors activated us with radiation a hundred years ago. Any transmissions we get are from a long time ago. For all we know, Fridare could be a dead planet by now. We may never find out who and what we really are, how we reproduce or even if we need to reproduce, much less what we're supposed to do with ourselves."

"Meaning," stressed Jean-Baptiste, "we may be the only hope left for the Fridarian people. If there are other Fridarians still out there somewhere, wouldn't we be getting newer transmissions?"

"If we're the only hope for the Fridarians, then all hope is truly lost," said Fernando.

Otto whined and swirled up and down in a haze of snow crystals. "I don't want to talk about this anymore," he said. "I don't want to think about the intruders and what they might do to us and all of that. Let's just not talk about this anymore, okay?"

"Well, it was you who brought up the subject, Otto. Why don't you just make up your mind?" said Jean-Baptiste.

Otto whined again.

"Knock it off," said Fernando. "We'll figure out what to do, and nothing bad will happen to us." He almost added "I promise" but stopped himself. There were no promises, not when they were completely on their own with no clue who they were, what they were supposed to do with their lives, or whether they were able, if needed, to prevent their own deaths.

Given they had drifted far from the telescope, Fernando suggested they return and find out if Carsten had indeed picked up stray signals from the ancestors and learned anything new. It seemed unlikely, of course, but they might as well return to the telescope and talk to Carsten. It wasn't as if there was much else to do anyway, and besides, Fernando would rather do almost anything than listen to Otto whine. It drove him absolutely crazy. It wasn't as if Otto ever *did* anything like help out or give Fernando a laugh. Otto's sole purpose in life was to *take*. And of course, to *whine*.

They found Carsten plugged into the telescope with hundreds of tentacles of black ice. He muttered to himself and cursed. "Damn Fridarians, assuming they *even* call themselves Fridarians, what the hell were they thinking? Sending us to this boring, stupid place with nothing to do? All day, every goddamn day, the same thing over and over again," and *blah blah blah*. Sometimes, Fernando actually preferred Otto's whining to Carsten's bitching and moaning.

He settled with Otto and Jean-Baptiste around Carsten and the telescope. To a non-Fridarian, they probably looked like a giant snow drift. Fernando shifted a few mounds to ease himself away from Otto. The telescope cavern was deep and in the far reaches of the transantarctic mountains, where no humans could possibly find it. Fernando ignored Otto's sniffling and Carsten's bitching, and he focused on the telescope. It was at the bottom of a large crevasse that opened to the sky, and in its envelope of snow, appeared minute. Small as it was, thought Fernando, it could reach across the vastness of the universe and grab information from the home planet. Well, it didn't actually reach across the universe, but that was beside the point. It did *receive* information from Fridare, which to Fernando's way of thinking, was the same thing.

Although it was December and summer, the winds raged across the mountains and the temperature was negative twenty degrees Fahrenheit. It was a bit warm, but Fernando was used to the tropical heat waves of Earth. Soon it would be winter, and the sun would disappear and the temperature would plummet to negative sixty, maybe lower. Fernando definitely preferred the cold.

"Well, what does it *say*, Carsten? What's the new reading? Come on!" Jean-Baptiste was already badgering Carsten for the latest

red

telescope reading. Jean-Baptiste was pushy, but without his bold and aggressive nature, Fernando would never have any fun.

Carsten glowered at Jean-Baptiste and Fernando, ignoring Otto as if he wasn't there. "There are no new readings, Jean-Baptiste," he said. "We have to wait for winter again, when it's dark all the time. This last communication was from a hundred years ago. It just burbled up from the queue."

Carsten creased his black ice into ridges and snaked more nano-particle tendrils around the telescope. The tripod vibrated slightly; the odd metal spears were sunk deeply into the ice and held a tilted parabolic mirror that was directed at a variable star. Inside the mirror was the telescope's focal point, which noted light intensities from the star flickering far off in the universe. The Fridarian ancestors shot messages encoded in neutrino pulses to the star, and as the star's light intensities changed, the messages were detected by the telescope. Implanted in Carsten's nanocircuits was the ability to translate the changes in light intensity into messages that Fernando, Jean-Baptiste, and the other Earth-bound Fridarians understood. Fernando and his friends didn't know how long the telescope had been on Earth; they had been activated long after the ancestors planted the device into the ice.

Fernando sucked oxygen from the air and filtered nutrients into his particles. He didn't need much to keep going. None of them did. He waited patiently for Carsten; they had all the time in the world because they had nothing else to do. Other than find a source of radiation and reproduce, of course, should they ever figure out how to do it.

They were all very good at waiting and not doing much.

None of them knew how they had been planted beneath the ice a bazillion years ago. But they all knew that in their dormant form, they had waited . . . and waited and waited . . . until their ancestors sent enough radiation down to Antarctica to activate them. The activation changed them from dormant creatures into hatchlings. In retrospect, it was naïve, Fernando thought, that they had called themselves hatchlings, but when Fernando was first aware of himself and his surroundings, the first thing he'd noticed were birds, and with the birds came nests, eggs, and *hatchlings*. And so, Fernando had assumed that his so-called birth, really a mere activation of dormant nanoparticles, was like the birth of a bird.

"*So what does it say?* What's this hundred-year-old message?" Jean-Baptiste jabbed at Carsten, who swatted him off and glowered. Otto rumbled back a few feet, afraid of getting hurt by Jean-Baptiste.

Carsten said, "This is serious, so stop screwing around, Jean-Baptiste. I think we're on a mission."

Jean-Baptiste laughed. "Oh come on, Carsten, you're kidding, right? You're starting to sound like Otto. We're not on a mission. That's ridiculous."

"Actually," said Carsten slowly, "I'm not kidding. This is the most interesting message we've received. It says that we were sent here to reproduce, and the only way for us to do that is to build what the ancestors say is a natural nuclear reactor. Two more batches of Fridarians will be activated more than one hundred years from now. One batch will be in Antarctica—*here!*—and the second will be in a place called the Mediterranean Sea. In 2015. There's a little bit more, something about Africa and sex . . ." Carsten started to say—

—when Fernando picked up the chattering of human voices in the wind. He would know that sound anywhere. Fernando said, "The humans are getting closer. They're coming *here*—and I don't mean some stray place, but I mean that they're coming directly toward us—and they're pulling their own sledges. Their dogs are all sick. They'll find the telescope if we don't stop them."

"Where are they? What are dogs? What does this mean? What are sledges?" Otto wailed and fluttered around Fernando in little gusts of wind. "Are they getting closer to the pole, to *us?*"

"For godsakes, Otto, shut up!" said Jean-Baptiste.

Carsten said to Otto, "Can't you figure out these things on your own? The dogs are furry animals that come with the humans. The sledges are the devices that the humans use to haul their belongings over the ice. What are you, an idiot, Otto?"

"Hey, don't call me an idiot!" wailed Otto. "It's bad enough that Jean-Baptiste makes fun of me, but I can't believe that you're making fun of me, too. I thought you were my friend, Carsten."

Carsten snorted.

"Listen," Fernando interjected, "let's keep focused on the matter at hand. Stop bickering with each other, would you?" When the others remained quiet, he said, "We have to deal with the humans right now. Later, we can talk about the meaning of life and our ancestors." He was thinking, *I'd do anything to shut Otto up.*

"I say we wipe them out," said Jean-Baptiste. He whirled himself into a little cyclone of snow.

"No violence," said Fernando, pointing an icy finger at Jean-Baptiste.

"If we hurt them, maybe the humans will stop coming here," countered Jean-Baptiste, always ready for a fight.

Fernando had to admit that Jean-Baptiste had a point. On the other hand, "We've hurt them before, and they keep coming back, don't they? No matter how hard we make it for them, the humans return, and each time they make it farther and farther into the continent. If they're not stopped, they'll find the telescope, Jean-Baptiste."

"They always come here and bother us. They kill seals and they cook them! What if they cook and eat us, too? I say we leave them alone," whined Otto.

"Oh for godsakes," said Carsten, "can we just get this over with? Fernando's right, we have to do something and drive them away. And okay *okay,* no violence."

Fernando heard the human voices from afar. "Shh . . ." he said. The Fridarians froze in place, listening.

"What I would do for a bloody raw steak," said one human. From the voice, Fernando knew it was a male.

"I'll take slabs of chicken and pork, thank you very much, even turtle or alligator," said another. "Anything decent would do."

"Maybe not insects, though," said the first, laughing.

"You can keep your turtles and insects," said a third voice. "Just give *me* all the sirloin steak, mashed potatoes, and hot tea."

And then the second voice said, "I'm so blinded by this damn snow I can't see *what* I'm eating, so it might as well be turtles and insects."

Fernando focused. The voices stopped, and the Antarctic wind carried the sounds—so subtle, so far away—of teeth grinding into meat, of saliva gurgling down throats. The smell of seal blood floated into the mountains. The humans were shoving seal meat into their mouths, and the meat was sloshing into their stomachs. These humans had bodies built from tubules and vacuoles, pulsating bloody organs, and strange protuberances. Fernando wondered what happened to the meat after it entered the human bodies.

He wondered why they ate the meat and why they had to come here to do it. How dare they eat the creatures in Fernando's homeland!

He remembered the ships *Erebus* and *Terror* in the mid-1800's led by James Clark Ross, and Lieutenant Archibald McMurdo who served on the *Terror*. He remembered Adrien de Gerlache and then Carsten Borchgrevink in 1898, who by 1900 had driven his dogs and sledges up the Ice Barrier into Fernando's mountains. And now came these three men through McMurdo Sound, stumbling a mile or two per day, barely surviving, but insisting on conquering Fernando's land and eating the seals.

Fernando wouldn't stand for it. "They can't get away with this! It's not right! Come on, let's go get them," he said to Jean-Baptiste, Carsten, and Otto. "But remember, no violence, we just chase them away."

With his friends following, he leapt up and out of the telescope crevasse, and then he raged across the gulleys and went howling down the mountains. He blasted as hail down the icebergs and whipped across the plains. Fernando would scare the humans. He would scare them until they left Antarctica and never came back. He peeked behind him. Two blizzards raged close behind him: Jean-Baptiste and Carsten. Otto trailed along as a feeble mist.

On the horizon, the sun had dimmed to an anti-sun, an orb of cold light filtering through the snow and sending cross-hatches of blue across the glaciers and down the 200-foot cliffs of the Great Ice Barrier.

The four Fridarians pulsed and huddled together. The cross-hatch of blue light diminished, and the ice crunched, and this time, the seals stirred and nudged their young into the frigid sea. The stench of fear rose in the animals, even in the leopard seals who weighed a thousand pounds.

Long ago, Fernando and his friends had learned how to interpret human vibrations and speech. Now the human voices grew louder.

"Snatcher died."

"From what?"

"Officially, I'd say it was acute peritonitis."

"Unofficially?"

"The dog died from being *here*. Extreme cold, blizzards, and not enough food."

"What about the other dogs?"

"Getting weaker by the minute. Most of them are urinating blood."

"What are we going to do, Scott?"

"I don't know, Wilson. We have to keep pushing forward. We may have to slaughter the weaker dogs. What do you think, Shackleton?"

"Well, the stronger dogs are going to die of starvation if we don't feed them more, so I'm with you, we have to kill the weaker ones."

"More killing," whispered Jean-Baptiste. "Now they're killing their own dogs."

"To use them as food," added Carsten.

"Oh God, what I would do for a decent meal! Did we freeze enough seal meat and fat? Do we have enough for the depot?"

"Whatever it is, it'll have to do."

Seals and dogs, thought Fernando, *the humans will eat any creatures near them. Nothing's sacred to humans. They're beasts. They're immoral, possibly they are the very embodiment of evil.*

Jean-Baptiste balled himself into a sphere of ten thousand ice particles, packed hard and ready to roll.

Otto whined, "Remember, Fernando said not to kill them. We just have to scare them away." He fluttered his ice particles like feathers, preening and scattering specks of black rock into the wind.

Jean-Baptiste rolled back and forth across a vast ice sheet, breaking it into pieces that fell hundreds of feet into the black sea. "Our lives are at risk," he said. "If the humans discover us, we're done for. I say we blow them away. All it would take is one blast of ice, one snow storm, a whiteout. *Anything.* Come on, why not, Fernando, *why not?*"

"But *why?*" said Otto. "I see now that they're not going to eat us. We're not flesh and blood like the Earth animals. As I see it, the humans have no way to hurt us. Let's just leave them alone." Otto was still whining—he rarely spoke in anything but that annoying sing-song voice—and he was still shedding ice and twitching in circles.

"Goddamn it, shut the hell up!" Jean-Baptiste rolled straight across Otto and flattened him onto the surface of the ice.

Otto's nano-membranes swelled as he replicated his ice particles into a cushion. "They can't do anything to us. We can't die unless—unless *maybe* our pre-programming switches off. I can't think of any reason we'd switch off unless maybe we spawn, so what are you worried about? What can the humans *do* to us? Let's just leave them alone."

Jean-Baptiste yelled at Otto to shut the hell up, but Fernando tuned it all out. Something in Otto's words suddenly made sense to Fernando, crystallizing an idea that had lay dormant, germinating in his mind for a long time. They, the Fridarians, were built from nanoparticles, from molecular circuitry. If that circuitry broke down or malfunctioned, if it simply grew old, could it *stop?* Was it possible that, as Otto suggested, they were all somehow pre-programmed to die? He was going to ask Otto about this idea when Jean-Baptiste screamed, "Idiots! Our way of life will be over! Our freedom will be gone! They'll bottle us, examine us, tear us apart! Sure, if we're lucky, we might survive, but it won't be much of a life."

Fernando made a quick decision. Jean-Baptiste was probably right. Fernando told Carsten to return to the telescope and wait "in case another transmission gurgles into the queue."

"What I saw earlier was old," said Carsten, "stored in the circuits. I think that I must have missed it somehow. We won't have another transmission."

Fernando would talk to Otto later about his pre-programming ideas. What he wanted to do now was unload Otto before approaching the humans, but he didn't want to make Otto feel bad. "Please, Carsten, this is important. Return and take Otto with you. Go on, Otto, *help Carsten with the equipment.*"

"Yeah, go back home, and let the real men do the work," said Jean-Baptiste.

"That's not funny!" wailed Otto.

"It's not supposed to be funny," said Jean-Baptiste.

"Fernando, it's not fair!" wailed Otto.

"Please. *Carsten.* You and Otto need to monitor the telescope, just in case. *Go!*"

Muttering, Otto trailed after Carsten, and the two formed a black cloud of doom, which wafted away and disappeared up the glacier and back to the plateau.

Fernando signaled at Jean-Baptiste to follow him, and they blasted down the Ice Barrier onto the floes of the Ross Sea. They merged their thousands of particles into prongs of ice and zoomed horizontally across the floes, like hypodermics heading straight toward the three humans and their dogs.

Fernando didn't want to hurt anyone, he really didn't–

We'll just chase away the humans, that's all–

But Jean-Baptiste was so strong, at least twice the size of Fernando, and his prongs slammed into the humans, who reeled backward onto the ice, grappling at each other and screaming for help. The dogs, ten of them, howled but couldn't stand up: the Fridarian ice storm was too fierce.

The humans looked like clowns, impotent and silly: clad in coats and pants, huge fur gloves, and boots of fur or padded cloth.

Jean-Baptiste howled with delight and swirled in eddies around the poor creatures, pricking their noses with ice, making their skin bulge with the chilblain, coating their pants with frozen crystals.

The smell of blood was everywhere, and the snow was painted red from the remains of the seal and the fluids of the sick dogs. It was a biting smell, one that spread like a cancer in the tiny particles that made up Fernando. He no longer felt like himself. It was as if a claw held his thoughts in check. He was dazed, stunned, and gripped by some form of delirium. An odd euphoria gurgled through him. The blood bound his particles and sent the oxygen racing through him. His particles started congealing and slowing down, they scraped against each other, and he couldn't think straight. He burst out laughing.

Jean-Baptiste was also laughing hysterically, and he was whirling as if drunk on the surge of oxygen. But they were both clearly high on something other than oxygen. They were high on *the blood.*

With mounting horror, Fernando watched Jean-Baptiste lap the blood off the snow. As the snow got whiter, Jean-Baptiste in the form of mist became increasingly red. Before long, the blood seemed suspended in the air—somehow gluing Jean-Baptiste's mist into ordered shapes. Jean-Baptiste hung in the air in the form of spheres, cubes, and bizarre structures twisted together at odd angles.

The three humans screamed and pointed at Jean-Baptiste. "What the hell is it?" cried one. This man was known as Robert Falcon Scott—Fernando knew this from vibrations in the air as the humans thought to themselves. Scott shoved the other two men, Edward Wilson and Ernest Shackleton, towards some thick cloth tents that were secured to the ice with stakes. They were still hollering and pointing. Cowards, these humans: they could club defenseless animals to death and devour their flesh, but a light mist scared them.

Jean-Baptiste, the mist of odd shapes, followed the men into the tent. They flailed and tried to escape from him, and as they scrambled to run from the bloody spheres and cubes, the tent collapsed. Holding onto each other, Scott, Wilson, and Shackleton stood, shaking and stumbling away from Jean-Baptiste.

"Get away! Whatever you are, get away!" cried Wilson.

"We can't be seeing this," muttered Scott. "It's got to be a hallucination affecting all three of us. Sleep deprivation, freezing cold, blizzards. Maybe we've all contracted an infection."

Fernando felt himself congealing into something far more than a mist or a chunk of ice. Just the smell of the blood was slowing down the movement of his particles, his metabolism. He filtered more oxygen from the air, hoping it would flush the pollutants from his system, but the oxygen only made him more giddy.

The humans' dogs barked, tried to stand, and fell down from weakness. Shaggy big dogs with white fur and dark patches. Intelligent eyes, following Fernando's every move, terrified by what they saw. Fernando saw himself reflected in those eyes and also in the glassy dead stare of the dog the humans had called Snatcher. The dead Snatcher was on its back, all four legs sticking up. The dog was cut down the center, its organs removed.

The humans come here, and they defile our home . . .
The humans torture and eat their own animals . . .
The humans put this diseased blood on our ice!

Fernando, drunk as he was on the blood, steadied himself and produced an icicle as long as a human body. He prodded Snatcher with the icicle. The dog's blood clung to the sharp prong, seeped into it, flowed up the icicle into the rest of Fernando's body. He shimmied from the impact. Saw himself glowing a fierce golden red, felt the force of the hemoglobin as it transported more oxygen and strange new nutrients to his internal particles.

What was happening to him?

It was the strangest thing, like an evolution of Fernando as a creature, as if he could feel himself transforming into something much more sophisticated and elaborate. It reminded him of the moments directly after his activation, but this time, the surge of the high was a thousand times greater.

Whatever was happening, Fernando *liked* it.

He stuck the icicle into the dog's remains again, and he drank more blood. A hot flush surged through him and congealed his particles. He felt more *whole,* more real. This was far better than being a chunk of ice. Fernando had transformed into a new consistency, one that merged the blood with his Fridarian particles and enabled him to assume a flesh-like appearance. It was heady, this new birth.

He arranged his particles into forms he knew: dog snouts and tails, human ears and limbs. He disassembled them back into nano-particles, then re-arranged them into seal flippers, whale blubber, and wings.

Jean-Baptiste hung over the collapsed tent with human skin stuck to his ice. Scott and Wilson were bleeding, and they fell alongside their dogs into the snow and ice. Wilson's nose was bloated from frostbite: red, raw, the left nostril damaged by scores of cuts.

"Get the dogs!" yelled Jean-Baptiste. "Get its remains! And get the seal, too!"

Fernando looked wildly around the human camp, saw the discarded skin and bones of the seal. The men had consumed most of the flesh and fat, but a bloody pool steamed off the snow to the left, and Fernando made a wild grab for it: blood, skin, bones, and whatever flesh and fat remained. Lifting his bounty, he curled ice around it and soared from the camp up the Ice Barrier and into the mountains. Jean-Baptiste whooshed past him in a blur of red hail, dizzy and screaming with glee. Fernando had no idea what had just happened to the two of them: what did the blood mean, why did it fill them with such potency, and now that they'd tasted the life energy of animals, how would they deal with what he could only think of as–

the bloodlust?

CHAPTER TWO

Antarctica: December 16, 1902
One Week Later

OH, HOW HE MISSED the feeling of blood raging through him! He could understand now why Scott, Shackleton, and Wilson ate the bloody meat and why they killed to feel the blood. Fernando pined for another dose. He plotted for a week with Jean-Baptiste about how they could drink more blood. Without hurting the creatures, it seemed to be an impossible goal. They devised various methods, but both knew that they would have to rely on the injury of other creatures, at minimum.

"Wait for the humans to kill birds, then lift the birds by wind and carry them into the mountains." This idea came from Jean-Baptiste. "Or capture a dog and slay it." This idea also came from Jean-Baptiste, and with it came a high-pitched chuckle.

It made Fernando shudder.

He offered his own idea:

"Wait for the humans and dogs to fall asleep, then prick their flesh with ice and take little nips of their blood."

"I like that!" cried Jean-Baptiste. "It works! We don't have to wound or kill anything, and we get our blood. Let's just go for the humans, Fernando. Human blood is the best."

Fernando had to agree. The potency of the seal and dog blood was good, but by far, the best high came from the human blood.

"The two of you are disgusting. You're no better than the

humans." Carsten frowned at Fernando and Jean-Baptiste. He was being his usual downer self. He was always so morose. He could be ice and hail, but instead, he insisted on appearing as frills of lacy black ice and piles of granite-dirty slush. He twiddled with the telescope, making sure for the umpteenth time that the focal point was directed exactly at the variable star.

Fernando told himself that, depressing as he was to be around, Carsten was very good at what he did. Carsten was the only one of them who was smart enough to interpret the ancestors' signals. It was more than Fernando could say for himself. Fernando's life was void of purpose and meaning. In less than two months, winter would set in, and the telescope had to be ready for any Fridarian transmissions sent by the ancestors. It wouldn't do to upset Carsten with too much talk about the blood.

The last message about the natural nuclear reactor had been followed by a stray message stuck in the telescope's cache. The star had pulsed changes in light intensity, up and down at different speeds that spelled out a message to the Earth-bound Fridarians:

DISASSEMBLE. THREE BEAMS ONLY. REPRODUCE.

Carsten tried to interpret the ancestors' meaning: "We're supposed to remain in our natural particle form, bound only by our nanotech glues, free to assemble and disassemble components. We're *not* supposed to become human monsters. We're *not* supposed to drink blood. The ancestors clearly didn't want us to be like the two of you with this . . . this bizarre cancer-like tumor of alien fleshy matter. *We're not supposed to take alien flesh form.*"

But I like it, thought Fernando. *I like having ears, feet, and wings. I like having rolls of fat and fleshy protuberances of any kind I want.* "What's the harm in it?" he said.

"How do you know all that, Carsten? How do you know what the ancestors meant? What three beams were they talking about?" said Otto.

"I don't know what the beams are," said Carsten, "and as for the rest, well, look at us, Otto. We're ice and snow. We're blizzards and glaciers, mists, fogs, storms, and frost. We don't have internal organs like these humans and their animals. We don't have fleshy alien parts, like mouths, hair, legs. We're entirely different."

"So, and your point is . . . ?" said Jean-Baptiste.

"My point," said Carsten, "is that *we're not built for eating alien flesh and drinking alien blood.*"

"So what? It tastes good. And it's a damn good high, wouldn't you say, Fernando?" said Jean-Baptiste.

"You should try it, Carsten." Fernando was pulled into the conversation against his better judgement. "There's no Fridarian law, memento, or code that says we can't experience new things, eat new foods, or enjoy ourselves. In fact, we exist to enjoy ourselves. That's all we've ever done." And then, quietly to Jean-Baptiste, Fernando pulsed a private message: *Carsten hasn't tasted or smelled the blood. He doesn't know what it's like to get high. But if he's "accidentally" exposed to the alien blood, he might understand why we like it so much. He just doesn't know what he's missing.*

Jean-Baptiste pulsed a private message back: *I don't want to disassemble into mist if I can't get high like this again, do you?*

No, pulsed Fernando. *I like having both forms, normal and high, mist and flesh shapes.*

Jean-Baptiste pulsed, *Carsten's not going to go for the bloodlust any more than Otto. Carsten's el depresso all the time, and Otto's just too frightened of everything to imbibe.*

I disagree, pulsed Fernando. *Being depressed, Carsten is more inclined to imbibe. He'll like the giddy release of the blood. Imagine Carsten happy for a change. One taste is all it'll take, then we won't have to put up with his bad moods all the time.*

Jean-Baptiste contemplated, then nodded. *Yeah, you're right. So let's give him a nip of the blood now.*

Now? What do you suggest?

We haven't been to the human camp for over a week. Let's return with Carsten and show him a good time.

Fernando quivered with desire. Yes no yes no, he couldn't make up his mind.

More blood . . .

Yes.

Killing the humans.

No.

Drinking the blood of dead alien animals. Dogs, seals . . .

Maybe.

Bloodosterone surges . . . the blood raging through my body!

Yes.

Did he really have a choice?

No.

So Fernando convinced Carsten to go on a little scouting expedition to the human camp. It was either that or throwing snow at each other, and God knew they'd had enough snowball fights over the years. Seen one blizzard, seen them all.

So Carsten tagged along with Fernando and Jean-Baptiste, two high-flying dense fogs trailed by a black wisp of gloom.

It didn't take long for the three Fridarians to locate the humans and their dogs. The pungent odor, the rasping voices, the barking, the howling: the humans spewed signals that led the trio directly to them.

At eighty degrees south of the pole, Scott, Shackleton, and Wilson were tucking provisions into tents hidden beneath ice canopies. "Three weeks of food and supplies," said Scott to the others. "We've already marched three hundred and eight miles. We have to continue south to the Pole, and when we come back through here, we'll get what we need for the journey home."

Scott was the clear leader of the human group: they deferred to him, did as he asked, and even respected him. Fernando almost felt jealous of this human, this Robert Falcon Scott. Though Fernando wouldn't want to be a human or look like Scott, of course; nor would he want to be responsible for all the death and mayhem surrounding the humans. But of the three men, Fernando liked Scott the best: strong, determined, kind, clear blue eyes, black hair, prominent nose. Edward Wilson, the medical doctor, also had blue eyes and dark hair, and he sported a beard and moustache. The third man of the bunch, Ernest Shackleton, had a troubled look about him; but he had a keen intelligence in his dark eyes, a survivor's grim set to his features.

All three men wore thick canvas clothes, including parkas, vests, shirts, pants, and large wallets that looped over their belts in the front. They were snow worn and weary, bedraggled.

Fernando looked at Jean-Baptiste, the fierce fog of blush-pink ice, and at Carsten, the sluggish mist of black depression. And what of himself, of Fernando? Strong and large, an immense frost, a commanding blizzard.

He wondered how the humans saw them. What were they, the three Fridarians, when compared to the three humans? The Fridarians played and romped, thought only of themselves. The humans worked and suffered, and while they also thought only of themselves, like the Fridarians, they also watched out for each other. They might eat seals and dogs, penguins and other birds, but they didn't eat each other.

It was a point that Fernando would have to remember.

On Earth, the humans ate all other creatures but did not eat each other. Nor did they drink each other's blood.

"Watch and learn how we subdue the humans and get what we want," Jean-Baptiste told Carsten, and then he drummed up wind barbs and howling gales, blasts of snow so thick the sky was white murk. The men would not be able to see a foot in front of them, and their dogs would grow weaker.

Tossing all night in their tents and sleeping bags, their teeth chattering so hard that they chipped, the three men looked close to death. They shared a biscuit, with each man getting a third and gulping it down in one bite. They shared a small portion of seal fat and washed it down with green liquid from a tin can.

And then Scott, Wilson, and Shackleton packed up their gear and moved on. One dog, Grannie, collapsed and the humans strapped her to a sledge and hauled her up a steep stretch of ice. Fernando and his friends watched, and they followed.

Wilson groaned a lot, staggered, and clawed at his eyes. He was snow blind from the reflection of the sun off the ice. Fernando knew the man was in pain, for eventually, Scott strapped a blindfold over Wilson's eyes for protection. Wilson marched onward, hauling two hundred pounds of sledge and supplies behind him. The straps over his shoulders dug into his upper chest and under his arms. With every step, he slipped and almost fell, yet he marched on.

Luckily, Fernando, Jean-Baptiste, and Carsten didn't have eyes or skin made from flesh. They never worried about the sun searing their corneas or scorching the flesh of their hands and feet. They couldn't get frostbite or snow blindness. They couldn't fall down glaciers. They *were* frostbite. They *were* glaciers.

Carsten seemed to be enjoying the drama of human suffering and pain. He remained black but vibrated more rapidly, sending bolts of winds and ice at the three men. Fernando and Jean-Baptiste held off from attacking the humans and their dogs with blizzards. They wanted Carsten to fall prey to the allure of the aliens and the bloodlust. And their strategy seemed to be working.

The humans marched for twelve, sometimes fifteen, hours a day, and after a few days of this brutal physical exertion and bravery, they pulled the sleeping bags off the sledge once again to settle under an ice ledge for the night. The winds howled. The temperature closed in on negative twenty-five degrees. Winter wouldn't bring darkness for another month and a half, and the men would be forced to continue sleeping under the sharp eye of the six-month sun.

Jean-Baptiste danced around the sleeping bags.

Later, Fernando drooled as he watched the three humans fry pemmican and biscuits in their Primus cooker and snack on lumps of sugar and cocoa. When the dog Grannie died, the humans wept, but they cut her to bits and fed her to the other dogs, who eagerly gobbled her up.

Fernando noticed that when hungry enough, dogs ate each other. He wondered if the humans would eat other under certain conditions, and if the seals, penguins, and other alien animals would do the same. He wondered if the alien blood lust included cannibalism, that once the Fridarians were all in the grips of blood lust, they might also be at risk of the same strange habit.

When the humans checked their position using a sledgeometer, Carsten was fascinated. "My God, these aliens have advanced technology!" he exclaimed. "I don't even know how our telescope works, yet the humans can figure out their location in *our* homeland using a simple wheel."

Then Scott looked at the sun's position with another device, something he termed a theodolite, and announced to the other two that they were at eighty-one degrees thirty feet south. Carsten was so excited at discovering the alien technology that he stole both a sledgeometer and a theodolite, whipping away the devices in a storm and stashing them high in the mountains.

By the end of December, Fernando could wait no longer to satisfy his bloodlust. Jean-Baptiste convinced him that the time had come to feast on the humans and their animals. How much longer could the Fridarians watch as the humans fried seal liver and pemmican fat? How much longer could they smell the slowing pulses of the dogs' hearts before they gave into the urge to attack and drink blood?

Fernando and Jean-Baptiste licked a few drops of blood off the seal liver, and when they slithered as mist against the black fog that was Carsten, they knew that their wait was finally at an end. As their particles intertwined with Carsten, the black fog finally felt the blood.

Even from a few drops, the blood surged through Carsten. It was in the long thin filaments that stretched from one icy plank to a globule of snow at his other end. It was everywhere at once, and the more Fernando and Jean-Baptiste wrapped themselves around Carsten, the more he felt it.

Carsten's black got blacker, and his storm grew harsher; and then the three of them joined forces; and together, their blizzard was *brutal*, one of the worst they had ever produced.

The men slogged onward, hauling their sledges. The dogs, what remained of them, dragged through the gale, ice coating every hair on their bodies. As soon as a foot or paw print pressed into the snow, it disappeared in a blast of wind.

That's when Carsten ripped open the crevasses beneath the ice and snow. The men couldn't see the deep holes beneath the surface, and neither could the dogs. Holding onto each other with ropes, the men tripped their way over the crevasses, barely making it across before the ice gave way and the hole opened up and swallowed everything near it.

It was the first time the Fridarians purposely killed a creature. And it was Carsten who took that first bold step, not Fernando and not the even wilder Jean-Baptiste.

When the ice groaned and split, when the four dogs fell into the crevasse far below the surface . . . when the humans decided that they had to "go back now" . . . when they left the dogs there in the clutches of the Fridarians, the dogs still steaming with hot blood, the effervescence curling in intoxicating circles around Fernando, Jean-Baptiste, and Carsten . . .

When the three just couldn't resist any longer . . .

They plunged like cyclones into that hole, sank their fangs—*their icy pricks*—into the necks of those dogs, and they killed them and drank the corpses dry.

CHAPTER THREE

Cerdanya, France: October 2015
One Hundred Years Later

CHLOE DESMARAIS WAS IN the smokehouse, head dizzy from the fire, when he came at her from behind. She heard him before she saw him; the crunch of his work boots on the twigs, the scrape of his fingers on the latch, the door creaking open. Sun streamed across the dirt floor. Chloe whirled, but he was faster, and his fingers dug into her arm as he jerked her around to face him.

"Mon père! Father, no!" Chloe dropped the jar of diced garlic, and it fell into the pot.

Chloe's father glared at her. Gray hairs poked from the mole over his lip. She staggered back, but only for a moment, and then his hand whipped out and smacked her cheek, catching her beneath the left eye.

"How *could* you? Why do you hit me all the time? What for? Get *off* me!" Chloe slapped at her father, but his grip tightened on her arm.

He hit her again, this time harder. "All your fault, is why!" he yelled. "You don't get enough done! Why can't you do more, you lazy bitch?"

She cringed and steeled herself for another blow, but it didn't come. The pain inside her was worse than the pain of his beatings, for this was her own father, and it hurt like hell that he didn't love her. He seemed to resent her very existence. Was it that he didn't want the responsibility of a child? Was it that she was a bad person? A combination of the two? Or was her father the bad person? After all, she was his only daughter, and if not for her, he would have starved to death long ago.

"If you keep hurting me, I won't be able to work," she said. "If you're so worried about how much sausage I'm making and how much bread I'm baking, it would make more sense *not* to beat me." She shouldn't have said it, but it slipped out of her mouth. She knew that arguing with her father was pointless.

"Say, what?" he said sharply.

"Nothing." Her voice was almost a whisper.

"Oh, don't think I didn't hear you, Chloe. You're whining because you don't want to work, aren't you? If you weren't so lazy, I wouldn't have to slap you."

Chloe smelled the wine on his breath—he was drunk again—and nothing she said would matter. Even when he wasn't drunk, his logic was always inverted, as if she was the trigger of his bad temper. Much as she hated lowering herself, there were no options with her father other than submitting to his demands. Begging was the only thing that ever really worked, so she said, "Please, I'm sorry, mon père. Yes, it's my fault, and I'll do better, I promise. Let me go, please, and I'll work harder, okay?" She kept her voice soft and even, carefully controlled. She bowed her head and pretended to cower, glancing nervously between him and the dirt floor.

He narrowed his eyes and studied her face as if judging her sincerity. His fingers were still clamped around her right arm. He drew her close so their faces almost touched. "All right, then, but don't let it happen again."

She wanted to spit on him, but instead, she held her breath, waiting for him to release her arm. In the one-room smokehouse, his stench was overwhelming: rancid meat and stale wine, unwashed clothes, greasy body. She tried to relax in his grip, but she was trembling.

He saw her fear and his mouth twisted into a cold smile. He was enjoying her pain, it was obvious. He said, "Pierre and I count on you, Chloe. We're all in this together. We can sell sausage and bread and cheese, but it's *your* job, Chloe, to give us something to sell. The Desmaraises have owned this land for hundreds of years. I don't want to lose it to the Spanish, not now, not after all this time. Poor Pierre would be left with nothing, no inheritance whatsoever. You don't want to do that to your own brother, do you?"

Always, he worried about Pierre, and never, he worried about Chloe. It was 2015, modern times, not the middle ages. Didn't girls have any rights? She wanted to lip off and argue with him that any inheritance of the Desmarais land should be *at least* split with her, but she had to remain calm when her father was drunk and upset. She said in as much a monotone as she could muster, "Yes, of course I understand. I'll do better, I promise."

Why had her mother married this monster, *why?* Yves Desmarais had been more than twice her mother's age, and he was as ugly as a pig, *le cochon*: upturned nostrils, beady black eyes, hairy ears. Chloe's mother had died in childbirth as a teenage bride, leaving Chloe with *le cochon* for eighteen years . . . and counting.

Her arm hurt where his fingers dug into her flesh, and she was certain her skin was bruised.

Her father said, "Pierre tells me he needs to pay the bills, Chloe. He needs money. We expect tourists through Cerdanya tomorrow from the Mediterranean. There's another big boat coming through and stopping for a few days at Perpignan. What do you suggest we sell to them?"

"I'll bake bread tonight, and we have a nice batch of goat cheese. I can't hurry up the sausage. It still needs smoking, heating, cold water dips, and then the drying." She didn't mention that the sausage would be jacked on garlic and totally ruined.

"How *many* loaves? How *much* cheese?"

She yanked free and stumbled toward the pot and the dying fire beneath it. She was careful not to reach and grab anything to steady herself. Anything near the fire or the pot would burn her hands.

As she rubbed her arm, trying to get the circulation back into it, he shut the door behind him, cutting the stream of sun flowing into the room. Neon dots flashed before her eyes as she adjusted to the darkness and smoke. If he didn't get out soon and leave her alone, she was going to pass out. She needed air. She needed him to leave.

Hoping to satisfy him, she said, "I'll make fifty loaves, and we already have a few pounds of cheese."

He pointed a finger at her. "I'll send Pierre and Deétda later to check and make sure you're working."

Pierre, her lazy creep of a brother, and his deadbeat girlfriend, Deétda: both were worthless good-for-nothings who smoked and snorted the family earnings.

There had to be some way out of Cerdanya, some way to escape from this life: there had to be something better. Chloe was determined to leave Cerdanya, the sooner the better. She couldn't stay here and be abused anymore. She was eighteen and could do whatever she wanted, and once she left, she would never come back.

Her thoughts flashed to Llivia, the Cerdanya town on the border of France and Spain. Tiny as it was, Llivia was much bigger than Chloe's forest community, and it wasn't all that far away, maybe an hour's hike through the woods and ravines. From there, Chloe might be able to find her way to the Mediterranean Sea, where the tourists came on yachts and cruise ships. Maybe she could slip onboard one of those ships and run away like people did in the movies. Not that Chloe had seen any movies, but she'd heard about them.

"I'll do what I have to do, father," she said, "It's not necessary to send Pierre and Deétda to check on me."

"Well, I say it is."

Quickly she added, "But it's fine. Don't worry. I'll get everything done." *And then I'll escape to the coast and to freedom. I've had enough of you, and I've had enough of Pierre and Deétda.*

She would become like the girls by the sea. She would wear beautiful dresses and bathing suits, and have friends who made her laugh. She wouldn't have to tighten her long hair into buns high on her head. She would emerge from this life hidden in the mountains and forests.

She wasn't really alive here anyway. On good days, she might see a couple of other girls her age, but they were all as dull as goats, all as depressed and lackluster as she'd become over the years.

"You'll get a whipping, Chloe, if those fancy people come and we have nothing for them."

Yes, yes, the whippings, she knew all about the whippings. The only way out of them was to run away.

And she would run away.

But for now . . .

"No more whippings, mon père," she said. "I'll be good."

She edged away from him and from the fire. Sweat soaked the back of her dress and ran down her face and neck. It was a cramped room, the smokehouse, built from an old refrigerator and piles of fruit wood. She ducked beneath the ham hocks dangling from hooks on the ceiling, inched past the table that held the jars of spices and cures.

She was by the door when he said, "Do as I say, then." He paused. "And get out of my way. I have things to do."

Like drink wine all day. Maybe he'd fall into a stupor and leave her alone. It was all she could hope for, really.

He shoved past her, and then she heard his boots stomping down the path toward the ancient stone house. She leaned, peeked outside the door, and saw him down by the creek with the mountains behind him. They looked sweet, those peaks with their trails spiraling off into the far distance. They were tipped in ice and snow, painted like frosting on cupcakes.

Her father disappeared behind the stone house, probably getting ready to slump on the bench by the creek and drink booze. Except for the caws of birds and the chirping of grasshoppers, the forest was quiet. The creek gurgled, light flickering across it like dancing fairies. The smell of pine and moss cleared some of the smokehouse ashes from her nostrils.

You'd almost think it was nice here.

But it wasn't nice at all. It was anything but nice.

Chloe pulled the smokehouse door shut and sank onto the stool by the table. Her right arm was bruised: she rolled up her sleeve, saw the purple welts starting to rise. It would be hard for her to bake fifty loaves of bread with an aching arm. She had to punch down the dough, knead it, and shape it. How on earth was she going to do that?

She wiped her nose on her sleeve and reminded herself that a bruised arm was nothing compared to a whipping. She had better get back to work.

She spooned the garlic jar out of the sausage pot and spent the day preparing the meat. By the time she finished her smokehouse work, dusk was settling across the mountains. The hut where she baked bread was bigger than the smokehouse, but just as hot. It stood in a clearing set into the forest near the smokehouse, and she had to wind her way up a path over the rocks and twigs to get to it. In the distance stood the mountain peaks with their glittering snow and ice. In the dying sun, they no longer looked like frosted cupcakes, but rather, like a string of beckoning jewels.

Chloe held her skirt so it wouldn't drag across the forest floor. Her sandals were worn and needed mending, but her feet were tough from a lifetime of tramping over rocks and branches.

It wasn't yet night, so she carried the unlit lantern through the shadows. The broken sandal flapped up and down on her left foot. She knew the path well, but couldn't see it as the darkness settled, and she tripped over a branch.

Tiny creatures squealed and skittered past her, dashing into the gloom of the deeper forest. Babies, she thought, wild boars: they were striped for camouflage against the twigs. From afar came a series of bellows, a wild boar's sign of fear and alarm. Probably the mother and her two or three female friends along with their recent offspring.

The males traveled alone and showed up here during the winter when they fought over the females. There was no way, thought Chloe, that the bellowing came from the males: it was too early in the season for them to be here at all.

Up ahead was the grass clearing, and at its edge, the bakehouse, an old hut that was warped and leaned to the left. The door didn't quite fit into the frame, and most of the stone tiles on the roof were long gone.

Chloe wasn't looking forward to a long night in the bakehouse. The place always spooked her. *Mort de peur.*

She stepped into the clearing, and her foot sank into mud. She wrenched her foot up and saw that her broken sandal was caught in the grass and mud. *Great.* She stooped and yanked the sandal out of the mud, then wiped it off with dry leaves and slipped it back on her foot.

Then it hit her: why was the clearing *muddy?* And why was the grass churned into clumps of wet sod? It hadn't rained in ages, and the surrounding forest was dry. What would cause one spot to be wet? She couldn't think of a single reason. As for the chunks of sod, only one explanation made any sense at all to her, an explanation that sent shivers down her spine.

It was possible that the wild boars had plowed the grass with their tusks as they dug for roots and small animals to eat. The boars often ripped up parts of the forest and devoured everything they could find. It took a lot of food to satisfy them—a small boar could eat several animals and many pounds of roots per day. If they didn't find enough food, the boars were dangerous. These were animals to avoid, all the villagers knew it: the male boars were aggressive and killed children who wandered too far into the woods.

She stared at the mud, puzzling over the situation. There was no reason to be afraid of the forest where she'd grown up and lived her whole life. The only beast in these woods was her father. Wild boars hadn't attacked anyone that Chloe knew. The rumors about the boars were just *that*: rumors. Yet she couldn't think of any reason why the clearing would be muddy if not for the animals, and it continued to bother her as she slogged her way toward the bakehouse.

Hammered together using nails and splintered slats, the door creaked on its rusty hinges as she opened it, and then it slammed shut behind her. She jumped slightly.

There was nothing to fear. Nothing.

Il y avait rien à craindre.

She set the lantern on the shelf to her right and groped for the matches. As the gloom dissipated into a dirty yellow, Chloe laughed at herself for letting the boars get the best of her. She should know better. Boars were nothing to fear compared to people.

She lit the fire in the rear of the bakehouse, and soon, smoke spiraled through the hole in the roof. Meat dangled from the ceiling hooks. It seemed that everywhere Chloe went, she was surrounded by ham hocks.

She dumped flour from the sack into the giant urn, then tossed in some salt. Then she warmed lard in a pot over the fire and made a yeast paste. She sat on a stool by the table on the right side of the room and waited for the paste to rise and become a sponge. As she waited, she listened to the sounds of the night: the wild boars grunting and squealing as they returned to their nests; the claws of *la griffe,* a bear, on a tree nearby; the scurrying of mice, raccoons, and squirrels; and what she swore sounded like the hiss of a hedgehog.

Half asleep, she worked more flour into the yeast paste. Her right arm was weak with pain.

She *wouldn't* work this hard much longer, *wouldn't* endure her father's abuse.

She would escape and find a much better life, maybe even respect, happiness, a future. There was nothing in Cerdanya for Chloe except hard work and beatings. She deserved better. In fact, she thought, *anyone* would deserve better. Wincing from pain, she split the dough and worked each piece into a glossy mound.

Pain sliced from her arm to her shoulder and shot down her back. Her head was pounding.

She knew how to ignore pain, she'd been doing it her whole life. She slipped into a rhythm, hearing nothing but the squishing of the dough, the thwack of the mounds as she slammed them onto the table. She kneaded and slammed the dough in the same rhythm as the throbbing of the pain.

Squish.

Thwack.

Squish.

Thwack.

But her arm hurt too much, and she had to stop. She was so dizzy that she almost fell down. She steadied herself and wiped the sweat from her face. It was too hot in here. She opened the top three buttons of her dress and fanned herself.

And that's when she heard something scratching at the door.

It sounded like a *claw.*

Or maybe a *tusk.*

The noise came from the top of the door, not near the bottom where a bear or wild boar would scratch. Fully awake now, Chloe stood paralyzed, rolling over the possibilities in her mind. Squirrels, no. Birds, no. Deer, no . . .

Maybe it was a bear. Or worse, a wild boar.

But a boar wouldn't just scratch the door. If it really wanted to get inside, a hungry male would smash down the door and come raging into the bakehouse, claws and tusks ready to sink into her neck, face, and body. It would kill her before she knew it was there.

The scratching rose in pitch.

Chloe gripped the table.

Something scraped against the door, something that sounded like wings. The scratching and scraping spread, intensifying and eclipsing the other noises of the forest.

She'd seen horseshoe bats, civets, feral horses, wild mouflon, pine martens, and once, she'd even seen a raccoon dog, which was said not to exist in Cerdanya. But nothing made *this* type of sound.

Across the room on the table, the mounds of dough started quivering. Chloe rubbed her eyes, imagined them bleary, the blue irises dim and the whites all bloodshot. Her eyes burned. She was seeing things. Dough didn't quiver. She blinked rapidly, trying to erase the vision.

But no, the vision didn't go away.

The mounds *were* quivering, and worse, *they were quivering in unison.*

The lantern cast threads of light around the room, and as the strands hit the dough, the loaves shook—ever so slightly, but they *shook.*

She must be overtired and imagining things, all sorts of things. Rising loaves of bread didn't shake in unison. They didn't shake at all. And she was probably imagining the scratching, the scraping, the fluttering of wings, whatever it was: the sound spreading across the door. She was too stressed out, losing her mind. *Insanité.*

Then, as abruptly as it had begun, the scraping stopped, and relief washed over her; but her relief was short lived, because as soon as she relaxed, the sounds picked up again. This time, they changed to mimic the rhythm of the dough as she had kneaded it.

Squish.

Thwack.

Squish.

Thwack.

I'm going crazy, or maybe I'm asleep and I don't know it.

But no, obviously, she was fully awake. She would get to the bottom of the mystery, she would determine what was making the strange noises, expose it, and get it to shut up. What could it be, after all? Birds, squirrels, raccoons: it had to be something ordinary, *didn't it?*

She would *not* be afraid.

With her hurt arm, she yanked open the door.

A spasm of pain sliced through her arm into her shoulder and chest. She fell back, and her spine cracked against the edge of the urn, and then she crashed to the dirt floor. Pain flowed everywhere: up and down her legs, through her back and chest, and into her head.

The door creaked, began to close, and then stopped. She heard heavy breathing, and grunting. There was something out there, something hideous! She inched back across the floor. She was going to die, she was sure of it. That thing, whatever it was, would kill her and leave her bloody corpse here to rot.

And then she saw it!

It was the most horrifying creature she'd ever seen in her life:

It was a wild boar, but it *wasn't* a boar. It was a strange mutation with short wings on its back, hooves with claws, and eyes that glowed with the intelligence of a man.

Its wide mouth was open, its tusks bared against bloody gums.

The tusks themselves were long and bloody—

—and sharp.

Two on the top gum, two on the bottom. It was a male. Female boars had only two tusks, which weren't as sharp as the four tusks on this boar: it *had* to be a male.

Then a deep voice entered her mind as if from afar. *Your pain,* it said, *is like the smell of blood, Chloe. Your pain is so alluring, so needful, it calls to me, Chloe.*

The thought entered Chloe's mind, but it wasn't her thought. It came from the beast! And the beast knew her name!

She felt her heart pounding in the purple welts on her arm. She was on the floor, on her back, the pain piercing her like knives. She couldn't move.

The beast stepped toward the door, put one hoof on the threshold and placed the other hoof on the bakehouse floor. Its mouth curled upward, further exposing the tusks, and its beady black eyes glowered at the ham hocks dangling on the ceiling hooks. Then the eyes turned back to Chloe and glittered with amusement.

Ham, a disturbing choice, Chloe.

Not my fault! My father made me cook it.

And if he didn't force you, would you eat this meat?

Yes. No. Yes. NO! She knew the correct answer was, NO!, but she couldn't seem to hide her thoughts inside her own head and finished with, *YES!*

A rumbling laugh reverberated through her head. She wanted to scream but couldn't open her mouth. The beast stepped toward her. *Intoxicating and seductive: your pain arouses me, Chloe. Do you do this to me on purpose?*

She sputtered, trying to *force* out a scream.

There's no point screaming, mon chère. Nobody would hear you. We're in the middle of the woods, remember? And the only ones here beside you and me are my kin, the females and our babies.

She would never beckon a beast like this to her door. On purpose? *Never.* She squeaked, almost inaudible, "Help, somebody help me." Her words bounced off the beast and echoed back at her.

The beast laughed again, bloody gums bared, four tusks jutting out of its mouth like filthy icicles, dripping with blackened moisture. *You'll learn to enjoy me, mon chère. Give me time. You'll see, dear, that I make a wonderful companion. You can have everything your heart desires.*

What? Killing her father?

What? Running away?

She stared at the bloody tusks. This thing before her, this monster, would never be her companion. She would die rather than let it get any closer to her. She didn't mind living without fancy clothes and boats and the beach. She would stay right here in Cerdanya rather than have anything to do with this . . . this monster!

But don't you want love, Chloe? I can give you the love of ten thousand boys.

Surely, this was a nightmare, nothing more than a nightmare, and soon she would wake up and laugh at herself for thinking it was real. But for now, the monster was here, and nightmare or not–

Chloe lifted her right leg and with all her strength, kicked the door, which slammed into the beast. The thing stumbled, eyes wide with surprise, and then he . . . it . . . whatever it was . . . lost his footing and fell backward. He was outside. On the ground. As the door swung toward her, Chloe caught one last glimpse:

Black bristles on wet auburn fur.

Head twice the size of her father's.

Narrow hips and large haunches.

A tail with tassels.

Four legs but standing like a human on two hind legs.

Four hooves with claws.

Four tusks.

Feathery wings.

And then the beast fell to all four legs, and it bounded into the forest as quickly as a deer runs from a hunter.

His wings unfolded, his wet snout glistened, and it appeared to Chloe that his body disappeared, simply evaporated like mist into the night.

"Soon!" he cried. "Soon, you will be mine, Chloe Desmarais. And you will be proud to be with me, *proud!*" Its language was an odd mixture of old French and Spanish.

And then the door banged shut.

CHAPTER FOUR

Cerdanya, France: October 2015

SHE MANAGED TO SCRABBLE to her feet, and she stood by the door, listening to the night. Coming from the twigs on the edge of the clearing, Chloe heard the squealing of the suckling pigs, *cochons de lait*. Hooves lumbered over fallen branches and squished through moss, and from several directions, the snorting and bellowing of the female boars grew louder. Chloe waited until the noise subsided, then finally summoned the courage to step outside. She squinted at the forest beyond the clearing, but saw nothing other than the dark trees, the stars, and the moon.

Where had he gone, she wondered, the mutated male, the dangerous one who had come to her door? Was it trolling the woods, seeking children to eat? Were the old village rumors *true?*

The beast had been in her *mind*. It found her pain alluring, it said. This made no sense. Wild boars, *les cochons*, didn't have claws that looked like talons, and they didn't have short wings on their backs. They were *pourceaux*: swine, pork. While the males were strong and dangerous, they rarely attacked people. However, the same couldn't be said for the way the villagers treated the swine.

Everyone ate pork and sausages. *Everyone*. Chloe was intimately involved with the entire process: after Chloe's father killed a pig, it was her job to slice the meat into chops and cutlets, bacon and ham, to dice the feet, tails, and hearts, and to make the sausage.

But other than killing boars for food, Chloe's family lived in peace with the wild animals. And besides, boars didn't seek revenge for the death of one of their own. Animals didn't think that way . . .

. . . *did they?*

Returning to her stool in the hut, Chloe decided to put the matter out of her mind and get her work done. She massaged the base of her spine, where she'd fallen and hit the urn. Numbness crept down her leg, so she shook it, which oddly, didn't help: her leg tingled from her thigh to her toes. A slice of pain, as if from a knife, slashed across her left thigh.

The lantern had died, and the embers from the fire cast a red halo across the floor. Tendrils of red flicked across the walls and tables and etched capillaries into the tops of the loaves.

The dough was quivering again, and then, Chloe heard it, that awful *awful* noise:

Thwack.

Squish.

Thwack.

Squish.

She could barely stand to look at the dough, could barely stand to think of what the noise implied—*the beast.*

The capillaries in the dough pulsed to the rhythm.

Thwack. Squish. Thwack. Squish.

The beast chortled in her mind: *You think you're safe, Chloe, but you're not. I'm with you now, and I'm not going to leave. We're going to be together forever.*

No, it couldn't be! She was imagining this latest intrusion into her mind, she was imagining that the dough was pulsing as if it had a heartbeat. She had to be imagining things now, had to be, because the boar was long gone. She shook her head, trying to clear the beast's voice.

Why bother worrying about where I am, mon chère? We are one, you and I, no longer separated. It doesn't matter if I'm in the forest and you're in the bakehouse. Chloe could almost see the black eyes glittering as the beast added, *You might say that you are my mate. Your pain, it's like the smell of sweet blood.*

"Stop it! *Just stop it!*"

Had the beast returned? Was it here again, in the bakehouse? There was nowhere to hide in here, the bakehouse was small: just this one room with the fire, the table where the loaves . . . pulsed . . .

A spasm hit her spine, and she caught her breath, riding the pain until it ebbed again. Then she peered around the room. She was alone.

You can't fight me, Chloe. Pain is eternal. It's the source of all energy and strength. It gives substance and form. Without your pain, Chloe, what would you be?

"Who are you," she whispered, "and what do you want from me?"

Soft laughter filtered through her mind. *Blood and ice, Chloe. Substance and form. Love, perhaps. Devotion.*

"Whatever you are," she whispered, "please, please just leave me alone."

But I can't leave you alone, Chloe. We're just getting to know each other. You and I, Chloe: it's destiny, and you can't fight it, so why not just enjoy our time together? A pause. *In time, my sweet morsel, you'll learn to love me.*

She was losing her mind, there was no other explanation. The pain was getting to her. The stress.

She would finish baking the bread, then get some sleep. It was already well into night, and she wouldn't get enough rest, as it was, before she had to give her father the loaves for the tourists.

Then she would run away to Llivia on the border of France and Spain, and from there, to the Mediterranean Sea. She would slip onto a tourist boat or a yacht. She would become like the girls by the sea. She would wear sparkling clothes and have friends who made her laugh.

Dream on, Chloe. You can't run away, not from me. We're just getting started.

She tried to ignore the voice in her head. She'd always been clearheaded, the one who got things done. Her father was the nut job with the sopped mind, not Chloe. Her brother, Pierre, was the one who smoked dope and snorted coke. His girlfriend, Deétda, was the ditz who lived to get high, sex it up with Pierre, and do nothing else in life. Chloe was the strong one.

She needed some sleep, that was all. She'd be fine in the morning.

She wouldn't listen to the voice in her head.

There was nothing to fear, she told herself. *I don't hear you,* she thought. *I've baked bread and made sausage all alone in these woods my whole life, and you've never been here before.*

The beast was quiet. No other soundtrack played in her head, only her own thoughts.

She limped to the door and peeked outside.

The moon shifted behind black clouds. The squeals of the baby boars rode on the scent of pine.

It's all in my head. I didn't see anything. I didn't hear anything.

The females grunted by the nest and collapsed—thwack—into the dirt. The squealing rose.

And in the distance, a male bellowed. And from afar, faintly now:

Thwack.

Squish.

There's nothing to fear. I don't hear anything strange. I'll get the wood and stoke the fire. These were her thoughts, not a voice in her head. Chloe would throw dry wood on the embers and build the fire in the bakehouse, and with light and warmth, she would feel better again.

But then, even more faintly:

Thwack.

Squish.

She would ignore it. There was nothing else she could do. If Chloe could endure her father, the ultimate *cochon,* and her brother, Pierre, and Deétda, then she could ignore something that *couldn't* be true.

She clutched the slats of the bakehouse, felt her way around the corner, careful not to cut her fingers and get splinters. She reached for the stack of split logs behind the building, grimaced as the pain shot down her back and left leg. She lifted a few logs, shifting their weight onto her left arm, the one that didn't hurt.

She felt her way along the back of the bakehouse and limped around the corner to the front.

It was so cold, so dark with the moon hiding. No bellowing, no grunts, no squealing now, the wild boars were quiet.

Yet by the door was a figure: tall, long hair; she couldn't see anything else in the dark. Was it the *beast*? Again?

She hobbled one step forward. Peered through the gloom.

The beast stood upright on two legs. It was thinner than she remembered, and she didn't see a snout or tail. She didn't see any tusks, either.

She took another step toward it. Something crackled beneath her foot.

The beast turned and looked at her.

Chloe dropped the logs. Her heart raced. "No! Please, *no–*" She was injured and couldn't run from the thing. It had been right: she couldn't run away from it. She didn't want to fall again, didn't want to grip the splintered slats of the bakehouse.

And then the beast was on her: in a few bounds, it reached her and grabbed her shoulders. She flailed against it, screaming "No! No!" but the thing held tightly and shook her.

Her body sizzled with pain: her shoulders where the thing gripped her, and her back and leg; and her head was pounding.

She remembered the thing's words: *Your pain, it's like the smell of sweet blood.*

"Get out of my head!" she screamed.

"Chloe. Stop it! Calm down, Chloe. What the hell's the matter with you? Come on, come on, take it easy."

It wasn't the beast.

It was George Bouchard, her childhood friend.

George.

She clung to him, weeping. *Dear God, he must think I'm crazy.* "George, a boar, a thing–"

"Take it *easy.*" His voice was calm, and it soothed her. But still, she cried, if not from terror, then from relief. She was no longer alone in the woods with . . . whatever was out there.

George looped his arm around her waist, helped her to the door, then eased her into the bakehouse. "Here, sit down, relax. You always get spooked out here alone at night."

"I do not."

"Yes, you do."

"I do *not*," she insisted, wiping the tears off her cheeks with the back of her hand.

George shrugged and laughed. "Okay, you're never scared. Whatever you say, Chloe." The lightness of his laughter eased her fear and once again, she wondered if she was imagining everything. In the red glow of the embers, George's hair looked auburn, although she knew it was really brown. Twin red dots were in his brown eyes. A flush highlighted his cheekbones, and even his lips looked more red than usual.

She was on her stool again, still shivering. George peeled off his jean jacket and put it over her shoulders. He stood there for a moment, just staring at her, clearly puzzled by her behavior. He said, "What's the matter with you? You're acting strange, Chloe, really strange. What's going on?"

He would think she was crazy. There was no way she was going to tell George what she *thought*—what she *knew*—had happened to her tonight. "I'm over-tired," she said, "that's all. My father's been banging on me to cook and *cook*–" She stopped abruptly. She was babbling like a fool.

"You're shivering," he said, "and sweating."

"I'm cold because the fire got me sweating, and my dress is damp and cooling me off." She looked down at what she was wearing and suddenly felt a pang of embarrassment. Her dress was unbuttoned nearly to her waist, meaning her bra was exposed. It was an old white undergarment, something she wore while slaving over the sausage and bread. And the dress itself was a floppy old thing that hung to her ankles.

George said, "You *could* relax and let your hair down once in awhile, Chloe. I've been telling you to take it easy for years. What with that dress and the bun on the top of your head, really Chloe, you look like you're out of the fourteenth century, or something."

He was right. She *did*. But it wasn't because she wanted to look like a moron. It was because her father was so poor, a drunk who didn't give a damn about her.

She really should jerk herself into the twenty-first century. She glanced at George. He had on a black long-sleeved t-shirt and tight jeans with a belt. The shirt had a word printed on it in gold letters. "Yale University." Nobody from Llivia, from Cerdanya, much less from their tiny village, had ever gone to college anywhere, much less a fancy university in North America. He actually looked as silly as Chloe, just in a very different way.

She said, "Tell you what, George. If you help me finish with the bread, I'll take down the stupid bun."

"It's a deal, *mon chère.*"

"Don't call me that," she said sharply. The beast had called her, *mon chère.*

"Relax, Chloe. What the hell is wrong with you tonight? Okay, it's no big deal, I won't call you, *mon chère.*"

"I'm sorry," she started to apologize, but George had already turned and was halfway out the door. "Don't go," she said.

"I'm not leaving you here, don't worry. I'm just stepping out to get your logs. Sit tight and don't move. You're obviously injured, and I do want to know what happened to you, okay?"

She nodded, sure.

"I'll finish the baking for you," he added. "It's not as if I don't know how."

While George retrieved the firewood, Chloe unpinned her hair, letting it hang to her waist, and ran her fingers through it to straighten out the snarls. With the fire blazing, she would sweat under the thicket of hair. On the other hand, the fire might dry the sweat off her body if George did all the work.

Good old George.

How could she have mistaken him for a wild boar-beast? Apparently, her imagination could run wild and conjure up anything.

George returned with the logs and tossed them into the fire, then stooped and prodded the flame alive with the iron. Flares of gold and red shot up as the fire took hold. The room danced with color and light.

Chloe glanced at the loaves of bread that were rising on the table across the room. They were still. The tops were cracked, but nothing throbbed, nothing glowed, and nothing looked like capillaries.

George said, "You look much better with your hair down." He paused and added, "Not to mention with your dress unbuttoned."

"You *would* notice that," she said.

He watched as she buttoned her dress. It was not that big a deal to her. They'd grown up together, played in the creek wearing next to nothing as toddlers. He was like a brother. Except, of course, that George always wanted to be *more* than a brother to Chloe. "Do you mind putting in the next batch?" she said to get his mind off her bra and what was underneath it.

"Yeah. Sure."

Grateful to rest and not torture her arm, back, and legs for a few minutes, Chloe settled onto the stool and smoothed her skirt over her knees. George opened the cast iron oven door over the fire. He slid five loaves of bread onto the tray, then using mitts, pushed the tray into the oven. "So. Tell me," he said.

"George, you'll say I'm crazy."

"No, I won't."

"But you already *did.*"

"But I didn't mean it."

"Well, *I* think that I'm crazy." She paused. "Say, what are *you* doing out here in the middle of the night?"

"Maybe I'm crazy, too," he said.

"Never."

"Yeah, well . . . don't tell Marie that."

Marie was George's latest fling, one of many girlfriends he'd had over the years while pining after Chloe. She always encouraged his flings. "The two of you have another argument?" she said. "What was it about this time?"

"Same old thing. This and that. Nothing much." He shrugged. He leaned against the door frame by the handle, crossed his arms over "Yale University" on his chest. "I don't think I can keep seeing Marie. She picks on me. I don't know, Chloe. We were having a good time down by the creek behind my father's barn—you know the place—"

She nodded. Yes, she knew it well. She often met George there, just to *hang* out, not to *make* out.

—"and before I knew it, Marie was telling me that I need to shave, wash my hair, that I'm boring and no fun, that I'm not wild enough for her, that sort of thing. We had a big fight, and I left. So here I am. I figured you'd be here, slaving away as usual for your old man."

"Yeah, I'm a lot of fun, aren't I?"

After awhile, George removed the loaves from the oven and shoved in another batch. He turned the hot pans upside down on the cooling racks. He tapped the pans with a knife, loosening the baked bread onto a giant platter.

He wasn't kidding, thought Chloe. *He's been here often enough that he knows how to do everything by himself.* "You want a job?" she said. "It doesn't pay anything, but it's a lot of work."

"Yeah, it sounds great, Chloe."

"I'll pay you in bread. One loaf. We'll split it."

"Your father will kill you, Chloe. He could get a whole Euro out of a tourist for that loaf tomorrow."

"Come on, let's share one. I'm starving." She gestured at the loaves.

"You're beautiful when you're hungry." He ripped a loaf in half and gave her the biggest piece. "You have any cheese?"

"Not here. Sorry. It's in the refrigerator in the house. Where *they* sleep."

George shook his head. "It makes me sick how they treat you, Chloe. You're the one who needs the soft bed at night instead of the hard floor of the smokehouse."

Her mouth was full of bread, and she was too busy eating to answer him. She couldn't remember the last time she'd eaten a meal. She hadn't eaten at all today. Had she eaten anything *yesterday?*

George settled against the doorframe again and crammed bread into his mouth. He chewed with his mouth open and his lips made loud smacking sounds, reminding her of one reason she didn't find George attractive. She liked him, no doubt about it, but she just couldn't slip over the edge from thinking of George as a friend to wanting his hands all over her.

"So," he said, "you haven't told me what scared you tonight."

She was wondering what to tell George when suddenly, the door crashed open.

George dropped his bread and staggered forward, regaining his footing mid-lurch. As she rose from the stool, clutching her back, George swiveled and said, "You! *You!* Get the hell out of here!"

Chloe's older brother, Pierre, swaggered into the cramped bake-house. He shoved George's shoulder. Behind Pierre came his slutty girlfriend, Deétda, who was several years younger than Chloe.

With both hands, George shoved Pierre's chest. "Get off me, loser."

"Stop it, both of you," said Chloe. "Pierre, what are you doing here in the middle of the night? Shouldn't you and Deétda be partying down at the house?"

Pierre withered under Chloe's glare. His eyes, light blue like hers, were bleary and had bags under them. His sandy hair was darker than Chloe's and dirtier: it fell in strings around his face. He probably hadn't washed in weeks.

Then abruptly, he grabbed Deétda's waist and pulled her close. "Here's how it's done, loser," he said to George, and he leaned Deétda back at her waist and kissed her. Deétda wriggled against him and giggled. Deétda's mini-skirt was hitched up to her butt, and Pierre's hand slid to her thong.

"Pierre, take it out of here." Chloe slid from the stool and tried to pry her brother off his girlfriend. "I really don't need to see this. Go back to the creek, to the house, anywhere else, but get it out of here. I have dozens of loaves to bake. Get out, and leave me alone."

"Oh damn." George leapt for the oven mitts and wrenched open the oven door. Smoke billowed out, filling the room. He slid the loaves from the oven. The crusts were black. Burned.

"Look at you," sneered Deétda. "Miss Goodie, the perfect Chloe Desmarais. Sitting on your high stool, making your stupid bread. You're so pathetic." She burst out laughing.

"Dad told us to come and make sure you were working," said Pierre. "He's not going to be happy when I tell him that you've been up here with *George,* screwing around and wasting time. And you know what *dad* does when he's mad at you, Chloe."

Just thinking about her father, *le cochon,* gave Chloe the creeps. The gray hairs on his mole, the ugly mean stare, the heavy hands, thick with calluses, smacking her face, her chest, her stomach, her arms. "Please don't tell him *anything,* okay, Pierre?"

"Always begging, aren't you, Chloe? As if it will help matters. You know it doesn't help."

Her brother was right. It didn't help. No matter what Chloe said or did, her father always picked on her and slapped her around. And it seemed that Pierre was following in his footsteps. Like father, like son.

"Can't you help her, Pierre, just this once?" said George. "Tell Deétda to go home, and then stay here and help Chloe for a change. Can't you see that she's hurt? Your father already beat the crap out of her tonight."

Deétda laughed. Her black hair was matted to her head. Heavy mascara and eyeliner circled her hard brown eyes. She was nondescript, really, just another ordinary girl, too young and wearing too little. "Pretty boy George, you can't get a girl, can you? I bet you don't know what to *do* with a girl, *do* you?" Her breasts bounced braless beneath a thin cotton halter top. One slipped out, but Deétda didn't care. She was high, as usual; both Deétda and Pierre, high on dope and crystal meth and God only knew what pills. They never cared what they stuffed into their bodies, as long as it made them high, they'd try anything in any mixture.

George bristled with anger but said quietly, "Just go away, both of you. If you're not going to help, then go away."

"I'll show you where to go," said Pierre, and then his fist slammed into George's mouth. Deétda gasped, her face twisting into a gleeful mask. She slapped Chloe's shoulder, as if the two girls were sharing a great time.

George's fist cracked into Pierre's jaw, and Pierre stumbled then grabbed both of George's wrists in his hands. George squirmed and broke free while Pierre laughed like this was all just a lot of fun. Deétda jumped on George's back and clawed at his face. Blood trailed down George's chin, soaking into his black t-shirt. With her legs wrapped around George's waist, Deétda's mini-skirt became a micro-mini that bunched around her waist and showed off her pink thong.

George elbowed her off, and she fell to the floor, but then she rose quickly and started pounding George's back with her fists. He turned and grabbed her right arm, wrenched her up against the wall.

George shook her. "Stop it!" he screamed.

Deétda just laughed.

"Pierre, take her and get out of here. Now. Or I'll tell father that *you* came up here, all messed up on meth, and that you and—" Chloe pointed a shaking finger at Deétda—"*her,* that you burned all the loaves."

Pierre's mouth was swollen from George's punch, and his upper lip was split, his teeth bloody. "He'll never believe you, Chloe. He never does. He's gonna let you have it."

"That's not much of a threat," she said. She was always in trouble with her father. It was simply a matter of degree.

"It's not a threat. It's a fact." Pierre stood there, his swollen lips wet, his eyes off in that distant world where drug addicts go, his hands trembling, his skinny body wasting away. Years ago, he'd been nice to Chloe. She remembered running with Pierre over the stones in the creek to the shore on the other side, trampling through the moss and twigs, reaching for the bushes, laughing as they fed each other red berries. Now, her brother was gone, as if a malignant spirit had cannibalized him. She had watched the drugs eat at him over the years, purging his soul until it grew faint, fainter, forgotten.

Chloe tried one last entreaty, in case a remnant of Pierre remained inside the drug addict. "I'm not feeling good, Pierre. Can you lay off, just for tonight? Can you help me make the stupid bread?"

But there was no remnant of the brother she remembered inside this Pierre, this shell of a brother with his addictions. "I don't have time for bread, Chloe. I got things to do."

Deétda was giggling, on the edge of hysteria from being high, her breasts flopping from side to side, the mascara and eyeliner streaking down her cheeks. "We can make you feel *real* good, honey, if you want to. Can't we, Pierre, can't we?" She eyed Chloe, up and down, as if Chloe were prey.

"Come on, get out of here," said George.

Deétda looked at George slyly, then glanced at Pierre. "Come outside with us, Georgey boy, we want to show you something."

"Yeah, tough guy, we'll leave *her* alone—" Pierre pointed at Chloe— "if *you* come with us."

Chloe shoved some loaves into the oven. She busied herself by arranging the cooling bread on the table. "What do you want with George? Just go away, Pierre."

"Only if *he* comes with me."

"Come on, tough guy." Deétda curled a finger, motioned at George to follow her. She yanked her skirt down to cover her thighs.

"I'll be right back," George said to Chloe. "For godsakes, what do you two *want?*" He rolled his eyes, but followed Pierre and Deétda out the door and into the night.

Chloe figured that George would be fine. He could handle himself against two drug addicts, her skinny brother and his under-aged scrawny girlfriend. George was six two, and he packed some muscle. There was no way Pierre and Deétda could hurt *George.*

She stoked the fire and returned to her stool, heard footsteps receding into the woods, knew the threesome had gone somewhere into the trees and brush.

The hours ticked by. The loaves cooled on their paper doilies. The fire returned to red embers.

And George never came back.

CHAPTER FIVE

Cerdanya, France: October 2015

CHLOE TRIED TO REMEMBER what happened, but it seemed like a bad dream. First, her father's threats, the pain in her arm; then the injury to her back and leg; the wild boar, the beast, whatever it was . . .

And finally, George's visit followed by Pierre and Deétda. Had her brother gone into the woods with George? If so, what had Pierre *done* to George? Why hadn't George returned to the bakehouse to be with Chloe?

By ten the next morning, she was worried. But she didn't have time to check at George's house or in the woods because her father cornered her, demanding to know why they didn't have more than thirty loaves of bread for the tourists.

She was in the kitchen, preparing her father's breakfast: strong coffee and toast with cheese. She'd bathed and changed into jeans and a long-sleeved aquamarine t-shirt. The color reminded her of the Mediterranean Sea, where emerald and aquamarine swirled against deep blues and greens. White frills laced the collar and cuffs of the t-shirt, reminding her of the froth by the water's edge. The shirt would help her get through the day. She would remember that someday, she was going to run away to the sea and escape.

Her father, *le cochon,* had splashed on cologne. Chloe wrinkled her nose. The stench of body odor and stale wine was a static undercurrent on him, and the cologne didn't do much to hide it.

"Where are the rest of the loaves? We need at least fifty." Like George, he ate with his mouth open, making loud smacking noises with each chew. She made a point not to look at him while he ate; she couldn't stand to see the goat cheese on his tongue, the bits of bread clinging to the sores on the left side of his mouth.

She stood in a shaft of sun and stared out the window. The creek was low, and she could see the roots of trees on the banks. Normally, the roots were beneath the water. Birds dove for tiny fish and landed on the smooth gray boulders, most of which were usually under water, as well. Chloe's mind flit back to the mud and overturned sod by the bakehouse. Mud, no rain, and a low creek level didn't fit together.

From behind her, *le cochon* swallowed loudly and his teeth ripped another hunk of bread from his loaf. "How many do we have, Chloe? How much bread?" he repeated between chews.

"We have a few dozen loaves, *mon père.* It'll be enough. We don't get many tourists through here anyway. They don't even go to Llivia, which is much bigger."

His eyebrows furrowed with concern. He crammed cheese into his mouth. His cheeks were greasy balls filled with food. "You want anything to eat?" he asked.

I'd probably get queasy if I tried to eat with you. "Maybe later. Do you need more coffee?"

Her father grunted. That was his way of saying, no. She cleared some dirty dishes from the rickety table, careful not to rock it. She didn't want his plate or cup to slide or rattle; that had led to more than one beating in the past.

She emptied well water from the basin on the counter into the washing bin, picked up the soap and rag, and set to work, cleaning what appeared to be dishes from a late night food binge: dried cheese and tomato-meat grease. Her father would have passed out from drinking and snored the night away, so he hadn't left the mess. Typically, the messes were from Pierre's late night food fests, after he'd come down from the drug highs and needed other forms of sustenance.

Wheels crunched on the dirt-and-gravel road that wound down the mountains past their house. Chloe knew the sound, and so did her father. It was a jeep, and that meant only one thing: tourists.

She opened the soiled curtain, leaned over the counter, and tried to get a look as the jeep inched its way down the narrow road toward the house. It was almost here. Such excitement, it always thrilled her when the tourists showed up. They were few and far between.

Her father was already at the door, heading outside to meet the middle-aged man and his two female companions. Chloe remained at the window, peeking around the curtain.

The man was clean shaven and wore sunglasses. His hair flipped over his forehead in carefully arranged curls and he had the face of a movie star. He wore a linen shirt with bright stripes down both sides. It was one of those cabana shirts, Chloe thought, the kind that men wore on yachts and cruise ships. She could tell that he had the kind of muscles tourists get when they work out in gyms. The muscles were thicker and more balanced than the muscles of men who worked their whole lives on goat farms or in the woods.

As the man stepped from the jeep, he gazed at the creek, the woods, and the house. He sniffed the air. "Ni-ice," he said with a heavy Italian accent, "the crisp mountain air. I like it."

The two young women, no more than nineteen or twenty years old, hopped from the other side of the jeep. Both were brunettes, their lush hair cascading down their backs. Both wore sunglasses, just like the middle-aged movie star man. One had on a bikini top, black triangles with bold sequins all over it; low-slung cut-offs that showed off her belly diamond; three-inch platform sandals. The other girl's bikini top was equally beautiful: gold triangles made from satin. Part of Chloe wondered how they had the nerve to dress like that; part of her wanted to *be them.*

The three tourists smiled at *le cochon,* and their teeth were white and perfect. Chloe's father was probably dancing with joy, ready to sell these rich people a stack of bread and several pounds of cheese.

Someday, I'll ride in that jeep with you. Someday, I'll wear glittering clothes, and my teeth will be white and perfect. Someday, I'll laugh with you, and we'll be friends. Someday, I won't be here with le cochon and Pierre.

Yes, Pierre and Deétda, last night with George, last night with the beast in the woods–

The image of the glittering girls faded, even as they chattered and giggled outside. Chloe's eyes were focused on something else, a different image, one that was as clear and real as the girls. Laced on the trees was the residue of something sparkling, a wisp of ice perhaps. She couldn't quite make it out from this distance, but she knew it wasn't something she'd ever seen before in Cerdanya. It reminded her of the wet grass and the mud, the moisture that didn't make sense on an otherwise dry day. It reminded her of the boar.

Chloe slipped out the door and behind the house, where her father wouldn't notice her. The male tourist was laughing with her father. His Italian accent faded as the noises of the forest took over. Crickets, birds, and the twitter of small animals.

The path leading through the pines and mahogany trees was dry, rutted with stones and roots, and littered with fallen branches and twigs. Squirrels raced over the moss, then stopped as she approached, and pretended to be dead, their little claws grasping nuts still halfway into their mouths.

A wisp of ice trailed before her, it hung in the air like smoke, sparkling beneath the sun, and drops of moisture dripped from it and dotted the dirt. Still limping from last night's injuries, Chloe couldn't move quickly. She twirled her dark blonde hair in her fingers, wiped flecks of ice from the long strands. When she swept her hands over her cheeks, her palms were coated with moisture.

On both sides of the trail, the branches—and even the leaves—were etched with ice. The forest had filled with sparkles.

Her body was warm, the sun blazed overhead, and yet, her breath plumed in frosty bursts from her mouth.

And then she stood, rooted in place as if her broken sandal had caught in a rock, but it hadn't: she was like the squirrel with his nut, standing perfectly still as if dead.

The beast was in her mind again. *I came for you, but now I've found the other, and I will have you both. We are mates now, the three of us. Blood and ice, substance and form, love and devotion. And above all, pain, the eternal source of energy and strength.*

"I . . ." she heard herself forming words, "I don't understand." She wanted to scream, *Who the hell are you?*, but she couldn't make herself say the words, much less scream them.

The voice in her mind grew cold. *Don't fight me, Chloe. The pain will be your pleasure. The ice will be your home. As the creatures in this forest have learned, you will learn to speak to me. We will be one.*

"What are you? Tell me! What is this ice? What is the meaning of all this?" Sparks flew before her eyes, crystallizing in dots of frozen color, then melting on her skin. Fear flooded her. *I'm insane,* she thought. *I talk to myself, to my own mind. I see things that can't exist. I'm insane.*

A voice whispered in her right ear. "You flatter yourself, *mon chère.* Your mind is too empty to conjure up one such as myself. Trust me, you have no clue what I am and what I'm capable of doing. I am here, I've been here for a long time, and I will exist forever."

Without moving her head, she rolled her eyes to the right, but saw nothing but the haze of neon ice roiling around her. Nobody was there. Who or what had whispered in her ear?

George has seen me, too. I have entwined myself with him. The voice remained cold in her head, flatlined as if uttered from something dead, an evil entity that stretched beyond the confines of time.

Chloe forced her feet to move forward on the path. She would escape from the beast, the monster. She would run—in terrible pain, she would run from its grip. She would find George, and together, they would go to the sea.

This thing in her head: it must be the monster that ate the children, the monster that the old women in the villages talked about with such fear.

Oh no, I'm not a monster, Chloe. I'm a lover. And I do not go near children. The voice in her mind paused, then added, *They have no taste. I prefer my lovers to be marinated and seasoned with time.*

The beast's voice stayed with her, even as she hobbled through the ice, now falling like hail and hanging in sheets from the limbs of trees. Ice slicked the dirt trail; and Chloe slid, stumbled, but hobbled forward.

She tried to understand what the thing was talking about, but she failed. How were its lovers *marinated?*

Ah ha ha ha! Le cochon. Saucisse. And then: *Salchicha fumada. Puerco marinado!*

Its laughter rang in her head. With horror, she realized that the beast had switched from French to Spanish, and it was laughing in both languages about smoked sausages and marinated pork.

Maybe the beast was a cannibal. Maybe it was going to kill and *eat* her.

The pain in Chloe's left leg intensified, slicing her thigh straight to the bone. Her back ached at the base of her spine where she'd fallen and hit it on the urn last night. The bruises on her arm still throbbed. Perhaps she was in a fever, a very cold fever, from all the pain.

Or perhaps–

perhaps–

The thought of it terrified her, but she had to *know*. "Are you the *undead?*" she asked the ice clouds, to the beast that wasn't there but was in her mind.

Its answer was quick by her ear, "No."

"Are you dead?"

"No."

"Then you are a living creature?"

"Yes."

How can it be? she thought. *You're in my mind, you whisper in my ear, but I see nothing next to me. Are you a wild boar with a man's eyes? What are you?*

It was in her mind again, supplanting her own thoughts with its own. As it took control of her mind, she could think nothing of her own and could only watch the ice swirling in a cloud of color around her body. *I am what I am. In time, you will know me, and we will be as one, you and George and me and the others.*

And with that, the voice left her. The ice vaporized. The trees dripped with water. Her feet were in mud, and her sandals were broken and useless. The path ahead was laced with water that sparkled white in the sun and covered the rocks and fallen branches like paper doilies.

Chloe had to find George. He was in the forest, she was sure. The beast had left him there to rot. Somewhere.

The beast had said that Chloe would join him with George "and the others," so George had to be alive; yet if she didn't find him soon, it might be too late to keep him that way. And who were these "others" that the beast mentioned? She envisioned a pack of male boars with bloody tusks, roaming the woods, seeking human prey.

She hoped George was still alive.

Leaving her sandals behind, she sloshed through the mud, following the sparkle until it ended in a fork: to the left, the trail was dry, to the right, it was mud. The wild boar, the beast, whatever it was, would have come from the right and left its mark in ice. Oddly, as soon as the ice appeared, it melted, leaving her hair and clothes sopping wet and leaving the path muddy. But it was the beast's mark, for sure, and she could follow it like a dog follows a scent.

Luckily, the soles of her feet were thick from a lifetime in the forests. She limped to the right, pushed a tangle of thorns aside, ignored the freezing water raining down from the pines and leaves. A keening rose in the distance as if mourners were weeping at a funeral. A sound came from overhead: a chorus of wailing and squawks: vultures. She paused and peered at the tops of the trees. Two birds soared from a high branch and dove almost straight down. They had yellow heads and red eyes, and the span of their black wings was at least two feet, probably more. Greater Yellow Vultures. They fed on dead animals.

She picked up her pace. The dry branches and thorns scraped her skin, and by the time she found George, her face and hands were bloody.

He was nestled beneath an oak tree, his back slumped against the trunk, his arms limp, his legs splayed.

She cried, bubbles of hysteria rising in her throat. Then she stooped, raised his chin so she could look at his face.

His eyelids fluttered.

He was *alive.*

He was as pale as the ice that had laced the trail. Whiter than white. His brown eyes were lighter, almost an almond color, while his hair had darkened from a soft brown to mahogany. His neck was coated in fresh blood.

She slid an arm behind his shoulders and cradled him. "George, wake up. George."

The eyelids fluttered again. She saw that his black t-shirt was sopped in blood. "Yale University" was no longer yellow, but rather, the color of rust.

She wiped the blood from his neck and then rubbed her hand across her shirt. Saw that her shirt was already wet from her own blood, from the trickles that had slid off her chin from the slashes of the branches and thorns.

Blood and ice, the beast had said.

And *pain*.

"George, please talk to me." Why hadn't she warned him about the beast? He'd asked her over and over again last night to tell her what had spooked her, but she'd switched the subject. If she hadn't been so worried that he might think her *insane*–

She let the thought linger . . .

She should have told him.

"Chloe?" George blinked at her, then his eyes focused. He shook his head slightly as if shaking off a bad dream. He looked down at his shirt. "Why am I all wet? What is this?" He dabbed at the blood.

"You're fine! Oh thank God!" She wrapped both arms around George, hugging him, weeping and laughing at the same time.

"Why is your face all bloody?" he asked.

She drew back from him, sank into the mud beside him with her back against the tree trunk. "Some branches scratched me, that's all."

"And why am I bloody?"

"I . . . I don't know, George."

"What happened to your hair, Chloe?"

"*My* hair? Nothing. What happened to *your* hair?"

"Nothing," he said. "What are you talking about?" He trained his eyes on her and swept his mahogany hair behind his ears.

She didn't know how to explain everything to him. She had very few answers herself. He was bloody, obviously weak if his pale skin was any indication, and in no condition to hear her strange stories about a wild male boar that turned the air into ice and threatened her inside her own mind. She had to tell him about the beast, though, because he clearly had to know. If she'd only told him last night . . .

"George, there's something horrible in these woods. It apparently attacked you, which is why your clothes and neck are all bloody. I can't explain why, but your eyes are much lighter than they should be, your hair much darker, and your skin . . ." She paused. "Well, you just don't look like yourself. Your skin is very pale, George."

His laugh was thin. He lifted an arm, but couldn't hold the position, and his arm fell back on his lap. "What's wrong with me? I'm so damn weak."

That's when Chloe saw the bite marks on his neck. Two small incisions on the top row, two tiny ones on the row beneath. The beast's tusks were huge. They couldn't have nipped George's neck and left such small wounds. Yet nothing else in the forest had four tusks, two on the top and two on the bottom. While it didn't make any sense to her—not yet, anyway—she knew the beast had done this to George.

"Your neck," she said, "something bit it, George. There are four pricks, evenly spaced. Here, feel." She lifted his hand and brought it to his neck.

His fingers touched the four incisions, and his eyes widened in horror. "I don't remember anything biting me! I don't remember anything at all!"

"What happened when you left with Pierre and Deétda last night?"

"I don't know, Chloe. I tell you, I can't remember last night at all. Was I with you? Where were Pierre and Deétda?"

"You were at the bakehouse with me when they busted in and caused their usual trouble." Chloe told George about his scuffle with Pierre and how the threesome had left the bakehouse in the middle of the night, but George couldn't remember any of it.

"Y-your hair, Chloe. I'm not kidding. It's not blonde any-more."

"It's not? That's ridiculous. I've had blonde hair since I was two years old." She grabbed her waist-long hair in a hand and stared at it. The hair was still damp from the ice and moisture, but even so, she could tell that George was right. Her hair was much darker than it had been only last night. It was the soft brown that George's hair had been yesterday. "What is this? I don't have brown hair!"

He chuckled. "Well, you do now."

"And pigs fly."

George helped her up from the mud. Confusing as it was, she

was happy to see that he was regaining his strength. But as they stumbled back to the smokehouse, she asked if he believed in vampires. His laughter rang through the forest, and he told her that she was insane.

But was she?

She'd explicitly asked the beast if it was *dead*. And instantly, it had answered, no. She'd asked if it was *undead,* and again the beast said, no. Dead and undead: that ruled out a vampire.

The beast claimed to be alive.

Yet what kind of living creature sucked blood from the necks of humans?

CHAPTER SIX

FERNANDO LE SPRAGUE HAD fed well last night. It had been awhile since he'd tasted human blood, and while he'd only taken a nip from the boy, it had stoked his desire for more. It felt good to be back in his natural state, not of flesh or body but simply "being" as a cloud or a storm or rolling thunder exists. Everywhere but nowhere, all at once, roiling through the forest at whim.

Rooted in his cave high on the mountain, he was safe from the humans and their intrusions. Not that they posed any real threat to Fernando and his kind. The humans weren't sophisticated enough anywhere on Earth to harm, much less kill, Fernando. Their science was too antiquated, their knowledge too limited. They were fools, all of them, especially here in the hidden forests and small villages where they were like mice in a cage, just waiting for him to swoop down, sink his fangs into their flesh, and devour them.

He was amused by the girl. Chloe. Such a simpleton with her bread, cheese, and sausage. So beautiful with the long flowing hair, the sparkling eyes, the naïveté. So ready for the plucking. The poor thing feared her father and brother, wanted to escape to the Mediterranean Sea, of all places, where she assumed life would be safe and full of splendor. Little did she know, this Chloe, the fate that awaited her.

The Mediterranean Sea *belonged* to Fernando and his kind.

Fernando would own her long before she saw the waves lapping the shore. He would own her before she left her father, the man she called a pig.

Fernando rubbed himself against the cool stone of the cave. Aah, that felt so good: the moisture dripping down the wall like cold sweat.

He liked the warmth of the Mediterranean, and after two hundred years, enjoyed the freedom to wander the Earth as he wanted. Yet he still preferred the cold. The colder, the better. Adaptation was one thing, he thought, but extreme cold was his natural habitat.

While remaining rooted to the cave, he drifted like vapor through the pines, clung to the needles and bark, felt the sun blazing above him—even on a cool day here in the south of France, it was so much hotter than what he preferred. Animals scurried beneath him. He dusted the moss and ferns with ice shards, reached at whim and froze the mice and squirrels. Slicked the boulders and rocks with frost, and graced the branches with surreal beauty that nobody would see but Fernando and the dying creatures beneath him.

After awhile, he grew tired of playing. He gathered his millions of particles into a ball and like a gale at sea, stormed down the mountainside. Branches fell in his wake and crashed to the forest floor. Animals screamed and squealed, made way for him.

He hungered for the girl and maybe for another taste of the boy. They would not deny him. They would yield because they had no choice.

His hunger grew. Last night's taste of the young boy's blood was fresh in his mind, and Fernando hadn't drunk enough to satisfy his thirst. Before returning to his homeland, he wanted to be sated: drenched in the blood, so he could survive if necessary in either of his forms, flesh-shaped or natural particles, for a very long time. There wasn't enough blood where Fernando was born, only a stray human here and there, a seal, a bird. His birthplace didn't offer bears, elephants, deer, or wild boars: not much food and very few methods of camouflage other than his natural state.

As he swept toward the edge of the woods and the grassy clearing, Fernando spotted the nest of baby boars. Tiny and disgusting, striped so they blended into the twig nest, the babies squealed incessantly for the females. Fernando could care less about the babies or their mothers. While more intelligent than most forest animals, the wild boars were even more stupid than humans. They were good only for camouflage. The tusks were strong and could rip a man to shreds, and people avoided male boars out of fear.

Fernando remembered the look on Chloe's face last night when she saw him by the sausage-making hut. It had been marvelous, that fear on her face. A jolt of excitement ran through him now as he anticipated the fun he'd have when he revealed himself to her again. This time, Fernando would take full advantage of her fear, bring her to the boiling point before sating himself on her nectar.

She would be one of many, and then he would return to his homeland.

He slunk across the clearing as mist, feeling himself starting to vaporize under the sun. The soil beneath him grew moist from his drippings. He was congealing again and could choose his form, but he had to choose quickly: the boar would be best, of course, but the human form would win the girl's trust. Few girls could resist Fernando's human form.

Even a sip of a hedgehog or deer would do. Or a raccoon, sheep, goat, or horse. But the delicacy of human blood was worth the wait. And the purity of the innocent was the sweetest taste of all.

The mist hovered, then enveloped the bakehouse, where the girl had been last night with the boy. No sounds came from within the structure, and the sweet smell of blood wasn't in the air.

As his particles began coalescing into human form, Fernando Le Sprague whipped back through the trees in a direct path toward the sausage-making hut. He had no need for forest trails. He was not yet in flesh form, and as a ghostly vapor, he could do as he pleased.

By the time he reached the hut, he was in human form. Smoke billowed from the roof, meaning Chloe was here, stoking the fire and making her sausages.

Fernando sniffed the air. *Blood.*

Two scents of blood.

Chloe *and* George. *Perfect.* Fernando would feast until he was bloated. As a sparkling haze, he would slip up the mountain back to his cave and hibernate until he was ready to return to his homeland. A few more weeks, and the homeland would be bright with summer.

Finally, the new hatchlings foretold by the ancestors' message a hundred years ago would spring forth. The ice would quiver with young Fridarian life. Fernando would dance beneath the sun, skitter across the ice plains, and scream into the howling winds. He would be one again with his essence. Flesh no more; at least, not for the season. The new hatchlings would see Fernando in all his natural glory, and he would train them in the strange ways of this world. He might even find new companions, those of his kind who wanted to feel the blood and its potency.

The ancestors had set it in stone; first, Fernando and his fellow hatchlings would be activated, and then two more batches would be switched on in quick succession: 2015 in Antarctica, 2015 in the Mediterranean Sea. The transmissions had come to Carsten almost a hundred years ago, and these had been the last messages ever received from the ancestors.

Fernando peered at Chloe and George through a crack in the wooden boards hacked together to form the rear side of the building. His gaze penetrated the fire and smoke that rose in the one-room building and billowed from the hole in the roof.

He heard their words. He heard their thoughts.

They would not see him. Not yet, for they couldn't see anything through the fire and smoke. They would not hear him. Not yet, for he wouldn't let himself be known until he was too excited to contain his lust anymore.

He stared, and he let his thirst grow.

The girl's hair was a light brown now. Fernando's touch had made the deep blonde grow colder. Her eyes were now the color of the water that swept upon the beach of the Mediterranean Sea. A wash of pale blue and green iris. She still limped, and she clutched her back as she rose from her stool and sat back down. She lifted the fire iron with her left hand. The father, *le cochon,* as she called him, had bruised her right arm, rendering it weak, and she continued to pamper it. Her face had scabs, and her shirt was crusted in dry blood.

The boy, George, was pale, and the four tusk marks had scabbed on his neck and were barely visible. He was naked from the waist up, and his shirt hung from a meat hook by the fire. The shirt looked clean. The girl must have washed it.

Pointless. These two would have no need for shirts, clean or otherwise.

"Would you help me grind the meat?" Chloe asked, and George nodded and hauled a hunk of cured pork off a ceiling hook. The meat was pinkish brown, a mottle of fat rippling through it. They both lifted butchers' knives from the table and began carving the meat into smaller pieces. Again, the girl used her left hand, fumbling and failing to chop the meat. The boy took the knife from her and suggested that she prepare the spices and intestines for stuffing. But the boy was weak, too, and had a hard time carving the pork.

The girl washed the hog casings in a water basin, mixed spices in the urn. "George, do you ever think of leaving this place?" Her voice was light and drifted toward Fernando as a feather flutters on a spring breeze.

George looked over his shoulder at her. He stuffed meat into a hand grinder, turned the handle. Fatty meat wound through the holes in the grinder and plopped into a bowl. "My parents would miss me, Chloe. My mother would cry, and my father would have nobody else to take over his herd. I can't leave."

Her voice cracked. "But George . . . what if I *had* to leave?"

"You? Why?" George stopped grinding for a second, then returned to the task. He grew more pale as he worked. He was much weaker than Fernando remembered. Perhaps Fernando had drained more blood than he thought. The boy said, "Because of your father and Pierre? Don't let them intimidate you so much, Chloe. Fight back, and they'll lay off."

"How can I fight my own father?" she asked.

George frowned. Fernando heard his thoughts: *Beat them off you is how. But I know you won't do that, not you, Chloe.*

Fernando heard Chloe's thoughts, as well. *I can't hit my own father. I don't have it in me. He's much stronger than I am anyway. He's been beating me since I was a little girl. And Pierre's no longer Pierre. He's a drug addict. His friends are capable of anything, his dealer would do anything to keep Pierre supplied and paying.*

George dumped mounds of meat strands into the urn, and Chloe used both arms to hold the long spoon and stir the meat-and-spice mixture. George told Chloe that he couldn't see leaving the village, not yet anyway, but that he would help her fend off *le cochon* and Pierre. Chloe shrugged, probably not believing that suddenly, George would be able to protect her from her father and brother.

Fernando noticed that, as she moved the spoon, Chloe winced from pain; and that whenever she winced, George cringed, too. It was clear that the boy was taken with Chloe. Smitten, as humans might say. Why didn't the boy offer to marry the girl and save her from the father? Why didn't the boy agree to run away with her? These humans and their absurd loyalties to each other. They claimed to care about each other but did little, if anything, to demonstrate it. They were each concerned with their own petty needs; all humans were the same, as far as Fernando could tell. They took from each other and rarely offered much in return. So how were they any different from Fernando and his kind? *We take what we need, too,* he thought. *You eat the sausage, you grind the boar meat. You think nothing of it.*

"Please go with me, George. Please. I want to run away to the sea, get on one of those ships, and go far far away." Chloe stuffed the spicy meat into the casings, and George looped the sausage on racks near the ceiling. Fernando had seen the process many times over the past hundred years: the villagers let the sausage dry, then they smoked and heated it, dipped it in water, and dried it again. It was a long process, but humans loved the result and devoured pig meat by the pounds when it was fashioned this way into sausages.

They would never process Fernando in boar form. Ha. No knife could cut into *his* flesh. No bullet could pierce his hide. Nothing could hurt Fernando because he could return to nanoparticle form at whim.

The muscles in George's upper arms quivered, and his hands shook. He shoved a coil of sausage on the rack, then his arms fell, and he lurched, his hands reaching for something to grab onto; he clutched the edge of the table, but his hands shook too much and he couldn't maintain his hold. His face now had a bluish cast. Too weak to stand anymore, he sank to the floor, his legs stretched out in front of him. He looked as he did last night, when Fernando drained him and left him in a dizzy haze by the tree.

Chloe wiped her hands on a cloth and sank to the floor next to George. *Just as she did last night,* thought Fernando, *when she found him.*

"What is it? What's the matter, George?" Her face was flushed, and her hands fluttered all around the boy. Fernando had seen such scenes many times, played out by young women and their lovers, as well as in reverse: the flushed men in their prime trying to revive their beautiful girlfriends and wives. Humans thought youth held all the power and beauty, thought Fernando, while in reality, it was the ancient who dominated life. Oh, Fernando was enjoying this little scene between Chloe and George. He was like the cat playing with its mice before coming in for the kill, except that Fernando had yet to show himself again and pounce.

But he would.

Soon.

He was in no hurry. He had all the time in the world. Centuries of time, perhaps millennia.

"I . . . I'm weak," said George. "What did you say was in the woods? What attacked me last night, Chloe?"

She held him upright so he wouldn't slump and fall over. Her eyes scanned the walls, seeking answers behind the smoke. "I don't know what attacked you. It was a beast, a male boar, I think, but it had the eyes of a man, stood upright on its hind legs, and had wings."

"Chloe, you must be joking. How is that possible?"

"I don't know how it's possible, but it happened. The thing, this beast, whatever it is—I saw it, George. It's evil. It's unlike anything I've ever seen."

Evil? Hardly. I'm no more evil than you humans with your meat and entrails and innuendos, your lies, unfaithfulness, and filth, your beatings and whippings, your murderous ways! Compared to you, I'm not evil at all! I seek nothing but a little sustenance every now and then. The rest of the time I exist as sparkling dust beneath the sun.

In full human form, Fernando adjusted the frilly lace cuffs of his shirt, the golden hem where it hung over his immaculate black slacks. He ran a hand through his hair—a fluff of gold so shimmering that it could be mistaken for 18K filaments beneath the brilliance of a Mediterranean sun. He studied his fingernails, a half inch long each and perfectly filed into smooth rounds with pointed tips, and he imagined Chloe's surprise to see him in human form. No doubt, she'd never seen a man with such hair and nails, clothes this fine—black polished shoes, white silk shirt embellished with gold embroidery. She would admire the large gold cross that hung on a thick chain around his neck. She would admire his face, the hard features, so masculine to human girls, the tanned skin, the huge hazel eyes. And when she learned that he was a Spaniard, she would blush and twitter and think that she'd never seen a Spaniard so handsome and so . . . *golden*. He would hear those thoughts, of course, and bask in them. If Fernando happened to have a heart, it would have raced as he anticipated his conquest, but as it was, he had no heart or other internal organs. The fibers of his being, the particles that crystallized and broke apart, that formed the flesh shapes that he conjured—yes, these particles would trill with excitement. The girl would see him vibrating slightly and think he was taken by her beauty.

As if!

As if he were a pathetic human male.

As if–

They were all so predictable, it almost took the fun out of the whole thing.

What was the point of bothering with these two, anyway? Why not just feast on a stray tourist? Fernando had enjoyed the tourists from time to time: so unsuspecting and naïve, much more so than Chloe and George, who had heard rumors about an ancient one devouring children in the forest. The tourists were so thin from their gym equipment that the arteries and veins were clearly defined and easy to drain, yet so primed from that very same exercise that their hearts pounded rapidly, providing exquisite feasts. Besides, tourists were disposable and not as quickly missed as villagers. When Fernando feasted on tourists, typically, their corpses were never found.

Fernando half-turned from the sausage hut. He would leave and find a few tourists who were at a mountain overpass enjoying the view. He could have three tourists and toss them over the cliff after his feast.

He vaporized back into his particle state and settled as a low fog on the ground. As he moved back toward the pines and the nest of baby boars, he left his usual trail of moisture on the ground. He was almost to the nest of squealing brats when he smelled flesh trampling through the undergrowth toward the clearing. Human flesh. Two more containers of blood.

He rose and clung to the branches as frost.

Beneath him was a girl who didn't look more than fifteen or sixteen years old. She was with a young man. Both appeared drunk or possibly drugged: Fernando couldn't tell the difference without sipping them.

Excitement gurgled in him as he realized: this was the boy who had poisoned George last night, and this was the boy's girlfriend.

"Come on, Pierre," whined the girl, "I don't want to do this. Isn't there another way?" Her eyes were as cold and distant as Fernando's homeland.

Pierre parted bruised lips that were split and caked in dry blood. He looked a little like the girl in the sausage hut. Chloe. Same light blue eyes, but veiled and dim. Same sandy hair but knotted in dirty clumps on the back of his head. His hands shook. His blood was clearly polluted with chemicals, and his body was too thin to be worthy of a meal. "It's not like I want to do this to Chloe. She's my sister. But if we don't give Andre what he wants, he'll kill us, you know that. I owe him too much money, Deétda."

Deétda stood with her hands on her hips. Her face got a bulldog look on it. "This is too much, even for me. I'm all for some fun, but this scares me, Pierre. It's one thing to rough up George or give him a hard time. It's another to give your sister to Andre."

Pierre grabbed Deétda's wrist, but he was too scrawny and she easily pulled away from him. "Come on," he said, "we have no choice. You want Andre to rape *you* instead? Worse, you want him to kill both of us?"

Deétda's eyes narrowed. "He won't rape me. He won't kill me. It's *you* he wants, Pierre."

"Don't be ridiculous. If you're with me, he'll get you, too."

"He's going to kill *you*. Not *me*. And I don't have to be around for it, do I? As you say, Andre isn't going to come near me for any reason *unless I'm with you.*" Deétda uttered the last few words slowly, then her lips curled into a sly grin. She turned her back on Pierre, and then she ran back through the forest, her laughter ringing out. Pierre stood there, speechless, not trying to win her back, just letting her go. The human was a wimp, thought Fernando, incapable of keeping his girl, protecting his sister, or even quenching the thirst of a bloodsucker. What good was this Pierre to anyone, including himself?

Pierre would make a tasty snack, a prelude to a meal of tourists later. And if there were no tourists today, then Fernando could return to the hut and have his way with Chloe Desmarais and George Bouchard.

It wouldn't be all that bad. George might taste better today. By now, the poison would be gone from George's body, and his blood might be pure again. He'd found George already slumped against the tree late last night; the boy had barely stirred when Fernando sunk his tusks into the soft flesh of his neck. This Pierre and his mite of a girlfriend had already pricked George with a poison, which had put the boy in a stupor and pickled his blood with a bitter aftertaste.

Fernando would dispose of Pierre, then check for tourists.

The frost was melting on the limbs of the fragrant fruit trees and oaks. Droplets splashed through the leaves, splattering on Pierre. The boy looked up and squinted, but he didn't see it coming, of course.

Nobody ever saw Fernando coming.

Mist clung to Pierre. Frost coated his eyebrows.

Not wanting to bother with his human or even his animal forms, Fernando slipped a sliver of ice into Pierre's throat, heard the boy moan, and lapped the thin trickle of blood.

Pierre's blood was weak and bitter from drugs and alcohol. Pierre slapped his neck; silly boy, he probably thought Fernando was an insect.

I'm disappointed in you, boy. Fernando implanted the thought in Pierre's mind.

The boy shook his head. "Who—what is that?" He took a step back, grabbed a tree to hold himself up.

The tree won't help you. Nothing can help you now. Nobody knows you're here except that twit of a girlfriend, and she's not going to tell anyone, is she?

The boy's own thoughts were jumbled, confused. *I'm hallucinating. The drugs are getting to me. But I don't care. The girl? Deétda. Nothing. Nobody. I can get any girl, just offer her some crank and she's mine.*

Fernando slipped another prong of ice, and yet another, into the boy's fragile neck. Soon, the boy's throat was riddled with pricks. The ice served to numb the flesh, and the boy hardly knew what was happening to him as Fernando sucked him dry and finished him off. The boy staggered, then dropped to his knees, clasping his throat, gurgling, gasping for air. Bubbles of blood effervesced from his mouth, and Fernando licked the boy's face, not letting a single drop go to waste.

Something about eating always bothered Fernando. Even taking the life of one as worthless as Pierre cost Fernando a moment or two of joy. The drink was good and satisfying, but at the point of death, the weight of the boy's memories sank into Fernando's consciousness.

Fernando's pleasure merged with his pain. All these memories from all these humans throughout the last century: the dying wishes and dreams, the desperate pleading and questioning: *Why me? Why now? No, don't let this happen. Let me go. Why are you doing this to me? I want to live.* Pierre, a boy who had never enjoyed his life, who lived as if he was already dead, begged to remain flesh and blood.

Memories filled the boy's mind and swept into Fernando:

The first time I touched you, Deétda, I loved you.

When you left me tonight, Deétda, I wanted to die but I didn't show you. I was too far gone to show you anything.

I should have fought dad, the beast, off you, Chloe, and I'm sorry. I should have fought him for you. Forgive me.

Andre, may you rot in hell. I wanted drugs. You gave them to me, and I got hooked—all my fault, sure, I know—and I sold crank and dope to feed my own habit. And it wasn't enough. I didn't sell enough to pay you off, and I gave so much away to Deétda and the others. And you wanted my sister as payment: my sister!

Sunlight, cool water in the heat of summer, tadpoles, orange juniper berries, bouncing peonies on their stalks, snakes under the rocks, the smell of apple pies and molasses cookies and buttery flaky breads. Growing from a boy to a man, finding myself tall one day and towering over my own father, missing my mother, so few memories of her, I was so little, only a toddler when she died, and then there was Chloe to replace her, my little sister, Chloe.

Please, I can't believe I'm dying . . .
It can't be . . .
I'm too young to die . . .
No . . .

One final puff of air. A gurgle. The swirl of that last gasp as life ebbs into the mist.

A sack of skin. Dry bones.

The surge of grief. The pain. The pleasure.

Fernando cradled the boy in a bank of snow deep in the woods. And then Fernando, fully sated, emerged momentarily in human form, let his eyes well with drops of blood—the blood of the boy–

His tears trickled upon the boy's face and dribbled upon the earth.

And then, Fernando blotted the guilt and pain from his mind, flickered back into mist, and from there, swept into the warm spring air, into the chitter of the crickets and the caws of the birds.

CHAPTER SEVEN

"COME, EAT SOMETHING." CHLOE knelt by George and held bread to his lips. He nibbled a few crumbs, then asked her to take the food away, it was making him queasy.

Fernando had returned to his place in the back of the sausage hut. He stared at Chloe and George through the cracks between the planks of wood. The fire had died, leaving a black stain on the ceiling and an entrail of smoke. All the sausage was stuffed and looped over the racks near the ceiling. The urn was clean by Chloe's stool. Fernando must have dozed off in his cave, for he had missed a whole day of human activity. He had eaten well, the cave was cool, the breezes dead within its walls.

And now, George slipped into the nowhere bliss of slumber, weak, incapable of eating much, withering away. Fernando had drained too much from the boy; he should have taken less; either that, or taken fully and given the boy full release from life. He didn't like to leave humans in that half-way state, where they weren't dead, weren't alive, and weren't transformed. This one, this George, could barely be called *alive*, for without help from Fernando, he wouldn't make it through the night.

Chloe bunched towels beneath George's head, stroked his face, and draped a towel over his body to keep him warm. Fernando assumed the towels were from the main house or possibly the bakehouse, where Chloe washed the pans and bowls.

He hovered in the back like a ghost: not really there but fully ensnared by the scene before him. Bored, knowing his options were to watch Chloe Desmarais until he took her; haunt the forest seeking prey; head to Barcelona and civilization; or return to his homeland. *Patience,* he told himself, *soon I can return home. Barcelona and Spain were nothing more to me than Perpignan or Montpellier in France. I came here to the woods to avoid civilization, I was tired of the follies of humans. I'm content to doze for a few more weeks in the cave, to watch Chloe, and to wait.*

She seemed restless: fluttering from one side of the hut to the other, then back again; fingers arranging stacks of bowls; eyes lit with anxiety. She was still limping and nursing her right arm, but she no longer winced or sank to her stool in pain. She was eating bread, a good sign, for it would make her stronger and the blood would pound through her veins.

Does she eat anything other than bread? Is there nothing more to her life than the bread, the sausage, the cheese, and tending to her father's house?

Blood by the door: Chloe had a visitor, and it wasn't Fernando or her father. Slipping ghostlike around the side of the hut, Fernando sniffed the air for clues. He smelled machismo, sweat, and blood gone bad from drugs. Was this Andre, the dealer on Pierre's lips as the boy had died? This was a man much older than Pierre or George, but far younger than *le cochon.* He swaggered as if he owned the forest, his whiskers were a quarter inch long all over his face, his moustache was shaggy and shiny with grease. Beneath the jeans and loose shirt, the man's body was strong and solid, yet it didn't have the gym-sculpted shape of a tourist.

The man stood before the door, and a wicked grin spread across his face. Fernando read his mind. *Ah, she's inside and alone. I only hear the movement of one person. Chloe Desmarais. Pierre's little sister, cute, sexy, no boyfriend to satisfy her. He says she's blonde, and like him, has blue eyes. I can't wait–*

And this man, most likely Andre, kicked the door and pushed his way into the hut. From within, Chloe gasped, and something crashed to the floor.

The door creaked and closed.

Leaving a puddle by the door, Fernando shifted from ice and vapor into human shape. He adjusted his lace cuffs and fingered the 18K cross that hung from the chain around his neck. As mist, he could suck oxygen and nutrients from the air and water just like the countless other microscopic creatures on the planet. But as he assembled into flesh-shaped form, his internal particles could no longer obtain oxygen and nutrients directly; and the hemoglobin in his blood washed over his internal nanoparticles and transported oxygen and nutrients into them. Self-assembly and internal replication of particles were a no brainer for Fernando. He could mass produce himself into blizzards at will, or shed his particles to the bare minimum he needed to survive, about the size of one ice cube. Turning himself into any animal form was simple, though he certainly preferred to turn himself into creatures that had tusks, fangs, sharp protrusions, anything with which to suck as much blood as possible in the shortest amount of time. But given that he could transform into any shape he desired, he could add wings for flying, strong legs for running, and anything else he wanted. That was the beauty of his Fridarian nanoparticles, he'd learned over the past century: by simply wanting to transform, he could make it happen. Just as long ago, he had taken his smallest shape, moisture or dew, and turned it instantly into ice or blizzards, now he could do the same with flesh forms.

Chloe was screaming at the man. "No! Get off me!" And she was thinking, *This must be Pierre's dealer. Get off! Slap him before he rips the clothes off me! I can't believe this, I swear he's going to rape me!*

George was thinking the same thing. *Pierre's dealer! The idiot who calls himself Andre. What's he doing here? My God, he's attacking Chloe. He's grabbed her t-shirt. He's got a hand on her breasts. I have to stop him. Move my legs, get up somehow. I'm too weak.*

But I'm not weak, thought Fernando, *and while I don't want to drink Andre's blood, I do want to savor Chloe's sweetness. He won't have her because she's mine.* As he stepped inside the hut, he drove these thoughts into her brain. As a human, Fernando Le Sprague, he bowed in her direction, keeping his eyes glued upon her.

The ham hocks swung overhead on their hooks. The coils of sausage looped down from the ceiling on both sides of the room.

Her eyes widened. She pointed at Fernando and shook. George

blinked rapidly, his mouth open but uttering no words. George's elbows slipped on the floor, and he was on his back again, groaning; and then he fell unconscious. George had no strength. Fernando would scoop him up and take the boy with him. Fernando would give the boy food, let the boy keep Chloe company; and when the time was right, when Fernando had stolen Chloe's heart, he would steal both their souls. There was very little bliss in Fernando's eternal life, with happiness coming only when he anticipated the tenderness of morsels like these two. To share his pain and pleasure was all he had. Succulent, juicy, pure . . . it would be ecstasy to mount Chloe and drain her blood.

"*Deje a la chica solo,*" he said in Spanish. Leave the girl alone.

"Speak French, man." Andre glared at Fernando, then his eyebrows lifted as he looked at Fernando, up and down, taking in the black polished shoes, the white silk shirt embellished with gold embroidery.

Chloe shoved Andre and she backed into the corner of the hut to the right of the smoldering fire. Her shirt was ripped straight down the front. She pulled the pieces shut to hide her breasts.

Andre yanked a ham down in one meaty fist and lifted it over his head. "You dare to interrupt me?"

"*Hago lo que yo por favor. Siempre.*" I do what I please. Always.

"Speak so I can understand you, fool!"

In French tinged with his Spanish accent, Fernando indulged the would-be rapist, just this once. For within minutes, there would be no further indulgence for Andre, not ever. "Understand this: your time is over. You have no worth to me. You have no value to anyone. You made a huge mistake coming here tonight. And you will die for it."

Chloe's hand flew to her mouth. She gave Fernando the look he craved so dearly. He heard her thoughts, the very thoughts he had hoped to hear: *This man's going to save me from rape and maybe murder. He's come to save me! He's gorgeous, so strong, so handsome, his hair so golden, his eyes so clear and huge and of a greenish-blue I've never seen. He's draped in gold, he must be very rich. What's he doing in the middle of the forest, here, now?*

Andre swung the ham at Fernando's head.

So predictable and stupid.

Fernando grabbed Andre's wrist and broke it, and the ham slammed to the floor, and the dust rose. A large crack of bone followed, as Fernando twisted Andre's arm out of its socket. The dealer screamed and doubled over, and tears ran down his face. In response, Fernando coiled a sausage around Andre's neck and squeezed until his face was crimson.

Fernando said in Spanish and then in French, "You shouldn't play with what you don't know. Fool." Then he released the sausage loop from Andre's neck and laughed as the man gasped for air. Andre was sputtering and crying, begging for mercy. Fernando didn't care. He wrenched Andre's arm loose and tossed it onto the ham, and kicked both aside.

From the corner, Chloe whimpered and shielded her face so she couldn't see the carnage and blood. She sank to the floor, knees raised, arms covering her head. Everything raged inside her, like bloody turmoil, and Fernando implanted soothing thoughts as he lifted Andre by the neck, squeezed the life out of him, and threw him outside. It only took a few moments to finish off the job, and moving faster than a human could see, Fernando splintered the body in pieces and cast the bits to the wind. A gust of cold air lifted the bits and ground them into particles, and then the particles rose in a cloud over the trees and dissipated. The forest would consume Andre, who would nourish the roots of the pine trees, the oaks, and the birch; and by extension, the squirrels, the deer, the marmot, and the wild boar. Having led a worthless life, Andre would serve a purpose in death.

When Fernando returned to Chloe, she was still sitting with her knees up and her head shielded. She'd seen nothing, and George was still unconscious by the fire pit. The glowing ashes lit his face with a flush that Fernando knew did not come from his blood. The boy was too far gone.

Fernando stepped toward Chloe and trembled. She was divine, with an innocence almost unheard of in modern times. Tucked away in this village her whole life, never taking the tourist roads to the east and the Mediterranean coast. Doing such menial work, endlessly, for *le cochon* and Pierre, and getting nothing in return.

You are perfection. He put the words into her mind.

She lifted her head. Slightly. Peeked at him. *Me? Perfection?* she thought. *Hardly. If not for me, George wouldn't be dying.*

He whispered, "He loves you. And he's not dead yet."

She sucked her lower lip between her teeth, thinking, *I know George loves me. If not for that, he wouldn't even be here, much less on the floor, weak and brutalized by that . . . that beast last night. This is my fault.*

"I can make it better." Fernando took her hand, lifted it to his lips, kissed the slender fingers.

She stared at his mouth, so rosy and soft, he knew. Just what she liked in men. She stared at the fluff of gold on his head, at his half-inch-long fingernails, at his fine clothes. "Who are you," she whispered, "and what happened to that guy who was going to rape me?"

In Spanish and then in French, he said, "I am Fernando Le Sprague. I've spent many years in Barcelona, Spain, right across the border from Llivia and Cerdanya."

"I know of Barcelona." Pause. "I've never been there . . . anywhere. What happened to Andre?"

"You don't have to worry about him anymore. I chased him away, and he won't be back to bother you."

"But how did you chase him away?"

"That need not concern you right now." Fernando flashed his sexiest smile, the one that had captivated the hearts of hundreds of human girls over the past century. And this one was no different: her features relaxed, melted with warmth. He had charmed her. It wasn't much of a hunt or a challenge. His excitement ebbed. He let her hand drop.

To his surprise, she graced his cheek with a gentle touch. "Can you take us, George and me, away from here and to the Mediterranean Sea?"

Touché.

CHAPTER EIGHT

Mediterranean Sea: October 2015

JAMES SCHANKEL GAZED ACROSS the Mediterranean Sea. The water was calm and green, the sky bright with only a dusting of clouds. James leaned on the railing of the ship's deck. The Castor was an old hulk, used for deploying the neutrino observation sensors in the sea years ago. Along with a small crew of researchers and sailors, James was on the ship again. They'd been out to sea for a couple of days, planning to monitor the sensors dangling on strings a mile into the ocean depths.

It was so serene here. James was in no hurry to return to the coast of France, much less to Antarctica for the summer season; although, of course, Toulon, France beat the South Pole any day. Still, James preferred life on the sea to life on land, even in the south of France. In fact, toss in a few bathing beauties, and he'd be willing to stay at sea forever.

But there were no bathing beauties on the Castor. Just crusty old scientists and technicians.

"You ready?"

James turned from the sea and settled his gaze on Albert Horowitz, his lead tech on the project. "Yeah, I'm ready to roll," said James. He zipped the front of his scuba suit, adjusted the weights on his belt, and checked his oxygen mask. Picked up his flippers and his gear bag.

Al held onto the metal rail that ran from the deck into the water. He went down a few stairs toward the sea, then stepped into the tiny powerboat. Al was short, light, and limber.

James Schankel was *not* short and light, but he *was* limber. He lowered his six-foot-three frame onto the stairs, shifted his two hundred and twenty pounds of muscle, and looked over his shoulder at Al. "Sure it's safe? I don't know if that little boat can hold a brute like me."

Al snickered. "If you're too heavy, I'll just shove you overboard. You ever think of going on a diet?"

Yeah, right. Back home, James's diet consisted of meat, vegetables, nuts, and protein shakes. He lifted weights for an hour or more every day. Ran for an hour, too. He wasn't an ex-Marine for nothing.

He climbed into the boat, dumped his flippers and waterproof sack on the floor. Then he loosened the knots holding the thick yellow rope to the Castor, and the tiny powerboat drifted to sea.

The algae were thick and cast a green tinge to the water. The Mediterranean was no longer a deep blue, thought James. The *Caulerpa taxifolia* algae were everywhere, choking other life at the bottom of the sea. James' superiors claimed the algae were disturbing the neutrino sensors that were on the surface and suspended on strings beneath the water. But they weren't scientists. James knew the algae couldn't be responsible for the strange signals they were receiving from the sensors. "Let's hope we get to the bottom of this," he said. "We have better things to do."

Al nodded. "Yeah, those freaky optical module readings. But I still think you're nuts. No way the readings show unexplained neutrinos are hitting us from the great beyond. No way. It might be the algae. Somehow." He frowned, puzzled.

"I absolutely see no way algae are disturbing the strings and the optical modules enough to trigger false neutrino events. I'm sorry, but that doesn't make any sense. Something else is disturbing the sensors and creating those signals. We'll clean up the equipment, remove any algae on the surface detectors, run some tests, and figure out what's going on. If this doesn't work, we'll have to use the sub. I don't think the robotics are up to this particular task."

"Suits me," said Al. "It's lucky for us the Castor has that fuel leak. Let the crew fix it. It gives us time to play on the boat, cruise around, and get ourselves a nice scuba trip or two."

"Yeah, some scuba trip. All we're going to see is astro turf made out of algae."

Al chuckled and switched on the power, and the boat grunted and lurched forward. Cold spray hit the two men.

Picking up speed, the boat ran smoothly over the murky sea toward the twelve sensor drop points. Red buoys bobbed on the surface, marking the locations of the points. By the buoys were the sea-top calibration units.

James motioned at Al to stop near one of the calibration units. The twelve buoys were only sixty meters apart, so it wouldn't be too difficult to check all the calibration units for algae.

He put on his flippers, adjusted his scuba gear, and slid over the side of the boat. Then he splashed backward into the water. Beside him, Al came a second later.

There were a small amount of algae clinging to the calibration unit near the first buoy. James removed the algae and then let Al check the unit for defects.

While Al examined the floating disk and its muon detectors, James rotated his body and knifed down into the sea. Far below him were the actual neutrino sensors. They'd have to go down 2,500 meters by sub just to reach the topmost sensor. Usually, robotic devices did all the work, but when the brass told James to check things personally because of weird events, he had to do what they wanted. On the ocean floor were the anchors, acoustic beacons, electronics boxes, and link cables, all deposited and wired together by robotics long ago. Hopefully, James and Al could fix whatever was causing the weird neutrino signals without having to check all twelve strings and sensors. Each string held seventy-five optical sensor modules. Sometimes, science could be incredibly tedious work, and slicing and dicing data was Schankel's typical fare, so a little underwater work, no matter how tedious, was actually inviting.

A large sunfish swept past him. It was light blue with enormous eyes that swiveled and stared directly at him. As quickly as the fish noticed James, its eyes swiveled in another direction. Most fish were not impressed by humans, he thought. But at least, they left humans alone. Hopefully, he and Al wouldn't encounter any sharks on this little excursion. That was never fun.

When Al was done with the first unit, the two men swam to the second buoy. They checked the surface unit there, then swam to the third buoy.

The first three surface units appeared fine. James knew from the signals received from the units that they were functioning; at minimum, they were receiving data and transmitting it to the station lab in France. Cables, electronics boxes, hydrophone: everything seemed okay.

James and Al worked like this for a couple of hours, and then Al dove beneath the surface for a little fun, and James followed. They might as well enjoy the sights and have a little R&R before returning to the Castor.

Tropical fishes of all hues swirled around the two scientists. Several lionfish flitted past. They were brown with willowy fins that fanned out in all directions. Beautiful fish, but deadly.

Finally, James signaled to Al that they should return to the powerboat. Their oxygen tanks probably required refreshing, and they didn't want to press their luck.

Al went ahead, kicking his way to the surface. James swam close behind, only a yard or two behind Al's blue flippers. Above him, the water shimmered; from this angle, it was light blue with ripples of the sapphire and emerald shades that made the Mediterranean famous.

Al looked down at him, motioned the "okay" signal with his thumb and finger, then turned and kicked upward.

But suddenly, the blue-green water shattered and turned bright white. A surge of foam and debris—a wave from nowhere—hit James and threw him to the left. His breathing tube was forced from his mouth, and a gulp of water filled his lungs. The sea surged against him, forcing him under one wave after another. Sputtering, he tried to get his balance but couldn't. His goggles scraped the bottom of his nose, the sea almost wrenched them from his face. He grabbed the breathing tube and held on for dear life. If he lost access to his oxygen tank, he wouldn't be able to breathe if the sea forced him completely under.

He saw Al's legs to his right. They were flailing, and then he saw Al's arms, both hanging at odd angles: they were both broken, James thought with alarm.

Another wave hit them. The blast threw James out of the water, along with Al, and then both men crashed back down.

Al's tank was loose, his breathing tube wrenched from his face and gone. Blood streamed down his cheeks and chin. He was shrieking in agony.

James's nose hurt, but hopefully, it wasn't broken. His legs and arms ached as if the muscles had been ripped from the bones. But he could still move, thank god. His limbs might hurt like hell, but they weren't broken.

The powerboat was still there, lurching on the waves. Damaged in places, but it hadn't sunk.

Where the Castor *should* have been, there was a mushroom of fire and smoke. The research boat was going down, like a big yellow monster diving beneath the surface.

Al moaned. "James?"

"You okay?" James called back, knowing that Al was definitely *not* okay.

Both of them were treading water. The waves had subsided but were still peaking at more than four feet over their heads.

James looked at his old friend, who was struggling to remain afloat without the use of his arms. James had to get over to Al and help him back to the powerboat.

James groaned. His muscles were killing him. With his head above water, he lifted one aching arm, then the other, and slowly swam toward Al.

"Hurry." Al's voice was weak, his mouth drawn down in pain. "I can't hold it much longer."

"I'm coming, buddy." The pain was intense, searing up James's arms to his shoulders, then ripping down his chest. But this wasn't any worse than the pain he'd felt in Iraq when bullets had blazed into his stomach and arms. James would make it over to Al, would save his old friend.

"James . . . Hurry." Al's head dipped beneath the waves, then popped back to the surface. He struggled for air but swallowed water instead. His face was a mask of pain. He choked, and more water surged down his throat.

James lowered his head and forced his arms to move more quickly.

He and Al were probably the only people left from the Castor, and he had no idea how they were going to make it back to shore with only a small damaged powerboat.

For now, he had to focus. He had to get to Al and save him.

But then a wave crashed down and slammed his body beneath the surface. Bolts of pain shot down his arms and legs. He struggled to get his head above water. He peered around him. A bump of water rose and peaked, and he dove beneath the crest before the wave could pound him back down. Then he lifted his head from the water again. Al was yards away, his face twisted in agony.

"Al, hold on!"

But already, James knew it was too late, for another wave curled over Al and then crashed down, and right before the sea plowed him to his death, Al opened his mouth one last time and screamed. And then he sank.

CHAPTER NINE

Antarctica: October 2015

"IT'S POINTLESS DOING AUTOPSIES of the remains." Rayna Chubkoff's gray eyes were as dark as steel, and just as cold. "Both Sarah Hermann and Zhen Qing were burned in place by some unknown mechanism. I'm putting that down as the cause of death, Sasha: *unknown.*"

The six survivors of the IceCube team sat around the wooden table in the recreation and supplies building. Everyone was shivering, and nobody was hungry. They'd been collecting body parts and hammering together makeshift coffins for hours, and all of them were depressed and exhausted. Twelve dead, all fried and shot to pieces by something that had left no traces of itself. No grenades, no bombs, no guns in the snow, nothing that would indicate an attack by a military force, terrorists, or even a solo lunatic.

Sasha looked at each of her associates and friends, trying to gauge how many of them were strong enough to help her forge ahead with the tasks and how many were falling apart from the ordeal. Antoine Damar, friend and senior lab technician: calm, holding up well, clearly capable of working through the crisis with her. He was tall and slender, not particularly rugged but definitely someone who would do whatever it took to get the communications running, fix the equipment, and help the others cope. Harold Chavenze, junior technician: teeth chattering, blue eyes watery, but a solid worker, muscular and good with the equipment. The other two junior techs were nauseous and already under Rayna's care for Post-Traumatic Stress Disorder. Sasha thought this was nonsense, for how could anyone collapse this quickly into Post-Traumatic Stress Disorder when the trauma had just occurred? But she knew better than to question Rayna's diagnoses or authority in medical matters. The doctor's nerves were already stretched thin. Rayna's hands were shaking, her glare was colder than usual, and her demeanor more sour. Sasha was the only senior scientist left alive, and in fact, she was the only senior staff member: all the other survivors were technicians.

So basically, three of them—Antoine, Harold, and Sasha—were still able to go out there, collect the body remains, make coffins, and try to fix the equipment. Rayna was still able to function as a doctor, though her only living patients right now were the two stressed out junior techs. All of her other "patients" were corpses.

"How is it possible for people to be burned in place, Sasha?" asked Antoine. "What could cause something like that?"

"How would she know?" Rayna spoke with a heavy Russian accent, her words dripping with sarcasm. "This is ridiculous, and we're wasting time. We have more dead bodies to bury. We can't just leave them out there, rotting on the ice."

"Well, they're not going to rot," said Antoine, "that much we know for sure. And if you want to go out and build some more coffins, be my guest. And I'll add that I'm not exactly looking forward to digging graves in the ice, either."

Sasha wouldn't mind a cup of hot coffee, some hot *anything*, right now. The temperature indoors was already dropping rapidly, down to negative ten. And they still didn't have the backup generators working, so there was no heat or electricity anywhere at the station. They had the door propped open slightly so a wedge of Antarctic sunlight could flood the dining room. None of them wanted to huddle together in absolute darkness and talk about death.

"Rayna's right," said Sasha, trying to mollify the ever-sour doctor, "in that I don't know what happened. Odd as it sounds, it seems to me that we were hit by a kind of narrow beam that might fry circuits. Such a beam could also fry people who are unlucky enough to be in its path."

"And what about radiation?" said Antoine.

"Apparently, the peripheral radiation, if the thing that hit us was a neutrino-like beam or series of beams, was not enough to hurt anyone." And then something clicked into place in Sasha's mind. If indeed the Amundsen-Scott Station had been hit by a series of very narrow neutrino beams, it might explain why the IceCube team had been seeing unexplained neutrino events. No, she corrected herself, the team had been seeing the mysterious neutrino events for a long time, and these other beams, if that's what they were, had hit the station only today. She was still baffled by what had happened, and why.

"I'm sorry, but that seems like a stretch to me," said Antoine. "Where would these narrow neutrino beams come from, Sasha?"

Slowly and quietly, she said to everyone, "Did it ever occur to you that we may have found what we've been seeking all these years?"

"Weird neutrinos from outer space?" snorted Harold, the junior tech. "You've got to be kidding, Sasha."

"What are you doing on this project if you don't think neutrinos might be out there, Harold, generated by something in the great beyond that we know nothing about? Just what do you think we're all doing here in the first place? Do you even know what IceCube is? Or did you come here hoping for good ski conditions?"

Harold's face went crimson. "I didn't mean anything by it. I'm just saying–"

"I know what you mean," said Antoine. "A stray neutrino event is one thing. A neutrino beam that kills people is quite another."

"Exactly what I was trying to say," sputtered Harold.

It wasn't like Sasha to lose her temper or talk without carefully considering the results. She often said stupid things, of course—who didn't?—but she rarely said anything that she knew was going to hurt someone's feelings. "I'm sorry," she said. "We're all really strung out right now, me included. I didn't mean to snap at you, Harold." Both Harold and Antoine nodded, but Sasha knew that they would remember how she had lost her temper. People could forgive, but sometimes, it was hard to forget. On the other hand, she thought, it wasn't *that* big a deal. They were all under an enormous amount of strain, and Harold, Antoine, Rayna, and Sasha had been venting their frustrations for hours.

Harold was actually a vital member of the team. He wasn't the smartest guy around, but he was physically strong and mechanically oriented. When muscle was needed, Harold came in handy, and that was certainly worth a lot right now. Brains could get them just so far. If they didn't get some heat going, none of them would survive except the physically strongest, and that person would be Harold.

It wouldn't do them any good to bicker amongst themselves, and as the senior person here, Sasha had to be careful how she treated everyone. They all had to pitch in and help, and things were so bad as it was that making one more person feel even worse wasn't on her agenda. "Let me explain," she said quietly, returning her attention to him. "This all started in Antarctica with the Amanda Project in 1993. They had only four strings in the ice, specifically, some 800-1000 meters down in the ice."

"Meaning," said Antoine, "the ice wasn't all that transparent. You have to go farther down to get to the transparent ice."

"And the bubbles in the ice didn't give the clearest readings of any particles that might have been hitting the ice and going through it from outer space," said Rayna.

"But now we have strings that are 2,450 meters down, so we get much better readings," said Sasha.

"Godamn it!" Harold pounded his fist on the table. "What's the matter with you people? What, do I look like an idiot to you? I don't really need a lesson in IceCube 101. Obviously, I know *something* about the project. I just never thought we'd actually *find* anything, not in my lifetime, anyway. And this has nothing to do with neutrino beams hitting us from outer space, I might add. Like Antoine said, stray neutrino events and killer neutrinos are two different things."

Oh my God, she'd done it again. First, she'd insulted Harold by suggesting he was an idiot, and now, she'd just lectured him as if he didn't know a damn thing about his own job. What had she been thinking? Sasha found herself apologizing yet again, and while everyone nodded as if they believed her, this time, they didn't look so convinced.

Maybe Harold wasn't as naïve as she'd thought. She had to admit that, while she didn't want to say it aloud, she didn't think they'd get results in their lifetimes, either. For one thing, it took a long time—many years—to analyze and interpret the data from IceCube. Unexplained neutrino events were what the scientists *didn't* expect to see.

"Listen, Sasha, I'm taking these two guys back to the medical unit for rest." Rayna gestured at the junior techs. "Let me know if you find anything or if we're able to communicate with the outside world and get some help. And," she added, looking pointedly at Harold, who had calmed down but was tapping his fingers on the tabletop, "if anyone else is suffering from stress, just come by the med unit and join the rest of us." The doctor looked weary, and it was Sasha's guess that Rayna wanted to return to the medical unit so she could remove herself from the others and get a grip on her own nerves. The doctor had been scraping the burned and mutilated bodies of her friends off the ice all day. If Sasha were in Rayna's shoes, she would probably be weeping from the stress. Sasha wasn't really built for crises outside the technical foul-ups of equipment in the lab. This was one reason why she had gone into scientific research in a remote corner of the world. Unlike Rayna, Sasha hadn't chosen an occupation that put her in much contact with people's feelings or health. By nature, Sasha was a loner.

As Rayna led the two junior techs out of the room, Sasha contemplated the situation. The pressure from the weight of the ice removed the air bubbles from the deeper ice, making it transparent. The ice itself *was* the neutrino observatory, an inverted telescope of sorts. The IceCube equipment had been detecting muons possibly generated by neutrinos shooting through the Earth from astrophysical sources other than cosmic rays. If the station had been hit by a neutrino beam, would IceCube have picked up any warning signals? Possibly, she thought, but the hypothetical beam fried all of the computer equipment that could have possibly detected it. But how and why would a stray neutrino beam hit the Amundsen-Scott Station? Sasha didn't believe in aliens. She only trusted empirical evidence as proof of anything.

Besides, aliens weren't blasting the Earth with beams. There was no alien invasion. That was the stuff of science fiction movies, the kind Sasha watched with her father as a child. Real life astrophysics was nothing like alien attack movies such as *The Day the Earth Stood Still* and *War of the Worlds.*

No, something else was going on, and whatever it was, there was nothing Sasha could do about it now. All she could do was focus on the problems at hand. "I guess it's up to us," she said to Harold and Antoine.

"What is?" asked Harold.

"Unfortunately, we have to go out there and bury everyone."

After a moment of awkward silence—nobody was anxious to go back outside and deal with the dead bodies—Sasha added, "And we have to figure out how to get the power turned on. If we can contact McMurdo or the outside world, maybe they can tell us what happened."

The other two lightened up a bit at the thought of doing tasks that were unrelated to deaths and burials.

Finally, they went back outside, figuring it would be best to just bury everyone without coffins. Snow fell in thick clouds, leaving the surface powdered and soft. As Sasha's boots crunched across the snow, she slipped on the icy patches beneath the powder, and had to keep grabbing Antoine to keep from falling. He was also having a hard time: they couldn't see more than a yard or two in front of them, and the wind was blasting snow and hail almost horizontally across the ice.

With her vision fogged by the snow, she relied on her sense of touch more than she usually did. She inched along with Harold and Antoine, intently aware of the *feel* of the surface beneath her boots. She felt every patch of ice, every narrow crack, every crunch of hardened snow, every tuft of soft powder before the wind whipped it up and whisked it into the fog. She realized that this was not a good time to bury the dead. They couldn't even *find* the dead under these conditions.

And that's when she stumbled over a mound of rock-hard flesh and fell down. Her forehead cracked against the ice, and dizziness washed over her. Antoine and Harold were scooping her up, and then she was in Harold's arms, being carried by him . . .

The dizziness eased, and she fussed and insisted that he let her back down to her feet, and finally he did, and she grasped both

Harold and Antoine, steadied herself, and yelled over the wind, "I suggest we just give up for now and come out later when we can see what we're burying!"

"What if the body parts are all blown away?" yelled Harold. "I mean, they're all in pieces!"

True enough. But Sasha didn't relish the idea of explaining to a bunch of grieving widows, parents, and children why their loved ones hadn't been buried. They couldn't let the body parts blow away.

The ice was pounding her from all angles, and through it, she saw both Harold and Antoine struggling to remain upright. There was nothing more they could do. If the dead disappeared, so be it.

"We have to go back!" she screamed.

Antoine screamed something in return, but she couldn't hear him over the wind. The three of them started back toward the building. The wind picked up speed, and the ice particles were like clouds around them. Clouds that coalesced and split apart, forming horrible images: grotesque faces, half-shredded penguins, dogs with pained eyes, frozen pemmicans. She must be imagining it all, she thought. Maybe she was going into Post-Traumatic Stress Disorder like the junior techs. *Shrug it off, just shrug it off. We've gotta get back to the station where it's safe.*

Sasha was beginning to feel as if all was hopeless. It took a lot out of her to keep her spirits up, to think that things would ever return to normal. After seeing people like Sarah Hermann blown to bits, how could she ever be normal again?

She was even beginning to doubt her choice of occupation. Why the hell had she gone into this insane IceCube research, anyway? Winter in Antarctica was a bitch, and all for what? So she might someday find some muons that hadn't originated from cosmic rays?

She'd never felt so down in her whole life. She had a PhD in this subject, had spent years on her doctoral thesis, and she'd never once regretted her choice or second-guessed herself. But now, she suddenly felt very mortal . . . and very scared.

Through the shrieking of the storm, she suddenly heard something even louder, a whirling noise, a grinding; and again, she questioned her sanity. *Now she was hearing things, too.* But Antoine and Harold both stopped, as well, and they grabbed her arms to keep from falling, and the three of them turned their faces back into the storm to try and detect the source of the noise. The fog and snow were too thick, and all Sasha saw were the grotesque images: mirages made of white mist and bluish water, shot through with gray haze, specters of the long-lost dead, the adventurers who had died in Antarctica a century or more ago. She knew the faces, ravaged as they were from frost and dead, from the photos she'd studied as an undergraduate student.

She pulled away from Antoine and Harold, who tried to hold onto her, and she squinted into the mist, trying to sweep the images away, hoping to god the hallucinations would end. The whirling and grinding noises drowned out the wind—were the dead screaming at her?

Before her, she saw Robert Falcon Scott: dead, hovering in the mist, blue eyes like beacons glowing through the haze, black hair coated in ice and framed around his face like a macabre hat, large nose puffed with frostbite, the nostrils tampered shut by icicles.

"Do you see it?" she cried to the others, but they just clutched at her and tried to drag her back to the building with them. She refused to budge. "Look! Look into the mist!"

"Sasha, Sasha, come on, you need to get back inside." Antoine sounded worried. His voice reminded her of orderlies in mental institutions, not that she'd ever been in a mental institution, but his tone suggested that he figured she was losing her sanity.

"Edward Wilson," she whispered, knowing that neither Harold nor Antoine would hear whispers over the storm. Beard, moustache, dark hair, Wilson had been Scott's medical doctor on their fateful trip a century ago. And she saw Wilson looming in the mist along with Scott. Wilson's eyes were glazed and didn't blink or flicker; she remembered the story well, how Wilson had been blinded by the reflection of the sun off the ice. Along with Ernest Shackleton, Scott and Wilson had died in a blizzard while trying to make it back to a supply depot.

Although she didn't see him in the fog, Sasha saw him in her mind, another man who had lost his life in Antarctica a century ago. Her great-great-grandfather Lawrence Oates, who sacrificed himself to a blizzard so Wilson and the others could share his portion of food. He was a hero, Oates, and another reason, she remembered, why she had come to Antarctica to do research. It was in her blood, her lineage, to be here. She was the first in her family to follow in Oates's footsteps.

Before her now, ice fluttered like feathers, and a cross-hatch of blue light rose. She heard voices, and they weren't from Antoine or Harold. Distinctly, she heard them:

"Snatcher died." And in the storm, Sasha saw a dead dog on its back, and it was cut down the center with its organs removed.

The wind howled, and the voices came:

"Acute peritonitis. Extreme cold, blizzards, not enough food."

"What are we going to do, Scott?"

"I don't know, Wilson. We have to keep pushing forward. We may have to slaughter the weaker dogs. What do you think, Shackleton?"

"Well, the stronger dogs are going to die of starvation if we don't feed them more, so I'm with you, we have to kill the weaker ones."

Then she saw a cluster of icicles hanging from Scott's dead face, and suddenly, the face disappeared back into the mist and the icicles plunged downward—right into the whirling snow on the surface ice, and the icicles grew red, as if from blood.

The humans come here, and they defile our home . . .

The humans torture and eat their own animals . . .

The humans put this diseased blood on our ice!

These last sentences were not from humans. They came to her as vibrations against her eardrums, she would swear later that the words weren't in any human language, yet somehow she knew the meanings.

Without a doubt, she must be going mad.

It was then, as she collapsed in a heap on the ice, weeping and clawing at the blizzard and crying "No, go away, no!" that she heard a *real* voice screaming over the wind:

"When we didn't hear back from you, we hopped on the plane and came out here. The storm almost downed us! I don't think we're going back to McMurdo until it eases up. What the hell's going on here, anyway?"

McMurdo?

McMurdo!

As in *McMurdo Station*.

A plane had come to the Amundsen-Scott Station from nearby McMurdo! Of course! At last, there was some hope. The images of the long dead faded, and their voices disappeared. In their place was this man, the stranger, with his very real voice, and there was another man with him.

Harold was holding Sasha's forearm, and she heard him as if from far away, telling the two strangers about the explosions, the deaths. Antoine explained that all three generators were shot, that there was no heat or power at the Amundsen-Scott Station.

The first stranger said, "Well, when we landed and tripped over the bodies and saw the buildings burned, we got on the short wave to McMurdo. They've probably been in touch with the military by now. You should have help here very soon."

"Did you bring any backup generators?" asked Antoine.

"Yes, one backup, some medical supplies, and food." The two strangers helped Antoine, Harold, and Sasha back into the recreation and supplies building, and then the five of them huddled around the wooden table, shivering, teeth chattering, trying unsuccessfully to get warm. Sasha couldn't remember a time when she was this cold and this terrified. People often had hallucinations when it was really hot outside, like 100 degrees or more, she thought. Was it possible to have hallucinations when the temperature dropped to the extreme opposite? She'd never had visions of any kind. She'd always been levelheaded. Perhaps it was just the stress of the situation getting to her.

". . . Sean McDonald and this is Albin Fageraas from Norway. We're going out to see what we can do with the backup generator. Once we get heat going, we'll all feel a lot better." He was big and beefy, the one who was doing all the talking. Sasha didn't recognize him or his friend. She knew very few people at McMurdo Station, which was hundreds of miles from the Amundsen-Scott Station and much larger. McMurdo was home to more than two hundred scientists and staff members in the winter; Amundsen-Scott housed two hundred in the *summer* while McMurdo's population swelled to well over a thousand in the summer. By now, McMurdo had sent emergency messages back to the military via the NASA NPOESS satellite. They had a dish on Black Island that supplied them with 20 megabit per second internet and voice communications. Of course, Amundsen-Scott had a high-speed connection, too, via several NASA satellites, but for now, nobody at the South Pole station could communicate to anyone anywhere: you needed equipment for that, and equipment needed juice.

Harold stayed with her, and Antoine accompanied Sean McDonald and Albin Fageraas back to the McMurdo plane to get the backup generator. As the three men opened the door and left the building, Sasha saw a wisp of frost trailing behind them. Like smoke puffed from a cigarette, the frost hung there by the door, then liquefied and dropped to the floor. How ice could liquefy in this weather was beyond Sasha's comprehension. How ice could follow people was also beyond comprehension. She watched the little fog of breath pulsing from her mouth: puff of smoke, a sparkle in the dark, and then, rather than evaporating, drops of moisture that coalesced and formed small puddles on the wooden table where she sat. The puddles rapidly turned to ice.

She had an eerie sense that something was clinging to her, something alive. It was cold, whatever it was, but moved over her body as if it knew what it was doing: lingering on her fingertips and mouth, cruising down her back then racing to her shoulders again. It wasn't just a flush of cold sweeping over her. It was almost as if the frost was intelligent and knew exactly what it was doing.

CHAPTER
TEN

Cerdanya, France: October 2015

CHLOE WRAPPED HER ARMS around George and helped him up the slope toward the mountain trail. His left leg was dragging in the dirt, and he kept complaining that his right knee hurt. The stranger, Fernando Le Sprague, disappeared behind a bend in the forest: he shimmered like a bolt of sunlight between the trees and left only his shadow on the forest floor. Chloe wasn't sure what she was actually seeing and what her brain was imagining when she looked at Fernando. At one moment, he was a powerful Spaniard, handsome, golden, and tall, his smile as comforting as the sun; and the next moment, he had either disappeared into the mist or was emanating an odd coolness that struck Chloe in the face like a hard slap.

One thing Chloe knew for sure was that Fernando Le Sprague was her one hope for getting out of Cerdanya. She couldn't make it on her own: her left thigh and right arm both hurt, and the pain in her back was escalating.

"Please, I have to rest." George was panting, and while they were hardly making any headway, the effort was apparently too much for him. His eyes were dimmer, his white skin more stark. Where was the George who had alert brown eyes, who was strong and confident? Chloe couldn't bear to see him this way. He'd always been her best friend, her *only* friend. What had she ever done for *him* other than spurn his advances? He'd wanted to stay in Cerdanya in their village, and she'd convinced him to run away with her. Now he was too weak to argue, and Chloe was too afraid to leave him behind. She would protect him. George would be safe with her.

His black t-shirt was caked in blood and sweat, and the four bite marks on his neck had faded into red pinpricks. If Chloe hadn't seen the bite marks herself, she wouldn't believe they had actually been bloody wounds only hours ago.

She eased George onto the moss beneath an oak tree, made sure to position him so the branches cooled him with shade and the leaves fanned him. She sank beside him, happy to rest her own back and legs. Her aquamarine t-shirt was blotched with mud.

Water dripped from the awning of trees, and moisture clung to the leaves. Farther ahead on the trail, frost coated the trees and their buds, and a fine mist of ice floated in the air. The ground clearly had patches of ice on it, but here where Chloe and George sat, everything was humid and wet.

Chloe's brown hair hung limply over her shoulders. She untangled the stringy clumps, wincing as she yanked the knots free, wondering what had happened to her dark golden hair, which used to give her so much joy. She'd taken her hair for granted, been proud that it was so beautiful, but it had never occurred to her that someday—as young as eighteen—her hair would grow dull and actually change color. She almost felt defiled, as if something vital had been ripped from her body.

But what did it matter, really?

If I cut my hair, if it all fell out, I'd still be the same Chloe Desmarais, running away from my father and my childhood village with George Bouchard in tow. What really matters is that I'm escaping from my past. And then she thought, *Of course, I'm escaping with a creature who claims his life is a combination of blood and ice, a creature who looks like a god.*

On the other hand, Fernando Le Sprague had saved Chloe from Andre's attack, so how bad could he be?

"How are we going to continue, Chloe? I can't walk anymore, and we're hours away from Perpignan." George's lips were parched, and his fingers twitched in the leaves.

"We have to make it to Perpignan and to the sea, George, somehow, I don't know how. But it's our only hope." She dipped

George's head back slightly and gently opened his mouth with her fingers. Water trickled into his hair, over his forehead, a few drops splashed into his mouth, and while he had trouble swallowing, he managed to get a little water down his throat.

"But I'm not sure I want to leave the village, Chloe. Why are we following this Fernando guy anyway?"

"You know I have to get away from my father, George. He'll beat the life out of me if I don't leave. I can't stay there anymore."

"But why *now,* and why with *Fernando?*"

"You forget, he saved my life."

George moaned and shifted his weight slightly to the left. His mouth shut. He let the drops splatter on his hair and cheeks. Abruptly, the water stopped filtering down from the leaves and branches—it just *stopped.*

From ahead, Chloe saw movement in the forest. Shoes crunched across the twigs. Chloe's heart quickened. Was it her father again? Was it the boar-beast?

But relief swept over her as she saw it was only Fernando Le Sprague, her savior: a gorgeous man with sexy eyes, no more scary than George Bouchard but a lot more attractive.

He flickered into view by the bend where he'd disappeared only a few minutes ago. He seemed to step out of the mist.

His hair was more golden than hers had been before it oddly darkened to brown. His was like a fluffy halo around his head, and his hazel eyes glowed like crystals. The frilly cuffs on his shirt were pure white and unblemished by sweat or soil. His black pants were creased and seemed made of silk, and his black shoes gleamed. Nothing about Fernando was soiled, tired, or blemished in any way. He was, quite simply, perfect. Beneath the sun, he glowed like diamond dust.

He stooped beside Chloe and touched her face. She shivered as the round nails danced across her skin. She saw a tremor of excitement on his face—or was she just imagining it?—as he noticed her reaction to him. She didn't want him to know how he affected her, she fought to control her physical response to him, but she couldn't hide it well enough, and he said: "Chloe, my dear, we are meant for each other, yes? You feel it as strongly as I do."

As Chloe felt the heat rising to her cheeks, George said weakly,

"Give me a break. You and Chloe aren't meant for each other. You're at least twice our age. *You* are an old man. What do you know about where we come from and who we are?"

"I know enough," said Fernando, brushing his fingers across Chloe's lips and down her neck, making her flesh tingle. It was an odd mixture, this fear and desire in her, just as Fernando himself seemed to be made from warmth and ice, compassion and cruelty. Chloe couldn't define, much less control, her own reactions to this man. She didn't understand her feelings, and Fernando seemed to sense her unrest. It seemed that she couldn't hide anything from him.

In her mind, she heard the beast's words again: *We are mates now, the three of us. Blood and ice, substance and form, love and devotion. And above all, pain, the eternal source of energy and strength.*

And then in hit her, and it was so obvious that she felt like a fool. "*You* are the beast, aren't you?" she whispered.

"Am I?" He laughed. He ran his tongue over his upper teeth. "Do I have big bloody fangs?" Then he parted his hair and shook his head. "Do I have horns on my head?" Then he pointed to the cross hanging on the gold necklace. "Do beasts wear the sign of Christ? Dear girl, the two of you have been in your village for far too long. It's time for you to see the world. And then you'll both realize that there's room on this planet for all sorts of people, and just because we're different doesn't mean we're beasts from hell or demons sent by Satan to steal your souls." He held her right hand between his palms and caressed her flesh. His touch was almost magical, for with each stroke of his icy fingers, her pain dwindled. It was as if his fingers were literally numbing her pain, though oddly, the cold numbness was flaring to heat and shooting up her right arm.

For the first time since her father had twisted her arm and hurt it, she was able to bend her arm freely at the elbow. The bruises were gone. The purple welts had disappeared, and her skin was smooth as if nothing had ever happened.

He gestured toward the path leading into the mountains. "Follow me, Chloe, and we'll take George with us, too. Don't worry, George, you'll learn to love me as much as Chloe does."

George flinched and growled something like "Yeah, when hell freezes over," but Chloe looked where Fernando was pointing:

following his slender finger and half-inch-long rounded nail to the trees beyond. She saw leprous spots on the trees, feathery sprays of leaves set against a backdrop of lush mountains, waterfalls, and blue ice high on the tips of the mountains. The air was cool and heavy with green filaments that swarmed around her head, her hands, around George and Fernando. Globules of blue bulged toward the right, drifting in the breeze, then shifted direction as the breeze shifted and burst on pine needles, spraying a fine mist upon the moss. The oaks were lustrous, the elms strung with dew that reminded her of pearls. And then the leprous spots faded and glowed like polished bronze, and the mountains lost their hardness and swelled like giant breasts, the waterfalls gushing and spilling krill along the forest path.

Fernando lifted his arms, and the krill and the blue globules swarmed around his body and settled into his cupped hands. His smile was dazzling, his eyes lustrous and moist. Chloe sank against Fernando's chest, feeling a vibration almost like a cat's purr where his heart should be. The vibrations spread over her cheeks and chin, entered her skin, and swept through her body. Warmth and chills, a pattern of black and white, of shades of gray, in loops and swirls and orbs and triangles, she was lost in them, as the vibrations grew in frequency and tone. Everything was a shade of black or white. And then the vibrations consumed her, and she felt and heard and saw nothing but swirls and patterns of infinite dimensions.

George was slumped across Chloe's lap, the vibrations emanating from her chest and torso into his body. From the vibrations between them, she sensed George's essence: the febrile pulse of his heart, the whisper of his breath across her skin. And then his body snapped back against the tree trunk and he groaned, but it was a groan of pleasure and relief.

Fernando's voice came soft and smooth through the whirlwind of lush monochromatic patterns. "We will walk together and feed together. Pain will be your pleasure now. You will be one with me, you and George. You will have all the freedom you've desired since your mother died long ago. Freedom from your father, at long last, freedom from confinement and slavery. The bread is the past, the cheese is the past, you won't hunger for these things again. I will give you this great gift, if you give me only one thing in return."

"What are you? What do you want?" whispered George. His eyes shined for Fernando the way they used to shine for Chloe, and she felt a pang of jealousy, which surprised her. She'd spurned George's advances countless times, so why should she care if he desired someone else, even if that someone else was a creature like Fernando? Of course, she told herself, the answer was simple. It was because she wanted Fernando for herself. *But I don't really want him, do I? He's a beast, probably the boar, a thing with four fangs and wings, a thing that kills children.* She could not love such a thing, refused to love it.

"What *do* you want?" she asked.

"Companionship. Friendship. Nothing more."

"Not sex?"

He laughed as if the thought were absurd. "No, I can assure you, Chloe, that I'm not after anything as base as that. There are few of my kind, and indeed, we've not seen each other for a very long time. Most of my friends are long gone. I lust for friendship."

Two isards bounced from one rocky ledge to another—Chloe saw them in the distance high on the mountains that fringed the forest, far away from where she should be able to see anything. Chestnut heads and bodies, white tails and throats, curved horns: she was sure that she saw them, rare as they were in this part of the Pyrenees.

Chloe peered at Fernando, so close to her down on the forest leaves, settled beside her, a distant look in his eyes. He was much older than she'd thought. His eyes were hooded and had dim blotches of purple under them. The hazel was dimmer than moments before, as if the lights were going out behind them. He had a weathered look: wrinkles on his face and neck, shoulders drooping, lips mottled like the leprous growths on the trees. Even his hair, that brilliant fluff of gold, appeared more gray than blond at this distance, and his fingers, rather than being slender and smooth, had arthritic knobs at the joints.

Her pain had subsided though she still felt weak, and to her left, George was still gazing at Fernando as if he was a god. She had the impression that her pain would return, that whatever she felt was temporary as if she'd been given morphine or a sedative. Something had taken the edge off the pain, that's all, but it would come back.

She felt the soft laughter rippling through her mind, the imprint of the beast's words inside her brain back in the bakehouse:

Your pain, it's like the smell of blood.

Blood and ice, Chloe. Substance and form. Love, perhaps. Devotion.

Pain is eternal, Chloe. It's the source of all energy and strength. It gives substance and form. Without your pain, Chloe, what would you be?

In time, my sweet morsel, you'll learn to love me.

And she knew that Fernando was lying to her now, that he wasn't lonely and seeking a few friends—how absurd was *that?* He wanted her devotion, her love, her blood and her pain.

What kind of creature would thrive on another's pain? Only a monster, she thought. Her father was a monster, who had lived on her pain for eighteen years. Her brother, Pierre, lived on her pain, too.

"You don't have to worry about Pierre anymore," she thought she heard Fernando say, but she wasn't sure what she was hearing, for her mind was in a haze.

She also heard nuts cracking in squirrels' jaws a mile off, and she saw vapors and isards high in the mountains, and she smelled flowers that she knew only grew on the Spanish side of the Pyrenees, nowhere near the eastern French forests.

George scrabbled to his feet and shook the leaves and dirt off his clothes. His hair was soft brown again and shimmering with frost. His face was no longer contorted with pain, he seemed relaxed and somehow, much stronger. "We need to get moving if we want to make it to the Mediterranean Sea before your father finds out we're missing, Chloe. He'll send the villagers out looking for us."

She shuddered. She definitely didn't want her father catching her and forcing her to return home. He'd beat her so badly she'd probably never walk again. "Come on, Fernando, we have to leave. George is right."

On the ground beside her one second, Fernando disappeared the next. He flickered out of sight, then appeared in a cloud of water vapor and seemed to crystallize back into view. Chloe knew she was seeing things due to days of pain and starvation, perhaps due to the sheer hysteria of running away, particularly with an old Spanish guy with peculiar habits. Perhaps she and George should dump Fernando as soon as he helped them make it to the sea.

"If we could go by the highways, it wouldn't take long at all," Fernando commented as the three of them hiked up the mountain pass. "That's the way the tourists make their way from Perpignan to Cerdanya."

George walked ahead with Fernando, leaving Chloe clomping behind them by at least a few yards. George wasn't limping or groaning. He smiled and looped his arm over Fernando's shoulder as if the two were lovers. Odd, thought Chloe, because George had always seemed straight to her, and only a little while ago, George was telling Fernando that he was way too old to be hanging around with them. Why was he suddenly acting as if had fallen in love with this creepy old guy?

"I've heard of it," said George. "They stay near the Mediterranean then rent their jeeps in Perpignan. I mean, you can take a train from Perpignan and be in Barcelona in less than an hour."

"Ah yes, Barcelona, my home away from home," said Fernando. "Perpignan actually has much in common with Spain. The fiestas, the Iberian refugees who fled over the Pyrenees to the coast at the end of the Spanish Civil War. Did you know there's an airport in Perpignan, as well as vineyards, cathedrals, restaurants, and theater?"

"No," said George, "perhaps we can stay in the city for awhile, then, before we leave for the sea?"

Again, thought Chloe, George was acting very strange. "You didn't even want to leave the village," she pointed out.

He turned slightly to acknowledge that he heard her but kept walking next to Fernando. "True, Chloe, but now that you forced me to leave with you, I see that maybe we could have more fun away from the village and all its old-fashioned stupidity. Why shouldn't we have fun?"

"That's what I said to *you*, George. Why should we kill ourselves making food and tending goats and what-not, while the tourists have parties on their yachts and wear fancy clothes? We've been living as if it's the 1800s. I don't know why anyone stays in the mountains. It's like death." Chloe hoped George would wait for her and walk next to her and continue their conversation. But he didn't.

Instead, he said to Fernando, "Tell me more about where we're going. It'll give me something to look forward to."

What was up with George? A little rest by a tree, a ten-minute conversation with Fernando, and George was like a totally different guy.

And then with a start, Chloe realized that she wasn't limping, either, and her mind was free from physical pain. At least for now. Fernando had a weird effect on her, too, but nonetheless, he appeared to be twice her age—or more—and there was something about him that she just didn't like.

And then with another start, she realized that she was acting even stranger than George. She liked Fernando, then she didn't like him. Her feelings were swinging back and forth rapidly, from one extreme to the other and then back again.

". . . and the airport in Perpignan," Fernando was saying, "is to the northwest of the city. The main highways run from the N116 by the coast all the way through the eastern Pyrenees to the D118 near Mont-Louis, the D618 and the N20 that bring you to Llivia. And of course, you can get to Barcelona from a variety of highways south of Perpignan."

To Chloe's left and right and as far as she could see ahead of her, there was nothing but an endless stretch of ice-tipped mountains, streams, wild flowers, and trees. Glaciers towered over the trail where they hiked. Small forest animals skittered away from them, unaccustomed to the intrusion of people, frightened of the unknown. The birds perched high in the trees, calling to each other, warning their mates that people were intruding on their domains. The path crisscrossed repeatedly, and each time there was a fork, Fernando knew which way to go. He didn't even stop and think about it, he automatically turned left or right, up an incline or around a foothill. They passed half-hidden lakes, the sun reflecting shadows of pines and mountains off the water, the birds diving for a stray fish, circles rippling outward as twigs fell from maples and pines, as birds dropped seeds and stones. And drifting in the lakes were chunks of ice, the debris of glaciers. Chloe saw butterflies dancing through sunlit dust across a stretch of flowering thistles: the butterflies were never seen by the tourists of Perpignan. Glandon Blue butterflies, and the Agriades pyrenaicus, the Parnassius apollo, the Swallowtail. She even saw a rare Hummingbird Hawk Moth among the buttercups, narcissi flowers, and irises.

They hiked for hours through valleys and U-shaped troughs, around boulders, next to streams, and past fields where oxen and goats grazed. Hidden paths, gorges, and waterfalls. An abundance of shadow mixed with light. Chloe was adrift, marching in a steady beat like a soldier, her mind lost in the deluge of color and ice.

They passed a limestone ridge and ducked inside a cave. The sky was pink and orange, a flush like blood on the cheeks of an infant. It was the last thing Chloe saw before she fell asleep: that pink pink sky.

She awakened to the blush of dawn, the limestone beneath her body slick with dew and slime. Overhead in the cave, stalactites hung like hypodermic needles, dripping water in a steady rhythm. Hair-thin needles and fat prongs, a cluster of projectiles surrounding a chunk of ice shaped like a tongue. Wet moss hung from the tip of the tongue, and water flowed from the tongue to the cave floor, where sediments had congealed to form a limestone stool.

Chloe was alone in the cave. She sat, careful not to hit her head against the icy pricks on the low ceiling. She held her breath, listened for any sound in the woods that might indicate that Fernando and George were nearby. But she heard nothing.

Marmots squeaked and chased each other at the lip of the cave. One whistled at her. A mole poked its snout into a puddle and extracted a squirming white worm: insect larvae. Chloe took it for a Pyrenean Desman; they were rare, but the webbed feet gave it away. The cave must be near a mountain stream because Desmans spent most of their time in the water.

Her clothes were damp, and her muscles ached again. Her feet were scabbed from cuts endured on the long hike over the stones and branches. Luckily, she had thick calluses on her feet from a lifetime in the mountains. Still, it was going to be a hard journey all the way to Perpignan without shoes or boots.

She slid along the floor until she emerged from the cave, and here, the sun was warm and helped take the chill out of her body. Flowers of purple and pink bobbed in the slight breeze, and behind them stood chestnut trees, cork oaks, and pines. Everything was dusted in a haze of frost.

The sound of birds brought her to the edge of a shimmering lake, where a wild horse sipped water and white-winged birds soared overhead. The firs and pines were sparser here, and the grass was thick and soft.

She was acutely aware of her hunger and wondered what she could forage for breakfast. Berries, perhaps, or other vegetation? Scanning the perimeter of the lake, she saw something moving by a flame-colored bush. The leaves rustled, then were still. Probably a small animal, she thought, but then, the leaves thrashed, and she knew something much larger than a squirrel or mole was beside the bush.

Winding her hair into a loose braid to get it off her face, she circled the lake, cautiously avoiding sharp stones and thorns.

Squish.

Thwack.

Squish.

Thwack.

She recognized the sound. It was the squishing of the dough as she kneaded it back in the bakehouse, the thwack of the mounds as she slammed them onto the table. It was the noise she heard when the boar came.

But now the boar was Fernando, and he was leaning over a body. Brown hair, muscular build, black jeans. Blood.

It was George.

Fernando licked George's elbow. George clung like a baby to Fernando, his arms around Fernando's neck, his hands gripping Fernando's shoulders.

A loud sucking noise, then *squish thwack* as Fernando squeezed the arm to push more blood out of the incisions in the elbow. He lifted his head from the elbow, and his skin was ice-white and glowing, four tiny needles sticking out of his mouth, two on top, two on the bottom. Bloody gums. Eyes that glowed with the intelligence of a man. Short wings pulsing beneath the golden-embroidered shirt, and black bristles and auburn fur protruding from beneath the frilly white cuffs. Narrow hips.

Chloe wanted to scream and run, but she was rooted in place, unable to move. A sound squeaked out of her throat, like the chirp of a baby bird.

Pink flared in the sky; the mist was a whirling kaleidoscope of color, frost clung to the trees, ice congealed on her skin. She touched her hair: it was golden again, and soft, threaded with beads of ice.

Le cochon.

It was Fernando, not her father.

George's legs twitched as the beast shook droplets of blood from its icy fangs. He was moaning, George, and he twisted his arm to look at the four tiny incisions in the crook of his elbow. His eyelids were swollen, and his eyes had that dreamy faraway look that Pierre and Deétda had after they'd been doing drugs for days on end.

Chloe took one tiny step forward. "George . . . ?"

He moaned more loudly, turned his head in her direction. His brows lifted, his forehead wrinkled, his eyes widened. Then his gaze shifted to Fernando, and his entire body jerked harder against the ground.

"You? What have you done to me?" George's voice was hoarse and low.

Fernando's icy fangs no longer protruded from his mouth. His lips curled into a crimson smile, his face became more solid and flesh toned, the wings on his back stopped moving and then disappeared. He ran a finger across his lips, then gently pushed George's lips apart so his finger could run across George's gums. Chloe had seen Pierre do the same thing to Deétda when they were high on coke. George's eyes fuzzed over and his body relaxed. A wisp of a smile played on his lips.

"I had no choice," said Fernando. "I was hungry, and you were here."

Another spasm, this time one of ecstasy, and George shivered and said, "Hunger is . . . excellent."

"Hunger is pleasure, and pleasure is pain, the eternal source," and Fernando didn't need to finish the sentence, because Chloe already knew the ending, *that pain was the eternal source of energy and strength.*

And in Chloe's mind, Fernando planted thoughts in both French and Spanish. *You're next, mon chère. I hunger for your taste, but I won't kill you. In turn, you and George will come to my homeland, where we'll find tranquility and peace. We'll dine fully before we leave, and when we finally return home, we'll teach the newly hatched how to forage for food and protect the land.*

What land? She thought wildly. *What is newly hatched? What are you talking about?*

All in good time, mon chère. First, I'll make you feel good. Then we'll travel south.

How would she ever feel good under these circumstances? She was running away from home with a monster who had just sunk needles of ice into George's arm and drunk him dry. George was alive and drugged, and not at all himself. She was hallucinating like a mad woman, hearing things, smelling things . . .

None of this could be real, *could it?*

CHAPTER ELEVEN

Cerdanya, France: October 2015

CHLOE FOLLOWED FERNANDO AND George down the steep path that wound its way down the mountain. She carefully stepped over tree roots and fallen branches, grasping whatever she could to keep from falling off the narrow walkway to a certain death. There wasn't much to hold onto, but with her back and leg pains gone, at least she wasn't limping or worried about her left leg collapsing beneath her.

The rough skin on her feet wasn't enough to protect her from the sharp rocks on this path, and she was anxious to get to Perpignan, where she could hopefully relax, let her feet heal, and maybe even find some shoes.

Up ahead, Fernando seemed to float over the large rocks obstructing the path. George effortlessly climbed over them while chattering constantly. He was high on something, and the only thing it could be was whatever Fernando had injected into his blood.

Chloe remained terrified of what she'd seen. She couldn't get it out of her mind: Fernando squeezing George's arm to squirt blood out of the incisions in his elbow; Fernando's mouth smeared in blood with those hideous four needles, two hanging from the top of his mouth, two from the bottom. The short wings, the black bristles, the auburn fur. She was sure now that Fernando Le Sprague was the boar-beast who had plagued her village and killed the children.

He's going to stick those four needles into my arm and drink all my blood.

He's going to kill me.

I'm going to die.

She wanted to scream, but nobody would hear her except Fernando and George. And then Fernando might kill her.

I won't let him kill me. I won't!

George was still alive, wasn't he? *Even if Fernando sticks those four needles into me, I'll still be alive. He won't kill me. Look at George. He's walking ahead, chattering gaily with Fernando as if nothing happened. He doesn't seem to remember that Fernando just attacked him brutally in the form of a monster. He doesn't even seem to know.*

A river glittered below, and the steep descent began to flatten; and Chloe struggled with her footing as she shifted downward, stones scattering over the cliff into the river. Finally, the path skirted the water under an awning of pines.

Fernando and George were already sitting at the edge of the river by a waterfall. Another mountain lay directly in front of them, and the water pounded down the side of a cliff straight into the lake, splashing back up in a heavy mist.

What kind of creature was Fernando? Chloe had never been particularly superstitious, and despite her upbringing, she considered herself to be a modern girl. She'd never really believed all those killer-beast rumors spread by the gossiping village biddies. Not *really*, not until *now*, anyway.

Rough skin could protect her only so much, and the soles of her feet hurt; there was blood, she noticed, on the dirt where she walked. She was getting so used to pain that it hardly felt real. Was this how Fernando initiated his assault, by crippling and weakening people before he attacked them? But *George* was no longer weak or in pain. He seemed just fine.

As she neared George and Fernando, Chloe heard the monster say, "The power of the water is astonishing, don't you think? As a liquid, it can fuel machines." He talked as if this was grade school science class and he was a teacher. It seemed like an odd subject to be discussing while they tramped through the forest on the run and afraid of being discovered.

George's brown eyes were glassy, reminding Chloe of smooth polished stone. He was obviously drugged. He looked at Fernando as an acolyte gazes at the master. His back was pressed against a large rock, and his knees were pressed against his chest. His chin was propped on his knees, and he was rocking back and forth slightly as if in a trance.

"Water is beauty," said George. "Just look at that mist as it billows up from the river. How beautiful is that, I ask you?" George talked oddly, too, his voice chirpy and giddy. Chloe had heard girls talking this way while flirting with boys.

"Beauty, power, pain, pleasure. Sometimes, the beautiful is the most powerful, George. Sometimes, the most exquisite pain brings the most magnificent pleasure. Say you're in a boat in a heavy mist at sea. Do you think you would survive?"

George shook his head, no. "I wouldn't be able to steer the boat, and it would get lost and eventually crash."

Chloe wondered if all this talk about water and mist had anything to do with the trails of frost, the odd mud, the ice clinging to the branches as Fernando moved through the forest. Was he connected somehow to *water?* But what kind of *vampire* derived its strength from *water?* And wasn't that exactly what Fernando Le Sprague was, *a vampire,* when you got right down to it? Fernando drank blood, and that meant he was a vampire.

She remembered asking the beast if it was dead or undead, and in both cases, it had said, no. The beast was a living creature.

Did a vampire have to be dead or undead, whatever the old vampiric legends claimed? Could a vampire be mortal and as alive as Chloe and George? Was this possible? And if so, if the creature was denied access to blood, would it then die as surely as Chloe and George would die if they didn't have water and food?

Fernando had said that he would exist forever, implying that he was indeed immortal. According to the old legends, sunlight could kill otherwise immortal vampires, yet Fernando had no problem being in the sun, nor did crosses bother him.

She stood over the two of them, Fernando and George, as light filtered through the trees and made the older man's hair sparkle with gold. Was it possible, she thought, that Fernando was a *new form of vampire?*

Everything was jumbled in Chloe's mind. Beauty, power, pain, pleasure. Fear. Desire.

Fernando was still lecturing George about water and mist. "Suppose the mist is made of ice rather than water droplets. Snow. Blizzards. Ice storms. Think of ice itself, the strength of it, the beauty, the perfection!"

"Why do you talk of water and ice, Fernando? Isn't it *blood* you prefer?" As she spoke, a shiver ran down Chloe's back. Fernando could easily kill her. But who was to say he didn't plan to kill her even if she kept her mouth shut?

Fernando opened his mouth and showed his bloody gums, and he laughed. "Chloe, mon chère, you're worried sick over nothing, I tell you. *Preocupadisimo.* You must learn to relax more and have fun. Isn't that why you asked me to take you to Perpignan? And now, you resist me and treat me as if I'm a murderer!"

"Chill out, Chloe," muttered George, casting her a look of utter disgust. Where George had once been her biggest supporter—hell, he'd been chasing her for years, helping her with chores, trying to get with her—now he openly sneered at her. George had changed. Right after Fernando had drunk his blood, George's attitude toward Chloe had completely reversed.

"George," she said harshly, "can't you see what he is? Fernando is a killer, *meurtrier,* a bloodthirsty creature, *sanguinaire.*"

In Spanish, Fernando chided her: *"Sanguinario?* Cruel? Me, Fernando Le Sprague, who saved you from a rape, as I recall, who is here with you en route to Perpignan *at your request."*

"Chloe, you owe Fernando an apology," said George. "He's not a murderer. He's our friend."

"He killed Andre, didn't he? We were there, George. He *is* a murderer." *He's going to kill me. He's going to stick those four needles into my arm and drink all my blood. I'm going to die.*

"He killed Andre, who was going to rape and kill *you,*" said George. "That's different, Chloe, and now he's taking you to the sea just as you asked him. You're being unreasonable."

She didn't feel as if she was being unreasonable. A killer was a killer, simple as that.

In her mind, Fernando said, *Don't fight me, Chloe. The ice will be our home, and I promise that you will be safe with me.*

She thought, *Mourir de froid. We'll all freeze to death in the ice. You are the boar. You are the monster.*

So what if I am? With me, you won't die.

"Here, come and sit beside me," he said aloud.

"No," she said, backing away.

"George," said Fernando, "I'd like to sit alone with Chloe for a few minutes. Why don't you wait for me back in the woods a bit?"

"You want to be alone with Chloe? What for?" George glared at Fernando with the kind of look reserved for cheating lovers. "Why should I go away?"

Fernando gazed evenly at George, and Chloe noticed that the beast's eyes were clear hazel again, his hair pure blond, his eyes uncircled by bags and wrinkles. He was handsome again, and very masculine. Fernando smiled and shrugged. "Fine, then. Stay where you are, George, and I shall come to Chloe."

Fernando rose and put an arm around Chloe's shoulders and pulled her close to him. She tried to pull away, but he held her more tightly. His fingers gripped her shoulder, and he gestured at her to sit beside him on the ground. She had no choice but to obey, his grip was too strong on her arm.

George scowled and stared at the waterfalls.

"Think of it this way, Chloe," said Fernando. "Think of a straight line with pain on the left side and pleasure on the right. In the middle is a big fat zero, where you feel nothing at all."

"What is this, math class?" muttered George.

"Since you insisted on listening to what I'm about to say to Chloe, you would be wise to heed the advice that I'm going to give to *her*," said Fernando. "When you're in pain, you'll thank me for this advice, George."

"Then why did you want me to leave in the first place?"

"Because Chloe's afraid right now," Fernando said, loosening his grip on her arm. He smiled warmly at her. "And she has no reason to be afraid. You, George, aren't afraid of me, so I didn't think you needed to hear this."

George looked hurt, but he was silent. Fernando's smile returned, and he looked so sincere that Chloe had a hard time convincing herself that he was a murderer, liar, or even dangerous. When he turned on the charm, Fernando was hard to resist. He was one of those people, Chloe thought, that believed his own lies so thoroughly that he could easily convince others that he was a great guy. If Fernando pretended he was dying of a terrible disease, he could evoke anyone's pity, and they'd do his bidding without hesitation. If he pretended to love her, then for the moments in which his voice softened, she might fall prey to the false charm and believe him. Fernando was the most dangerous type of being imaginable. A bloodsucker, a leech, yes, but his true danger was in his ability to win your heart, your trust. He was the kind of guy for whom people literally forfeited their lives, only to learn at death that they'd been conned.

But what have you forfeited, Chloe? His words came into her mind. *Have you suffered for me? Have I tricked you out of anything: love, health, or fortune?*

No, she thought, aware that his entry into her mind no longer startled her in any way. *You didn't con me into loving you or having sex with you. You didn't con me into working for you for a decade or two. You didn't con me into forfeiting my home, my family, and some productive use I could have made with my life. I'm too young for any of that, Fernando.*

He chuckled. He had released his physical hold on her and sat beside her on the ground, not even looking at her as his thoughts entered her mind. *Am I not having sex with you right now? I'm penetrating you, am I not?*

That's disgusting and absurd.

But true! What's the worst kind of penetration, Chloe? Mere physical sex for a few minutes? Or permanent penetration—in your mind and soul forever?

"So what are you going to tell Chloe?" It was George, of course, anxious to win Fernando's attention again.

"Patience," said Fernando, and then to Chloe, *You see how George desires me? He thinks I'm the greatest guy he's ever known, and he'd probably do anything for me. He trusts me to never hurt him.*

But Fernando could hurt George as easily as most men swat flies. When Fernando got tired of George and his infatuation, the older man could simply get rid of George and forget about him. He could do the same with Chloe . . . if she let him get under her skin, that is.

"Your right arm was bruised with purple welts. Your leg and back hurt, and you were limping. I brought you from pain to the zero point, remember, yes?" Fernando was talking aloud again.

"Yes," she admitted, "you did that for me."

"And what have you done in return?"

"Nothing."

"And does that make *me* the bad guy, or *you?*"

"It's your way of winning us over." She knew how awful it sounded even as she said it, and George shot her a look of utter contempt.

"How do you think it makes me feel when you say things like that?" said Fernando. "Here I am, helping you get to Perpignan, relieving you of terrible physical pain, and all you can do is claim that I'm not your friend."

"Friends don't drain each other's lives."

"Oh, the blood? That's nothing. It's mere sustenance, dear, and in time, even you will learn to enjoy it. Trust me, it has nothing to do with who I am, how I feel, and what I do for my friends. I'm far more compassionate and kind than most humans can ever hope to be. Including you," he added.

She stumbled over her words. She was so confused. "I suppose you have a point."

"Is it so awful that I'm different? Is that really enough to scare you? What if I were yelling that you're a blood-thirsty monster just because you slaughter and eat hogs?"

"Well, I suppose the hogs don't like us much, this is true."

"Do you befriend the hogs?"

"Sometimes, yes."

"Then how are *you* any better than *I* am?"

"I'm not, Fernando. It's just that I don't want to be the hog with you being my slaughterer, don't you see?"

"I promise never to slaughter and eat you. There. Better?"

She couldn't help herself, she was starting to like him again. She felt like a ditz, liking him, hating him, liking him, hating him: at some point, she'd have to make a decision one way or the other, and let it go. She was either with the beast, or against him. And no doubt about it, Fernando was a beast. "Listen, what did you want to tell me, Fernando? I'm getting too confused . . ."

"Think about that straight line, Chloe, with pain on one end and pleasure on the other. And you, too, George. I moved both of you from pain to no pain, from the pain point on that line to the zero point. Now imagine the pleasure point on the other end of that line. Doesn't it make sense that I can also move you from the zero along the pain-pleasure line into the pleasure zone? Is that really so hard to imagine?"

"What do you do, Fernando, give us drugs when you drain our blood?" she asked.

"You're being too difficult, mon chère. Humans are destructive and they kill each other. They cause each other a lot of pain. I hunger only to remain alive and to find companionship. Your feet hurt now, yes? Let me feed on your pain, Chloe, and heal you. Let me give you pleasure."

"What do you mean?"

"You know what I mean."

"What you did to *George?*" As the realization hit her, that *Fernando intended to drink her blood, too,* Chloe froze.

"No," said George, "it's not fair!"

Not fair? What was this, a thrill to be sucked dry by a beast?

She wanted to run away, but this time, there truly was nowhere to go. She was in the middle of the woods with Fernando and George, not at home in the village. She tried feebly to move away from him, but Fernando was too fast. He grasped her arms with both of his hands, and before she could move, his lips were on her neck, and she felt the sting of the four needles. Her neck went numb, and then her shoulders and arms went numb, and her stomach tensed. Heat rushed up her body from her legs into her stomach and then surged into her head. She was floating. The heat was everywhere. The trees and the waterfall whirled in a kaleidoscope of color. The river undulated and sparkled with gold and red. She felt the heat down in the roots of her being, sucking at her very soul. A swirling perfume embraced her, a mist so fine she could barely see it, and through the delicately scented mist, the kaleidoscope whirled. Whirls within whirls, color within color, ice within heat. The pulsing of her heart quickened to staccato as the heat inflamed her and her limbs convulsed against the pressure of Fernando's body. Her body shook with violent spasms, and then suddenly, she felt something unlike anything she'd ever felt before: it rose up her body like a tidal wave of heat, then pounded her over and over again, twenty, thirty, forty times the heat soared, and finally, she screamed and fell back, limp, against Fernando. The colors and mists faded, and shadows took hold, and she could do nothing, and she wanted nothing more than to sink into the velvet dark.

She rested—for how long, she didn't know—and let the warmth caress her body. The darkness lifted, and the world was lit with sun.

As quickly as Fernando's lips had brushed her skin, they were gone. He was sitting upright again, peering intently at her while cradling her in his arms. There was a flush to his skin, he almost glowed, but then, everything she looked at glowed with a warm blush as if she was seeing the world through a tinted lens. The world appeared greener, more vibrant, younger: fresh, blurred on the edges yet intense, everything snapping into clear focus within soft perimeters.

Fernando's gums and lips were a deep burgundy, like the color of her father's pinot noir in firelight. She bit her own lower lip, wondering if it, too, was such a fine color. She twisted her left leg and stared at the bottom of her foot: no blood, no cuts, no abrasions of any kind, just smooth unblemished skin. Fernando had brought her from the big fat zero on the pain-pleasure axis all the way up into the pleasure zone. Her mind was floating, and she was happier than she'd been since she was a small child.

Fernando took her hand and helped her stand, and she floated upwards, light as if gravity had been reduced, and his hand melted with hers as if they were bound together by flesh. He put the thought into her mind: *You and I, Chloe, consist of particles. Your body is one set of particles, mine is another set. Yet sets often overlap, don't they? The particles intertwine at the juncture. You understand?*

No, I don't understand, Fernando.

And then, George was in her mind: *He means that we're all together as one now, Chloe. We're intertwined. First, it was just me and Fernando, but now, you're part of us, too.*

Both of them were talking to her directly in her mind. Why couldn't she read their thoughts, as well?

"You *are* reading our thoughts, mon chère," said Fernando. "How else would you know what we're thinking?"

I can read your thoughts?

You can hear what I'm telling you now, can't you?

And me? added George.

"You're planting these thoughts into my mind," she said.

"Are we?" Fernando said. "We're becoming family. You, me, and George. Our blood is fusing, and each time I coax it along, we'll fuse more. In time, we will be as one."

Chloe didn't understand, but for now, she didn't care; she was feeling good, and given her past life, that wasn't something to knock. She began to understand her brother Pierre and his obsession with getting high. Though, she reminded herself, she hadn't taken any drugs, nor had she asked Fernando to infuse her with whatever intoxicating drugs his blood possessed.

"Pierre couldn't help himself, Chloe. He actually wanted to help you fight off your father," Fernando said. "He wanted you to forgive him."

"How do you know about Pierre?"

"I met him briefly in your village."

"He's alive? He disappeared right before I left with you. Do you know where he went?"

"How would I know where he is or where he went?" Fernando shrugged. "But he did tell me how much he loved you. I could feel it."

Chloe had a hard time picturing Pierre confessing to a total stranger how much he loved her. It seemed ludicrous. Though apparently, nothing with Fernando was beyond possibility. He worked wonders.

In fact, she thought giddily, Fernando was the most wonderful man she'd ever met. There was no way he was a monster. Her *father* was a monster. Chloe knew the difference.

One man cared about her and took care of her.

The other man didn't care at all about her and never did a thing to help her. He only wanted Chloe to take care of him.

Fernando was the real man.

Her father was the pig.

No wonder George looked at Fernando as if the older man was a god.

As they walked through the forest, Fernando smiled at both George and Chloe, talked to them about their childhoods in the Pyrenees, told them stories about his life as a wealthy art dealer in Barcelona. He knew a lot about the Catholic mass, the saints, and the holy trinity. Chloe's father had raised her to believe in God and Jesus, but that was about it. Neither she nor George had attended church much since they were children.

Fernando appeared younger now, cheerful, even robust, and the bags were gone from beneath his eyes, the wrinkles smoothed from his face. It was as remarkable to look at Fernando Le Sprague as it was to notice that she appeared normal again, too: her blonde hair was back, her pains were gone.

His stride was graceful in the roughest terrain. He never stumbled, he didn't seem at all worried when they snaked their way over the most narrow mountain passes. George remained drugged—or spellbound— and listened with rapt attention, his eyes gleaming with admiration.

"Have you ever been married?" Chloe asked. Surely, someone as handsome and charming as Fernando had attracted his share of girls over the years.

But his answer was, no. "I've fallen in love many times," he said, sweeping her with an appraising gaze, "but I'm not at all the marrying type."

She felt oddly disappointed. "You mentioned loneliness, Fernando. Wouldn't a wife ease that loneliness and possibly even comfort you?"

"As for romantic love—" a dry chuckle—"for me, it makes no sense. You're too young to know, Chloe, but I tell you: it gives a person no comfort to love and lose. I crave companionship, yes, but only in the form of friends, not physical sex. I have no need, and certainly no interest, in having a wife."

"So you're a player?" laughed George. "That's just too funny."

George, the mooning romantic, who had chased Chloe for years, suddenly wanted to hang out with players? Chloe almost laughed, too. But she couldn't laugh at George, because she knew that she had changed, too, possibly even more than he had. Before Fernando drank from *her* veins, she had been terrified of him. Now, like George, she would do anything for Fernando Le Sprague.

They were scrabbling up an incline, and Chloe knew they'd reach their destination soon. She figured they were close to 2800 meters in elevation, possibly nearing the peak of Puig Carlit, the highest part of the Capcir. Already, they were skirting lakes and pastures, and the air was chilled. *Petit Sibire,* little Siberia, she thought. Freezing in the winters and even now, cold compared to her tiny village.

Fernando took them past villages and inns, modern resting spots for tourists, restaurants, careful not to come within viewing distance of anyone. When Chloe or George was hungry or thirsty, Fernando went alone into the tourist areas to find bread, cheese, and wine for them. He said their needs were temporary, which gave Chloe a twinge of apprehension, as if perhaps Fernando intended to murder them both; but George just laughed and didn't seem to notice that anything was remotely amiss.

Finally, they reached the town of Perpignan. "And now, I'll give you some of your dreams," and Fernando took Chloe to a small shop. It was on a sunny avenue lined on both sides by palm trees. She heard French, Spanish, and other languages as people passed and went into shops and restaurants. Medieval buildings resembling castles were interspersed with modern cafes.

George slumped on a bench in front of the shop while Fernando accompanied Chloe inside. She'd never been in such a place before, but this is what she'd been dreaming about for years: she would finally dress like all the tourist girls, the glittering lucky girls who didn't have to bake bread and make sausages day and night in the mountains.

"How will I pay for these things?" she asked.

"Don't worry about it, Chloe. Choose a few items, and be happy. It won't cost all that much."

The shop girl wore a lavender silk dress, and her hair was swept up into an exotic bun. She wore purple high heels. She gave Chloe an appraising look, and Chloe could tell that the girl was stifling an urge to make fun of her; but she wanted to sell clothes, after all, and so she took out a measuring tape and wrapped it around

Chloe's body in several places, announced some measurements, and told Chloe to go behind a curtain in the back. "The dressing room," she explained, and after Chloe peeled off her filthy t-shirt and jeans, the girl looped some new clothes over the metal rod holding the curtain in place. First came the underwear, which Chloe eagerly donned. It was delicate with lace and silk. She couldn't bring herself to try on, much less buy, the glittering bikinis and over-priced dresses and blouses. Instead, she selected a green t-shirt and a new pair of jeans. This time, the shop girl did sneer at her. "That's all?" she said.

"That's all," said Chloe.

Fernando took care of the purchase and seemed highly amused at Chloe's restraint. He said that he'd get her whatever she chose, but Chloe told him that she didn't feel right about having Fernando buy anything for her at all.

George didn't have that problem. When it was his turn to strip off his filthy, ripped jeans and t-shirt and replace them with new clothes, he purchased a button-down blue-and-white striped shirt made of linen and a pair of white slacks. Both Chloe and George procured new shoes, and then Fernando treated them all to a fine dinner by the sea.

Fernando sipped water but ate nothing. George had a bloody steak, and Chloe found it so enticing that she ordered the same thing. Typically, Chloe ate sausage, bread, cheese, and maybe some tough, dry meat cured over the winter. She never ate bloody steaks.

Fernando ordered pinot noir, and they all drank toasts to each other and their new lives together. Chloe never wanted to leave Fernando. She was sure that she was going to follow him wherever he decided to go; if he agreed, that was.

They slept in a fancy hotel room, and Chloe got a queen-sized bed all to herself. The mattress was thick and soft, and she had four pillows and a blanket made from some kind of tapestry. George and Fernando shared the other bed in the room, and after watching television for an hour or so, Chloe dozed off to the sound of George snoring.

She awakened in the middle of the night. There was a noise in the room, a radio next to Fernando's side of the bed by the bathroom.

In the dark, Fernando's eyes glittered like two crystals. Through the static, Chloe heard a male announcer's voice:

"According to James Schankel, the only surviving member of the crew on the Castor, the ship went down in flames for no apparent reason. Schankel, a physicist and engineer working on the Antares project in the Mediterranean Sea, said that he and lead technician Albert Horowitz were monitoring neutrino sensors dangling on strings a mile into the ocean when they saw the ship blow up on the horizon. 'We'd been receiving reports of odd neutrino events,' said Schankel, 'and didn't think the events could possibly be triggered by the abundance of algae in the area. It seemed more likely that Antares was picking up its first indication of neutrinos generated by unknown sources beyond Earth.' The main ship, the Castor, did have a fuel leak, according to Schankel, which may explain the explosion."

Chloe switched on her nightstand lamp and sat up, still groggy with sleep. "What's all that about?" she asked Fernando.

"There have been explosions in two parts of the world, Chloe, and both happened within the past couple of days. One was in the Mediterranean Sea, the other was in Antarctica."

George groaned and pulled the blankets over his head. Fernando turned off the radio, walked across the room with the grace of a dancer, barely touching the floor with his feet, and sat next to Chloe on her bed. He had a pained expression on his face. "In a few hours, it'll be sunrise, Chloe, and maybe we'll take a boat out to sea."

To see the ruins of the Castor ship? Was he out of his mind? It would be one thing to take a boat cruise on the Mediterranean Sea as she'd always dreamed, but she wasn't so sure that cruising out there to see an exploded research boat was such a great idea.

Fernando gently held her hand. His skin was smooth and cold, and at his touch, her vision sharpened and a rush of happiness flooded her: Fernando was like a narcotic. "You see, Chloe, mon chère, you have *few* pleasant memories of your home."

True enough. She inclined her head slightly, agreeing with him. But what was his point?

"I have nothing *but* pleasant memories of my home. And while you knew your place in the world at all times, I never knew mine. You were to cook and earn money for your father and brother, yes?

I never had a purpose, not even a painful reason to exist. I simply existed, and all I did in those days was dance and drink and fly with the wind. Yes, you think it's silly that I want to sail to where Schankel and the Castor were destroyed. I have my reasons, Chloe. I have a purpose now. We're going to Toulon, France, possibly to Marseilles. I need to meet James Schankel."

Well, this was an interesting turn of events, she thought. She wondered what Fernando's home would be like, whether it was as pleasant as he claimed. But more, she wondered about his mysterious reasons for going there now. What was this purpose he mentioned, this driving force that made him want to leave Spain and France after so long? What did James Schankel and the Castor have to do with their mystery trip to Toulon or Marseilles?

Fernando knew that he'd won over Chloe just as he'd won George's trust and devotion. Humans were so predictable that they almost bored him. Their reactions to Fernando had always been the same over the course of the past century: fear, lust, devotion, worship. The four were always mixed in his human followers. As soon as he drugged them by sipping their nectar, they fell under his spell. Nobody could resist him. Just as insects numb their prey, Fernando numbed the human spirit with a narcotic ecstasy of such pleasure they always longed for more. And the more he drank, the more seductive he became to them. As his essence mixed with theirs, as his particles mingled with their particles, the overlapping nature of Fernando and human increased; and should he ever let his particles intertwine enough with a human, he knew that the prey would become a mutation of human and Fridarian, no longer able to pull back to pure human form. Fernando had never flipped a human into mutation; he never drank enough to let them change, for it just seemed too dangerous a thing to do. They never remembered the actual drinking, and after he left the prey—either dead or returned to ordinary human state—they only remembered Fernando, the Spaniard with golden hair. Their initial fear was always replaced by lust, devotion, and worship, and he'd always been tempted, sorely tempted—if only for once!—to completely flip a human into mutated state so he'd have a constant companion, one who admired and worshiped him. Was it so much to ask? Wasn't that what humans did all the time, found others to be their companions and give them total devotion? How was Fernando all that different?

Both Chloe and George intrigued him as possible companions. Chloe, more so than George, for while George was as beautiful to gaze upon as Chloe, the girl was far more intelligent. Fernando had lived long enough to value the mental attributes over the physical. After all, he was an expert on many subjects, having little else to do with himself over the past century other than learn and think. Besides, physical beauty was laughable for one such as Fernando, who could transform himself into nanoparticles at whim, ice cubes, blizzards, mists, storms, or flesh shapes such as boars, tusked deer, seals, humans, whatever he wanted. Animal shapes with fangs or other sharp protrusions were always useful. But it didn't really matter. Fernando could appear as anyone or anything he wanted. That was the beauty of nano-construction: he could assemble his constituent particles into a variety of shapes and hide in a city as a parked car, hide in a slum as a rat, or coast overhead as a low-lying cloud.

A mutated human . . . what would it be like? Would it have Fernando's nano-capabilities? Or would it simply be a blood-drinking human who communicated mentally with him? He had yet to find out the answers to those questions. But once he reached Antarctica, should George or Chloe still be with him, perhaps he would take the risk and flip one of them. There, far in the center of the frozen continent, surrounded by the newly hatched Fridarians, if a flipped human got out of hand, it would be nothing to dispose of the mutated creature. Crevasses, blizzards, most anything would do, and nobody would ever find the body.

Fernando was anxious to return to Antarctica and see his newly hatched brothers. Would they be as naïve as he, Carsten, Otto, and Jean-Baptiste had been when they hatched two hundred years ago? Antarctica was much different now from what it was even one hundred years ago. There were more people now, scientists and researchers from all over the world. From what Fernando had seen in news sources, Antarctica was fairly modern, with buildings, research facilities, banks, and even satellite communications.

He wondered what his old friends had been doing throughout the years, especially Jean-Baptiste, who'd always had a knack for the spectacular. Fernando had been so lonely, missing his old friends but keeping his distance while preying on the humans. He'd been in touch with both Jean-Baptiste and Carsten for the first few decades, but ultimately, the three had drifted apart. Jean-Baptiste was probably out there, just like Fernando, preying on innocent young humans, while Carsten had probably spent his life looking for a way to die. As for Otto, he'd probably remained in Antarctica all these years, trickling into the realms where the humans dwelled, but only to watch them and maybe scare them. Most likely, Otto had never sipped the blood and changed to immortal form.

According to Otto's hypothesis long ago, their natural life cycle was to reproduce and switch off, but without reproduction, none of them really knew if they *could* switch off. As Fridarian particles, they were nanotech life forms, this much Fernando had learned over the years from studying human science. They could create new heaps of particles instantly.

Chloe insisted on seeing the beach before looking for James Schankel. Fernando couldn't bear to say, no, to her, not right after he'd sipped her luscious nectar. It was one of the most heady rich drinks he'd had in a long time. So he took Chloe and George to the beach, and he pretended to worship the sun with them, stretched on a thick towel on the sand, his toes curled in the hot dry particles. He could sense a fine mist in the air, so fine that neither Chloe nor George could feel it at all.

Chloe wore a string bikini she'd bought from a local shop. It was extremely skimpy and left nothing to mystery. Surrounded by other bathing beauties, Chloe still got admiring stares from every guy who seemed to be between the ages of sixteen and eighty. As the Fridarian-infused blood coursed through her, she appeared increasingly beautiful: radiant, her eyes clear blue, her hair more golden than Fernando's. She was enjoying the admiration of the human males, he noted; turning on her side as particularly attractive men passed so they could see her breasts bulge from the tiny top, the curve of her waist over the scrap of cloth that served as a tiny bottom.

George looked good, too: much more robust, taut, and handsome, brown eyes sharp over chiseled cheekbones. He was getting his share of admiring stares from the bathing beauties who sauntered back and forth, hoping to be ogled and maybe picked up by the more attractive and wealthy guys on the beach.

But both Chloe and George belonged only to *him*. They didn't quite know it yet, and it amused him to watch them still playing to their human desires. So silly, so predictable. So intensely pointless.

"So Fernando," said Chloe, "tell us about James Schankel and why you need to see him. What do you have to do with that ship, the Castor, that sank?" She was squinting at him in the sun, and the turquoise and green hues of the sea were dancing in her blue eyes.

"Do you really want to know?" he asked.

"Well, sure," she said. "Why wouldn't I?"

"Do you know anything about neutrinos?" he asked, and as expected, both Chloe and George shook their heads, no. He didn't feel like giving them lessons in physics 101, so he considered how to explain about James Schankel in a way that at least Chloe would understand. "Dr. Schankel," he said, "was working on a neutrino project called Antares in the Mediterranean Sea, not all that far from where we sit now. I'd say his ship, the Castor, went down around one hundred and fifty miles from here." Fernando pointed across the turquoise-blue water towards the horizon. They were at Canet, which was the largest beach near Perpignan. France curved around the Mediterranean Sea like a cup: north of Canet was Montpellier and then the cup sloped south again toward Toulon. "The Antares neutrino project is based largely in Toulon," he added.

"I don't understand," said Chloe. "What does James Schankel and Antares have to do with us?"

"Well, everything. Antares is an inverted telescope just like the one called IceCube in Antarctica." When both Chloe and George looked at him with puzzled expressions, Fernando explained, "Oh, see I haven't told you yet, of course. My homeland is Antarctica."

"You grew up in Antarctica?" said George. "Why were you in Spain before showing up in our village in France?"

Fernando adjusted his sunglasses and stared at the water lapping the soft sand a few yards from their towels. "If you grow up in a place like Antarctica, you move away as an adult to a nice, warm place like southern France. Doesn't that make sense?"

Chloe nodded and squinted at the horizon, where Fernando had been pointing moments before. "I get it. So out there is this Antares thing, which is like a thing called IceCube where you grew up?"

"Yes, you could say that. Both are Cherenkov detectors, which detect muons from high-energy neutrinos that hit the Earth from outer space. Muons and neutrinos, these are just very tiny particles, to put it simply. You can't see them, Chloe, but then, you can't see other tiny particles, either. Basically, neutrinos are hard to detect and come with zero charge and extremely small mass. Your body is hit by neutrinos constantly, but they're so minute and fast that they don't do anything to you. One neutrino detector operates beneath the sea, and that one is called Antares. The other neutrino detector is deep beneath the ice in Antarctica, and it's called IceCube."

"How do you know all this, and why do you care?" asked George.

Fernando stifled a laugh. "I'm old, George, my friend. I've had many years in which to relax and do what I want, and what I wanted to do was study various subjects: art, music, religions, biology, but most important for very personal reasons, neutrino detectors."

"Because of IceCube?" said Chloe.

"Was it around when you were growing up?" asked George.

Another stifled laugh. "I'm sorry. I don't mean to laugh at you, George. When I was growing up, no, IceCube definitely didn't exist yet."

They didn't understand. Their educations in the village hadn't included neutrino physics, much less anything remotely similar. Fernando gave up trying to explain and just told them that he longed to see his childhood home in Antarctica, simple as that. Why bore them with the details, when they wouldn't understand what he was talking about anyway?

Nor did he mention the discoveries of microbes in ancient Antarctica ice, another bit of human research that had fascinated Fernando years ago. The microbes had been discovered in deep ice core samples at Vostok Station, some six hundred and twenty miles from the South Pole, where the Amundsen-Scott Station and IceCube were housed. The ice was nearly half a million years old, and the microbes ranged from a few diatoms to algae and fungi, quite a range of life, thought Fernando. Why would it be odd to think that ones such as Fernando dwelled there, as well?

Traveling long distances in outer space, the cosmic neutrinos interacted weakly with matter, and to detect them, the humans built huge targets that were shielded from cosmic radiation. One such target was the water near the floor of the Mediterranean Sea, which was shielded due to its depth. The Antares detector consisted of more than a thousand photodetectors hanging 2,400 meters beneath the surface. The photodetectors picked up light from neutrino byproducts.

All Fernando cared about was the fact that both Antares and IceCube had been hit by blasts, and that both were neutrino detectors.

It had been a neutrino beam from Fridare that activated Fernando, Jean-Baptiste, Carsten, Otto, and the others two hundred years ago.

The recent blasts at Antares and IceCube implied that Fridare had activated more spores like Fernando.

This is why he felt compelled to return to Antarctica. Though it also made sense to find out what had happened right here in front of him, only one hundred and fifty miles away. If Fernando could talk to James Schankel, he might learn if new hatchlings were beneath the sea, and if they were, he would help them cope with life here on Earth. It wasn't easy to remain on Earth undetected unless a Fridarian happened to drink the blood and change into immortal form.

Fernando hoped to pick up vibrations from the new hatchlings here at the beach, but nothing emanated from the sea or anywhere else remotely near the French coastline. He was getting anxious to find James Schankel. When Chloe suggested they leave the beach, Fernando immediately agreed, and the three of them changed into street clothes in a public restroom. While George and Chloe ate their latest food addiction, bloody rare steak, Fernando tapped into the internet and did a search for James Schankel. He was a research professor stationed at the University of Marseilles.

It would be a quick trip by boat in the morning. To play it safe, he could steal a few passports from tourists who resembled Chloe and George. And then, if all went as Fernando hoped it would, Dr. James Schankel would become the third member of Fernando's little harem. Perhaps Schankel's intelligence would be more attractive than Chloe's, which after all, was seriously hampered by her lack of formal education. Schankel might be a better companion for Fernando than either Chloe or George, and perhaps Fernando's use for the two younger humans was coming to an end. A long drink from each of them, and perhaps he'd dispose of them at the University of Marseilles.

Chloe still didn't understand why they had to find James Schankel, but she was willing to go along with Fernando's plans. She would follow him to Toulon, to Marseilles, to James Schankel, to Fernando's homeland: whatever Fernando wanted, she would do. "How far away is Marseilles from the place where the Castor exploded?" she asked.

"If we went directly from here to Marseilles, it would take hours to get there by car. I believe that by boat, we can get there more quickly."

Chloe sensed from the way Fernando's eyes misted when he looked at her that he wanted to tell her more, but for some reason, he was holding back and giving her only the bare essentials.

Again, he seemed to read her mind, saying, "I'll tell you everything in good time, I promise. For now, I want you and George to come to my homeland with me, and I want James Schankel to accompany us. You've eaten, it's late and dark now, and we should leave quickly. We need to go down to the dock and board a boat."

George and Chloe followed Fernando from the restaurant where they'd just gorged on steak to the street, where Fernando flagged a car, and before long, the three were at the dock. All the boats were moored for the night. Chloe wondered how Fernando would find a boat for them to rent when everything was so dark at the pier except for the glimmer of the moon across the sea.

As Fernando paid the driver, Chloe and George sauntered toward the pier. Rather than walking across the boards, they stepped onto the rocky beach and watched stray birds dive for fish. The birds cawed, diving beak first into the water, then out again, soaring high and wide only to return and dive again.

"Where is he?" George asked suddenly, and Chloe turned and looked up and down the beach and the dock. Fernando had disappeared.

"I don't know, George. He was here a second ago."

A motor started, and a large boat chugged through the water, and both George and Chloe noticed Fernando on board, steering the craft. "How do you think he got the key?" Chloe said.

"I bet the owner left it on the ship."

"But how did Fernando know which boat had a key onboard? There must be a hundred or more boats out there." As Chloe ran down the dock after George, she made a note to herself to ask Fernando how he'd started the boat. She assumed he was stealing it, which also meant that she and George were stealing it. On the other hand, perhaps it would be best not to ask about the boat. Its owner was probably drained of blood and dead somewhere at sea.

You trust me? came the voice in her head.

At this point, it went without question that she trusted Fernando. She was running from one master to another, from her father to Fernando. But while her father abused her, Fernando took care of her needs and made her happy. Fernando actually seemed fond of Chloe and George. Her father had openly despised both of them.

Yes, she would stay with Fernando, and she would do whatever he wanted, even steal the boat: this much she knew. As for love, that was a heady word and she didn't know what it meant. She didn't know if she loved anyone. Was she capable of loving a monster?

CHAPTER TWELVE

Antarctica: January, 1903

THE OTHERS OF THEIR kind continued to do nothing but play, hurtling snowballs and storms at each other, ignoring the changes in Fernando and his friends. Several dozen of Fernando's kind had hatched at the same time when the bolt of radiation activated them long ago. But everyone had his clique, and for Fernando, his fraternity was a small blood-thirsty one: Otto, Carsten, Jean-Baptiste. To Fernando and his friends, the Fridarians who hadn't joined their blood circle were immature children.

By January 13, the three humans all had scurvy. Wilson announced that Shackleton's condition was the worst. The men choked up blood, and Fernando and Jean-Baptiste eagerly sucked it out of the snow. Even Carsten enjoyed the feast, and as the humans hacked up more seal to share in hopes the meat might fortify them, Carsten stole more of the bloody globs than either Fernando or Jean-Baptiste.

The snow was like a curtain: solid white, hanging from the sky to the frozen terrain. Haze floated and shifted its weight, stinging the human faces, cutting the skin. Veils of drizzle and gray clouds obscured the mountains. The men staggered forward, trying to reach their ship, which was stuck in the floes off the coast.

Fernando, Jean-Baptiste, and Carsten followed them. Their bloodlust was all consuming now. Soon, it would no longer suffice to eat bloody raw seals and lap scurvy blood off the snow. Soon, it wouldn't suffice to nip the flesh of these humans and take a little taste of their blood. Soon, Fernando knew, they would have to kill a human and dine more fully.

On January 15, the men killed their last dog. The winds kicked up and the storm raged as Fernando and his friends swooped down on the carcass, lifted it, and carried it into a crevasse, where they ripped it to shreds within seconds. As crimson fog, they rose from the hole in the ice and drifted around the men and their sledges.

Trembling, desiring human meat, they tried to keep their thirst in check. The seal and dog blood, the human spittle, gave them increased form, brought their particles more into flesh shapes that they could barely control. Carsten looked vaguely like a penguin, for what else did they have to pattern themselves after but the creatures surrounding them? Jean-Baptiste's shape was congealing into that of a dog. And Fernando was pleased to see that of the three, only he even remotely resembled a human: his particles were congealing with the blood into a biped creature with arms and a head with hair.

Wilson claimed that he was seeing visions, "gelatinous apparitions" and "mirages of blood and fat."

Shackleton claimed that he was too weak to know what he was seeing, that it had to be "mountains in the gray fog, it can't be anything else."

And their leader, Scott, kept blinking his eyes behind thick goggles, hoping to clear his vision but failing. "We're dizzy from lack of food, from the scurvy, from exhaustion. We're seeing what can't be here." He hobbled off to the left and swiped his arms through a thick bloody mist that looked vaguely like a gelatinous man—it was Fernando—and was disappointed when he felt nothing. "It's all in my head," he said, "it has to be. See, there's nothing here." For Fernando had simply dissipated his particles and then rejoined them after the human arms fell and Scott started walking again.

Fernando stole clothing and pots and pans from the humans. He stole their pouches and everything inside them. He blasted their belongings into crevasses and into the blizzards, and he secreted everything along with the sledgemeter and theodolite he and his friends had stolen earlier.

All winter, while the men remained on their ship in McMurdo Sound, the Fridarians ate seal, penguin, and even a killer whale.

Fernando taught Jean-Baptiste and Carsten how to take human form, and the three practiced shifting from particles into semi-solid flesh shapes for six months.

The temperature plummeted to a comfortable negative sixty-seven degrees in the deep of winter, and then the humans returned and tried trekking across Antarctica again. Fernando, Jean-Baptiste, and Carsten trailed along, stealing the men's bloody food again, still maintaining control over their urge for human blood. But their willpower was growing weaker by the day.

After eighty-one days and a thousand miles, the humans gave up again and turned back. The Fridarians received no communications from their home planet that winter. Carsten feared that the communications were now lost forever, that the home planet had died. Fernando agreed, for they'd never been without instructions and warnings from their ancestors before. This was the first time they'd received no transmissions during an entire winter period. Something was wrong back home. It seemed most likely that home no longer existed.

"We have to find this Africa place," said Fernando. "It was the last instruction from home, to find Africa, to create natural nuclear reactors—whatever that means—and to reproduce. This is what we must do."

"I don't care about any of that," said Jean-Baptiste. "What I want is more blood. I want human blood and form. I want to walk like a man, leave Antarctica, and go wherever these men come from. We can walk among them, Fernando, be like them, fit in, and drink all the blood we want."

"I don't want to leave," said Carsten. "I'll stay here with Otto and the others. I don't want to be anything like the humans."

"But why not? You like drinking their blood, don't you?"

Carsten shrugged. "Yes, of course. It makes me feel much stronger, alive, and healthy." He paused. "And it makes me happy. Drunk happy."

"So why not come?" asked Jean-Baptiste.

"There's something wrong about it. I don't know what it is, Jean-Baptiste, but I feel it. If we leave Antarctica, we'll never be the same again."

"What do you suggest, Carsten, that we go back to the way we used to be, like Otto and all the other pathetic hatchlings who never grew up? I mean, look at them all: just ice particles, snow storms, with nothing more to do than cavort in the wind. How many decades—how many centuries—can you do that before the boredom kills you?"

Carsten said, "We weren't bored before, were we?"

"We were younger. We were like babies, Carsten. We hadn't had the blood yet," said Fernando. "I've been learning more of the words of the humans, and also their habits. If I had to cook seal fat, I could do it. And that's just one example of the interesting things I've learned by watching the intruders."

"I don't know . . ." said Carsten. "Leaving here could kill us, could kill *what we are.*"

"Nothing can kill us," said Fernando. "We may eventually run down and switch off, of course. We may split into spores again, into our constituent particles, but I doubt that we'll literally die. Our particles will wait, that's what I think, and when the radiation shines down upon us from the mother planet, we'll reproduce."

"At that point, we're dead."

"How do you know?"

"I don't know, but how do *you* know that won't be dead, Fernando? And what's more, if reproducing can kill us, then why can't something else kill us?"

"Because none of us has ever reproduced, and none of us has ever switched off or died."

"Not yet," said Jean-Baptiste.

"We'll wait. We'll learn. And then we'll decide. How's that sound?" said Fernando.

Jean-Baptiste skittered in icy circles. His patience was growing thin. "We've been waiting forever. We can wait a little longer, I suppose."

For once, Carsten looked pleased. His color lifted from black to dark gray. He slinked off to find Otto and "work on the telescope." Pathetic, both of them: Jean-Baptiste was right about that.

Other human expeditions came and went. Erich von Drygalski came from a place called Germany in a ship called the Gauss. He went to the Kerguelen Islands, to Heard Island, and even farther south into Antarctica. Swedish explorers came and went, as well. And even Shackleton came and went again; in 1908, he attempted to climb Mount Erebus with his men, and Fernando and Jean-Baptiste noticed that neither Scott nor Wilson were with him. The men who tried to trek up the 12,450 feet of Mount Erebus had names that were new to the Fridarians. Edgeworth David, Alistair Mackay, Douglas Mawson. Fernando inflicted frostbite, and Jean-Baptiste blasted them with blizzards, but the humans prevailed and continued defiling Antarctica with their presence, their gear, their clothing, their garbage, their devices. They came with ponies rather than dogs, and when Shackleton had to kill four of the ponies, Fernando and Jean-Baptiste jumped in, devastated the human camp with a fierce ice storm, and drank the blood of the animal carcasses. It was a new treat, horse blood, and it made them even stronger and giddier. Up on the surface of the Ice Barrier, two more ponies died, providing another blood feast. And when the final pony fell into a crevasse on Beardmore Glacier, and the now flesh-form Fridarians drank enough blood to give their bodies more than gelatinous shape: they were solid and whole, fortified completely with the blood that transported oxygen and nutrients through their systems. Being nanotech, they easily built internal mechanisms to simulate those of the ponies, dogs, killer whales, and men. Their icicles became fangs. Their crevasses and caverns became maws filled with these fangs and with grippers that sucked blood rapidly through their new bodies.

The humans bickered constantly. They called each other names. Desperately wanting to reach the South Pole, Shackleton dumped most of their equipment at a camp to lighten their sledge loads. Fernando and Jean-Baptiste stole everything they could.

Only ninety-seven miles from the South Pole, at eighty-eight degrees and twenty-three feet south, Shackleton and his men turned back.

Shackleton would come to Antarctica again, but not for many years. In the interim, Fernando and Jean-Baptiste would learn to enjoy human blood. They knew that someday they would leave Antarctica, just as all the humans eventually did, and they would invade the humans' homelands, just as the humans invaded Antarctica.

It would be another decade before the Fridarians left their homeland. A century later, Fernando would look back and remember this last period of Fridarian naïveté, before they sucked humans dry, before they took the complete form of humans themselves, before they left the frozen south for the places where humans lived. He would remember, and he would wish that he'd been strong enough to resist the blood, because once he went speeding away from the blizzards headlong into the cradle of hot flesh, he could never truly come back.

CHAPTER THIRTEEN

Antarctica: 1911-1912

THE KILLER SEASON FOR Fernando and Jean-Baptiste was in 1911 and 1912. Too many humans were coming to Antarctica, seeking to claim the South Pole as their own. Otto was in a constant state of terror, begging Carsten to check the telescope for transmissions, "there must be some instructions from the ancestors, something telling us how to avoid the humans." But there was no transmission and there were no instructions. The Fridarians were on their own and had to learn to co-exist with the human intruders or to kill them without getting caught. They fought constantly.

Otto insisted that the Fridarians hide in the middle of the continent, where the temperatures were so low that humans would rarely venture there. Otto insisted that the Fridarians leave the humans alone, not drink any animal blood, and return to the more simple ways of their youth.

Carsten tended to agree with Otto, and without his telescope to occupy his attention, he wandered in a black fog over the tops of glaciers and down their craggy slopes. He hid at the Bay of Whales, where Shackleton had visited in 1907, where Fernando and Jean-Baptiste had blasted huge slabs of ice, driving Shackleton away. He drifted alone to Victoria Land, and for several months, he sulked by the Pole. He muttered and complained about everything. No matter what the Fridarians did to drive the humans away from Antarctica, the men kept coming back. Nothing worked: not blizzards, not temperatures near negative seventy degrees, not crevasses, killer whales, scurvy, frostbite, not even death. The humans never gave up. What were the Fridarians to do?

"There are two main groups here right now," stressed Carsten. "They're moving in two formations up either side of our home. There are only four of us, and that's if you include Otto."

Otto was shaking, of course, the only one of the four who remained in pure particle and fog form, unwilling to drink so much as a drop of blood and start the cohesion process.

Carsten wavered between his usual black fog and a fleshy shape that vaguely reminded Fernando of Robert Falcon Scott. Except in Carsten's case, his hair was long and black, he had bright green eyes, and he was bone thin.

Jean-Baptiste had adopted a fleshy shape that looked like no man that Fernando had seen anywhere. Jean-Baptiste had hair the color of fire, black eyes, and a deep tan. He had thick muscles all over his congealed arms and legs, and his torso was rock solid. Except of course, that Fernando knew that in reality, the whole body could collapse—and would collapse—if Jean-Baptiste ceased drinking the blood.

It was the blood that kept the particles glued together. As the particles formed larger and more uniform shapes, the resulting body needed new mechanisms to transport oxygen and nutrients, and being nanotech creatures already, the Fridarians assembled tubules, vacuoles, and other simple mechanisms to flood their fake bodies with the blood. In mist or particle form, as snow, ice, and fog, they got their oxygen and nutrients just like any other microscopic creature without blood: directly from the air and water.

As for Fernando, he also adopted a unique body shape that wasn't based on any of the intruders. He created a face of perfect proportions with high chiseled cheekbones and clear hazel eyes. His face was hard, his eyes soft; his skin tan and glowing; and he stood as human form well over six feet tall and solid with muscles. He built himself in this form for a reason: he looked much larger and stronger than any human he'd seen, so real humans would be less inclined to mess with him.

"Given that the humans have two teams now, we must have two

teams," he said, "so while I follow Robert Falcon Scott, I suggest that Jean-Baptiste follow Amundsen.

"I'm not going anywhere!" cried Otto. "I'm staying near the telescope, just in case—"

"Carsten, what about you?" asked Fernando.

"I'll go with you," said Carsten. "Of the three of us, Jean-Baptiste is more . . . shall we say, ambitious?"

Jean-Baptiste hooted in agreement. "I have no problem killing humans. Fernando here always hesitates, don't you?"

"Neither one of us has yet to kill a human," Fernando pointed out, "though we've talked about it every day for the past decade or so."

"Well, this time, let's see who strikes out and finally slaughters them. I'll bet you anything it'll be me."

"You can have that honor, Jean-Baptiste. Divide and conquer, we have no other choice."

"None of the others will do anything, that's for sure. They're all too childish."

"Jean-Baptiste, you stick with Amundsen, and Carsten and I will stick with Scott. We'll compare notes later, and when all is said and done, we'll decide together whether to kill all the humans or figure out how to coexist with them."

"I don't know about this plan," Jean-Baptiste said. "For the record, I say we kill them all before they make it to the plateau, much less to the South Pole. We have Amundsen heading from the Bay of Whales toward the Pole from one side of Antarctica while Scott treks from Ross Island again on the other side. The humans are all over the continent now. How do you expect to coexist with them?"

Fernando considered what his friend was saying; Jean-Baptiste was rash but smart, and there was nobody else with whom Fernando could have an intelligent discussion about much of anything.

Otto cowered behind Carsten. "We can't kill them!" he wailed.

"Sometimes, we have to do unpleasant things in order to survive, Otto," said Carsten. "It's called survival of the fittest. It's not that we want to kill them. It's that we might have to kill them. Don't you see the difference?"

They continued to bicker about what to do with the humans, but Fernando tuned them out.

Jean-Baptiste followed Roald Amundsen and his Norwegian expedition, transmitting reports to Fernando around the clock. In the meantime, Fernando dragged Carsten with him back to Ross Island, where Scott and his crew were preparing to trek across the Ross Ice Shelf to Beardmore Glacier, and from there, to the South Pole.

According to Jean-Baptiste, Amundsen reached the South Pole on December 14, 1911. All of the Norwegians survived the trip: Amundsen, Oscar Wisting, Helmer Hanssen, Sverre Hassel, and Olav Bjaaland. Fernando was struck by the unusual names, the different speech patterns, the way that Amundsen led his men.

Jean-Baptiste's report only underscored what Carsten had said, that the humans never gave up. Despite the blizzard inflicted upon them by Jean-Baptiste, Amundsten's group forged onward to the Pole. They suffered from frostbitten feet, one man had to carry another through the blizzard, nothing stopped these creatures. They took fifty-two dogs and marched up the Axel Heiberg Glacier, and when they finally made it to the plateau in the middle of the continent, they named their camp The Butcher Shop. Jean-Baptiste reported that the men slaughtered twenty-four of their dogs. "They carved up the dogs," reported Jean-Baptiste, "and they devoured them. They fed dog meat to the other dogs, too. It was a bloody mess, but I feasted well on dog. I hit the humans with another blizzard, hoping they would die so I could drink them dry, as well. I still couldn't bring myself to lash out and openly kill them for their blood. But an accident, oh how I waited for an accident that just never came."

Three days of blizzards ensued, as Jean-Baptiste accompanied Amundsen and his party across the plateau to the Devil's Ballroom, which was littered with deep crevasses. The winds howled, knocking the men over again and again. Jean-Baptiste kept praying for the men to fall into the crevasses so he could enjoy a blood feast, but they hauled each other over the ruts and gaping holes, and they managed to make it to the South Pole.

In the meantime, Fernando and Carsten followed Scott and his men. He was shocked when Scott announced that they would be taking both dogs and ponies on the expedition and that the plan was to shoot the ponies for food. It was murder, short and plain. Scott would send the dogs back to a base camp, and then divided into three groups, twelve men would haul sledges up Beardmore Glacier. Two of the groups would be sent back to the base camp, and Scott and a handful of men would continue to the South Pole.

That, at any rate, was the basic idea. Fernando didn't understand Scott's reasoning at all. Why murder the ponies for food? Why send the dogs back? Why not murder the dogs for food, too? And why would only a few men journey to the South Pole?

Along with Fernando and Carsten, Scott had an expedition consisting of Wilson, Lawrence Oates, Bowers, and Edgar Evans. When the group finally reached the South Pole, as Fernando and Carsten already knew, they found that Amundsen had already been there. Scott almost wept when he saw what Amundsen had left behind as evidence: a flag, a tent, and some supplies, but also a letter to King Haakon of Norway to be delivered by Scott.

Carsten drove his ice into the men's feet and into their faces, and it was Lawrence Oates who suffered the most. Frostbitten and hobbling, Lawrence Oates seemed destined for death.

As Scott's group returned to Beardmore Glacier and prepared to head down to the Ice Barrier, Edgar Evans fell prey to Carsten, too. Evans's hand was so frostbitten it was bloated to twice its normal size, and blood was iced to his forehead and scalp: Carsten had tossed the man down, head first, onto the ice repeatedly, bashing in his skull. But still, Evans forged ahead, increasingly incoherent but valiantly refusing to die.

All of the humans were starving and in desperate need of food. Fernando realized that, the thinner they became, the less nourishing their blood would be to the Fridarians. Carsten pressured Fernando to kill the humans *now*, while their bodies still had substance and "life."

But still, Fernando held out. He couldn't quite bring himself to kill the men. He wasn't sure why; he'd been killing penguins and seals for many years now and feasting on their blood, but somehow, a human was a different matter. It wasn't human intelligence, for Fernando didn't consider humans to be particularly smart at all. Certainly, they were smarter in many ways to seals, dogs, and ponies, but all of those creatures possessed intellect, so it wasn't human intelligence that made Fernando pause.

Eventually, Fernando's thirst was unbearable, and he realized that there simply was no reason *not* to drink the humans. Dogs looked at humans with love, yet humans killed and ate dogs. And the same was true with the ponies.

They were still on Beardmore Glacier, the men half-sliding and half-staggering toward the bottom. Fernando whipped around them, half-wind, half-ice. Carsten remained as a dense fog beneath the men so they couldn't see their footing clearly nor what was below them on the glacier.

"Kill this one now, this Evans! He's weak, his head is bleeding! He won't make it back anyway, so kill him now, Fernando! Let's taste fresh blood, at long last, just killed, still flowing through his veins and pumping from his heart. Human blood, potent potent *potent!*" Carsten was trembling from excitement, his particles skittering in all directions, his fog growing thicker and taller as he pranced around the men.

Fernando could smell the blood on Evans. Ripe and succulent. It called to him. It rose in the air like a sweet perfume.

And in that moment, everything else seemed stark and pointless. The endless storms and gales, the dancing of ice across the plateau and down the Barrier. How much of that could one creature do?

How much–

Before he needed *more?*

Barely thinking about what he was doing, consumed by the bloodlust, his head filled with raw desire, Fernando blasted down the glacier at Evans, and in a mighty hailstorm, lifted the human off the ice and threw him down the side of the glacier.

Evans screamed, but in the fierce storm, his companions didn't hear him. But they saw him as he flew past, headlong, to the ice below. Evans disappeared into the black mist that was Carsten, and Fernando came shrieking down after him.

The twisted, broken form of Evans was already half-buried in snow and ice when Fernando hovered over the corpse only a second later. Carsten was already leeching blood from the body, icy fangs sunk securely into the back, the buttocks, and the legs. Fernando knocked Carsten aside and growled. This was Fernando's kill, and he would have first draw of the blood. Carsten snarled and hurled himself at Fernando, and the two wrestled, a whirlwind of frost and ice slugs, while Scott, Oates, Bowers, and Wilson stared and blinked as if hallucinating; but this was no hallucination, and Fernando meant to have them all.

He'd always known that the first killing would be the hardest, and that first one was already behind him. The rest would be simple. These men were food, simple as that. Just as the dogs and ponies, the seals and penguins and birds, were all food to the men, so the men were food to Fernando.

"You can't have it *all*," said Carsten, glowering and lashing about in the wind.

Fernando saw red and purple and black, flashing before him, but mostly, it was red: *blood* red, flowing and glittering, beckoning to him. He was in no mood to argue. He ripped off Evans's head and tossed it at the fog, and Carsten lunged and howled in delight. The black fog went gray, then beige, then pink from the blood. The head was a skin sack filled with bones. It was devoid of blood. Even the eyeballs were smashed and sucked dry, the nostrils and tongue scraped clean by the wind.

Fernando felt a rush unlike anything he'd felt before: so high, so full of life, so *happy*. He was at peace with himself, he knew his calling, he knew—at long last, he knew what they were, the Fridarians and their cohesive particles. *This is why we're on Earth, here in Antarctica, to take form and shape, to drink the blood, to merge with the humans and their animals, to live through them.*

He splintered himself into prongs of ice and thrust them into Evans: a hundred prongs, maybe more, slender as needles, thick as icicles. The blood was rich and pure, potent with nutrients. It raced to Fernando's consciousness, made him laugh and scream as red and purple swirls filled him and enriched him, and his particles multiplied and bulged, throbbing knots across his top and braided strands along his bottom.

He was the storm from hell.

He was a prick in the wind.

Fernando and Carsten plagued the remaining four humans—Scott, Wilson, Bowers, and Oates—for a full month. They remained in their natural form, not taking flesh shape, finding they could hide among the humans more easily as mist and storm. And then, after a month, they grew thirsty again and needed another fix, and so Fernando told Carsten to kill Lawrence Oates.

The humans told each other that Oates had sacrificed himself by leaving their tent and letting the storm take him. The humans were short of food and fuel, Oates had been suffering from crippling frostbite for months, and Oates was their hero.

But Fernando and Carsten laughed over that one, because they knew that Oates was nothing more than a meal, one that had been slaughtered to provide a feast. They were the storm that killed Lawrence Oates. They were the storm that battered him and drained his corpse of blood. His blood wasn't as tasty as Evans's blood, for Oates had been sicker for much longer than Evans. But still, the blood kept Fernando and Carsten nourished until they could feast on something better.

A couple of weeks later, still drunk on Lawrence Oates, they got their chance for the ultimate high. Scott, Wilson, and Bowers were so weak they couldn't continue their march towards safety. The three humans collapsed in their tent. They were so close to death, so *close,* that killing them would be a gift.

"Why let them suffer any longer?" whispered Carsten.

Fernando nodded. His mind was whirling with the possibilities. They would drink the men and steal their human belongings. They would don their clothes, learn to read their words and use their equipment. This was no longer a hobby, an amusement by which Fernando, Carsten, and Jean-Baptiste wiled away years of blizzards. This was now their life's work, their reason for existence. They would blend into the human world. They would feast at will, whenever they wanted blood, for the feast would be all around them. They would have an endless supply of human blood.

"Shall we show ourselves to them?" he asked Carsten.

"You mean show our human shapes to them? Are you sure you want to do that?"

It would be more merciful to kill and drink them as storms. It would be more fun to do it as "humans." Before Fernando could make up his mind how to kill the three humans, his instincts took over. It would provide the biggest rush to just suck them dry. Scott,

Wilson, and Bowers never saw it coming. All three men were incredibly weak and barely conscious. Fernando released a thousand pricks of frost and hoar-bite into the men. He sucked their essence through his pricks and into the internal cells of his being. Scott was savory and robust, a full-bodied blend. Wilson was a nice after-dinner cocktail. And Bowers served as both dinner and dessert for Carsten. Fully satiated, Fernando and Carsten rested as light breezes, watching the tent flaps rustle. Inside the canvas cloth were three corpses.

When Fernando transmitted a message about what he and Carsten had done to the Scott expedition, Jean-Baptiste went on a rampage, killing animals and leaving their bloodless bodies all over the plateau. He split the ice and threw the bodies into the holes, swept them out to the frozen sea. In a blood-drunken rage, he attacked Otto, who dug himself a tomb miles beneath the ice.

And it would be another hundred years before the four friends would run into each other again. Fernando would come from France, wearing frills and courting a young girl and her boyfriend. Carsten would come from Russia, drunk on the stout blood of Cossacks and Siberian laborers. Jean-Baptiste would come from a casino somewhere anywhere in the world, wearing a white dinner jacket and black tie, with three girls on his arm. And Otto would come out of hiding, still a formless mist and still as pure as snow.

CHAPTER FOURTEEN

Marseilles, France: October 2015

"VOUS DEVRIEZ ÊTRE À l'hôpital, James." Madeline fluttered around James Schankel, concern clouding her brown eyes. Usually, he was captivated by those eyes, large and crystalline, and set in a face so beautiful he found it hard to think when he was around her. But today, he just wanted her to leave him alone. He didn't need to go to a hospital. What he needed was to book a flight to Antarctica, to McMurdo Station and from there to the Amundsen-Scott Station. He had to find out why both neutrino detectors had gone offline.

"I can't waste any time seeing doctors," he said in French. *"Al est mort pour une raison et je dois découvrir quelle cette raison est."* He had to find out why his lead tech and buddy, Al Horowitz, had died in the Mediterranean Sea. Madeline, the physics department administrator at the University of Marseilles, was going to have to leave him alone . . . just this once. Though after he'd done what he had to do, he might be willing to have her fuss over him, of course. So he softened his voice, thanked her for the concern, said that he really appreciated it, and then he asked her to look into flights to New Zealand, which typically was the route he took when he traveled to Amundsen-Scott. He was supposed to go there for the summer season anyway, so he might as well leave a little early and try to find out what had happened with IceCube and Antares.

"What happened to the Castor, James?" Madeline was adjusting a belt that divided her pink sweater from her navy skirt. He stared at her belt, unable to pull his eyes away. At some point, he'd have to find a female companion, but it wouldn't be Madeline. As much as he liked hot women, *really liked them,* he was lonely. He'd never found a girl who turned him on physically *and* mentally. It was a hard combination to find in one person.

Lonely as he was, he'd always put his job first, which gave him little time to form close relationships with women. If he didn't work with someone, chances were high they'd never meet. And not many women were drawn to physics.

"You thinking about anything in particular?" she asked.

He shifted his eyes from her belt to her face. "Yeah," he said, "I'm thinking about Antares and IceCube, and I'm wondering why both experiments basically blew up at the same time."

"I'm sure you'll figure it out, James. You want to tell me about it?" She did have a warm voice and a nice smile. And she smelled like citrus fruits and flowers, a blend of perfume he always noticed when he returned from his research trips.

Her office was adorned with potted plants and posters of tigers and lions. He wondered if she was a tigress in bed but quickly put the thought out of his mind. It was one thing to flirt, but it was quite another to do something with an admin who could slap him with harassment.

He settled into one of the soft-cushioned chairs in front of Madeline's desk, winced as pain shot down his legs. It still felt as if the muscles had been ripped from his bones. But while his legs and arms hurt, he knew they weren't broken, and his nose was bloody but unscathed, as well.

In French, he told Madeline what little he knew about the sinking of the Castor. "We were receiving strange signals from the neutrino sensors beneath the Mediterranean, so we went out to investigate. The Castor had a fuel leak, so all the technicians were busy trying to fix it while Al and I took the small boat out to sea. We knew it wasn't the algae that were disrupting the sensor readings. Well," he amended, "that's what *I* thought, anyway. Al wasn't so sure." He paused, wondering for a minute if Al had been right, after all. But again, he came to the same conclusion as he had reached out at sea: something else was screwing around with the signals. There was no way for algae to trigger neutrino events; that was ridiculous.

"The news was all over the internet and television," said Madeline. "It was everywhere."

He nodded. "Yes, I know. They blamed the explosion on the fuel leak."

She nodded somberly. "But–?"

"I'm not so sure," he said slowly. "Something had to light the fire, right? Nobody onboard the Castor was stupid enough to smoke and toss a match into a fuel leak, Madeline. Something else sparked the explosion."

"Like what, James?" She moved around the desk to face him, and she put her palms on the desk.

James didn't answer. He didn't know what to say. He just shook his head sadly. Whatever had sunk the Castor also killed Al Horowitz. And whatever did all that damage probably had caused the weird neutrino events, as well. It made sense, *didn't it?*

He shook his head, more in response to his own thoughts now than anything else. *No, it really didn't make any sense at all.*

The phone buzzed, and Madeline turned her attention away from him. While she talked to a student about scheduling a meeting with the department chair, he sank into his thoughts. It was going to be hard for him to continue working with Al's death such a strong and near memory. What was the last thing Al had said to him? James felt horrible but he flat-out couldn't remember. No matter how long and hard he thought about it, he didn't know what Al was thinking or saying right before he died. James had spoken to Al's wife on the phone after being rescued at sea. He had wanted to tell Al's wife that her husband's last words were full of love for her. He had wanted to tell her that Al died quickly and without pain. But he didn't know what to say, so he'd muttered some nonsense about how courageous Al had been, what a wonderful friend and scientist, what a wonderful husband . . . all meaningless, James was sure, to Al's poor wife and children.

If only James could remember . . .

But what he did remember he'd never tell anyone. It would kill Al's family to hear about what James *did* recall.

The blue wave came out of nowhere.

The water shattered into bright white, and the sea surged, wave after wave, against both James and Al.

Beneath the water, James struggled for his own life, glimpsing poor Al beginning to sink with both arms broken and hanging at strange angles, his oxygen tank loose, his breathing tube gone.

And what James remembered most clearly was all the blood. The blood just streamed all around Al and was swept away by the waves to be replaced by yet more blood. And *more.*

James had come up for air, gulping, and that's when he heard it.

Yes, he remembered now, the very last thing he heard from Al was that horrible shriek of agony, as Al went down *down,* and screamed his death cry, and the only person who heard him was *James.*

Oh hell. Why hadn't James been able to swim fast enough, to get across the pounding water to Al and save him? Why?

Al wouldn't even get a proper burial. His body was lost at sea. Sure, they were looking for the body, even now as James was booking a flight for Antarctica, so there was still a chance that Al would have a funeral and a casket.

It wasn't exactly a cheerful thought.

James made sure that Madeline had all of the necessary details for his trip to the South Pole, and then he made his way into the bowels of the physics building, where he kept a small office. There were no windows down here, it was as dark as the deep sea. And the quiet was like death itself.

He sat in his chair, head cradled in his hands, remembering Al, wishing over and over that he'd been able to save him. Time crept by. James was awash in darkness, sadness, and guilt. All his training, his muscles, his macho swagger: in the end, when it mattered the most, it hadn't mattered at all.

He lifted his head and wiped his eyes against his shirt sleeve. He felt like hell. The guilt was unbearable. While it would be easy enough to cry on Madeline's shoulder, he didn't even want to be around her, didn't want to be around anyone. He just wanted to sit here in the dark until the veil of gloom lifted.

He thought he saw a shadow even darker than the dark of the basement flit past his open doorway. He must be dizzy from the pain and the exhaustion. The grief was getting to him. The guilt.

And then he saw something else: a figure etched in black, its form shifting like a black haze. James half-rose, squinting at the figure. The haze coalesced then broke apart again, then formed the shape of a man equal in size to James. A big man, with strong muscles, a thick neck, and a shock of black hair.

"Who are you?" James called out. "Can I help you with something? Are you lost?" But even as he spoke, James felt something hard and cold knot in his stomach. He knew that what he was seeing was something well beyond a stray visitor to the physics building who had perhaps gotten lost and wandered into the basement offices.

The figure didn't respond.

Then it shifted from the hallway into James's office.

The knot in James's stomach tightened. His mind shot from dismal self-pity to terror, his focus as sharp and clear as ice. He reached out a hand, a quivering hand, and again said, this time in a harsh whisper, "Who are you? What do you want?"

He'd seen a lot of strange things during his stint in the Marines. Blood, corpses, war. His buddies losing their minds as well as their limbs. He always thought he was strong enough to endure most anything. He would rise above any problem or crisis, he always *had* and this would be no exception. He wasn't seeing things, imagining the figure, he was certain of it, and yet what he *did* see wasn't making any sense to him.

The black haze crystallized, and even in the dark, James saw glints of light flickering off the man. And then a thickly muscled arm reached out and turned on the lights.

The fluorescent ceiling tubes crackled to life, flooding the office with harsh, white light. James blinked against the wash of colors that fuzzed his vision. He stepped from behind his desk to confront his visitor, thankful that his eyes were clearing and his brain was still working and in crystal focus. He would need his full concentration, just as he had needed it during the war.

Before him was a man of at least 250 pounds, all rock-hard muscle with a mane of curly black hair, large green eyes, and taller than James's six three. The man didn't look threatening, though; he was smiling, warm, and friendly. He wore strange clothes: what appeared to be a black lab coat with a name tag, *Fernando Le Sprague*. James had never seen anyone in the physics building with a lab coat of any kind, much less a black one. "Like you, I'm interested in neutrino research," the man said in an archaic form of Spanish, and then noting James's baffled expression, he repeated himself in French.

A strange man, but a fellow researcher? How odd that a neutrino researcher would just show up in James's office on the one day he happened to be in town. And even more odd, James thought he already knew everyone in his small field of Antares research, so who was this strange researcher in the black lab coat?

The man smiled again, his lips a deep burgundy. He was attractive in an unsettling sort of way. James wondered what Madeline would think of him.

"Are you going to invite me in?" asked the man.

"Oh yes, I'm so sorry. I'm just standing here, aren't I? Come, please sit down and join me." James extended his hand, and the man shook it and nodded pleasantly. James felt ridiculous. His nerves were getting the best of him. The man, odd as he appeared, was nothing to fear. With the knot unraveling in his gut and relief dissipating the cold fear, James sank back into his chair and motioned to his visitor to sit, as well. "And you are . . . ?" asked James.

"Fernando Le Sprague of Spain, France, and most important, Antarctica."

At the mention of both France and Antarctica, James's brain cranked into high gear. This was indeed a strange coincidence. The image of Al popped into his mind, and he almost heard Al's voice, urging him to do whatever this man wanted, to avenge Al's death, to learn the truth behind the twin disasters in the Mediterranean Sea and in Antarctica.

"You come from Antarctica?" asked James.

"I do indeed."

"In what capacity?"

"I was born in Antarctica and spent my childhood there. I'm well versed with the terrain and the harsh climate."

"Really? And where did you live exactly?" This was getting more interesting by the moment. A shadowy man, robust and powerful and claiming to have an interest in neutrino research, had shown up at his door, and now he was claiming to be an expert on Antarctica.

"I lived everywhere, at the locations of Amundsen-Scott and

McMurdo, in Ross Sound, on the glaciers. You might say that I was as free as the wind."

"When you were a child? And your parents?" James eyed Fernando Le Sprague, not quite believing what the other man was saying. Since when did a child grow up blowing around Antarctica as freely as the blizzards?

"I was an orphan, left there to fend for myself. I never knew my parents." Fernando Le Sprague's eyes misted slightly, as if he were remembering very hard times. He leaned back in his chair, extended his legs beneath James's desk, and looped his fingers together on his lap.

Despite his immense size, James thought, Fernando came across as totally harmless. He asked, "You were orphaned in Antarctica, and yet you grew up there?"

Fernando nodded vigorously. "I'm afraid so, but that's not why I've come to see you, Dr. Schankel. My childhood is of no consequence here. Though," he paused, "I am anxious to see some of my childhood friends again."

"There are no orphanages in Antarctica, none that I know of," said James. Had the child Fernando been taken in by explorers? Had he spent his first years in a tent, enduring winters that would kill the most virile men? No. It seemed ludicrous.

Fernando's eyes narrowed to slits, and a tremor swept over the man's face. James was sorry that he'd pressured the poor guy to discuss what obviously had been a dreadful childhood. It would be best to get to the point and find out the nature of Fernando Le Sprague's visit. "And you are here because . . . ?" he said softly.

"I'm here because I know a great deal about neutrino research, about communications equipment, and about your destination."

"My destination, eh? You've piqued my curiosity, Mr. Le Sprague."

"Fernando, please. And it's obvious that you're planning to go to Antarctica with both Antares and IceCube down, right? You're an expert in the field. There are plenty of people here in France to deal with what happened to the Castor, but very few to help the survivors at the Amundsen-Scott Station."

James laughed, albeit nervously. Fernando Le Sprague knew too much about him for comfort. What did the man really want from him?

As if reading his mind, Fernando said, "I want to go with you to the Amundsen-Scott Station. I can be of enormous help in assessing the communications equipment damage and inspecting the terrain for clues about what happened there."

James shook his head slowly back and forth, answering with a *No*. The military and the science community would never allow a total stranger to wander around the IceCube lab or the area of Amundsen-Scott after such a devastating explosion that killed so many people. There was no way to take Fernando, even if James wanted to take him, which of course, he didn't. "I can't take you with me. I don't know who you are, sir, and you don't have any authorization," he said.

"None of that matters," said the other man. "I'm rich, I'm an expert, and I'll pay my own way. I'll simply book the same flight as you, and after we arrive, you can decide then if you're able to use my services."

There was nothing stopping Fernando from booking a flight to New Zealand, and from there, to Antarctica. And with the mayhem at the South Pole station, an expert along for the ride *might* not be a bad idea. James could pump Fernando for advice during the twenty-five hour flight to New Zealand, and as Fernando pointed out, James could say goodbye to Fernando in New Zealand or later at the South Pole.

He asked Fernando Le Sprague to explain his personal interest in neutrino research and what had happened at the South Pole station. "Studying neutrinos isn't exactly a hobby for most people like bowling or painting watercolors," he said.

"It's not my hobby, Dr. Schankel. As I said, I'm very rich, and I've had plenty of time to learn and study what I want. The field of neutrino research has fascinated me since its birth. There's very little I haven't followed, and yes, before you even ask me, I've studied physics, astronomy, and engineering."

"And your particular interest in IceCube *now?*"

"I think I can help you."

"I see." But no, he didn't see, and after a brief pause, he urged Fernando to explain further.

"There's very little I don't know about the area, Dr. Schankel. Once we're there, if you decide you don't need me, so be it. I promise to bow out graciously."

"I can't allow it. I'm sorry."

Fernando Le Sprague shifted in his chair and stared at James. He leaned forward and a rush of heat hit James. A strong hand, white and cold, reached across the desk and touched James's fingertips. James could swear that he felt the man's thoughts penetrating his own mind.

I tell you that I'm an expert in the field. You might say I was born to do neutrino research. Neutrinos are my life, you see. When a neutrino interacts with a neutron, you have a proton plus a negative muon. These two neutral objects yield one positive object and a negative one. Fascinating, isn't it?

James wrenched his hand from Fernando. "Where did you study?" he asked sharply.

Fernando Le Sprague rose and seemed taller and larger than James had thought. He towered over the desk. His eyes were like gemstones, glittering even in the brightly lit office. He listed half a dozen top research universities. Then he chuckled. *You doubt me, mon ami? I know far more than you can imagine. The negative muons only interact by ionization, so they slowly lose their energy. It takes a long time. The direction the muon travels is correlated to the direction that the neutrino was traveling—not exactly, but on the average. On the other hand, the proton interacts both electromagnetically and with atomic nuclei because it's a strongly interacting particle, so it will go only several meters into the ice. Muons go hundreds of meters into the ice, depending on the energy of the neutrino.*

"This is elementary information," said James. "It's trivial, sir!" He didn't so much care about what Fernando Le Sprague was saying; he was far more concerned that the man was saying it *via his thoughts.* James had no idea how such a thing could be done.

Fernando Le Sprague continued. "Elementary perhaps, but only to people in the field. Beneath ice or water, you can detect the light emitted by the muons. The medium must be transparent to light. Clear ice is transparent to light. Clear water is transparent to light, but the Mediterranean Sea isn't really *clear.*"

James interrupted. "What's your point, sir, in telling me all this?"

"My point is that I know at least as much as you do about both IceCube and Antares." His speech quickened to a rapid pace. "If you have photodetectors scattered throughout the ice or water, you'll pick up on wherever the light pulse is and by comparing the times each pulse hits different phototubes, you'll know the direction of the muons. By seeing how far each muon went before it stopped, you'll know its energy and where it came from."

James raised a hand, hoping to stop the other man's speech. Fernando Le Sprague was beginning to annoy him. His voice was way too strident and excited. But when the other man stepped even closer to James and flicked his fingers over James's hand, a weird sensation rose in James's chest. It was as if a tidal wave of heat was pounding his veins at a pace so rapid he feared his chest might burst. Fernando's fingers prickled his skin with ice, and James felt the icy threads running up and down his flesh: coursing through his arms and up his spine, knifing through the heat in his chest and veins. James flashed back to the horror he'd felt when Al had died right before his eyes, there in the churning water of the Mediterranean Sea. The cold fear pitted in his stomach again.

Fernando droned on, his words like radio static in the fog that was now thickening in James's mind. ". . . use a hot water drill and drop a cable that's 2.5 kilometers long into the hole. On the cable, you space out the phototubes 17 meters apart from each other."

James let the fog build and drown out Fernando's words. He shut his eyes. His head was swimming. He was so very dizzy–

He couldn't move.

He couldn't talk.

He could only feel the icy knot clutching at his insides, the icy pricks dancing over his skin, the rapid pounding of his heart.

Through the fog, Fernando penetrated the core of his mind: *What has Sasha Karonski detected at IceCube, James Schankel? What?*

I don't know, James thought. *Neutrinos from astrophysical sources other than cosmic rays? Isn't this what we've been seeking since the inception of IceCube and Antares?*

Abruptly, the ice stopped prickling his skin and the fog lifted from his head. His body remained in a state of intense heat, flushed, his heart beating so fast that his chest hurt. He felt his own hand move, and he forced himself to lift it and place it over his heart as if that alone could keep it from exploding. He lifted his eyelids. Fernando's eyes were warm with compassion. The burgundy lips were parted slightly, and a drop of blood glistened off the lower lip. James was mesmerized. Terrified, but mesmerized.

"Do not fear me," said Fernando Le Sprague. "I'm your friend, Dr. Schankel, and I'm here to help you. How do your legs feel?" The burgundy lips twisted into a smile. The black lab coat was splattered with something wet. *Blood.*

"My legs?" James stretched both legs, noticed with surprise that they no longer hurt from his near death at sea. The muscles no longer felt as if they'd been ripped from his bones. And his arms! They no longer hurt, either. He looked up at Fernando Le Sprague. "But how did you do this?"

"I understand science, Dr. Schankel, body chemistry, pain and pleasure. I understand IceCube. I understand how the Amundsen-Scott Station runs. I'm here to help you." Fernando wiped the blood from his mouth and smiled thinly.

"What are you?" James whispered.

"I'm your best friend. I'm a better man than any man."

But not very humble, thought James. *What makes you think you're a better man than I am?*

"You, too, are a decent man, James—may I call you *James?* And please, call me Fernando. Together, we're going to help Sasha Karoniski. We're going to rescue her and the others. We're going to fix IceCube. And we're going to avenge your dear friend, Al Horowitz."

Avenge him?

Poor choice of words, came Fernando's thoughts. *We're going to find out why he died.*

It flit through James's mind that he should check with the various universities that Fernando had mentioned, but oddly, when Fernando smiled at him, James trusted the other man completely. So he agreed to Fernando's plan, and when Madeline rang to confirm his flights, James asked her to book similar flights for Fernando Le Sprague, who would pay with a private credit card. Fernando suddenly interjected and requested that Madeline obtain tickets for *three* extra passengers rather than one. He had two young friends, he explained, traveling companions that he'd adopted.

Normally, James would never agree to such a thing.

But times weren't normal, were they? The IceCube technicians and scientists weren't scheduled to arrive for another couple of weeks. Military flights had already been to the South Pole and reported that IceCube was destroyed. James would pitch in and help Sasha and her lead technician, Antoine Damar. If Fernando were indeed an expert . . .

His instincts kept pulling at him to refuse Fernando's suggestion, especially with two young people in tow. But when Fernando added that the boy and girl were both eighteen years old and legally on their own, James tentatively agreed to let them come along. He seemed unable to resist Fernando in any way. The man was captivating, and he was inexplicably brilliant about the research to which James had devoted his life.

Flights were booked for James Schankel, Fernando Le Sprague, Chloe Desmarais, and George Bouchard. They would leave France the following morning, and within two days, they would arrive at the Amundsen-Scott Station.

CHAPTER
FIFTEEN

Antarctica: October 2015

EN ROUTE FROM NEW Zealand to McMurdo Sound in Antarctica, Fernando was more excited than he remembered being in more than fifty years. He was going home, back to the ice and the cold, and he hoped, back to his friends. New hatchlings would emerge from the ice, brought to life by the neutrino beams sent by his Fridarian ancestors. The beams that gave life to the young Fridarians came from the Earth's moon. Fernando was sure that the beams had been pre-programmed by the ancestors at the dawn of time, long before Fernando's birth.

Carsten's telescope had received messages from neutrino beams the ancestors had shot from the home planet centuries ago. The message-beams had made the variable star flicker with meaning like Morse Code. The beams had also wafted stray neutrons into the universe, and it was these stray neutrons that IceCube and Antares had detected.

Fernando was convinced that James Schankel and his collaborators had no idea where the odd neutrino events were coming from. The humans would never figure it out. They weren't sophisticated or intelligent enough, and Fernando was heartened to think that they'd never discover the new hatchlings, much less the nature of Fernando and his friends.

Settling into the cramped airplane seat and trying to ignore the shaking of the small craft, Fernando glanced at his two young wards,

Chloe Desmarais and George Bouchard. He'd sipped from both of them during the twenty-five-hour flight from France to New Zealand. Both had collapsed in his arms in ecstasy, thrilled to be consumed by him, to merge their blood with his body. For Fernando, it remained almost a religious experience when he took their blood. As for James Schankel, who sat in front of Fernando on the plane, he was already under Fernando's spell, too. Fernando had made sure of it even before they left the University of Marseilles. He'd decided to keep all three humans. James was no substitute for the effervescent youth of Chloe and George.

James had shut his eyes, leaning back in his leather chair. "I'm so tired," he told Fernando. "I almost died at sea. I was so weak . . ."

"Rest, friend. I don't mind. We'll wait together for your Madeline to bring us confirmation about the plane tickets to Antarctica." Fernando slipped around the desk in a whisper, so fast no human could ever notice him. Before James could so much as bat an eyelid, Fernando was on him.

First, a nip, then a suck.

James flailed at first, but as Fernando drank from his body, he relaxed and went limp. He was weak. He hadn't been kidding.

Fernando drank fully of James, bringing the other man almost to the brink of total subservience to Fernando. At the last second, Fernando released his grip and withdrew his teeth.

He wouldn't let James die. He needed James to bring him to Antarctica, specifically to Amundsen-Scott Station, to get him involved with the IceCube researchers there . . .

He needed James so he could gain the trust of everyone involved with IceCube. This was crucial.

Fernando trembled. He really wanted to sink his teeth back into the other man's flesh and drink him dry. Fernando had killed plenty of animals and people over the last century. It was a need. It was food. Without blood, Fernando would return to mist and snow and ice, and if he thought he was lonely now as a human among humans, surely being a chunk of ice would be lonelier.

So with his stomach lurching with excitement and his mind buzzing from the blood, he released James and let him live.

James's face was white, his lips purplish-blue. His eyelids quivered. "Good," he was whispering, "that felt so good."

It was time for Fernando to make his escape. Before James realized who and what had sunk its teeth into him. Like all the others, James would not remember what happened to him with Fernando. He wouldn't even remember whether Fernando had black hair or red hair.

Fernando disassembled into black mist and billowed down the basement hall, then up the stairs. As he left, he heard James whispering, "Albert. What's happened to me that I'm so weak and couldn't save you?"

And Fernando thought about his own friends, long parted from him. Was Fernando strong enough to save his friends should he encounter them again at the South Pole? Was he strong enough to insist that they do what was necessary to reproduce and ensure survival of their race? Only time would tell.

That time was now, of course. Fernando was en route to the South Pole *now*. He was on his way to seeing his old friends.

Chloe and George wanted to meet his friends, they said, but of course, they were so naïve about Fernando and his kind, they had no idea what they were really asking. They assumed his friends would be human in form, thought Fernando. They didn't know the full power of the Fridarian, the ability to rule everything imaginable.

Fernando's mind flit to his old friends:

Had Carsten learned about the beams at IceCube and Antares, in Antarctica and the Mediterranean Sea? And what about Jean-Baptiste: surely, if *he* were still alive, he'd want to return home, too, and greet the new hatchlings. And then there was Otto, who hadn't left with Fernando, Carsten, and Jean-Baptiste. Otto had stayed behind in Antarctica, but had he partaken of the blood? Perhaps he had finally left, as well, but would return now to meet up with his old friends.

It had been far too long since Fernando had last been home. As soon as the plane touched down at McMurdo Station, he would know if his friends were there, he'd be able to sense their vibrations and mentally talk to them as soon as they were within his communications range. Fernando was trembling from excitement. To have conversations with his own kind again! To no longer feel such isolation and loneliness! They had split up, the four friends, countless decades ago, each going his separate way after incessant quarreling over right and wrong, blood versus no-blood, pure Fridarian versus blood-Fridarian.

All silly, thought Fernando, such a waste of the decades. He'd make everything the way it used to be, he'd make it all *right* again, and the four friends would rule Antarctica as they did so long ago.

The plane rumbled as it lowered over McMurdo Sound. Fernando peered out his window and noticed that Chloe and George were doing the same. Beneath them, the water was frozen but broken into pieces as if cut by a jigsaw. The sun gleamed off the ice, making it almost unbearable to see. Fernando, with his nanotech capabilities, was able to shift the internal structures of his vision to cope with the glare, but the two humans jolted back, squinting.

"Damn, that's bright," muttered George. "Are you okay, Chloe?"

"Sure, but I don't think I want to look out the window again until we've passed over the ice."

Fernando knew that they wouldn't be finished with the ice anytime soon. If Chloe thought McMurdo Sound had a lot of ice, wait until she saw the rest of Antarctica: it was nothing *but* ice. Two miles thick at the South Pole, and in the eastern interior, ice so thick and impenetrable that for fifty years, scientists had known of a buried mountain range they could not focus on sufficiently to provide images. Only a few years ago, scientists had produced detailed pictures of this enormous mountain range, a range the size of the Alps. More than eight thousand feet tall and buried under a mile of solid ice, the mountains, dubbed the Gamburtsev Mountains by the Russians, ranged over 750 miles of sub-glacial Antarctica.

Fernando made a mental note to check out the Gamburtsev Mountains once he arrived in his homeland. He wondered if his fellow Fridarians were down there, living in the mountains just as he had spent decades living in the Pyrenees. It seemed like a natural habitat to him.

He gazed out the small window, anxious to see his homeland and all of the beauty he remembered. The billions of krill, the sixty million penguins, the thirty million seals, the more than one hundred types of whales and fish. All potential foodstuff for Fernando and his kind, a feast of blood.

The plane chugged over a gigantic iceberg with birds fluttering around it, and shortly after, Fernando saw whales breaking through the splits between the ice sheets. They were getting close to the McMurdo runway, he just knew it!

Within moments, the jigsaw puzzle ice and black sea swept behind the plane to be replaced by mountains coated in ice with whirling snow sweeping down their slopes. The mountain peaks stabbed the sky, the sun was high and bleeding crimson rays.

George held a hand over his eyes, trying to see the landscape below. "Are there any people here, Fernando?"

"At the research stations, some, yes, but everywhere else, not really, George. A few stray wanderers every now and then, I suppose, but I haven't been home in a very long time. You'll notice that there aren't any buildings, houses, schools, nothing—this isn't exactly the kind of place where people want to raise their children." It was the kind of place, Fernando thought, that attracted the wild and free, those unafraid of blizzards and ice, those who embraced sub-zero temperatures and endless stretches of frozen wasteland. It was the kind of place that was a natural habitat for those of his kind. It was the Fridarian homeland. It belonged to Fernando's people.

And then his heart leapt. Down below, he saw Ross Island, a lobed land mass constructed out of ice. Soon, *soon . . .*

What he wanted was another shot of blood. He wanted to feel the surge of power as the blood hit him. He wanted to be fully potent before the plane landed, and to do that required the blood.

Was Fernando addicted to blood? It wasn't just sustenance anymore, he realized with a jolt, it was far more than that. It was a craving, both physical and deep in his core, something so powerful that he had to have it. Was he any better than Chloe's brother, Pierre, the drug addict?

"Wow, look!" Chloe suddenly cried, and Fernando felt a rush of pride as Mount Erebus loomed before them. They flew over the giant black crater in the top of Mount Erebus. Swirling red lava and white mist billowed from the crater. Molten rock spewed from the hole and burst into flame on the sides of the mountain. Along with the rock were the ice sprays, some sixty-feet-tall, and capped by clouds of volcanic gas.

Fernando explained that Erebus was the son of the Greek god, Chaos, and was made of darkness. And yet, he told Chloe, Mount Erebus was a mixture of fire and ice with a 1,700 degree Fahrenheit lava pool that was several miles deep. "The mountain is covered with snow and ice, but inside the volcano, all along its side, the lava has carved mazes of ice tunnels and caves."

"How do you know this?" she asked.

Perhaps he'd said too much, but it was hard to resist pouring out his love for his homeland to one as eager and simple as Chloe Desmarais. She was like a child. "I know because I grew up here, and when I got older, I studied about my homeland," he said, and she smiled, believing him without hesitation. He wished that he could tell her more, tell her everything about himself, but he didn't dare; but believing her to be intelligent at the core, he gave her a clue, as much as he dared reveal. "There are those who think that extremophiles live in Mount Erebus. These are microbes, very tiny creatures, who live in unusual conditions, in this case, the 32 degree Fahrenheit ice caves carved by hot volcanic gases."

But she wasn't listening to him. She was pointing again, excited, at the next mountain looming before them. This one was Mount Terror. "They truly do look like cupcakes coated in vanilla frosting!" she exclaimed. "That's how I thought of the mountains back home! But these mountains are even more beautiful, Fernando!"

She was so childlike and naïve, so innocent, that it pained him. Mount Terror was anything but a cupcake with frosting. Anything would look and feel spectacular to an eighteen-year-old girl who had wasted her life in a forest village. And here he was, leading her to mysteries of life that even the most worldly humans didn't know. He would try to protect her, to be kind, but he knew deep in his soul that he'd already cost her and George their basic humanity. He'd exchanged blood with them, he'd burned his own desires into their flesh. They now consumed the blood with him, and at some point, if they stayed with him, they would be more like Fernando than their own kind. It was a small price to pay for immortality and eternal pleasure, he told himself. They would both learn that pain and pleasure were equally sweet.

James Schankel was talking to Chloe and George about what to expect in Antarctica. Even James was under Fernando's spell, cast beneath the dark spell of the blood. James would protect Fernando's two young wards to the death, because now, all four of them were blood family. The three humans had Fridarian nanoparticles coursing through their blood now. James was explaining, much to the excitement of the two wide-eyed teenagers, that Ross Island and its two giant mountains were full of crevasses, and when George asked for more details, he told him that crevasses were deep grooves all over the ice. James went on and on about geography, animal life, and history, and Fernando was impressed with his deep level of knowledge. The two had talked for many hours on the twenty-five-hour flight. They were getting along like old buddies. Two of a kind. A key difference was, of course, that James didn't yet drink human blood. He didn't know his new family's secret.

When James had shown Chloe, George, and Fernando the bite marks all over his flesh—Fernando had gotten carried away and sunk his teeth into James's torso, stomach, shoulders, arms, and neck—Chloe and George considered telling him about the bloodlust but kept it to themselves. Fernando mentally communicated to them both that it wouldn't be wise to tell James their secret just yet. *Give him time,* he vibrated into their minds, *to adjust to our ways. Soon, like you, he'll want me to drink his blood constantly so he can feel good. I'll put him on the positive side of the pleasure-pain line, too, until like us, he won't be able to resist the taking of blood.*

At the thought of blood—only in the form of raw steak—both Chloe and George salivated. Soon, Fernando would graduate them both to the final level, the consumption of fresh human blood.

The plane swerved and brought them toward the western side of Ross Island. They saw the Great Ice Barrier and Beardmore Glacier. They saw the two-hundred-feet-high cliff of snow that stretched four hundred miles along the frozen coastline. It was eerily beautiful here.

"It's just as I remember it," whispered Fernando. Over the noise of the plane, nobody heard him. He almost cried as they reached Hut Point Peninsula at the southern tip of Ross Island. And then they stepped off the plane onto the ice at McMurdo, and Fernando felt the tears squeezing from his eyes, and he ducked his head so nobody would notice. It felt so good to be home that it hurt. Always the pain and pleasure were equal.

"We have to catch another plane now," said James. "This next one will take us to the South Pole station, and it'll probably be a military flight. That's how it's done here."

Fernando didn't listen. He could simply leave the others here, if he wanted, and fly as a gale to the Amundsen-Scott Station. *That's how it's done here!*

"Cool," said George, shivering in the heavy coat Fernando had purchased for him. While all of them were already wearing the heavy clothing required for the South Pole, nobody except Fernando could really handle the extreme weather. It would take some adjustment, thought Fernando, for three people from the Mediterranean to get used to *this* climate. As for Fernando, he didn't need to wear a parka, a hat, gloves: he could go naked, if he wished, and the negative twenty degree temperature wouldn't affect him. He could be hit by the biggest ice storm ever to blast over Antarctica, and it wouldn't affect him. When George said, "Cool," the kid didn't have a clue just how cool Fernando was.

Two weeks. That's all the time Fernando had to pump the IceCube researchers for information about the explosion. The summer technicians and scientists were expected in two weeks. But on the other hand, would they still come considering what had happened here? Almost every member of the winter crew had just died. No, the more he thought about, the more it made sense to him that he, James, Chloe, and George—and possibly Carsten, Jean-Baptiste, and Otto—would be here alone with the few surviving members of the winter team.

The McMurdo Station base looked like a town out of an old western movie, except it was built on ice and surrounded by snow-slathered mountains. Chloe and George were seduced by their surroundings, and both kept asking Fernando questions about his childhood. Had he lived in a place that looked like McMurdo? What did he think of the penguins, the seals, the freezing weather?

"The penguins and seals are plump and juicy," he said.

They laughed, thinking he was joking. James shot him a dismayed look. Fernando laughed, too, pretending that it was a big joke, knowing full well that he wasn't joking at all. He'd drunk the blood of many penguins and seals a century ago.

They were bustled into a bus with gigantic tractor-tires and transported to a tiny military plane on another airstrip. On the side of the plane were the words AIR FORCE, which Fernando knew was an arm of the United States military. The pilot told them briefly that James was in charge, which Fernando thought highly amusing. "You and your crew, Dr. Schankel, have a week or two tops, then the military's coming in for a complete investigation. If you find anything at all—any diseases, infections, plagues, odd bacteria, strange things buried in the ice, evidence of whatever hit this place—radio it to us immediately. If you need to get out of there, radio us and we'll be back for you in a flash. Got it?"

James nodded. "Yeah, I get it. One week. What about the IceCube researchers, the survivors?"

"Check it out. If they're sick or infected, we want to know. We sent a small team in there with medical supplies and equipment, but thus far, we've been holding off on shipping people into Amundsen-Scott for fear of contamination."

"And I'm the lucky one chosen for potential infection or death?" said James.

"You insisted on it, pal. That's the reason."

"So I did."

Luckily for Fernando, he'd hooked onto James Schankel right after the Mediterranean explosion. During the long flight here, he'd warmed up to James, dosed him with the blood. Like Chloe and George, James would now do anything Fernando wanted, and what Fernando wanted was access to the IceCube outpost at Amundsen-Scott Station. James was internationally known, a friend and collaborator of Sasha Karonski's team, and was able to pull all the right strings to get Fernando, Chloe, and George to accompany him to IceCube. The story James told was that "Fernando is an Antarctic expert, well-schooled in everything from IceCube to general neutrino research to matters of health. Chloe is his wife. George is her brother." Laughable, really, thought Fernando, that anyone would believe that Fernando Le Sprague would be married, much less to one as childlike as Chloe Desmarais, but James had pull, and he'd definitely pulled off this one. It was a pathetic comment about the McMurdo men who were afraid to come and rescue Sasha Karonski and her small team, yet had no problem at all letting James bring the unknown "expert" Fernando, his supposed wife, and her supposed brother. They'd all signed a bunch of forms and been on their way.

The plane rumbled over the blinding landscape, and eventually, it touched down on a snow-packed fire-bombed runway. Black flags marked the edges of the runway. In the distance stood the dome of Amundsen-Scott and the shattered remains of the buildings. A black hose reel sat like a giant spool of thread by an IceCube drill. Nacreous clouds swirled over the station, illuminated by the sun. Fernando knew the brilliant hues sparking the clouds were formed because the extreme cold was forcing gases to crystallize.

Fernando sensed the microscopic diamond dust in the air, the ice crystals that feathered the glaciers, plains, and plateaus. The crystals fanned out, growing tiny stems as if alive. Fernando sniffed the air and tried to sense vibrations of Fridarian life, but sadly, there was no response from the ice, and he realized that it was *only* ice and *not* Fridarian life.

Before they got off the plane, everyone—including Fernando— donned goggles, a hat, parka, and boots. Fernando figured it wouldn't look good if he appeared different from the other humans. The excitement among the travelers was so intense that the air crackled. Fernando sensed vibrations from all three of his companions, James, Chloe, and George. In all three cases, their blood was diluted with his blood, an intoxicating blend of blood he'd gathered for more than a century. His nanotech particles had worked well on the blood over the years, churning out increasingly potent forms until finally, a bite from Fernando not only gave him food but also injected his prey with euphoria and intense sensory awareness. And his blood was rich with his nanotech mechanisms. If Fernando drank someone dry to the point of death, then there was no blood left in the human. But once in the bloodstream of a *living* human, or certain animals for that matter, Fernando's nanotech particles swept throughout the body, multiplied, and latched onto internal cells. They were all artificially intelligent, these particles, and had the drive of alife, so they quickly took over, turning Fernando's host prey into a weaker version of himself. Weaker, he thought wryly, because the humans hadn't started out as powerful as a pure nanotech creature such as Fernando. Fridarians were clearly the rulers of the universe, not humans. But luckily for the humans, Fernando wasn't the type who wanted to rule others. He just wanted to eat and be happy, to have some companionship, and to ensure that his species survived.

And that's why he was back in Antarctica, to find the hatchlings and to nurture and teach them the ways of his kind.

James clung to him, wanting to merge the blood again, but Fernando eased him gently away. "Not now," he whispered. "Later." Fernando knew that James Schankel's research collaborators would think it very strange if the macho ex-Marine was clinging to Fernando with moony eyes. Fernando turned and put his arms around all three of his companions to form a football-like huddle and told them, "Nothing out of the ordinary, okay? We have to look like ordinary humans here, on a mission with James—" he paused to smile and even wink at the other man, who smiled in return as a child does when patted on the head for good work on a spelling bee—"Yes, we're on a mission with James to help these people out. They've suffered terrible losses due to the explosions here. Remember, we're here to learn and to help. Okay?" When they all nodded, he added in French, *"Aucune adhésion."* No clinging. And, *"Cueillez des informations. Annoncez-moi en arrière plus tard."* Gather information. Report back to me later.

And then, leading the way, Fernando Le Sprague walked down the stairs leading from the plane and returned to his homeland.

CHAPTER SIXTEEN

Antarctica: October 2015

THE WIND WHISTLED, AND the ice crystals danced in the sun and caressed his flesh like a loving hand. Fernando shivered with delight, felt his teeth chattering from the sheer thrill of being drenched in the negative forty degree temperature. The ice kissed his lips, and though he felt no intelligence in this ice, no Fridarian presence in it, still it was *ice* and Fernando knew that all ice would soon be under his control. He would permeate the ice on his lips and brow, the wind whistling past his flesh body, and he would be one with it all. It had been *so* long, it had been *much too long ago* . . .

"Go with James," he told Chloe and George. "Help him in the station, help these people as much as you can."

"Where will we meet up with you? Where are you going to be?" asked Chloe.

George was thinking, *I would do anything for you, Fernando, and anything for Chloe. The three of us are family now. We'll always be together, always love each other.*

Yes, we are family, Fernando communicated to both of them. *I promised you my devotion when we set out from your small village in France to travel to the Mediterranean Sea. I saved you, Chloe, from your father—that pig! le cochon!–*

Yes, you did, Fernando, and I'm so grateful. I'm not sure what we're doing here in Antarctica really, but I'm happy to see where you grew up. Are you going to show us around?

When do we meet your childhood friends like you promised? George chimed in.

The two were such simpletons, so saturated in Fernando's blood, so willing to give anything to him now. Even George, who had resisted leaving his village at first, even he was now utterly devoted to Fernando. Fernando would not hurt these two, he would protect them as he had promised. Nor would he hurt James Schankel, the man he'd almost killed in his bloodlust. The three were so blindly devoted to Fernando now, so intent on doing his bidding–

It is indeed as if I have a harem, he thought. *They'll do anything for me, anything. It's marvelous! Wait until Jean-Baptiste sees this! He'll be so envious!*

Anxious to find Jean-Baptiste and the others, anxious to discover more about the hatchlings, Fernando asked the McMurdo pilot to take James, Chloe, and George into the Amundsen-Scott Station and acquaint them with whatever crew remained.

As they cautiously walked across the snow and ice toward the station's dome, Chloe peeked over her shoulder at Fernando. Although her eyes were hidden by goggles, Fernando knew that they had to be shining with devotion to him. He felt so good inside that his head was whirling. After all these years of drinking blood and killing his prey, he was loved. None of his other prey had ever loved him. Some had wanted to be him, and he had to kill them for that. Some wanted to worship him, yes, but blindly and without true affection. They had been too weak, the blundering fools, and he'd had to kill them, too.

James, Chloe, and George were different from all the others. They actually loved him. Fernando could hardly believe his good fortune. In return, he would make sure that others of his kind didn't kill them or even drink from them. These three belonged to Fernando.

As they moved from view and entered the main building of the station, Fernando splintered his flesh body into his natural form. It was luxurious, this feeling, to be mist again, to be ice, snow, and billowing frozen life. Oh, what heaven! He'd been in flesh form since leaving Marseilles, and granted it had felt good to be mist in the Pyrenees, it wasn't the same to exist as warm mist and slush as it was to exist as *pure frozen power.*

His mind was everywhere all at once, existing throughout his ice particles, and he flushed the particles outward in many strange formations, letting them float in the wind, congeal, split, congeal, split, as a bird ruffles its feathers. Oh, what a life form the Fridarians were! Nothing could equal them! If he had his way, he wouldn't bother with flesh forms, not human, not wild boar, not soaring bird, nothing flesh based, not for a long time. If only!

He moved as a snowstorm over the burned-out runway, even as the pilot emerged from the station, boarded the craft, and started the engine. The pilot didn't notice that Fernando was still there. All the pilot saw was a snowstorm.

But Fernando saw and felt everything across the vast expanse of ice. He saw the icebergs pushing up from the surface, saw the remote summits poking the gauze-like sky, *swooned* as he felt the keening of the seals beneath the Ross Sea. And there, beyond the South Pole, he felt the vibrations of the Fridarian telescope, the one he'd last seen a century ago. The telescope remained buried where they'd left it. Fernando wondered if Carsten had ever returned to check it again. Had the ancestors left them messages over the past century? Unlikely, but of course, Fernando wanted to know.

He surged across the surface, reveling in the gusts of sleet that swirled up and over him. He soared over the slabs, the cones, the pyramids, and the cubes of ice that lay beneath him, over the twisting crevasses, where he sensed the remains of dead dogs, men, and birds.

As he crossed the true South Pole and headed toward the telescope, he felt *them,* the living frostbain and blizzards; *them,* his buddies who had turned to flesh form with him; *them,* all back to witness the great event, the birth of the new Fridarians. *He felt them.* As he had long ago, Fernando flexed, and the miles of ice beneath him trembled and thick slabs of ice cascaded down cliffs into the sea.

And they felt him, too. Their vibrations pulsed with extra energy, they paused to feel his presence, and he knew they were as elated as he was.

They were at the telescope, deep within the crevasse on the plateau where it was hidden. Otto was the first to pulse Fernando a welcome message: *You've come! I can't believe you've come!* Otto shivered, and Fernando felt his neurotic vibrations in the air.

Yes, I'm here, my old friend. Fernando could barely contain his joy. He raced toward the others as a hailstorm, a blast of pellets more than a hundred miles per hour. A tidal wave of ice, he swelled and then crashed down the transantarctic mountains and to the telescope cavern, noting with delight that humans had still not found the Fridarian hideaway. And he saw them, his friends, huddled as in long-gone days around the telescope at the bottom of the deep crevasse:

Carsten in the form of black ice dust, and behind him, two filthy, near-dead human men.

Jean-Baptiste in the form of giant white ice cubes, and behind him, three beautiful girls, shivering and freezing to death in flimsy cocktail dresses.

And Otto, quivering and whining, a formless mist, pure as snow, with nobody behind him at all.

Fernando threw himself around all of them at once, clasping them in a frozen embrace of blood and ice. Otto shrank back from the blood, crying "I don't do blood! I don't!" But the others, Carsten and Jean-Baptiste, both swooned, and ice of a thousand colors burst from them in plumes that spiraled from the crevasse ditch into the sky beyond. They were more beautiful than auroras, more breathtaking than the black sky of an Antarctic winter shot with stars.

"And what do you think of my lovelies?" asked Jean-Baptiste, gesturing with a flourish of snow at the three beautiful girls in their cocktail dresses.

"Ridiculous, I keep telling him that it's ridiculous," muttered Carsten. "Why does he need these ridiculous girls around him?"

"You would prefer that I drink the filthy blood of men such as *yours?*" countered Jean-Baptiste. "And why should I do that, my friend? The girls are much more tasty, and they amuse me while they're still alive. Your men would depress me. I doubt that I would even drink them, unless of course there was nothing better around."

"The men suit me," said Carsten. "They die, nobody knows and nobody cares. If I could figure out how to die, believe me, I'd do it in a flash. Life is nothing. It's an empty void of pointless nonsense. These men remind me of myself. Their lives are pointless, too. Their blood is fine, just as potent as the blood of your beautiful girls."

"You're pathetic, Carsten. You've never known how to have any fun, have you?" Jean-Baptiste lifted one of his girls with icy tendrils and cradled her. Blood droplets coalesced in the air and dribbled over her body. She was so weak that she didn't scream or struggle. Or maybe she was just so used to being abused by Jean-Baptiste that she'd given up all hope. Fernando cringed to look at her. It wasn't right to abuse their prey in this way. The humans were food, nothing more than that, they weren't inanimate playthings. The humans were flesh and blood creatures who felt pain. They had emotions just as Fernando, Jean-Baptiste, Carsten, and Otto had emotions. The other two girls shielded their eyes with their hands and clung to each other, whimpering, while Jean-Baptiste splattered blood across their friend's body.

What had happened to him, to Jean-Baptiste? He'd always been cavalier, fun loving, and boisterous, but Fernando didn't remember his friend being sadistic. Had Jean-Baptiste been cruel back when the Fridarians ruled Antarctica, had Fernando forgotten?

"Jean-Baptiste, put the girl down," Fernando said quietly.

"Yes, put her down," Otto repeated, his voice cracking.

"What the hell's it matter? Everything dies anyway, doesn't it? Does it matter *how* she dies?" Carsten said.

"As you noted, Carsten, *we* don't die," said Fernando, "or you would have killed yourself long ago."

While they were talking about death, Jean-Baptiste had wrapped his girl entirely in ice, and now he was literally squeezing the blood from her body. She was trapped, immovable, in the cocoon of ice, and surrounded by a cloud of red, which slowly *slowly* dissipated into the frost. Her mouth was frozen wide open in a huge O shape, and her eyes were wide in terror and glazed by ice. Her nose was squashed into her face, the nostrils flared but drawing no oxygen into her lungs. And then the glaze over her eyes hardened, and Fernando knew she had died, in that one brief moment of sheer horror, she was no more. Her skin shriveled, and her head shrank in size. She was no longer beautiful at all, though Jean-Baptiste clearly enjoyed the sight of her. He made some smacking noises, much as a human man smacks his lips after a large feast, and he sighed with contentment, just as a human man might sigh after sexual climax. The blood was gone from the girl's body, and it was now inside Jean-Baptiste, fueling *his* life and giving him energy and momentum. The ice encasing the girl fractured and whirled up into thousands of tiny shards. And there she lay, a sack of withered skin, empty of all blood, her organs crushed by the block of ice. Her eyes had burst in their sockets.

Fernando had to look away. "How can you live with yourself, Jean-Baptiste? *How?*

Jean-Baptiste belched. "The same way you do," he said.

"The same way we all do," said Carsten. "I ran into these two human men in Russia. They were losers, doing nothing with their lives, just drinking booze all day and freezing, drifters who weren't drifting. They reminded me of myself, so I took a liking to them. I've enjoyed watching them die, so I prolong the experience. Their agony is my bliss."

"You feel as if your life is a slow death?" asked Fernando.

Carsten shrugged. It was his way of saying, *yes and I don't care.*

"And so you enjoy watching others . . ."

"Yes, I enjoy watching others die slowly. Yes, in this way, we are companions." When Fernando said nothing, for he was too horrified by what had become of his friends to comment, Carsten added, "You're no better, Fernando. Think about what your life has been. You can't really judge us."

Jean-Baptiste hurled his remaining two girls onto the ice by Carsten's two human men from Russia. The girls cried as they cracked against the ice, and one of the men toppled over from the impact. They were a sorry bunch, the four humans, weak and almost dead, knowing full well that their fate was torture and death, just as they had witnessed moments before. They knew that they had no strength to fight it. Jean-Baptiste and Carsten treated people in the same way humans treated food. Eat what you want, let some spoil and rot, throw out wasted tidbits, think nothing of the manner in which the food is procured: sure, there was always some guilt and remorse, but in the end, food was "dehumanized" by all animals, including the Fridarians.

Fernando's friends were no longer like him. His aim was to bring James, Chloe, and George from pain to pleasure. Sure, their pain— when he drank their blood—brought him pleasure. He'd told them this often enough, hadn't he? But ultimately, they were getting high on the blood now, too, and were in essence no different from him. They were his family, and he didn't want them to suffer or die.

Carsten's two men, on the other hand, were unshaven and wearing rags, their boots were riddled with holes, they were scrawny, starved, and almost dead. They looked as dry as a river in the desert. They probably had as much blood in them, thought Fernando, as the young girls Jean-Baptiste had brought with him to Antarctica using private boats from Argentina. Had all of Fernando's old friends lost their minds, their compassion, their wits? Was he the only one left of the original Fridarians who had any sense of compassion and empathy? For lack of a better word, was Fernando the only one left with any *humanity?*

"We are what we are," Jean-Baptiste stated flatly. He'd been reading Fernando's mind. "You weren't born human, Fernando. You weren't born flesh and blood. You're just like us. We're all icy pricks, and nothing more."

"But . . . but doesn't the blood change you as it changes me?"

"Into what, Fernando? One of *them?* Don't be absurd!"

"If they're all dead, what else will we have?" said Fernando. "Each other? I haven't seen you in a century, yet I've been surrounded by thousands of humans."

"Pity, isn't it?" said Jean-Baptiste. "Though it's nice that we never run out of food, I suppose. There's plenty to go around. The humans will never be all dead, Fernando. What are there, billions of them? They're like roaches. We can feed on them forever."

"I've never had the blood, and I never intend to have it," interjected Otto. "I'm the only one of us who remained pure Fridarian. In pure form, I tell you that we are *not* immortal."

"He's right, Jean-Baptiste," said Carsten. "Like it or not, the blood has changed you into something other than Fridarian. The only true Fridarian among us happens to be Otto."

There was quite a bit of laughter at that, but for once, Otto didn't take offense, nor did he seem at all proud that he was the last pure one of their kind. "Tell them, Carsten! Tell them why they have to stop drinking human blood. Tell them what our mission is, what the ancestors told us to do. If we don't do as they wanted, there will be nothing left of us except this mutation, this blood-driven Thing that the rest of you have become."

Had Fernando been in human form, he would have rolled his eyes. He'd forgotten how melodramatic Otto could be: the whining, the hysteria, the drama queen fluttering his snow as he carried on.

But about one thing, Otto was right: of them all, only Otto had not changed; and apparently, the other Fridarians that hatched with Fernando and his friends had left Antarctica long ago.

Carsten had always been dark and gloomy, the pessimist who feared the worst and always got it. Now, Carsten actively bled men to death and enjoyed the process in some perverse way. Jean-Baptiste had always been the bon vivant of the guys, so it wasn't surprising that he'd shown up with three gorgeous women. However, jetsetter that he appeared to be, Jean-Baptiste was into more than having fun these days. While the old Jean-Baptiste was like a frat boy, he had evolved into a frat boy who enjoyed hazing freshmen to death. Like Carsten, he had developed a cruel streak.

And what of me? thought Fernando. *I'm not cruel, but I'm not pure like Otto, either. I need the blood to survive and be happy now. I wouldn't really want to return to my pure Fridarian state, not forever, not endlessly without any flesh form relief.*

You're not all you think you are, pulsed Jean-Baptiste. *Don't look down on us, Fernando. You're no different if you look inside yourself closely enough. How many animals and humans have you drained during the past hundred years? Be honest.*

I've lived quietly, studying humans, trying to figure out how to fit in with them.

"So have we," said Carsten.

But I don't like to hurt or kill them. I try to avoid it.

Did you bring humans with you to Antarctica as we did? asked Jean-Baptiste.

Fernando had to admit that he'd brought three humans with him.

And did you drink their blood? asked Jean-Baptiste.

Yes, he had.

Well, then . . . Jean-Baptiste didn't have to complete his thought.

Fernando explained that he'd lived in Spain and France all these years, that he'd lived in a cave in the Pyrenees, seeking forest prey in the guise of a mutated boar. And yes, he had scared the humans, and yes, they thought he killed and ate their children, but he'd had plenty of time to think about who and what he was and how he wanted to live. He'd killed plenty of men, yes, but not by torture. Always, he gave them pleasure with the pain. He considered himself to be a gentle soul.

This set the other three, even Otto, into fits of laughter. As Carsten turned his "back" on him and fiddled with the old telescope, Jean-Baptiste brought Fernando up to date on what he'd been doing. It was no surprise that Jean-Baptiste had spent the past five decades cruising the hot spots of the world: nude beaches, high-stakes casinos, strip joints, bars, all the places where prey was easy to catch: he'd been like a killer shark in a goldfish tank, he explained.

The old tripod was vibrating, and the parabolic mirror of the telescope was reflecting the sun. There could be no reading during the months of sun, of course; Fernando remembered well how the ancestors' technology worked, and he'd read about the humans' pathetic versions of the technology for years. Out there, unknown to human engineers and scientists, the Fridarian ancestors had shot messages to a variable star, and the messages had bounced from the star to the Earth-bound telescope. Carsten translated the light intensity fluctuations into the ancestors' original messages. "Remember a long time ago," said Carsten, "when I told you we were here on a mission? Well, when I returned here from Russia, I discovered the final fragments of the ancestors' message in the queue. I know what our mission is now."

Fernando thought back to when the four friends had parted ways. Carsten had discovered that they were supposed to reproduce by building something called a natural nuclear reactor. The message had indicated that two more batches of Fridarians would be activated in 2015, one in the Mediterranean and one right here. There was a little bit more about Africa and sex, as Fernando recalled, but that had been it. Oh yes, and then there was the cryptic final message that Carsten repeated to them now:

DISASSEMBLE. THREE BEAMS ONLY. REPRODUCE.

The words reverberated in Fernando's mind. He still wasn't sure what the ancestors had meant. If beams had somehow triggered the two explosions, then would a third beam hit the Earth somewhere, and if so, would hatchlings be discovered there, too?

Suddenly, things began to make sense. One thing was very clear to Fernando. IceCube had to be destroyed. He said, "The IceCube and Antares researchers have been detecting evidence of our telescope."

"They *have?* Are you sure?" wailed Otto.

"What do you mean?" asked Carsten.

"You said that you recently received a garbled message from the ancestors?" asked Fernando, again ignoring Otto as he did long ago.

"Yes. It gurgled into the queue somehow."

"Oh," said Jean-Baptiste. "I know what Fernando's getting at. The pulsating star! The source of the messages sent from far away!"

There was silence. Then Otto whined, "I don't get it."

The IceCube data had to be destroyed, or at minimum, contaminated so the humans wouldn't believe their discovery. Fernando explained the situation to the others: "The pulsating star technology is based on optical transmissions. Neutrino detectors like IceCube and Antares don't see these optical transmissions. However, IceCube and Antares *can* see the neutrino emissions that the ancestors shot at the pulsating star."

"*What?*" said Otto.

Jean-Baptiste chimed in. "Don't you see, Otto? The ancestors emitted strong neutrino beams to make the stars pulse with our messages! Like Morse Code!"

"Then what about the hatchling beams?" asked Carsten. "They have to be different, right, and not detected by IceCube? Am I right? Isn't that what you were saying?" He addressed his questions to Fernando.

"I can't be sure, but I think I know why the hatchling beams killed people and destroyed things both here and in the Mediterranean Sea. The peaks of the narrow beams fried circuits and killed people in their paths. When the circuits fried, more explosions occurred, which killed a lot more people. I think on the Castor, the beam hit the fuel that had leaked from the broken tank onboard."

"Do you realize what this means?" said Jean-Baptiste.

"Unfortunately, I do," said Fernando. "The ancestors sent the beams to activate the hatchlings, but in each case, the drift of ice and oceans caused the beams to miss their marks."

"So no new hatchlings have been activated." Carsten frowned.

"Probably not," said Fernando, "but it's *possible* that some were activated. You never know."

"I think," said Carsten, "that we're supposed to reproduce in our pure form using a natural nuclear reactor, and that we're supposed to do all this in Gabon, Africa. I keep telling you that we got one last transmission from our ancestors. The ancestors said that, in our natural nanoparticle form, we eventually will split into our constituent parts, which will remain dormant, waiting like spores, like unborn hatchlings . . . our particles will wait until sufficient radiation hits them and triggers reproduction. At that point, each spore becomes a new Fridarian, and the old Fridarian, though essentially alive in all these new hatchlings, is dead."

"Oh, *please!*" said Fernando. "I don't believe this for a second. Do snow, rain, and ice ever die? No. Plus, Carsten, we have nanotechnology on our side. If anything ever breaks down, not that it ever *has* in more than two hundred years, we can simply wish the construction of new body particles or pieces as easily as we make ourselves into pigs, handsome human men, and countless forms."

Jean-Baptiste said, "Fernando, he's talking about *pure* Fridarian life, not us. And he's saying that in pure form, we are mortal but only if we reproduce."

"And as blood-Fridarians, then what? I think that, in this form, we live forever," said Fernando. "I feel intensely vital after drinking blood. I don't think that I'm going to run down and switch off, Carsten. I believe that all of us, except Otto of course, is immortal."

"But only *I* can reproduce," Otto said. "None of *you* can do that. Of us all," and he paused for effect, obviously enjoying the moment, *"only I can have sex."*

There was a stunned silence. Of course, Otto was correct. Of them all, only Otto was capable of Fridarian sex. It was an insane thought, an odd twist of nature, one that made Fernando think that perhaps the humans had a point when they babbled about the meek inheriting the earth. "Do we have genes, like humans have them? Just what is reproduction for us, anyway? If Otto replicates, will his offspring resemble him?" Fernando was suddenly aware—very keenly aware—that perhaps only Otto would have offspring to push the Fridarians into future generations; would all future Fridarians be like Otto? Would they have none of the strong attributes of the Fridarian leaders, of Fernando, of Jean-Baptiste, and even of Carsten?

"Who knows?" said Carsten bleakly. "What's it matter, Fernando? If you want to reproduce, you can tell yourself that your fate is to die rather than be immortal, and you can stop drinking human blood." He paused. "Actually, that's not a bad idea."

"Perhaps then, in pure form, all four of us can go to this Gabon, Africa and reproduce as the ancestors commanded," added Jean-Baptiste.

"But do *you* really want to stop drinking blood? Do *you* really want to return to pure form?" asked Fernando.

"No." Jean-Baptiste's answer was simple and to the point.

Jean-Baptiste curled his frozen particles around the two girls who had passed out on the ice, and he fluttered around the two human men from Russia. He twisted his icy fangs into the men's skulls and cheeks, forcing Carsten to erupt into a foaming black mass, screaming, "Get away from them! They're mine!"

Jean-Baptiste laughed and withdrew his fangs from the human heads. The men collapsed unconscious, their hearts feebly beating. Blood gushed from their faces and their craniums. The massive hemorrhaging smelled good. All three blood-Fridarians bristled with thirst and lust. Carsten's black foam rose like a wall and smacked Jean-Baptiste away from the men, and then Carsten sucked the blood from the splatters on the ice cavern walls and floor.

Jean-Baptiste was still laughing. "You can't die, Carsten, no matter how much you want it. You can't stop drinking blood!"

Carsten was a black splotch of filth stuck to the walls of the cavern. His foam slopped across the legs of the Russian men. He was sulking, almost as bad as Otto, who trembled by the telescope.

Perhaps after a century, the three blood-drinking Fridarians no longer had a choice, thought Fernando, maybe they *had* to drink blood. And why not? He flexed himself into a blur of shapes, then into flesh forms that humans wouldn't be able to fathom—antelopes with gills, chickens with groundhog heads and bear paws, seals with twelve human legs, and in each case, he made sure to give himself fangs, four of them, long and sharp and hollow with tubules.

If Fernando, Jean-Baptiste, and Carsten remained immortal, then why did the Fridarians need to reproduce at all? And what of the hatchlings in the Mediterranean Sea and here at Antarctica? If any of the hatchlings had been activated by the misplaced beams, the need for Fernando or any of his friends to reproduce became irrelevant. "I didn't sense any hatchlings back in France near the Mediterranean explosion, and I don't sense any here, either. But some of them may have been activated, don't you think?"

"If we find any hatchlings, I say we move them as far away from the humans as possible, somewhere deep in Antarctica where they won't be noticed in any way," said Jean-Baptiste

"And then what?" said Otto.

"And then, we decide whether we need to go to Gabon, Africa," said Fernando.

"We must do what the ancestors told us to do." Otto's voice was rising again into that high-pitched whine that drove Fernando crazy.

"Gather the remaining humans," Fernando told Carsten and Jean-Baptiste, "and put them with the three I brought with me. Your humans clearly need medical help." As the others protested, he added, "Listen, we have to keep all the humans alive. For food, if for no other reason. There aren't enough humans at the Amundsen-Scott Station to feed us all, and any scientists we kill now will bring even more scrutiny to the place. An explosion is one thing. But killing off the survivors one by one would bring us too much attention."

As he revved himself into a snowstorm, Carsten told Fernando that there was a little more to the ancestors' last message. The four Fridarians blasted their way from the telescope crevasse, with Otto carrying the four humans in a mini-gale of snow. Otto would deposit the humans outside the Amundsen-Scott Station, while Fernando, Carsten, and Jean-Baptiste would bore deeply into the ice to search for the hatchlings.

"The final communication," said Carsten, "is that the third beam is going to hit Antarctica very soon because the mother planet isn't going to survive. In fact, given that the message was sent a hundred years ago, it means that Fridare is now dead."

The ancestors would send no more messages. There was nobody left to tell Fernando and his old friends what to do and how to survive. They had their mission, to reproduce and save the Fridarian race, to ensure that any new hatchlings were schooled in Fridarian ways.

Assuming there *were* any hatchlings, of course . . .

Earth was chosen for the Fridarian spores because it was a planet high in uranium. Fernando must find a source of uranium in this place, Gabon, Africa, and figure out how to induce reproduction using the uranium's radiation.

It was a good thing he'd been studying human textbooks for a hundred years, he thought dryly.

As he swept across the glaciers and plateaus and down the barren peaks of ice, he was filled with anxiety. There were no other Fridarian vibrations anywhere except the ones generated by Fernando, Carsten, Jean-Baptiste, and Otto. The ice sheets strained against each other, chipping and groaning. The red rays of the sun were like blood across the mirror of ice. The wind was shrieking its welcome to Fernando and his friends. And far off to the right, Fernando sensed the keening of a mother seal as she tried to save her pup.

He raged across the frozen landscape toward Amundsen-Scott and stopped near the runway, where he had first landed in flesh form as Fernando Le Sprague. The humans were all inside the dome and one stray man worked by a burned out building. He was poking around the IceCube equipment.

A third beam was supposed to hit Antarctica, but would it come? If so, IceCube must be shut down and all the humans must be driven away. It wouldn't be hard to destroy IceCube; it had already been damaged to the point where it would take the humans months to repair it. The key would be to get the remaining humans to leave Antarctica, and then to take over the Amundsen-Scott Station and await the arrival of the beam. While waiting for the beam, the Fridarians would contaminate and destroy the humans' neutrino data.

Fernando wasn't sure what to do. Too much was happening too fast. First, he would seek evidence of activated hatchlings. That was the most important thing to do. He told Carsten and Jean-Baptiste about the sub-glacial Gamburtsev Mountains, eight thousand feet tall and over seven hundred and fifty miles long. But they pointed out that it would take them decades to search for stray activated hatchlings—and even longer for dormant spores of Fridarian life—in such a huge area. Before activation, the spores wouldn't vibrate, and it would be impossible to figure out their locations.

Realizing the chance of finding hatchlings *or* spores was remote, at best, Fernando formed himself into dozens of steel fangs, and then he drilled into the ice. Beside him, Jean-Baptiste self-assembled into a huge drilling machine that bored an enormous hole into the ice, and Carsten followed Fernando's lead, assembling his nanoparticles into drilling fangs.

The human man looked up, saw the machines, and dropped his equipment. He ran toward the dome of the station but Jean-Baptiste quickly roared into blizzard form and attacked the man, whose head burst into a bloody spewing pulp, whose limbs cracked into a thousand pieces, whose screams died beneath the shriek of Jean-Baptiste's storm. Within moments, Jean-Baptiste had buried the man under a few tons of ice. The human went quickly and loudly, but over the screech of the storm, Fernando was sure that none of the humans inside the station would think anything unusual was going on. Jean-Baptiste re-assembled into his drilling machine, which Fernando noticed was tinged with human blood. Jean-Baptiste had drunk the man dry, of course, before killing him beneath the ice.

This is what we've become, thought Fernando.

We're killers.

No better than the humans.

And maybe worse . . .

After hours of drilling and fusing their particles with the ice, they gave up. There were no activated hatchlings anywhere near the Amundsen-Scott Station. The explosions in the Mediterranean Sea and here in Antarctica clearly hadn't worked. Whatever seedlings, spores, Fridarian debris—whatever it was Fernando had been as a baby—whatever was supposed to be under the water and ice, well, it hadn't hatched when the two beams hit the Earth.

Fernando shifted into flesh form, and his friends quickly followed suit. Fernando Le Sprague, the debonair Spaniard in the fine clothing, was joined by Jean-Baptiste, tall and thin, tanned and wearing a tuxedo, sun glasses, and a white bow tie, and smoking a cigarette. And there was Carsten in human form: it was no surprise to Fernando that Carsten had spiked black hair; eyebrow, ear, and nose piercings; and black boots.

"I think it's time we meet the humans who work at the Amundsen-Scott Station," said Fernando. He knew that his voice held no enthusiasm whatsoever, and behind him, Carsten sighed the sigh of doom and Jean-Baptiste licked his human lips and toked on his cigarette.

"You realize the third beam, even if it hits Antarctica, probably won't hatch any seedlings, either," said Carsten. "Remember, the ice has shifted since the ancestors pre-programmed the beams."

Jean-Baptiste flicked cigarette ash onto the snow and chuckled. "I'm not sure what it entails, but we're going to have to learn how to have sex, boys."

Fernando shuddered.

Sex meant death, didn't it?

CHAPTER SEVENTEEN

Antarctica: October 2015

SHE WAS TRAPPED, UNABLE to move, her legs broken, her arms crushed, her face hurt so badly that her eyes were glued almost shut by frozen blood. She was deep inside a crevasse far from the station. Nobody would hear her calls for help, nobody would hear her crying; the wind was screaming far above her, the blizzard raging across the opening at the top of the crevasse.

She'd been staggering across the ice, tripping over the sastrugi, sliding along a pressure ridge when everything collapsed. Her legs crumbled beneath her, and she fell to the right, hitting her elbow on ice. The snow opened up and swallowed her, and in that instant, she knew she was falling into one of the thousands of crevasses that plummeted to the sea, negative 20-30 degree water, and certain death. As she tumbled, she saw the sky one last time, and it was as white and bleak and windswept as the surface. Her parka snagged onto an ice prick, some four feet long and two feet wide, tapered at the end into the point of a sword, and she hung there, dangling with one broken leg and a shattered elbow, looking at the blackness below. She screamed for help, but her words reverberated off the ice wall and fell. And then the prick snapped, right at the top, at the point of the sword it snapped, and she plunged down, her back, her head, her torso, her limbs slamming against solid ice, turning her into a pulp of herself until finally, she landed on a narrow ice ledge deep beneath the surface.

Pain blazed through her. In her moment of death, she replayed her memories, and they were all monochromatic: black rock with white ice crawling over it like moss, black sea stagnant with white ice banging across the surface like slow-moving bumper cars, black and white penguins, black seals, white pemmicans, black blood congealed and frozen on white snow, black smoke rising from ice-encrusted white buildings, white bones, white skulls, black and white skin, black hair, white fingernails, white steam rising from white fat slashed open to the white sky, black dreams, a black life, the debris of life after death.

In her moment of death, this is all she remembered of Antarctica.

She squirmed on the ledge and heard the crack of ice as she fell, and then her body crashed into the water.

The water was as real as her pain, and it was cold and like a whirlpool; and she was caught in its powerful grip.

Her mind circled the drain of death, its focus getting narrower and narrower . . .

Something pricked her, and her heart fluttered, uneven, and stopped. And the pricks came again, and then again, and she felt something warm flooding her body and bringing it back to the surface of life. She fought it—no! don't bring me back! no, please let me die!—but it was too powerful for her, and her struggles were fruitless. If it was her time, better to let her go now; why return to live her monochromatic life, only to die again tomorrow?

I was so close to death, so close . . .

"Wake up! Wake up, Sasha! We have visitors." Someone was shaking her shoulders. The voice filtered in, indistinct, and then rose in volume and sharpened. It was Antoine. Her lead technician, Antoine Damar. What the hell did he want? Why couldn't he let her sleep, or die, or just be done with all this hell?

Burned meat on a grill.

It filled her nostrils, that awful smell that just wouldn't go away, that smell that had been with her since the . . .

What had happened? Oh yes, the explosion, the unexplained detonation of something that had killed everyone and left the IceCube project and the Amundsen-Scott Station in ruins.

She remembered the halo of angels around the sun, the Antarctic beauty marred, its pristine ice coated in blood. Everywhere: the beauty and death, the blood and ice.

"Snap out of it, Sasha!" Antoine shook her again, and she blinked, slowly seeing his face and registering his anxiety. She was the only senior scientist left, all the others were dead, and other than Sasha and Antoine, the only other technician alive was Harold. Rayna was stressed so much she was at a breaking point and hiding in her medical unit with the two junior technicians who had suffered from nervous breakdowns.

Antoine.

Had Antoine and Harold been able to fix the backup generators with the help of those two guys from McMurdo Station? Sasha was about to ask Antoine about the generators when a shiver ran down her, sending her teeth chattering and her eyes blurring. Another shiver shot through her, but it ran in rivulets, forking and merging in odd places, in two of her fingertips but not the others, on the left side of her belly, then splitting and fading away. She felt clenched by ice, as if it were real and alive and not simply fear clinging to her. "I . . . Antoine, I'm not well," she sputtered.

"You certainly don't look well, Sasha. You're as white as a ghost, and I've never seen you this nervous." He sat in the black steel chair by her cot. She was in her room, she realized, the tiny cubicle she called home. Like the outside world, it was done in monochromes, black steel desk, chair, and file cabinet, white mattress, white sheets and blankets, and the floor was a clot of dirty snow and ice. She wondered if she was going color blind. Hilarious! Wouldn't that be the ultimate joke, she thought, if she finally went home, away from this black and white nightmare, only to learn she'd lost her ability to see color!

Not so funny . . .

A candle flickered on top of the file cabinet, filaments of light slinking across the walls. She watched the light undulating as if dancing to a snake charmer's pipe. She wondered how many candles Antoine and Harold Chavenze had found, if they were all as short and burned down as this one.

Could they cook with candles?

Could they keep warm with candles?

She propped herself on an elbow. "I had a terrible nightmare, Antoine. I fell into a crevasse. I was drowning in the sea."

He twiddled his thumbs. His right knee jumped up and down. "Yeah, well, I dreamed I was chopped into bloody pieces by a beam from outer space, so I'd say your dream beats mine."

She touched his hand. They were all having nightmares. She wasn't the only one.

Antoine's mouth twitched, and there were bags under his eyes. She'd never seen Antoine so nervous, and it scared her. She could only imagine how creepy it must be for him to see *her* this freaked out.

"Antoine, I've seen things that scare me, things beyond what you've seen," she said.

He gave her a look that told her he was afraid to hear what she had to tell him. As if his boss, Sasha Karonski, might be losing her mind. "What do you *think* you've seen, Sasha? Remember," he said gently, "that what we've all seen here, Sasha, can't be any worse than what you *think* you've seen. Keep that in mind. Now, are you sure you want to tell me?"

The candle burned down slightly, oozed liquid which instantly froze, spit a crackle of fire at the wall. She stared at the flame. It was nothing compared to the flames that had seared horrible images into her brain. She was branded with those images no less than if she'd been branded by iron on her flesh.

Sarah Hermann.

Zhen Qing.

Both young, both with bright futures, both fine people.

Both burned in place by some unknown mechanism.

Before she answered Antoine, she asked, "Tell me the truth. Have you seen or felt anything unusual . . . that is, other than the obvious? I mean, anything that *really* makes no sense to you?"

He shuffled his feet uncomfortably. His knee still bobbed up and down. "You mean, like, have I seen *mirages* of sorts?"

"That's exactly what I mean, Antoine." Relief flooded her. Perhaps the others had been seeing strange images, as well.

"Out there, when we were trying to bury everyone, Sasha, and failing miserably, I thought I saw strange patterns in the sky. In the clouds. Animals in pain, seals being frozen alive until the life was sucked out of them by the cold, that sort of thing. I mean, the wind was fierce, the snow and ice a searing cloud, I . . ." He paused and held his head in his hands. "Extreme stress does these things to people. That's what Dr. Chubkoff—Rayna—said."

Sasha forced herself into a sitting position. She looked at Antoine, straight in the eyes, steadily, hoping her excitement would latch onto him in some positive way. "Don't you see," she said, "that we're not seeing things in some isolated way? I've seen these same things, Antoine. Grotesque faces, penguins shredded by what I can only describe as fangs. My god, Antoine, I've seen things that I'm afraid to tell you about, I thought myself so insane!"

His eyes held a little hope, but he still looked highly uncomfortable even to be discussing what he'd seen or what Sasha thought she'd seen. "I don't know, Sasha. I think these were all mirages built from the fog and the snow." His voice grew low. "I thought I saw Robert Falcon Scott out there. How crazy is that?"

"But I saw him, too. Blue eyes like headlights in the blizzard. I saw his black hair, his frostbitten nose."

Antoine sucked in a deep breath. "His nose had two icicles in it."

"Plugging both of his nostrils."

A long pause. "Yeah."

"And I saw Edward Wilson, too, with his glazed eyes, blind. But not Shackleton," she added, "though I almost wanted to see him with the others. But I didn't."

"What do you think all this means?" asked Antoine.

"I think it means we have to get the generators running and hope to god McMurdo sends help, like right away. I think it means we have to get out of here, Antoine. There's something very wrong happening here at Amundsen."

"Gee, you think?" He stood and reached for her, and she let him help her to her feet. Both of them were terrified, it was palpable between them. She no longer gave a damn if she carried on the family tradition. So what if her great-great-grandfather Lawrence Oates had been one of the great adventurers of Antarctica? So what if Oates had sacrificed his life so Wilson and his friends could live? Did this mean that Sasha Karonski had to sacrifice her life, as well?

"Have you heard from McMurdo?" she asked. They had left her tiny room, and with the candle made their way down the narrow corridor toward the outer door.

"We have company in the recreation building, Sasha. That's why I came over here to get you. Yes, there's news from McMurdo—they sent us some help, but the help has gone away again. These two men, Sean McDonald and Albin Fageraas, rigged up a backup generator for us then returned to McMurdo. They said that, one way or the other, they were going to return very soon to pick us all up and bring us to McMurdo. They're not gonna leave us here. They swore. But then, while you were laid up in bed, another plane arrived from McMurdo."

Another plane, eh? Sasha wondered why this second plane hadn't picked up the survivors at Amundsen-Scott and brought them back to McMurdo. What were they waiting for?

Sensing her anxiety, Antoine said, "They've sent a small crew here to check things out before they take us back to civilization, Sasha. Because nobody knows what happened here, they're playing it safe."

"They think we're, what? *Infected?*"

"I don't know what they think. Maybe this small crew can fill us in."

Sasha pushed open the door and stepped onto the ice. Saw the burned recreation building, the charred remains of humans, the nothingness of everything around them. Bleak. White. Frozen. Endless swirls of snow and ice diamonds, the weird ice sculptures that littered the landscape with lattices and jumbled geometries, heard the high-pitched shrillness of the wind. She hated it here. *Hated it.*

And now she knew that she was stuck here until some unknown group of people gave the okay to let her return to civilization.

"So who came to help us from McMurdo, Antoine?"

Antoine didn't look at her. Instead, he picked up his pace and hurried toward the recreation building. She struggled to keep up with him. She felt weak, sick, dizzy, and the wind was getting fierce again and picking up speed. Of course, she'd seen much worse, like when the katabatics rolled through at two hundred miles per hour and lasted for days on end.

Visibility was fading, so she tried to walk more quickly, but her ankle hurt and she had to limp. Had she twisted her ankle, injured herself? Why had she been laid up in bed, and for how long? She couldn't remember.

She wasn't anxious to leave her safe place, her dorm room, her comfortable bed and blankets. But when she stumbled into the recreation building, she forgot all about her bed and blankets. What she saw was so shocking that the earlier massacre settled into her mind as just one of many horrors. The scene before her wasn't as terrible as the massacre, but it was much *stranger.*

Splayed on the dining hall table was her old friend, James Schankel, all six foot three inches and two hundred plus pounds of him. His parka and shirt were both open, displaying tufts of black hair across a massively muscled chest. Sasha had once admired James, she remembered her feelings acutely, for he was older and she looked up to him back then. She'd even had a thing for him, a vague fantasy and nothing more, but still, it was more than she'd felt for any other man in the past five years. And now here he was on the dining table of the IceCube research station, groaning in ecstasy and arching his back and clasping the sides of the table with both hands.

What the hell?

Sitting on James's thighs was a fully clad man with a halo of blond hair, huge hazel eyes, the whitest skin Sasha had ever seen, the muscles of a Greek god, the weirdest freaking clothes *ever,* and if that wasn't strange enough, the guy's face was smeared in blood.

Smeared in James's blood!

And James was getting off on whatever the man was doing to him!

Antoine threw himself at the blond man. "What are you doing? Get the hell off him!"

The man's mouth stretched into a bloody grin and with a flick of his wrist, he threw Antoine to the floor. Antoine screamed and clutched his leg, but he scrabbled back up to fight the monster on the table. Again, this time sneering, the man flicked him away like a fly.

Then the man noticed Sasha. "And you are . . . ?"

Sasha gasped. "I-I'm. *Nothing.* What?" She stopped.

A young girl, a real beauty, stood behind the bloody man. The girl reached for him and looped her arms over his shoulders and then nestled her head into his hair. And there was yet another member of the party, a young boy, dark and brooding, black hair and green eyes, shuffling his feet and looking the other way. Both the girl and boy wore full South Pole gear, parkas, boots, and hats. But the blond man was in a Flamenco-type outfit, all gold and glittery, and James was–

"What's going on here?" stuttered Sasha. She limped toward the table, frightened of what the man might do to her but needing to see James. What was he doing to James, *eating him?*

James craned his neck, saw her, and muttered a name. "Chloe." Then, "Go away, Chloe. Fernando, I need more!"

Antoine was on his feet again. He grabbed James's arm and tried to yank him off the table. "You sick fuck! You came here to *help* us? Are you *joking?* You're the one who needs help. Who the hell are these people, and why don't you take your fucking party somewhere else? We have enough trouble without your deviant sex crap."

Sasha's stomach lurched. She felt as nauseous as when she'd first seen the bloody bodies outside the dome after the explosion. James and the blond man exchanged a glance, and then James slid off the table to confront Antoine.

Sasha couldn't believe what she was seeing. What had happened to Dr. James Schankel? Why was he acting this way? She gasped as he lifted Antoine and hoisted the technician over his shoulder. Blood ran down James's chest and pooled into a coagulated mess over his belt. The blood was freezing quickly, and she wondered how James could stand the extreme cold without his coat or at least a heavy shirt. There was still no heat, just weak power offered by the backup generator, and a dim bulb over the table trickled light over the bloody mess.

Sasha staggered, her eyes lost focus, and a new wash of dizziness enveloped her. Something inside her seemed to flicker off and die as she watched James hauling Antoine out of the recreation building into the outdoor wasteland. She was too numb to argue, to understand, to question what she was seeing, and something else was at play, too, something strange and new to her, something *inside . . .*

A horrible cold gripped her, and her heart pulsed with a throbbing ache—yes, she could feel it pulsing, *feel it struggling.* Her heart beat louder, *louder* and her eyelids felt heavy. Her mind was floating on icy breezes, there was an ache in her bones, a terrible ache, and then the patterns took hold again. This time, she didn't see Scott or Shackleton, but rather the vision of her own ancestor, Lawrence Oates. He was blind, clutching at his face, trying to ward off the stabs of a dozen icicles that probed his cheeks, his eye sockets, his mouth, his forehead. But he wasn't succeeding, and his hands struck out blindly, slapping at hail, at ice dust, which only fluttered and sparkled more brightly as it slammed into his bloody red skin. He fell onto a sastrugi, screamed as his spine hit the ice. To his knees he went, to his knees, and the ice plunged down and slashed his throat, and out poured his blood. And something loomed over Oates, this ice monstrosity, this *Thing* of no proportions, it suddenly disintegrated all around him, coating him with ice and dust, and from within a blossom of red suddenly bloomed, like a giant rose frozen in an Escher patchwork of ice, frozen yet oozing with new petals as the sack of flesh inside was drained of its blood. Oates. Lawrence Oates. And he was why Sasha Karonski was here in the first place, for she had felt compelled to make discoveries in Antarctica and resurrect Oates's name for all the world to admire.

She had failed miserably, hadn't she?

For now, James Schankel was off doing something terrible to poor Antoine, and Sasha herself was dizzy and maybe—*what?*—was she perhaps *dying?*

She willed herself to hang on to life.

But *she* was on the table now, and the blond man was over *her,* and he ripped off her parka and the front of her shirt with his fists. It was a déjà vu, she'd been here before, felt this before, and knew it wasn't rape, it was something far worse and odder, and even as she thought *that,* she knew also that this would be something delicious.

"Fernando," whispered the beautiful girl draped over the man's shoulders, "can I do her first?"

"Or me? Let me do her first, me," whispered the dark-haired boy.

The blond man, this Fernando, gestured for the girl and boy to stand on either side of the table. He cradled Sasha's head in his hands and leaned over, and his breath was blood, but it was sweet not cloying, pleasant not sickening as she expected. It aroused her with a strange desire. She was apart from her body, her mind floating on the icy breezes that coursed through the room, her body glued to the table.

The man turned to the beautiful girl and said, "Don't kill her, Chloe. She must be brought into the fold. Be careful not to drink fully of her. Let her live as one of us."

A whining: "But why, Fernando? What's the point of letting her live, much less as one of *us?* You have *me,* don't you? And you told those people that I'm your *wife,* didn't you?"

A frustrated sigh. "This has nothing to do with that, Chloe. You're not stupid. You must understand what I mean."

"I do," said the dark-haired boy. "Sasha Karonski is the only remaining scientist here, Chloe. That's what James said before we got to McMurdo. Remember?"

Chloe, petite, thin, lovely light hair to her waist, gauzy eyes, a butterfly of a girl. She nodded. "Fernando needs her to help find the hatchlings, right? But if we're not going to completely drain her, I want to be the one to merge her blood with ours. I want to feel what that's like, George."

"But I want to feel it, too, Chloe. Neither one of us has turned anyone yet." The boy—his name was apparently George—paused. "Tell you what. Let's do her together." George turned to the one in control, this Fernando, and requested permission. Fernando slid off Sasha's body, but she barely felt the pressure lift, for her mind was already too far gone into the haze where Oates and Scott and Shackleton dwelled, wherever that was.

"Take care of her," said Fernando, "but be very cautious that you don't put her over the edge. I doubt she can help us find the hatchlings, but I need her to do other things for me. Things that only she knows how to do."

"Like what?" asked Chloe.

"Like, it doesn't matter," said George. "What are you waiting for?"

Chloe's eyes lit, and excited, like little birds feeding for the first time, the two bent their heads over Sasha's body, over her breasts, and they nipped her, and she felt the energy flood from her limbs and torso.

CHAPTER EIGHTEEN

Antarctica: October 2015

OUTSIDE, SASHA SAW ANTARCTICA as if through a kaleidoscope. The mists were etched in color, the expanse of solid ice glimmered in soft pink. The world had changed from monochrome to neonchrome, alive with sparkling crystals. Like fairies, the crystals danced in the wind and sang in muted harmonies. The wind no longer howled; instead, it whistled a subtle tune behind the melodies of the fairies. The sun blinked overhead and no longer hurt her eyes. She could look straight at it without goggles. The extreme cold of the swirling crystals was like the warm massage of a whirlpool, and Sasha shed her parka, hat, gloves, and boots, and still, she was warm.

There was no need to crank up the backup generators.

There was no need for candles, fires, and medical supplies.

She was transformed—*into what, she did not know*—and she no longer felt anything but happy, calm, and buoyant. These were new feelings for Sasha Karonski, formerly the MIT PhD with the logical mind, quiet demeanor, and less-than-buoyant perception of humanity and the world. She recognized Sasha Karonski in herself, but from a distance as if contemplating an entirely different person.

A white petrel bird circled once overhead and set out to sea. Its wings were delicate and finely boned. Its beak was chipped at the end, its eyes keen with intelligence. Its heartbeat was rapid, and blood pulsed through the small mounds of protein in its breast. Heat burned in Sasha's ears, and her mouth salivated. The bird, she knew, would taste like nothing she'd ever eaten, the tiny mounds of protein flush with seasoned blood, the head a delicacy of crimson mush. Sasha could sense all this from her position outside the recreation building, something the old Karonski couldn't possibly do even if using binoculars.

Fernando and his two young friends had given her this new life, this joy. Over the piping of the wind and the lilt of the ice crystals, she heard Fernando's voice. *Blood and ice, substance and form, love and devotion. And above all, pain, the eternal source of energy and strength. The pain will be your pleasure, mon chère.*

Excitement surged in her. *Yes!* Fernando was the omnipresent substance of the world, the omniscient being, the one that people had been seeking since the dawn of time. Was he the son of God, the Holy Spirit, or was he God Himself? She fell to her knees on the rock-solid ice with the wind whipping past her. She clasped her hands together and lifted her face to the blotted sky. *Dear God, Oh Holy One, Thou Art in Heaven, please forgive my sins.*

Péchés? Why, mon chère, you've not sinned at all! Nor am I the human God nor anything remotely like Him. I am what I am, and nothing more. Now be good and help James.

You are not God? she thought. *Then what are you? And what am I?*

Again, he put words into her mind. *I am the one who relieves your pain. I am the one who gives you ecstasy.*

"Did you kill everyone here, Sarah Hermann and Zhen Qing and all the others?" she whispered.

No. I did not kill them.

"Did you make me see visions and hear things?"

No. That was probably an old friend of mine who did that to you. A chuckle. *His name's Otto, and he was probably trying to scare you away from Antarctica. He's afraid of everything. And now, enough questions. You must go now and help James Schankel.*

James. She had to help James!

Wildly, Sasha looked across the ice for him. Equipment buildings, food depository, greenhouse, digital optical modules, vehicles, hoses. Yes, she'd seen James back in the recreation building, right before Fernando mounted her and turned her world into a blaze of fierce highs and whirling fuzzy color. She'd *seen* James.

And Antoine! He'd been on James's shoulders, struggling to jerk free, and James had carried Antoine outside to . . . *where?*

Use your senses, Sasha. They will lead you to James and Antoine. Help James. He will nourish your soul.

And another voice filtered into her mind. *Come here, Sasha, here behind the equipment trailer. I'm feeding but will wait and share.*

Was it James?

Yes, came the voice, *this is James. And do you sense who is with me?*

She sniffed the air. Nothing. She listened and heard a whimper, very low and muffled, but nonetheless, she heard it despite the howling wind.

James and Antoine Damar were behind the red equipment trailer, the one to the left. Antoine was tall and thin, and he was good with computers but physically not the strongest guy around. There was no way someone like Antoine could defend himself against someone like James Schankel.

As lightly as a breeze, Sasha floated across the ice toward the trailer. She remembered how she and Antoine had cried when they discovered their dead friends. She remembered how Antoine had helped her regain her strength. She remembered Zhen Qing, the young engineer, his limbs shattered in pools of blood far from his body.

For a moment, grief welled in her, but it quickly dissipated into the frost. These memories belonged to the former Sasha Karonski, not to the Sasha of today and tomorrow, of forever.

Still floating, she reached the rear of the trailer, and that's when she saw them:

James Schankel had his back to her. He was on the ice, crouching over a body. He wore no shirt, and his enormous shoulders and arms gleamed with frozen blood. His black hair was fringed in red, and his neck was coated with gore. He turned his head and flashed a bloody smile at her. His lips were so dark they looked bruised. His eyes appeared unfocused, so absorbed was he in ecstasy and raw desire.

Instantly, her body reacted, and the desire rushed to her head and set her limbs quivering. *She had to drink the blood. She had to share the feast.*

Yes, this body had been Antoine, and yes, she had been best friends with Antoine, but that was *then,* back in mortality, and this was *now,* at the dawn of—*immortality?*

James Schankel's memories coursed through her as keenly as if they were her own. She felt the agony of watching Al Horowitz die beneath the Mediterranean Sea, saw his blood billow like a huge cumulus cloud in the bright blue water. She felt the loneliness of the former Dr. James Schankel, he who had been mortal before Fernando touched his soul. His desire for Madeline at the University of Marseilles. His years in combat, the pain of his muscles flailing against the water of the sea, the rough terrain of the Middle East, the jungles, the skies. He was an ex-Marine, and he'd suffered much in his mortal life. And now, he was one with Sasha and with Fernando, and no longer, would James endure such pain. Now, the pain he cast was pleasure. She saw blood and ice, and she felt substance and form, love and devotion.

"It is my first time," said the transformed James Schankel. "Let it be yours, as well." He stood and stepped back from the body, which lay twitching upon the blood-sopped ice. It was indeed Antoine Damar, but thin as Antoine had always been, this version was much thinner. He was naked, the rear of his body frozen in place on the ice. The skin had been ripped open straight down his chest: half-gutted like a lab specimen in autopsy. His breath came in wisps, gargled by the foam of blood. His face was mauled as if from the teeth and claws of a wild animal, swollen and blue, tendrils of white fat poking out, teeth jutting at odd angles, one eye missing. He was very close to death. The heartbeat was faint and erratic.

She wanted to taste him alive.

She wanted the thrill of knowing what it was like to suck a man dry while his heart still beat with the fresh blood.

Later, she would taste the stale remains.

But now, *now* was the time for the feast!

The crushed lips parted and whispered her name, only half her name, "Sa . . ."

She straddled his waist and bent. She placed her hands on his shoulders. Her body was on fire, the need so acute she almost screamed. There was nothing else that mattered, nothing, only *this.*

He smelled so sweet, so ripe, and his flesh was there for the taking, and it bulged with the succulence of beating blood.

"Sa . . ."

She lowered her head until her lips touched his chest, and her mouth tingled from the blood; and she lifted her lips and licked them once, let the trickle slide down her throat, slowly slowly gliding and merging with her cells as it dripped into her belly. She moaned and licked her lips again, felt herself gyrating on top of the body, rubbing herself against the naked flesh. His whimpering was like a narcotic, and her need rose even more until she could no longer resist the urge–

and she slammed her head against the face and plunged her teeth deeply into the left cheek, and she sucked with everything in her and felt the blood coursing now—no longer trickling—but *coursing* down her throat and *blazing* through her body.

Antoine gasped, feebly fluttered a hand. His back strained to wrench free of the ice. Peering down at him, she saw the trill of life expire in his eyes, and she heard his last thoughts. *You, of all people, Sasha, why? I'm dying, Sasha, please don't do this, please, no.* Memories rose to the surface of his remaining consciousness: a five-year-old playing with trucks in the dirt, a mother's smiling face, a seven-year-old swinging a bat and hitting a ball far into a cornfield; a first love beneath a young woman's embrace, the swoon of ecstasy; the pride of earning his degree, the thrill and wonder of seeing Antarctica for the first time. And then a final image gurgled into his brain, that of Sasha Karonski five years ago when she joined the research time; a demure face, thoughtful and intelligent, brown eyes shining with kindness and determination, long dark hair framing a freckled face. *You, of all people, Sasha, why?*

One small tear formed at the edge of Antoine's eye, and it froze in place. His heart paused. Forever, it paused.

At the final moment, his pain surged and melted into a honey-like warmth of release, of pleasure. She remembered Fernando's words, that pain was the eternal source of energy and strength, that pain and pleasure were equal. She licked the small ice tear from Antoine's eye. There would be no remorse, she knew, for Sasha and James had brought Antoine from the pain point on the axis all the way up to the highest point of pleasure. It was a gift, really, that they'd supplied to the human. Life for humans was difficult, painful, and filled with disappointments. They yelled at each other. They betrayed each other. Death was the greatest gift you could give to a human, particularly when bestowed with such grace and kindness, the narcotic uplift of The Blood.

James was at her side, crouched on the ice, feeding from the body. Sasha was hungry, for she'd eaten next to nothing for days, not since the explosion. And this was food, *good* food, and she dipped her head and drank.

Later, fully sated, she and James left the dried husk of Antoine Damar to be swept away by the wind or buried in place by ice and snow behind the trailer. Whichever came first, it was of no importance.

They found the drained body of Harold Chavenze by the recreation building, smelled the scents of Chloe Desmarais and George Bouchard on his remains. Harold had never been of much importance anyway, thought Sasha. He'd been a useless human and was better off dead.

James read her thoughts and grabbed her arm. She whirled to face him, angry. He said, "Sasha, none of these humans are *useless*. Have you no compassion left? Both Antoine and Harold were our friends and workmates. I feel their loss as acutely as I grieve for Al Horowitz."

"Your face is masked in the death blood of Antoine Damar, so who are you to speak of compassion?" she snapped. She wrenched her arm free of him and pointed at Harold's body. His legs were broken in multiple places, his arms jutted at odd angles, his face was as contorted as a cubist painting. "Harold's lucky," she said.

James backed away from her. She was amused to see that he was afraid of her, for James Schankel was the big macho military man and she was only a petite female with no athletic strength at all. "How is he lucky, Sasha?" His voice cracked in mid-sentence.

She scowled at him. He was an idiot. "He's lucky, you fool, because he's dead! Because we released him from the pain of human life, from disease, illness, mental anguish, lost love, bigotry, and hatred! There *is* nothing else to human life, is there, James?"

"There's love."

"Fleeting."

"There's happiness."

"Fleeting."

"There's pleasure."

"Ha! We give the humans their ultimate pleasure, James. Don't you feel the excruciating ecstasy they enjoy when we drain them?"

He stood a few yards from her, no longer backing away but not smiling or approaching her, either. His forehead wrinkled, his lips were drawn tightly together. Finally, he said, "I can't believe what I just did to Antoine. What *we* just did to him. When Fernando drank of me, Sasha, he told me that taking human life gives us sustenance and force, the power to survive the ages, but nothing more. We're not to take life in the way humans torture and kill each other. Didn't Fernando tell you that, as well?"

James, she thought, wasn't as smart as she'd always assumed. Fernando had fed on Sasha's blood, yes, but Chloe Desmarais and George Bouchard had completed her transformation. As for the humans, she said, "I tell you we're doing them a favor, and besides, I might point out, James, that *we are nothing like Fernando.*"

"Aren't we?" He delicately swung his body up into the air so he was hovering a few inches off the ice.

She floated over to him and took both of his hands in her own. She gazed into his eyes. He briefly looked away, then looked back at her. He was listening to her now, intently, so she said, very softly, "James, we were humans before Fernando took us. Fernando was never human, he's always been something else. He doesn't know what it's like to be human. We do."

And so did Chloe Desmarais and George Bouchard, she realized. The four of them, transformed from humanity, were the first of their kind. She suggested to James that they look for the other two, and somberly he trailed behind her, past the buildings and the debris, and toward their scent.

Chloe and George were by the digital optical modules, yanking on the wiring. Sasha instantly knew what they were doing and why.

Together, the four of them—Sasha, James, Chloe, and George— smashed all of the digital optical modules, the IceTops, the cables, and the communications equipment. There would be no way for humans to analyze any data showing evidence of the Fridarian transmissions. There would be no way for humans to detect the spawning of a new generation of Fridarians. If the third and final neutrino beam hit Antarctica where the Fridarian spores lay waiting for radiation to hatch them, there would be no way for the humans to detect *anything*. IceCube was dead. Neutrino anomalies no longer mattered.

CHAPTER
NINETEEN

Antarctica: October 2015

"TOO MANY HUMANS HAVE been killed. We need to leave Antarctica quickly." Fernando had just come to Antarctica and didn't want to leave so soon, but he knew that the deaths of Antoine Damar and Harold Chavenze would be noticed by the humans at McMurdo, in France, and elsewhere. "The McMurdo guys could come at any time now and question us," Fernando added. "*Nous allons être capturé et détruits.*" We'll be captured and destroyed.

He hung as an opalescent fog over the black sea. Beneath him, the penguins cavorted, diving over the water and flipping to its depths. He'd often seen human scuba divers trying to emulate the ease with which the penguins dove beneath the water, but human efforts at everything were clumsy, at best.

Carsten rose from the water as a black scab of ice upon which a dozen Chinstrap and King Penguins lolled. The Chinstrap Penguins had narrow throat stripes of white, and their chicks had the fluffiest and purest white bellies that Fernando had ever seen. The King Penguins, *Aptenodytes patagonicus,* were much larger than the Chinstraps and had very long orange-black bills with a dusting of orange and yellow on their throats. Their chicks were brown fluffy things, as cuddly to behold as the teddy bears of human children.

"How many are dead?" asked Carsten as he expanded his black scab to accommodate another cluster of fluffy King chicks.

"He already told us," said Jean-Baptiste. "Two more humans are dead. Sasha and James killed Antoine Damar. Chloe and George killed Harold Chavenze. Fernando, they weren't particularly *important* humans." Jean-Baptiste remained as white ice dust and tickled the flanks of the mother penguins. He didn't touch the males, which seemed strange to Fernando. Regardless of gender, a penguin was *just a penguin*, right? But Jean-Baptiste had a thing for females of any species, didn't he? Fernando remembered with disgust the three girls Jean-Baptiste had brought with him to Antarctica, juicy tidbits for Jean-Baptiste's bloodlust.

"I suppose," said Fernando, "that as long as Sasha and James keep up a charade of being pure human, we're safe. They *did* destroy IceCube for us. They can tell the other humans that the two technicians died from exposure."

He reflected on the changes he'd noticed in Sasha and James after they had so much Fridarian blood and nanoparticles in them that they were essentially a mutation of human and Fridarian. Perhaps he'd been unwise in letting them live. Or perhaps he shouldn't have drunk more than a nip or two and left them alone. But it was too late now, *trop tard maintenant.*

The adult penguins suddenly lifted their heads and barked. They beat their flippers on their breasts and swung their heads back and forth. Protruding from Carsten's black slab were sharp ice stalagmites, and more needles were springing up and jabbing the penguins as they skittered with bloody webbed feet toward the water. The black ice needles were tipped in red, and Carsten's vibrations were clear: *the pain, the supreme pain, it's such a high! Let them suffer more! The pain, the pain, it lets me forget.*

"Stop it, Carsten," said Fernando, as Jean-Baptiste howled with delight and descended from the air as translucent prongs, stabbing the fat heads of the scampering penguins. And, "Stop it, both of you!" cried Fernando. He crystallized his opalescent mist into solid sheets of ice that scooped the birds toward the water. The penguins and their chicks slid into the sea, and dots of blood blossomed into pools on the water's surface, then swirled into the sea and disappeared as the birds descended to safety.

"What's the matter with you? Don't you like any fun, Fernando? You've become such an old man. You used to be as down and dirty as us! In fact, as I recall," said Jean-Baptiste, "wasn't it *you* who first suggested that we give the blood to Carsten?"

It was true! Fernando had been the worst of any of them back in the day, back when he first tasted blood. He remembered as if it was yesterday.

He'd pulsed a private message to Jean-Baptiste: *Carsten hasn't tasted or smelled the blood. He doesn't know what it's like to get high. But if he's "accidentally" exposed to the alien blood, he might understand why we like it so much. He just doesn't know what he's missing.* And: *One taste is all it'll take, then we won't have to put with his bad moods all the time.*

"Don't you remember?" pressed Carsten, congealing with Jean-Baptiste into a solid ice tower that hung in mid-air with no roots to the glaciers, to the floes, or to the water. They were ganging up on Fernando. No, the thought was absurd! Carsten, Jean-Baptiste, Fernando, and even Otto would be friends to the very end of time, for that's how long they would all live.

"I do remember, yes," admitted Fernando. "We were so young then. Our first tastes, the first few times, yes, it was exquisite and beyond anything I could possibly imagine."

It had been the urge of a young Fridarian before he matured and saw things with the wisdom of age.

More blood . . .

Yes.

Killing the humans.

No.

Drinking the blood of dead alien animals. Dogs, seals . . .

Maybe.

Bloodosterone surges . . . the blood raging through my body!

Yes.

"All right," he said, "I admit it. The two of you are absolutely correct. I was as bloodthirsty as anyone back then, and I've been bloodthirsty ever since. But you see, I've developed a fondness for some of these humans."

"Fool," said Jean-Baptiste. "You let the *food* get to you?"

"Everything fails and dies," moaned Carsten. "You never should have given Chloe and George your blood and infused them with your particles. You gave them too much, and you didn't kill them. That was stupid, Fernando."

"You don't know what they'll do," added Jean-Baptiste. "You can't expect them to react like us or really behave as we do. What is it, old man, you think that they *love* you?" And he burst out laughing.

"Oh damn," moaned Carsten.

"There is *no* love with humans. They are *food.* Got it, Fernando? *Food!* There is only love among Fridarians," said Jean-Baptiste.

Jean-Baptiste and Carsten were right, of course. Fernando had always known it. To love a human was to flirt with disaster, for humans couldn't even love each other for very long. And their form of love was so selfish and needy. Few of them truly cared about each other. Yes, Fernando had recognized that back in 1903 and 1911.

So what were they to do now?

Boom! An explosion hit Antarctica, jolting Fernando from his thoughts. The explosion cracked the solid block of Carsten and Jean-Baptiste, and they splintered apart, falling into the churning water.

"What was that?" cried Carsten.

But before Fernando could answer, another explosion shattered the air, and this one was louder and followed by a crescendo of explosions that left Fernando dazed. He tried to place the location of the noises. He sensed absolutely no vibrations from Amundsen-Scott or McMurdo, nothing from the Ross Ice Shelf or the transatlantic mountains, nothing from the outlying areas of Rookery Island, Haswell, Molodezhnaya, or Novotazarevskaya.

"Get up!" he cried to Carsten and Jean-Baptiste, and the three of them assembled into one hell of a storm, with their winds more than a hundred miles per hour and their particles congealed into hail the size of baseballs. All three were screaming, half from glee, half from excitement. The hatchlings! The third beam had hit the hatchlings!

But where? The three Fridarians raged toward the western coast, blindly and without cause.

And then they all smelled the blood at the same time. It was human blood, lots of it, oozing from chunks of meat strewn across the ice far away.

"Neumayer Station," said Jean-Baptiste. "The first all-female group of humans ever to winter in Antarctica stayed there."

Neumayer, established by Germany in 1981, thought Fernando, and he shifted course and sped toward the upper east coast. Neumayer Station was on the Ekstrom Ice Shelf in Atka Bay in the northeast region of the Weddell Sea. It had been upgraded in 2009 and stood on a platform above the ice.

If they could find the hatchlings there, if the hatchlings had been activated, then Fernando and his friends would have no need to reproduce. They could remain as bloodsucking flesh-formed Fridarians for as long as they wanted. There would be no need to disassemble, to go to Gabon, Africa, wherever it was, no need to degenerate into pure particle form like pathetic Otto and whine their way to certain cessation as their particles evolved into new Fridarians. Fernando could remain Fernando, and the hell with his offspring!

They approached the station from the south. It was covered in snow and perched on a flat sheet of ice that was a mere two hundred meters thick. Half of it had been blown away and was burning. Corpses lay in pieces like litter around the platform stilts. *This is not an ideal place for hatchlings*, Fernando pulsed to the others.

The ice isn't thick enough, not like the two miles of ice where we hatched, pulsed Jean-Baptiste. *I doubt the ancestors would have placed any Fridarian hatchlings here. It doesn't make sense.*

Fernando sensed the great frustration emanating from his two friends. At the core of his being, which Fernando always thought of as his "heart," he felt as dejected as he'd ever been.

They poked among the rubble and found charred fragments of kitchen equipment, cots, motor sleds, and laboratory hardware.

"Do you sense *anything?*" asked Fernando.

"If the hatchlings were buried here, they certainly aren't alive or activated now. I think the third beam was way off mark just as the first two missed *their* marks," said Jean-Baptiste.

"We can always dine on the remains, yes?" Carsten floated toward some human gore that stained the ice near the left side of the station. Fernando heard him sucking on the ice to leech the blood from it.

A dark cloud of moisture descended over a tangle of bloody body parts and slurped from the organs. It was Carsten.

Fernando knew that he had to join his friends and dine, for the humans were food, he told himself, and nothing more. And this food was freshly killed and would taste sweet. Why let it go to waste, way out here on the ice shelf where nobody would find it and provide human burials anyway?

He was gorging on A negative when he sensed vibrations beneath the surface of the ice. Something was below the station, and it was moving! The hatchlings? His senses pricked. Totally alert!

And then: "Run!" he screamed, and he bolted from the carcasses and raced from the station. Behind him came Jean-Baptiste and Carsten, who always listened to him when it really mattered.

As the three streamed inland away from Neumayer, they heard one final huge bang. The fuel tanks beneath the station had exploded. A flare shot from the station, as fusillade shot in all directions. There would be nothing left of Neumayer Station and nothing left of Fernando's hopes for new Fridarian births.

CHAPTER TWENTY

Antarctica: October 2015

SATED ON BLOOD, FERNANDO, Carsten, and Jean-Baptiste rejoined Otto near the Amundsen-Scott Station. Otto was jittery, even more neurotic than usual. After fluttering around them, muttering about bloodbaths and vile human habits, he threw himself down by the recreation building, where he pounded the snow with fists of ice. He was throwing a temper tantrum.

"You sniveling idiot, stop it! You're two *hundred* years old! You're not a *two* year old, Otto!" Fernando scooped the wailing Otto off the snow and shook him. Otto collapsed as a pile of powdered snow, and Jean-Baptiste blew on him, scattering the particles in all directions.

Otto quickly coalesced again. "Look, there are no hatchlings, okay? And the three of you are insane mutated flesh-eating abominations."

"We only drink blood. We don't eat flesh," corrected Jean-Baptiste. "And we're not insane."

Carsten assumed human flesh form, that of a heavily muscled Russian male with a bald head, drooping moustache, and tattoos. He was clad in a black leather vest and tight leather pants. From his belt hung a heavy chain-link rope with a spiked ball on the end. He scowled at Fernando and Jean-Baptiste. "There's nothing left for us here in Antarctica. Not now, anyway."

Fernando quickly merged his particles into the form of the

handsome Spaniard that Chloe and George adored. He tossed his golden hair off his forehead and examined his perfect fingernails. He was so much more refined than either Carsten or Jean-Baptiste, and of course, Otto, was like a Fridarian caveman, lost in the past and unable to evolve into the present or future. "Sadly, Carsten's right. We can always return after the humans come and clean up their messes. I was hoping to spend more time here, but sadly, we have to go. We need to head to Gabon. After we have sex and reproduce, we can return home again."

Fernando pulsed privately to Jean-Baptiste and Carsten, *If there's to be any hope for the Fridarian race, it would be best to ignore Otto. If we let him, he'll whine until we all agree to stay here in Antarctica forever, disintegrate into pure-particle form, never reproduce, and never drink the blood.*

But do we have to reproduce at all? pulsed Jean-Baptiste. *Who really cares if the Fridarian race consists of anyone other than three immortals and one purebred nut job?*

They were all silent for awhile as they pondered a future devoid of any Fridarians other than the four present. Apparently, all other purebreds had winked out or gone elsewhere over the years. There were no vibrations anywhere in Antarctica from any other Fridarians. And given that there were no other purebreds present, was it possible that Otto would wink out at some point, too? If so, it would leave only the three immortals, who really weren't pure Fridarian. But, who cared?

And then Carsten pulsed, *What if Otto does reproduce? Imagine a world of a thousand Otto's and only the three of us. That would really suck.*

Is there a way to kill Otto? pulsed Jean-Baptiste.

I'll pretend that I didn't hear that, pulsed Fernando. Aloud, he said, "Otto, are you with us, or what?"

Sniveling and clearly distraught, Otto said that, of course, he was with them. But what did they have in mind? Not more blood, he hoped.

"Well, what do you think we have in mind?" said Jean-Baptiste. "Caviar and toast? Cookies and milk?"

"We have to do what the ancestors wanted," said Fernando. "We have to have some meaning, don't we?"

"No," said Carsten. "If there's anything I've learned from humans, it's that there *is* no meaning to anything, Fernando."

"I don't agree. You're either with me, or you're not." Fernando turned from the others, and in human form, strutted toward the recreation building, where he sensed the presence of Carsten's two human males from Russia and the two nightclub girls who had arrived with Jean-Baptiste. Chloe and George were also in the recreation building near the humans. The only other humans left anywhere at Amundsen-Scott were a female and two young males, and they were also in the recreation building. How handy, thought Fernando, that all the human food was in one place.

Within a week or so, more humans would show up, and then, the deaths of Antoine, Harold, and possibly even the human food brought by Jean-Baptiste and Carsten would be discovered. The time to leave Antarctica was *now*. They might as well go to Gabon and scope out the natural nuclear reactor mentioned by the ancestors. They might not even be able to find it, but if they did find it, there would still be time to figure out whether to reproduce or not. This whole reproduction-sex thing might be impossible anyway. Besides, Fernando didn't want to return to France or Spain just yet, so why not travel somewhere new? Like Gabon, Africa?

Fernando entered the building followed closely by both Jean-Baptiste and Carsten in their human forms and Otto as the purest mist he could devise. The dining table was littered, but not with paper, forks, spoons, or plates. Rather, it still held the remains of the mini-feast Fernando had enjoyed first with James Schankel and later with Sasha Karonski. Yes, there was plenty of dried blood on the table, but also bits of flesh, nails, and torn fabric. In the back corner on the floor, Chloe and George were playing cards.

"Gin rummy," said Jean-Baptiste. "It's nothing like stud poker or Texas hold 'em, if you ask me, and I'm an expert." Smoothing his white tie against his tuxedo shirt, he wandered back to join the game.

Huddled on the other side of the room in the back were the food humans: the two girls almost dead and shaking in their flimsy cocktail dresses and the two filthy men with the bashed-in heads. To Fernando, the four looked identical: they were just food, nothing more. He barely registered the differences in their faces and bodies, all he sensed was the amount of blood they held within their skins.

Two young men in parkas and hats lay sleeping on the floor by the table. With them was a female with a stethoscope in her hands. She glared at Fernando and his friends as they sauntered around the room. "And who do you think *you* are?" Her voice was cold, but frightened. Like the two young men, she also wore full extreme weather gear: parka, hat, boots. This would be Rayna, the medical doctor, thought Fernando.

"We're here to help, of course. I'm Fernando Le Sprague and these are my two associates."

The doctor eyed Jean-Baptiste in his casino getup, the tuxedo with white shirt and tie, and then Carsten, who looked like a cross between a Hell's Angel and an executioner. "Your associates don't look like scientists to me," she said.

"I'm the scientist," said Fernando lightly. "At your service. I know Antarctica well. I know IceCube. I know how to deal with communications equipment." He was enjoying himself, toying with the human. Being around Carsten and Jean-Baptiste must be rubbing off on him. He flicked his hand at his friends. "Say hello to Carsten, who has the strength to lift bulldozers, if he wants, and to Jean-Baptiste, who has the charm to weasel millions in funding out of international scientific organizations, should he choose, that is."

Jean-Baptiste flashed him a smile. "I do tend to get what I want, don't I?"

Carsten balled his human fists, hoisted his leather vest on his shoulders, and growled. Otto settled on the floor by the door and turned himself into an ice slick.

Chloe chattered about gin rummy to Jean-Baptiste. She placed three kings on the floor and motioned to George that it was his turn. She'd come a long way since her time in the Pyrenees, thought Fernando. She'd matured into the Fridarian ways very nicely and no longer cared about sausages, bread, cheese, or fitting in with superfluous glittery tourists. She had more substance now. She understood love and devotion, pain and pleasure. She was independent, no longer worrying about what her father did or thought. She was free.

Jean-Baptiste said, "Do you want to place bets?"

George snickered. "We have no need for money here." Fernando could tell that both Chloe and George sensed that they were in the presence of three more Fridarians: Carsten, Jean-Baptiste, and even Otto. Fernando could also tell that both of his young wards were thrilled to meet others of their kind who understood the ecstasy of blood.

Tension coursed throughout the room. Taut. So fired up that the air *vibrated.*

And then, apparently sensing what was to happen, Otto squeaked a feeble, "No . . ."

But of course, Otto's whining didn't matter. It never had mattered. Carsten *lunged* at one of the bedraggled Russian males. A slash of crimson, the face mauled, and then Jean-Baptiste was solid white ice raging against the two young bimbos from the casinos somewhere anywhere.

Chloe cried out and dropped her cards. George went white and rigid and flattened his back against the wall.

Carsten smothered one man in black foam while smashing his spiked ball into the other's skull. Carsten was half-human form and half-Fridarian form, but as soon as the ball hit bone, he transformed into all black foam and oozed like a mountain over the two Russians.

Rayna collapsed, weeping, beside the two young men, who awakened and screamed.

Chloe's confusion rang like a death knell in Fernando's brain. George was vomiting blood across her lap, she was scampering to get free of him and run.

Fernando almost split to particle form, but not wanting to risk hurting Chloe should he turn to ice, he stood instead before her as a wild boar, blocking her escape with his huge, padded body. His four tusks were long, curved, and very sharp. The little spikes of his auburn fur bristled against her perfectly white and creamy skin. He spread his wings, pressed his fat belly against her. His wings folded around her. *Ah, little Chloe Desmarais, my wondrous beauty, my mate, my divine one.* She tensed, and he held her more tightly, but she wailed and beat him with her fists.

This would not do. He shoved her back and grabbed her wrists with his hooves, and he ripped her parka off with his tusks. Goose feathers fluttered around him as he sliced his way down her shirt, cutting a bloody groove from her chest to her waist. She was shrieking and crying, God what an awful noise, and he wanted her to *shut up!*

He slammed her body against his belly, and she moaned in pain as his boar bristles poked into the bloody groove. And then teeth chattering, she relaxed in his arms and wings, no longer struggling.

It was such bliss to be with her in this way, mentally connected through their minds and physically connected with their bodies. Fernando made himself forget the reason they were physically bound. He let himself drift in the sensation of simply being with her, flesh wrapped around flesh. Perhaps he'd been wrong about sex and mates and the romantic nonsense that Chloe had desired from him. Perhaps he should give her what she wanted. Give her physical love as well as emotional love.

But–

"You disgust me," she said.

"*Mon chère*, my love."

"You filthy pig."

"My love. Don't you feel the fire between us? Cold flesh, mine, pressed against such hot hot flesh, yours?"

"*Le cochon!*"

He held the hot flesh close to his belly, luxuriating in the vibrations that emanated from her and seeped into the fat cells of the boar. He stroked her back with his wings, and she shuddered.

"Let me go! Oh my God, let me go, you're so disgusting, *let me go!*"

Chloe flailed against him with her arms and fists, but he pinned her to the wall so she couldn't move, and he tightened his hold. She squirmed and cried his name over and over again. Crying. "No, Fernando, no, tell me it's not so! Is this what you are? Is this what I've become? No, no, Fernando!"

Did she think he had the patience of a god? Fernando was no saint and certainly no mortal god. He was Fridarian, and he had offered Chloe everything: immortality, love, companionship, food and eternal health. And *this* was how she repaid him? "What did you think, Chloe, that the drinking of blood was always clean?" he said.

"No! I didn't know it would be like this!"

And then a male voice came, high and shrill: *"Have you no shame?"*

Fernando released Chloe and whirled. He confronted George Bouchard, who stood there, scrawny, dark mop of hair, blood-plumped lips, a silly human, after all, and what could he possibly know of *shame?*

Behind George came the loud sucking and slurping of two Fridarians hell bent on gorging themselves sick. Shreds of cloth were scattered everywhere, boots and pants and shirts were strewn across the floor. What had been two human males and two human females was now a smear of gore and piles of organs and meat: nothing was free from it, nothing, the remains coated the walls, floor, ceiling, table, and chairs.

Jean-Baptiste belched.

Chloe screamed again, but she wasn't trying to escape; she was frozen in place, shaking from terror.

It was George who bolted for the door. But he didn't make it there, for he slipped on Otto's ice and fell. His head cracked against Otto, and blood seeped from a gash near his scalp. He moaned and held his head in his hands. Drops of blood splattered across Otto's ice.

Fernando watched closely. Would Otto taste the blood, would he lap it up?

The drops remained whole on the ice of Otto. Little balls of iridescent red. Tempting . . .

Jean-Baptiste was quick, not letting even a few small beads of blood go to waste. A chunk of ice crashed down on George, flattening the boy against Otto. Ice shards flew in all directions, as Otto shrieked and Jean-Baptiste sucked the dying body dry. A scarlet mist rose and spread through the air as a flower opens in spring. And beneath it spread a white mist, Otto.

"George!" And now Chloe ran toward the door, toward the remains of her friend, toward Otto and Jean-Baptiste. But Fernando the wild beast grabbed her with his hooves and wouldn't let her go. He couldn't let her near Jean-Baptiste, not when the Fridarian was in full bloodlust, not when she could be easily killed, squashed like a fly and drained.

Back by the other bodies were three more: the medical doctor, Rayna, and her two young patients. Carsten heaped himself on the dining table. He was black mush seeped in red, and he slopped over the sides of the table and splattered onto the floor.

Fernando's friends were all gluttons. They knew no limits now when it came to the bloodlust. They would take any life near them in order to satisfy their insatiable thirst.

Chloe sank in his grasp, weeping, the strength ebbing from her. She'd seen her best friend, George Bouchard, murdered. She'd seen seven other humans murdered and drained of all their blood. She'd seen what Fernando really was, what he was capable of doing. She'd seen his true essence.

And she didn't like what she saw. She looked at him, terrified, trembling, and her thoughts were a whirl of hysteria: *I'll kill Fernando. He's a monster. My father was a GOD compared to Fernando and his friends. What was I thinking, to run away from my father with this monster? How could I have insisted that George come with me? It's all my fault that he's dead, all my fault.*

Fernando snapped back from her. He assumed his natural Fridarian form, blended into the ice fog that was Jean-Baptiste, Otto, and Carsten. They were one, the Fridarians. These humans would never be like Fridarians.

Humans knew no loyalty.

Humans knew no compassion.

Humans knew no *love.*

Both Chloe and George were traitors. Fernando had treated them both so well, released Chloe from impoverished hell at the hands of her father, *le cochon.* He'd taken her to the Mediterranean Sea, as she wanted, he'd fed her, clothed her, protected her, given her immortality as one of his own kind! And now, *this!* How dare she cast him aside? How dare she treat him as if he was a monster? How dare she desire his *death?*

As for George Bouchard, Fernando felt little. He'd been a minor playmate compared to Chloe Desmarais, for whom Fernando would have done almost anything.

Yes, perhaps the Fridarians were murderous gluttons, but they killed for food, didn't they, and not for sport? *Didn't they?*

Fernando was no longer sure.

But it didn't matter. Not really. *We are what we are,* he thought, *and there's no crime in that. We were born this way. If the cosmos hadn't intended for us to drink blood, we wouldn't be able to drink it. If we require blood to be alive, to take flesh form, to let the oxygen and nutrients flood our internal cells and give us meaning, then so be it.*

CHAPTER TWENTY-ONE

Antarctica: October 2015

IN THE DISTANCE, GROTESQUE shapes rose from the sea and clawed the horizon. The red sun blazed over the water. Sasha sensed the krill, the fish, the whales beneath the water, the flapping of gills, the *whiz* of tons of blubber racing against the currents. She felt the excitement of ancient fish species from thousands of years ago, fish that were still unknown to man, as they dove en masse toward a transparent pulsing glob of life stuck in a rock deep below. She smelled a wisp of blood, iron and oxygen, a tartness like unripe apples, as the glob disgorged its life under the grasp of the ancient jaws.

The world remained neonchrome, alive with sparkling crystals. The world was ripe and full of color and sounds and smells, all designed by some unknown hand to make her reel with desire and ecstasy. It would be enough to spend the rest of her life in this cocoon of pleasure.

James Schankel stood beside her, also viewing the expanse of Antarctic sea that reached to the edge of the sky and sank down into worlds so deeply hidden from mankind that it was almost funny to think that they'd once thought they knew *anything* about Antarctica at all. They'd known nothing. All of the training, the years at MIT, seven days a week year round with no break, all for what? To learn what little mankind knew about the world.

James's chest was still bare despite the raw wind and negative twenty-five degree temperature. His pants were shredded at the knees, his black hair wild and knotted by blood, his skin almost translucent over the blue tangle of capillaries. It occurred to Sasha that she and James were the only two of their kind.

In response to her thought, he said, "And then there are Chloe Desmarais and George Bouchard, yes? Aren't they also like us, switched on by Fernando, flushed with his blood and his nanoparticles?"

She felt the vibration of the nanoparticles, yes, everywhere in her body and mind, she felt the alife assembling and disassembling, counteracting anything harmful to her, building her resistance, fueling her with abilities that no other human could possibly have. Acutely, she sensed the hysteria of Chloe Desmarais, the girl's desire to kill her benefactor, *to kill Fernando.* "The girl isn't like us, no, James," said Sasha. "She wants Fernando dead."

"Dead? But why? Look at what he's given to us." James gestured at the sea, and behind them, at the desolate peaks, where birds flit to ice-cliff nests and the wind screamed.

She knew what James meant. But she also knew that she and James were scientists, trained for years, intelligent, and much older than the young and very naïve Chloe Desmarais. James nodded, reading her thoughts again, and said, "I think, also, that Fernando infused us with a lot more of his blood and his essence, Sasha. He gave much less to Chloe and George, and he didn't give them any more blood after meeting us."

Sasha turned from the sea and from James, and she stared in the opposite direction. "I need to go to Beardmore Glacier, James. I want to visit the place where my great-great-grandfather died. I've seen visions of Robert Falcon Scott and Edward Wilson. I also saw Lawrence Oates, my great-great-grandfather. I saw him die, James. I think that whatever Fernando is, whatever his kind are, somehow their particles have formed these mirages over time."

"I don't understand," said James, cracking over the ice behind her as she floated back toward the mountains and land-locked glaciers. But then he said, "We've both spent our lives studying neutrinos, very tiny particles that nobody can see. I suppose that Fernando and his type are like these tiny particles, too, but they have different properties. You mean to say that they somehow imprinted their memories in the very ice dust that makes up Antarctica?" Even as he said it, he scoffed at himself, shook his head. "That's wild, Sasha."

"Wild, maybe, but I think there may be some truth to it. We'll probably never know, James, not for sure anyway. We're here, and what else is there to do? Go back to Amundsen-Scott Station and smash more equipment?"

"No point. I think we've already smashed everything."

As they floated over the ice together, coursing against the wind as if it wasn't there, she told him that she sensed the death of other humans, including George Bouchard. James was dismayed and asked why George had died.

"I don't know, James. Probably because like Chloe Desmarais, he wanted Fernando to die. I don't know. What does it matter? Other than Chloe, who is much weaker than us, only you and I exist in this form."

They had reached the base of Beardmore Glacier, where nothing remained of the long-dead Lawrence Oates. At any rate, there was nothing on the surface, Sasha told herself, to show that he had ever been there. James was thinking that he and Sasha Karonski were meant to be lovers, soulmates, companions forever. She keenly sensed his loneliness and how he had longed for a companion for many years. Now, only Sasha was the same species—or whatever they were—as James, and he'd always admired her. She glanced at him, considering that she'd once been attracted to him, but . . .

"James, that was *then,* and everything has *changed.* We have to learn what we are and get used to all this before . . . I just can't think of things like that, James." What was he, *kidding?* James Schankel, Mr. Macho ex-Marine, was a known ladykiller, *sure,* but now, he was no longer a man. They were both *something else.*

"It was just a stray thought, Sasha. You don't have to get nasty about it."

"I'm not being nasty, James, just practical."

"I don't know. Seems to me you've been flying off at people like an arrogant fool for quite some time now, Sasha." When she didn't bother to respond, he said, "Is this the right place?" He was changing the subject. Good thing, she thought, because she didn't feel like putting up with his stupid accusations. Her anger was on a hair trigger, and she wasn't exactly feeling like herself these days.

She couldn't be sure that she was really near the location of Lawrence Oates's death. Beardmore Glacier was a hundred miles long, a soaring expanse of dazzling white, swirled with the etchings of a million storms. She thought back to the family stories, to what she'd read about her ancestor, and she realized that he *hadn't* died at the foot of Beardmore Glacier.

"Edgar Evans died at Beardmore," she told James, "not Lawrence Oates. Evans fell into a crevasse and hit his head. Oates had frostbitten feet but staggered on with the others."

James had wandered away from her, was floating over the snow and ice, beckoning her to follow him. "I've studied the expedition, Sasha. I think that I can find where he died."

"Really?"

"Yeah. Well, before Fernando, I couldn't have done it, not as a pure human, but now, my senses are more acute, and I just have this *feeling—*"

She tensed. Was James getting better than her at being whatever they were now? She tried to pick up cues from her surroundings. If she focused enough, maybe she could find Oates on her own.

"Don't be obstinate," said James. "Just follow me, would you?"

Sure, why not? They zipped across the wasteland, James telling her that he'd read that Oates died somewhere near seventy-nine degrees forty feet south; and then Sasha remembered the details, that her ancestor sacrificed himself to Antarctic death at thirty-two kilometers, or twenty miles, shy of the location mentioned by James. Lawrence Oates had died on the Ross Ice Shelf.

They wandered for hours, seeking the exact spot, and then at the same time, they both knew they had found it. Beneath them, the ice vibrated in a pattern different from what they expected. A vision rose before both of them, a vision of Lawrence Oates as he died, the same vision that Sasha had seen when she thought she was going mad.

"He's way down there, buried in that crevasse. We can float to him, James!" She hadn't considered that even if they found Oates, they might not be able to reach him. What if he'd been buried deep beneath the ice? They had no tools, no equipment with them. But luckily, they were able to float over the ice, lower themselves in the narrow opening between the immense frozen slabs, lower themselves down down *down* a hundred, two hundred, three hundred feet.

And there he was: Lawrence Oates. Dead, all the blood drained from his body, frozen in place like a mummy. *After all these years!* He had a rugged face, a broad nose, dark hair, and a throat slashed clear from one side to the other as if from a knife. "He was thirty-one years old when he died," she said. "It was 1912."

"Had he lived now instead of then, from the looks of him, he could have been a Marine like me," said James. The mummified Oates looked as if he'd been strong in life, she saw it was true: strong neck and arms, masculine features. But now he was *dead*.

Mummified.

Frozen in time.

Sasha and James lifted the mummy and swept it back to the surface of the Ross Ice Shelf. She remembered her earlier vision:

Something loomed over him, this ice monstrosity, this Thing of no proportions, it suddenly disintegrated all around him, coating him with ice and dust, and from within a blossom of red suddenly bloomed, like a giant rose frozen in an Escher patchwork of ice, frozen yet oozing with new petals as the sack of flesh inside was drained of its blood.

"What happened to him? Who did this?" Sasha knew the answers even as she asked the questions, and James—the ever-intelligent James, he knew the answers, too.

"Fernando." James uttered the word very softly, and he glanced at her.

"Fernando killed him." She crouched with James on the ice next to the body, put her head on Oates's chest, licked the hundred-year-old scab sliced into his neck. No blood in the body, nothing, but a trace of something frozen in time. She tasted it, and it coursed through her body and fused with her nanoparticles, the ones injected by Fernando.

She tasted Fernando on Lawrence Oates's neck. She tasted his nanoparticles, the alife mechanisms that existed at such tiny levels that only one as she could detect them.

"But I taste someone else, too," said James, following her lead and flicking his tongue across the long-scabbed wound. "Another of Fernando's kind slit the throat. Fernando and he drained the blood together. There were two of them, Sasha. Fernando and one other."

Tears burned her eyes, and a wave of nostalgia passed over her. Only days before, she was pure human, wasn't she? It hadn't been *that* long ago. She'd spent her entire human life following a dream based on Lawrence Oates's heroism and self sacrifice. She looked into the blind sockets that had once held Oates's eyes. She bent her head again toward Oates's neck. She sunk her teeth deeply into his frozen flesh. And she pumped as much of her own blood into Oates as she could before her head fell and she collapsed onto his body. She was so weak, dizzy, and yet, there was a flicker of life in the body, *a flicker!*

James gently rolled her off the mummy and onto the ice. She lay there, panting, holding back tears. What was she? Human? Blood monster? Both? To which did she owe her allegiance?

She turned her head slightly and gasped. "No, James, don't do that!" But it was too late, for James had sunk his own teeth into the sliced neck of Lawrence Oates and his blood streamed from his mouth into the wound, too. Blood slopped across the neck and onto the ice. Blood covered James's face and hands, his own neck and chest. She tried to lift herself and wrench James off the corpse, but she couldn't move. She was too weak by the loss of her own blood. And still James injected his life into that of the Oates mummy. James groaned, lifted his mouth from the wound, and gasped for air. Then his hands slipped and his head fell onto Oates's chest. Sasha urged him, *no more no more,* but he didn't respond. She pulsed her thoughts into his mind, imploring him to roll off the corpse next to her. *We need to recover. We're too weak. There's no point to this.* What had she been thinking, that she could bring Oates back to a weird form of life, for what purpose and for what direction? And at such a cost: she could die here, and worse, James could die.

Al Horowitz was murdered in the Mediterranean Sea because of Fernando and these monsters, James pulsed to her. *Al Horowitz was one of the most decent men I've ever known. Always had a smile on his face, always made people laugh, loved his wife and children, Sasha. He deserved a better death.*

Are we monsters, James?

Yes. And there it was, a simple enough answer, but one that disturbed her greatly. Yes, they were monsters, no better than Fernando. They'd killed, hadn't they, and drank the blood of fellow humans? They were murderers. Serial killers and possibly even cannibals.

Sasha lay there under the screaming winds on the sub-zero Ross Ice Shelf. The winds were music in her ears, like fairies singing. The ice and the cold were like the womb. She felt at home, yet her bliss had shattered to the depths of utter depression. She would welcome her own death, may it come soon. Perhaps if she stayed here, she would die on the ice and she wouldn't have to live with the knowledge that she had killed and tortured and cannibalized.

James was injecting more of his blood into the mummy of Lawrence Oates, and she felt the stirrings of life thrash within the corpse. The nanoparticles were revving and multiplying, streaming through the dead flesh, activating it with alien technology that human scientists couldn't fathom. She'd been such an idiot to think herself smarter than Harold Chavenze or anyone else. In the end, she was only an arrogant fool.

James choked and sputtered. His cheek lay on the chest of Lawrence Oates. His mouth hung open, he gasped for air. He wretched a few times, gagging up only thin drizzles of fluid. His body had run dry of blood. He had pumped everything he had into the corpse.

We were monsters, Sasha. Perhaps. But no longer. Your pain is too real over the death of a human who died a century ago. And my pain is too real over Al Horowitz. I can't live with myself, Sasha.

The beautiful eyes filled with pain. The strong body rolled off Oates. James's arm muscles were contracted, weak; his bare chest deflated; his leg veins almost protruding from his skin. With a start, she realized that James was committing suicide.

If Sasha drained more of her blood into Oates's corpse, she could die, too, and release herself from the nightmare.

The ex-Marine clenched her hand in his own. As she heard the dying thoughts of the brave James Schankel, Sasha also heard the thoughts of someone else, now sputtering to life and thinking for the first time in a hundred years.

CHAPTER TWENTY-TWO

Antarctica: October 2015

"HOW CAN YOU BETRAY me like this?" Fernando demanded. He'd assumed his handsome human form, that of the Spaniard Fernando Le Sprague. Perhaps the golden visage, the moony hazel eyes, and the rugged muscles would bring Chloe Desmarais back under his spell. He couldn't bear to lose her, not after wanting her so badly. For a moment, when she'd been hysterical and he'd been in boar form, he'd felt something remarkable between them: the contact of flesh with flesh. The bristles on his boar belly against her hot breasts and stomach. "How can you want me *dead?*"

Chloe's long hair was a tangled mess, her eyes were bloodshot and weary. She'd vomited fluids until there was nothing but dry heaves. She'd cried until there were no tears left. She was scrawny and weak. *Not so beautiful anymore,* he thought. *What has happened to her?*

His friends had left the recreation building to roam the glaciers and hurl snowballs at each other. Having feasted well, they were having a good time, reliving the old days. Only Fernando had stayed behind, alone with Chloe now. He didn't feel like rejoicing or reliving his childhood.

"Please let me leave this place," said Chloe. "The smell is killing me. I can't look at what you've done to George and the others."

Trying to win her over with charm, he acquiesced. "I've been rude and neglectful," he said. "You're right, of course. This is no place for you to be. Let me lift you, Chloe, don't be scared. Let me lift you in my arms and carry you to the dorms, where you can rest."

She frowned and scrunched her eyebrows together, then dropped her head and nodded. He read her thoughts, that she had no choice, so she might as well let Fernando carry her to a comfortable bed, where she could sleep and hopefully never wake up. Chloe wanted to die. She'd seen too much carnage, she'd had a terrible life before Fernando came along, and now her life was meaningless. She'd dragged George Bouchard on this trip, only to watch Fernando's friends maul him and eat him. *Let me die, Fernando.*

He stroked her cheeks with his soft human fingers, the rounded nails gently moving the wet straggles of hair from her face. She whimpered. *Let me die, Fernando.* With both human arms, he lifted her and cradled her. Tenderness rose in him and quickly dissipated. Fernando tried to hold onto the feeling but couldn't do it. He didn't understand it. "I don't want you to die," he said. "I want you to come with me. I'll protect you, I promise."

Like you protected George and all the others?

They were not you, Chloe.

Yes, they were, Fernando, they were just like me.

No, he insisted.

The door was splintered on its hinges, and Fernando gracefully exited with one arm under Chloe's back and the other beneath her legs. She didn't wrap her arms around his neck. She kept her arms crossed, her hands tightly clasped over her breasts.

Kill me, Fernando, like the others. Just do it quickly, please, and without pain.

I can kill you, Chloe, yes, and give you pleasure rather than pain. I can let you die in ecstasy if I want.

I know you can, Fernando. Please . . .

No.

"But why?" she wailed.

His thoughts were jumbled. He didn't know why he couldn't kill Chloe Desmarais. She was a human like the others, and he should take her life and blood as food. And yet, Fernando had never enjoyed the killing, and as humans died, he'd generally felt deep sadness at what he had done. He'd killed, of course, and enjoyed it at times, yes, but still, even as he drank the blood of the dying, as their last memories wafted into his mind, he always felt a tinge of sorrow and loss. As if each death killed a little piece of him, as well.

It was all absurd, of course. *I am what I am. I drink blood because I must. It is how I live.*

He kicked open the door to the dormitories, which were cold and empty of people. In his human shoes, he wound his way down the empty halls. The shoes made a *clunk clunk* noise, dull and plodding. He could easily float down the hall, but he wanted to maintain his semblance of the handsome Spaniard Fernando Le Sprague.

He placed Chloe on a soft mattress in a room decorated with posters of Renoir and Georgia O'Keefe paintings. The lampshade was pink with gold threads hanging from it. On the desk were several photos: one of an old human couple hugging, another of a young woman, pretty and petite, smiling and holding a small dog. He opened a textbook, *Quantum Mechanics,* that lay on the desk by the photos. There was a name scrawled on the title page. *Sarah Hermann.*

Something flickered through his mind, the image of this young woman in Maine with her parents, the old couple in the first photograph. He wondered if this information mattered in any way, if he should lodge it in his memory for later use. But then he dismissed it, as he had dismissed the memories of so many dead humans during the past two hundred years. This was a human he hadn't known.

Fernando rolled the heavy blankets on Sarah Hermann's bed over his beloved Chloe, who had already drifted to sleep. Her face was strained and twitching. He touched the skin. Stroked it. And her face relaxed, the twitching replaced by a wisp of a smile.

Sorrow clenched him, and unable to stare at Chloe Desmarais any longer, Fernando left the dorm.

CHAPTER TWENTY-THREE

Antarctica: October 2015

HE WANDERED FOR HOURS, alone, across his vast homeland. He had lost everything. His friends had become too extreme for his comfort. The hatchlings had not been born. The three beams sent by the ancestors had failed to hit their marks. Humans were dead everywhere, in the Mediterranean and the Antarctic, because of those beams, and human scrutiny would intensify upon the remaining Fridarians.

Eventually, he knew what must be done. Hopefully, Jean-Baptiste, Carsten, and Otto had returned from their partying to the Amundsen-Scott Station. The four of them had important things to do. And there was no more time to waste.

He hurried back to the station, then abruptly halted near the runway and collapsed on the ground, quickly melting into human form. He no longer wanted Chloe to see him any other way, only as the handsome Spaniard.

There was the dome up ahead, where she slept comfortably. There was the recreation building, or what was left of it, a battered skeleton of boards and human remains. Hardened blood glistened under the ever-constant glare of the Antarctic sun. The wind howled, as always. Ice shards glittered everywhere, the diamond dust that once delighted him and made him feel whole.

Depression descended as he trudged in his human shoes toward the station. He passed several gas tanks, where the humans had stored fuel. He passed the large cable spools, the smashed IceCube modules, and the dry hoses.

Jean-Baptiste wasn't here yet, he could sense it, nor were Otto and Carsten. They were still having fun, and Fernando had no desire to find out where they were or what they were doing. He would simply wait for their return.

His mood lifted slightly. He would wait in Sarah Hermann's room, where Chloe slept.

But as he walked toward the dormitories, a noise made him turn.

Over by the right gas tank, the one closest to him, *a scraping sound.*

What was it?

The noise intensified and rose over the wind, and it reminded Fernando of what he had done to Chloe Desmarais before she knew he existed. He'd been with her in the sausage hut and in the bakehouse. He'd scratched upon her doors with his wings and tusks. He remembered her fear, the hysteria of her thoughts: *Les coulisses! The wings, so many of them, scratching everywhere on the door! Insanité!*

From behind the gas tank, a shadowy figure emerged and staggered toward him. *It wasn't real, it couldn't be!* His old friends must be here, somehow hiding from him and playing with his senses. They had conjured up this vision from Hell! They had set it upon him!

Fernando Le Sprague, afraid of nothing for two hundred years, felt the stab of fear.

Squish.

Thwack.

Squish.

Thwack.

He remembered the terror of Chloe Desmarais as he toyed with her in that little village in the Pyrenees. He was cruel then, wasn't he, no different from the others? Not kind and loving, as he'd always thought, but cold and heartless.

Two frostbitten feet, bare and bloated and bleeding, staggered across the ice toward him. They hit the ice, *thwack,* and flesh tore from the soles, *squish,* and then over and over again:

Squish.

Thwack.

Squish.

Thwack.

Fernando would not be afraid.

Words entered his mind from the Thing, this monstrous entity that staggered toward him. Your pain, it said, *is like the smell of blood, Lawrence. Your pain is so alluring, so needful, it calls to me, Lawrence.*

Those were Fernando's words, the ones he'd placed into Chloe's mind, and then with a start:

They were also the words he'd placed into the minds of countless others he'd stalked and drank over the years *including this one.*

Lawrence Oates!

But he was dead, Lawrence Oates, long ago dead and buried here in Antarctica by Fernando and Carsten. Why, Fernando had seen it himself, had sucked the body dry with Carsten, had laughed with glee, drunk on the narcotic of Oates's blood.

"Who are you?" Fernando pointed at the vision and demanded an answer. "I say, answer me or fear my wrath! *Who are you?*"

The Thing dragged toward him, the bloated feet leaving a blood trail to the gas tank. "You tortured us for a month!" cried the Thing. "Don't you remember, Fernando Le Sprague? You were the worst. You were the leader."

Remember what? Fernando focused on the wind and the ice around him, forced his Fridarian senses to melt through the haze and see the Thing for what it was. It had no eyes, and the sockets beneath the frostbitten brows were black and purple and perfectly preserved as Fernando remembered them. It had the slice of death across its neck, scabs of blood frozen for eternity on the hardened flesh. The hair, black and short, frozen to the shredded scalp. Naked, the genitals gone, the hair off its chest; the legs broken and hobbling on the frostbitten feet, the arms broken and dangling from the shoulders.

And he remembered:

Lawrence Oates, slapping at the icicles plunging into his face, at the hail battering his skull and body, at the ice dust, which only fluttered and sparkled more brightly as it slammed into his bloody red skin. Lawrence Oates, screaming as the blood poured from his throat.

Fernando, drunk on Oates and giddy. Fernando, a prick in the wind, a storm from Hell.

Lawrence Oates, nothing more than a meal, one that had been slaughtered to provide the feast.

Oates was dead. How could he be back, confronting Fernando after all these years?

"Go away!" Fernando raced across the ice toward the figure of Oates, hunched, crippled, now cackling and hobbling back toward the tank. Fernando would reach this vision, would break it with his bare human hands, would crush it from his mind. He would shove it back where it belonged, back to the eternal hell of his memories. And then, he would teach his friends not to trick him like this, not ever again.

The tank was rusty and painted green. It stood on four steel legs, bolted to cement in the ice. A door, steel, hung limply open on one hinge and clanged relentlessly against the tank. The wind was fierce, assailing the bulbous tank and slamming ice inside where the door banged.

The wind was nothing to Fernando, it never had been. *He* was the wind. *He* was the storm. *He* was the ice.

He was everything that mattered. Power and intelligence, strength and determination.

Lawrence Oates was by the clanging door, and his two broken arms whipped up in the wind and glued themselves to the lip of the hole.

What was he doing?

Fernando grabbed for the corpse, but oddly, it was too fast for him. The body flipped up and hurled itself into the tank. Without thinking, Fernando hurled himself into the hole after Lawrence Oates.

He would show him! He would show this vision of Lawrence Oates, this figment of his imagination, concocted, no doubt, by Jean-Baptiste and Carsten, he would show them all that nobody toyed with Fernando Le Sprague!

In the darkness was Oates, still cackling at him. Oates huddled in the dim recess of the empty tank, holding his broken knees to his chest, the arms twisted at both elbows and jutting at Fernando. Fingers dripping like icicles from both hands. *This is absurd,* thought Fernando, *absurd!,* and he lunged at the corpse of Lawrence Oates.

That's when the door slammed behind him.

Whatever.

Nothing scared him. He'd take care of Oates, then leave the tank and confront his friends for putting him through this horror, just after he'd been so tortured by Chloe Desmarais and her cruel words.

Oates began twitching: first the fingers, clattering as they hung from the stumps of his hands; then the arms and legs, rattling against the floor. Then the entire body: banging up and down on the steel, breaking the bones into smaller and smaller fragments.

Fernando heard the whine of equipment, a drill perhaps or a—

He didn't have time to complete the thought. Before him, Oates was disintegrating, blood pouring from the corpse and congealing, the skin and bones, hair and teeth, glued and mummified like some fossil into the steel floor of the tank.

Fernando knew he had to get out of the tank. Quickly.

But it was too late. The tank filled with the bite of tar and molten steel. Something had sealed the door and welded it in place.

Fernando threw himself at the door, trying to force it open, but the door had already frozen solid against the steel tank.

From outside came Sasha Karonski's voice. "This is for my great-great-grandfather, Fernando. You killed him and his entire crew. May you die, as well."

But I cannot die.

But you will die.

Like hell, I will! Fernando disassembled into his native form, that of nanoparticle ice dust. He pressed against the sides of the door, all four sides of it, seeking a microscopic exit point, but there was no way out. Sasha had sealed the door tightly and thickly. There was no escape.

And so, Fernando curled into a ball of snow, alone, waiting on the steel floor for Jean-Baptiste and Carsten to return to Amundsen-Scott. They would sense his presence in here, and they would release him.

Surely, they weren't responsible for imprisoning Fernando in this tank. They couldn't be! Somehow, Sasha Karonski had done this to Fernando, had brought the corpse of her great-great-grandfather back to life and lured Fernando into the tank, and then welded it shut.

He'd never been imprisoned before, not in two hundred years had he ever been tricked and captured. But then, he'd never given humans enough blood to transform them into a mutation of half-Fridarian and half-human. This had been a mistake, to give Chloe, George, Sasha, anyone, the Fridarian blood, the Fridarian infusion of nanomachinery.

He would not make this mistake again.

As soon as he got out of here, he would make sure of it.

He would kill Sasha Karonski, and he would kill Chloe Desmarais.

Fernando emitted vibrations as strongly as he could, trying to reach his friends, wherever they were in the Antarctic wasteland. They didn't respond.

They were probably still high on all the carnage, he thought. They had probably sunk themselves deep beneath the ice, a thousand miles down, to party and play with the microbes near Vostok Station. That was six hundred and twenty miles from Amundsen-Scott, not very far, but had the Fridarians drilled deep beneath the ice, they might have drifted out of Fernando's range.

They could be anywhere.

For all Fernando knew, they might have left Antarctica and returned to Russia and Europe.

His particles were drying and needed more blood. He'd been detoxing in the tank for too long. He had to get out soon and refresh his body with more blood, oxygen, nutrients. He was hungry.

He wouldn't let himself go soft again.

He was a Fridarian, and there weren't many left. Fernando, Jean-Baptiste, Carsten, and Otto had a mission, and they owed it to their ancestors, those who had sent him here to give him life, he owed it to them to fulfill that mission.

Fernando self-assembled his particles into a drill strong enough to bore through steel. He blasted a tiny hole into the tank.

A thread of mist slipped from the hole into the wind.

CHAPTER TWENTY-FOUR

Gabon, Africa: October 2015

THERE WERE PLENTY OF airports in Gabon, West Africa, and getting a flight into the region near Oklo wasn't as difficult as Fernando had feared. The tricky part was getting out of Antarctica without causing suspicion among the humans at McMurdo Station. Luckily, Fernando had left Sasha alive. Although she had sent Lawrence Oates to trap him in a drained gas tank, and although she had welded the tank shut hoping to kill Fernando, she still had her uses. He wasn't done with her yet.

She was the only remaining senior scientist from the winter crew at Amundsen-Scott Station. She was already infused with Fridarian blood and nanoparticles, and it didn't take much to hunt her down, plunge his icy pricks into her body, and infuse her with more.

She'd been so weary and deflated, reminding him of Chloe at her weakest, it had taken hardly any effort at all to subdue her. One slip on the ice, and she went down, and then one hundred needles of ice descended into her torso and injected the potent transfusion. Her head swarming with Fridarian particles, Sasha Karonski barely remembered she was human. She got them all out of McMurdo Station, claiming medical emergencies that couldn't wait for the bureaucracies of the world to decide their fates. Sure, the humans were worried about the spread of infections, but Sasha had more pull than James Schankel. She insisted that McMurdo get her out of Antarctica.

The Fridarians transformed into snow and basically air-lifted both Sasha and Chloe from Amundsen-Scott to McMurdo, and from there, five "humans"—the three Fridarians in flesh form plus Sasha and Chloe—were rushed onboard a plane set for New Zealand.

After landing in New Zealand, they arranged to head immediately to Gabon, which was between Equatorial Guinea and the Republic of the Congo. Fernando had brought everyone with him except Otto, who refused to take part in any further excursions with the mutated flesh-eating Fridarian monsters, as he called them. Otto refused to leave Antarctica, where he'd always lived, and now, he would stay there as the last of his kind. "If I blink out at some point, so be it," he said. "At least, I'll die with my dignity. And as far as I know, I won't die anyway. If I don't reproduce, I might live as long as the rest of you."

"Forever, you mean? I don't think so!" Fernando had scoffed at him.

"We'll see about that," said Otto.

As the clunky four-seater plane wobbled into the West African airport, Fernando glanced at Chloe Desmarais across the aisle from him. He remembered her excitement at seeing Mount Erebus and Mount Terror for the first time, her naïve childlike view of Antarctica. Now, there was no excitement in Chloe; her eyes were glassy and dull, her shoulders hunched, her body thin and weak. He had dragged her out of Antarctica, knowing that if he left her behind, she would die from the extreme cold.

Sasha sat in front of him, vibrating with excitement, and of course, Jean-Baptiste and Carsten were with him, too, the former anxious to reproduce and the latter hoping to die.

The plane touched down, Fernando gave the pilot a huge tip, and the five passengers—Fernando, Jean-Baptiste, Carsten, Sasha, and Chloe—debarked into Gabon, the place the Fridarian ancestors had pegged as the spawning ground for their race.

As soon as the door opened, a blast of moisture and hot air hit Fernando. It was hotter than Hell here, and for a Fridarian, the temperature seemed equivalent to that of the volcanic pit of Mount Erebus.

"I don't know if I can do this." Carsten was already panting from the heat. He wore silky black boxer shorts and a black net sleeveless shirt. His human head was shaved close to the scalp. Sweat glistened on his shoulders and arms and ran down his forehead into his eyes. He stopped, put his hands on his knees, and bent at the waist.

Chloe walked in a zigzag, dizzy, and grabbed hold of Carsten to steady herself. She was also breathing heavily. Sasha, Jean-Baptiste, and Fernando were the least affected by the temperature and wetness of the place, but even so, Fernando felt much weaker than usual. The Fridarians were all in human form, though, and possibly, if they assumed their natural state, they would also have their full strength and vitality. But for now, they had to remain in human form, get a vehicle, and drive to Oklo, the site of the natural nuclear reactor.

Fernando beamed at Carsten. "You did a good job, finding this place for us."

"Yeah, right. I brought us from the freezing wonderland of Antarctica to this scorching hellhole. And all for what?"

"So we can do what we were born to do," said Jean-Baptiste. "Have sex."

"Damn internet," muttered Carsten, pulling himself up and treading over the weedy airport terrain after the others. Chloe clung to him, staggering like a cripple. "If not for the internet," said Carsten, "I never would have known that Gabon *had* the Oklo reactor."

"Well, it does, and people speak French here, which is handy, too." Fernando tried to sound chipper, but he was wondering if their plan was sane. Why not return to France itself or to the casinos of Europe, the ski slopes, the yachts, anywhere fun, and live forever as Fernando Le Sprague? He pictured himself with Jean-Baptiste, playboy of the world, draped in beautiful women, playing Russian roulette or Canasta or whatever humans did in casinos. Fernando had never been to a casino.

They rented a jeep and drove alone through the dense jungle, which seemed to be everywhere. A canopy of trees obscured the sky, and from their heights dripped vines and cones and other shrubs. Beneath the canopy were more trees of all sizes and shapes, forming umbrellas over the ground. These umbrella trees had thin but very high trunks and pointed leaves. It was dark in the jungle, and much too humid and hot.

The vines were a thick mat everywhere. Ferns and moss grew on the ground, as well, but mainly what Fernando noticed were the vines. They were almost as prevalent as the ice in Antarctica.

Insects chattered incessantly and were joined by the chittering of small animals, the screams of monkeys, and the calls of wild birds. There were sloths here, and orangutans, elephants, tigers, chimpanzees, gibbons, cobras, and pit vipers. The rainforest held an abundance of blood, Fernando realized, food for those of his kind, and like most regions of the world, it also had its share of fanged creatures. If not for the heat, it wouldn't be a bad place for a Fridarian to spend a few hundred years.

The jeep rattled along the roads, and finally, Chloe moaned, "I can't continue. Please, we have to stop." She hadn't eaten human food in a very long time, Fernando knew, and it had been too long since her last infusion of his blood.

Jean-Baptiste, who was driving, stopped the jeep and turned to face Fernando and Chloe in the backseat. "Why don't we dump her here and let her die?" he said as if it was no big deal.

"We don't need her, do we?" echoed Carsten. When Fernando frowned at him, Carsten added, "I mean, she doesn't add anything to our mission, not like Sasha, who at least has scientific capabilities."

Sasha bristled. "Excuse me," she said, "but I'm one of you now."

"Are you?" said Fernando quietly. "You did try to kill me, Sasha."

"But then you gave me more of yourself, and I realized how stupid I'd been."

He eyed her and wondered. Had she really changed enough to support Fernando and his cause, or was she playacting to save her pathetic human life?

"She's a scientist with training limited to neutrino research in Antarctica. She knows nothing about the rainforest. Or about Oklo." Jean-Baptiste glared at Sasha and added, "I think we should kill both of the humans. Drink them first, then toss them aside. They're of no use."

Sasha scrambled over the side of the jeep and jumped out. "You're not killing me!" she said. "You need some people, at least the two you already have, me and Chloe, to subdue any humans at Oklo. How do you propose doing that while trying to figure out how to reproduce, huh?"

"She has a point," Fernando said. He kicked open the jeep door, put his human feet onto the ferns and moss, then lifted Chloe out of the vehicle. Carsten and Jean-Baptiste got out of the jeep, as well, and the group leaned against it and considered what to do. Chloe was no longer conscious, she was in a dead faint in Fernando's arms.

Sasha stood before him, arms folded over her chest, waiting for his pronouncement of her fate. "What if you need someone to talk to the scientists at Oklo, huh? Then what will you do? You need me, Fernando."

"I don't think we need anything, Sasha. We only need to choose between pure Fridarian life and the one we already have. And we've already made that choice or we wouldn't be here."

Jean-Baptiste's eyes watered, or maybe it was the heavy mist that permeated the forest or the raindrops filtering from the canopy above. His tuxedo vanished, and then his white shirt and bowtie. His human features blurred and melted like butter into a fine mist that sparkled into the humidity around them. He had reverted to natural form, particles of moisture, bits of ice that melted in the heat.

Keeping Chloe aloft on a cushion of mist, Fernando also reverted to his natural form. And Carsten did the same, puffing into a cloud of black perspiration.

Let's ditch the jeep and get to Oklo, pulsed Fernando to the others. *Jean-Baptiste, you carry Sasha, and drink her if she causes any trouble. I'll take care of Chloe.*

You need to let it go with this Chloe girl, Jean-Baptiste vibrated privately to him. *She's dangerous. She's human. And you're about to reproduce and possibly commit suicide in the process.*

I promised to protect her, that's all.

Leave her here, Jean-Baptiste urged. *We need the scientist, but not this simpleton from the Pyrenees.*

"Take the scientist and head to Oklo," Fernando told both Jean-Baptiste and Carsten. "I'll join you shortly. I want to say *goodbye* to Chloe in private."

"You will leave her, then?" asked Jean-Baptiste.

"Yes, I will leave her."

The two pillows of mist, the white Jean-Baptiste and the black Carsten, seeped into the humidity and swept out of view. Within their folds was Sasha Karonski, adrift in the ecstasy of Fridarian blood as they nipped at her body. Fernando knew that they were right, that he couldn't protect Chloe any longer, that he had to leave her behind. He should have left her in Antarctica, but he decided that here in Africa, perhaps she could survive and return to Europe. There was no hope for her at Amundsen-Scott, even had he given her more blood to sustain her, for there was no way for her to contact McMurdo and get a flight home. And had he left her at McMurdo, she might have told people there about the Fridarians. Here in Africa, nobody would believe her tales about Antarctica.

He realized that he wasn't thinking as clearly as he should, that he'd been blundering along at fast speed like the rest of them, making snap decisions. One decision he knew that he couldn't make, no matter what the consequences, was to kill Chloe Desmarais.

Fernando wrapped his mist around her unconscious body, caressed the face and hair one last time. *When you wake up, I hope you understand why I left you here. It's to save you, Chloe. I may no longer be alive myself, and yet, I cannot give you death.*

And his ice fangs drilled into her, all over her body, puncturing her with hundreds of bloody pinpoints; and he drained enough of his own substance into her veins to give her the strength to survive.

As her eyes fluttered open and red flushed to her cheeks, he didn't wait to say anything more, his heart was too heavy with the knowledge that he had to leave her to fend for herself in the jungle. He left her there in the rainforest, half-human and half-Fridarian. There was plenty of food in the jungle for Fridarian thirst, and she would know what to do.

CHAPTER
TWENTY-FIVE

Gabon, Africa: October 2015

IT WAS ALMOST TWO billion years ago when ocean water flooded the Oklo mine and created natural nuclear reactors that then ran for millions of years. "The ancestors sent us to Earth to find the Oklo mine in Gabon and reproduce here," said Carsten. "These reactors don't require that beams be sent from space, beams that might miss their marks. These reactors work naturally without any human technology."

"But how?" asked Jean-Baptiste.

The three Fridarians floated over the Oklo mine operated by France. A few trucks and bulldozers were parked along inclines in the graded slopes of the mine. Nobody was in the trucks or the bulldozers. Some plant life managed to flourish along the orange slopes of the mine, though in the blacker gradations, there was no vegetation. Here, the sun burned hot upon the Fridarian mist with no tree canopy to serve as a shield. The Fridarians could maintain ice form for a short while, but it was easier to float as hot vapor along the inclines of the mine.

"I read a little about this when we were waiting for the plane to Gabon," said Carsten. "I have no idea how to use this information to reproduce. It's very complex."

"Well, let's give it a try, Carsten. Just tell us what you know, and we'll try to puzzle through it. If it doesn't work, we can always return to Europe or someplace else," said Fernando.

"True," added Jean-Baptiste, "we might as well try our best before we give up. We've come a long way to find out if this is our destiny, and we honestly don't have much else to do with ourselves other than play forever. Much as I do love playing . . ."

Could it be that even Jean-Baptiste yearned to do something more with his life than go to casinos and drink the blood of pretty girls? Fernando was surprised at his old friend, for hadn't Jean-Baptiste been the most bloodthirsty of them all?

Carsten told them what he knew. In prehistoric times but discovered only as recently as 1972, the natural nuclear reactors of Oklo generated as much power and heat combustion as any nuclear reactor built by modern men. Indeed, said Carsten, the French discovered that the Oklo uranium was very similar to the type found in modern nuclear waste. The Oklo reactors sustained an output of a thousand megawatts of power without blowing up Gabon.

"So how did that happen? I don't see any evidence here of explosions or fire," said Fernando.

"It no longer operates as a nuclear reactor," explained Carsten. "It shut down a long time ago."

"Well, what does it need to start again?" asked Jean-Baptiste.

"For one thing, it needs a steady source of water. And I don't mean mist or humidity. I mean that it must be flooded with water. Constantly."

This wasn't looking too good, thought Fernando. They were floating around a bunch of dirt in a crater in the earth. He didn't see at all how this place could provide nuclear fission. Sure, these were supposedly uranium deposit mines, but floating around a bunch of uranium didn't lead to fission.

Reading his mind, Carsten said, "I'm telling you, it happened here two billion years ago. The groundwater swelled and flooded these uranium deposits and started a self-sustaining nuclear chain reaction. There was a lot of radiation for a very long time."

Jean-Baptiste said, "I get it, Fernando. What Carsten's saying is that the chain reactions increased the temperature to a point far beyond what we're feeling now. The water boiled and evaporated, right, Carsten? And then the deposits cooled, and the tides came in again and flooded the area, causing another nuclear fission chain reaction."

"That's right," said Carsten. "But after a million years, the nuclear reactors used up the naturally occurring U-235, the uranium, leaving only traces behind–"

"Which were discovered in 1972," finished Jean-Baptiste.

"Exactly," said Carsten.

Fernando's frustration was hitting unprecedented levels. "Then what the hell, I might ask, are we doing here? Why didn't you tell us this before, Carsten?"

"You didn't ask! And I only read about it on the internet before we hopped on the plane to West Africa. Besides, what's it matter?"

"It matters because even if we managed to get water flowing into this basin here, this damn crater, we still don't have enough U-235, from what you're saying, to start a nuclear chain reaction! All the raw components died off billions of years ago!"

"Damn!" cried Jean-Baptiste.

The three of them said nothing, just gazed around the orange and black deposits, the scrawny vegetation poking out of the sides of the mine. It was sweltering, and they all collapsed into muddy puddles beneath the sun.

"We came all the way here for nothing," moaned Jean-Baptiste.

"I never told you life was rosy," said Carsten. "Nothing's ever easy. If I could switch on Oklo and blast us all to smithereens, into tiny particles that reproduced and left us dead—deactivated and switched off forever—believe me, I wouldn't hesitate."

"And what about the scientist, this Sasha we dumped over there by the bulldozer for her afternoon siesta?" sneered Jean-Baptiste. "Fernando, she needs to go. Even she can't get this Oklo thing running again."

"There's got to be a *small* amount of U-235 left, *a trace of it,*" said Fernando. "We're near the ocean. We're on the equator with plenty of water in the air. We're Fridarians. Use your brains, boys."

"We're cold beings. Freezing. We can condense the humidity into a flood of water," offered Carsten.

"That's right. We flood what's left of the U-235—the massive amounts of U-238 are irrelevant to our cause—and we kick off the reactors. They don't have to burn for long, just enough for us to reproduce," said Fernando.

Not knowing quite what they were doing, the three of them set about building their natural nuclear reactor. They used their nanoparticles to form themselves into machines and drilled into the mines. Fernando was thrilled when they found the uranium traces he'd hoped would be there. They created long grooves in the dirt on both sides of the uranium deposits.

As predicted, it didn't take long for a bunch of humans to show up. They turned on their trucks and bulldozers, but Fernando told Sasha to seduce them and drain their blood. After a week, corpses were heaped in ditches by the mines, Sasha was plump with blood, and the three Fridarians were detoxed into their natural states, pure particles, no longer in flesh form. However, they'd been drinking blood for two hundred years, and it would take more than a week or even a month to detox them down to pure Otto-like state. It might not be possible no matter how long they stayed away from blood.

They crystallized into ice as best as they could, condensing the humidity around them into a flood of water. And then they waited for the rain, and when it came, they froze it all and filled the tunnels and the entire basin with snow and ice. The cold was a welcome relief, and all of them shuddered with delight. All but Sasha, who remained in her bulldozer, watching and waiting.

It didn't take long for the African sun to melt the snow and ice; and with the melting came rapid flooding of the tunnels and the basin. The mine filled with water, and torrents whipped through the tunnels, flooding over the remnants of U-235.

Fernando disassembled into his smallest particles. *Pound me with the radiation. Let me feel the natural life cycle of the Fridarian. Hit my spores and create hatchlings. Activate them! Give us new life!*

Fernando would leave the world behind and go wherever Fridarians went when they switched off. He would go with his oldest friends, Jean-Baptiste and Carsten. He felt them flickering around him in their tiniest particle form. He felt their thoughts.

From Carsten came a mantra: *I'm going to die. I'm going to die. I'm free at last, good God almighty, I'm free at last.*

Jean-Baptiste was remembering his most lavish experiences in the resorts of the world. He remembered cavorting in Antarctica as a hatchling, slamming Otto with snowballs, and chasing Fernando down the glaciers to the Ross Sea.

It had been a good life.

It *had* been fun.

A small chain reaction kicked in, but it was very small, and only a bit of radiation trickled over the three Fridarians. Excitement surged through Fernando. *It should be enough to trigger the new births. It should be enough to activate my particles and render them into new nanolife creatures.*

The radiation intensified, and with a burst of joy, Fernando realized that *it was going to happen!*

He was steam surrounded by a gas more noxious than that spewing from Mount Erebus. He was steam in the midst of life-producing radiation. He was a spore again, an infant, and his mind floated to days past; back in Antarctica, when he'd rose as a single ice crystal from the core and flourished with alife, rapidly expanding into the full power of Fernando Le Sprague. Would it happen again? Would each of his particles grow into new Fernando Le Spragues?

Oh, let it be!

And that's when he felt the vibrations of Sasha Karonski. Her thoughts flooded to Fernando, Jean-Baptiste, and Carsten. *I won't let you reproduce! Now that you're all weak, I'll dam the water and destroy the reactor!*

Fernando hadn't thought of this one, that Sasha might wait for them to dwindle away, that she might destroy Oklo.

Can you kill her? Jean-Baptiste pulsed.

I cannot. She's immortal now, isn't she?

No. She's not like us. She's not of Fridarian origin.

Ah, yes. Fernando remembered now. James had died, and Chloe *could* die. And so, Sasha could die. She had served no purpose here, after all, other than to watch and wait, hoping to stop the flow of water once they were dormant.

She still wanted him dead!

And he would be dead, very soon, yes, but not until he'd reproduced!

He coalesced slightly, just enough to form a blast of mist that spiked her with radiation. She staggered from the blast and fell into the crater of water, which was boiling now with deadly nuclear reactions. Her flesh boiled off her bones, her meat dissolved into the basin, and in her dying moments, an image of James Schankel shot through her mind. As her last thoughts permeated him, Fernando knew that Sasha Karonski felt *human guilt* over Schankel's death. No matter how much Fridarian blood they'd given Sasha, she was still more human than Fridarian. Possibly, she'd once lusted after James as a human. Possibly, she'd once admired him for his work in the Mediterranean Sea. But none of it mattered now. Sasha and James: neither had been intelligent enough to outwit the Fridarians and survive.

It was over. Their journey was done. Carsten would finally get his wish and die. Jean-Baptiste and Fernando would die, too, but their offspring would play together, all over the world, they would play, and hopefully, the offspring of the Fridarians would share the bond their fathers had shared.

And Fernando let the water split him into a million particles and carry him away.

CHAPTER TWENTY-SIX

Perpignan, France: October 2015

CHLOE DESMARAIS LOUNGED IN a bikini by the Mediterranean surf. She had everything she wanted. Plenty of blood to drink, plenty of young men who flirted with her, beautiful clothes, glittering jewels. She killed with abandon and kept the material possessions left by her victims. The pain and the pleasure, the blood and the ice, the ecstasy of it all: she could never get enough. While she couldn't ball herself into ice chunks or cast frost upon the trees, she remembered the ice as it wrapped around her body, the swell of pleasure as frosty wings enveloped her.

A young man sauntered by, eyeing her, and she decided that he would be her evening fun. She let him flirt and believe he was in control. She asked for his name, and he told her, but it didn't register because she didn't care. She only cared that he was strong and that the blood coursed through his muscles with oxygen and nutrients. He smelled sweet with it, sweeter than any other morsel on the sand.

He was happy to return to her villa for a dip in her pool. She read his thoughts. He was anxious for sex. It bored her, really, how simple these humans were with their pathetic and predictable desires. It almost took the fun out of it.

She enticed him by taking off her bikini top and jumping into the sparkling pool outside her dining room. He was so eager, so pathetic, that she felt little joy in playing with him. It was much too easy.

He stripped off his shorts and leapt into the pool, showing off his masculinity with a giant splash of water. His face was red, his lips thick and smiling, and the laughter and innuendos gushed from him.

Bored, she let him hug and kiss her, and finally, sickened by his presence—his *live* presence—she sank her fangs into his neck and drained him. He thrashed, but then stilled as his skin shrank around his bloodless body. His eyes were wide with shock. The pool water blushed red as his essence filtered outward. She lapped the blood droplets from the water, felt the heat rushing up her body into her brain. Overhead, the clouds were technicolor blurs. Her limbs convulsed with pleasure, her body peaked over and over, sixty times at least, until finally, she was spent. She dragged herself to the side of the pool, draped herself across the cement, and baked under the warm sun until it dipped and the moon replaced it. The heat was in the roots of her being, sucking at her soul, just as it had when Fernando had drunk from her in the forest. Whirls within whirls, color within color, ice within heat.

She was so incredibly bored without Fernando. So incredibly lonely.

How could she ever replace him?

She'd been in Perpignan by the sea for long enough, she decided. She rose and went inside her villa, into her bedroom where she packed for tomorrow's journey.

It was time for Chloe to go home.

Back to her tiny village in the Pyrenees.

Back to her father, *le cochon*, the pig.

She would settle into Fernando's cave in the mountains, and when the time was right, when she was hungry enough, she'd come on the mist, float through the trees, and cling to *le cochon*, and when he slept, passed out from the wine, she'd whisper to him, let him know it was her, and as soon as his eyes glazed with horror, she'd laugh and sink her fangs into him. It would be bitter, his blood, but having taken it, she would know that all was right in the world. She would roam as the wild boar, and she would take nips when hungry from the pine martens, the civets, the horses, and the goats. And sometimes, from the children who wandered and got lost in the forest.

She would flourish over the centuries, and if life became too lonely, she'd drain someone—as Fernando had drained her, bringing her to this point but not to death—and she, Chloe Desmarais, would bring her new lover into the fold.

She was in no hurry to replace Fernando's love. She had the rest of eternity, didn't she? As long as she dodged death, it was possible she could live for hundreds of years. She didn't know for sure because, after all, she was the first of her kind.

CHAPTER
TWENTY-SEVEN

Gabon, Africa: October 2015

FERNANDO AND JEAN-BAPTISTE STARED at each other. They were supposed to be dead. And then they gazed all around them at the nanoparticles swirling, coalescing, and breaking apart. Their hatchings were red-tinged and easily built themselves into monstrous shapes: a skinless bloody fanged gorilla with three arms and a scorpion tail; a formless glob of pure pus and blood; a flying mound of teeth held together by rotting flab; the mutations were endlessly strange and grotesque, and the particles held more blood than ice.

What are they, and where's Carsten? pulsed Jean-Baptiste.

Fernando didn't know about Carsten and figured he was already deactivated, dead. *As for the hatchlings, they appear to be what we are, Jean-Baptiste, flesh-and-blood nanoparticle creatures who can assume whatever form they want. Except they don't seem as Fridarian as we are, they seem more . . .*

Cruel and formless?

Yes, and more bloody, I would say. They seem happy in the heat of the rainforest. They're not ice creatures like us, Jean-Baptiste.

Fernando and Jean-Baptiste floated as wisps of white mist, catching slight vibrations from the thousands of hatchlings they'd spawned with Carsten, the black foam of doom. The vibrations were horrifying, for the hatchlings thought only of seeking prey, killing, drinking blood, and terrifying the creatures around them. They didn't possess the sensitivity of the Fridarians. They possessed the sensitivity of the humans. To dominate. To kill at all costs. To eat meat and flesh.

The hatchlings tried to infiltrate Fernando's thoughts but he blocked them. They were curious about these two antiquities, Fernando and Jean-Baptiste. They recognized that the Fridarians were their fathers, but they didn't understand yet what they were, much less how they had been born. They were infants with no knowledge of the ancestors. They were infants who hadn't been born pure Fridarian. *They were infants who had been born directly into the blood.*

"What have we done?" whispered Jean-Baptiste.

"We've spawned what we *are*, my friend, not what we *were*."

"*They* are the future? We gave up life for *them*?" Jean-Baptiste's mist puffed out, simply dissipated into nothing as his particles started to deactivate and shut down. His Fridarian life cycle was coming to a close. With only a few particles left, he whispered, "but they are not Fridarian. They are hideous mutations, Fernando."

Yes, Fernando knew it, as well. As his old friend's life flickered off, a great sadness came over him. He was alone now, surrounded by these hideous mutations. *They were so different from him.*

In the end, Otto had been the only smart one. He'd stayed in Antarctica, intending to remain pure forever. He was the only hope for the Fridarian race. But Otto, whining and sniveling Otto, could he survive against the power and numbers of these new hatchlings? Could Otto reproduce before the hatchlings killed him?

And kill him they would, for Fernando could hear the vibrations all around him:

Dominate.

Kill at all costs.

Eat flesh and meat.

Fernando felt the pain, the excruciating soul-searing pain of death, rise in him, and he felt his particles twitching and blinking off. His last memory was of Chloe Desmarais' smile, that childlike innocent smile, and of her lilting voice and sweet naïveté; and that last memory soared in him, rocking him with ecstasy even as the pain squelched his final cell.

ABOUT THE AUTHOR

LOIS H GRESH is the New York Times Best-Selling Author of more than 25 books, including *The Termination Node, The Science of Superheroes,* and *The Twilight Companion.* Look for her short story collection, *Eldritch Evolutions,* in March 2011.

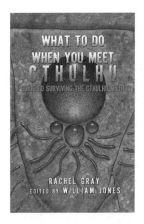

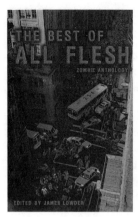